Joseph Allen

Life of the Earl of Dundonald

Joseph Allen

Life of the Earl of Dundonald

ISBN/EAN: 9783337332976

Printed in Europe, USA, Canada, Australia, Japan

Cover: Foto ©Raphael Reischuk / pixelio.de

More available books at **www.hansebooks.com**

LIFE OF
THE EARL OF DUNDONALD.

LIFE

OF

THE EARL OF DUNDONALD,

G.C.B.

REAR-ADMIRAL **OF THE** UNITED KINGDOM,

AND

ADMIRAL OF THE RED.

BY

JOSEPH ALLEN,

AUTHOR OF "THE LIFE OF NELSON," ETC. ETC.

With Illustrations.

LONDON:

ROUTLEDGE, WARNE, & ROUTLEDGE,

FARRINGDON STREET;

NEW YORK: 56, WALKER STREET.

1861.

TO

MISS ANGELA BURDETT COUTTS,

THE EXEMPLARY DAUGHTER AND REPRESENTATIVE OF

SIR FRANCIS BURDETT, BART. M.P.

THE STANCH PARLIAMENTARY ALLY AND FIRM PERSONAL

FRIEND OF

THE LATE EARL OF DUNDONALD, G.C.B.

This Biography

IS, WITH HER KIND PERMISSION,

RESPECTFULLY DEDICATED

BY

THE AUTHOR.

PREFACE.

THE necessity for this little volume will be obvious
to all who set a right value upon the achievements
of British sailors. It is true that the public is not
without full and authentic particulars of the career of
the late Earl of Dundonald. Two comprehensive
volumes **were** published in 1859, containing an account of his services in Chili, Peru, and Brazil, written
by himself;* and the second volume of his " Autobiography "† was published shortly before his death.
Those who are more than commonly interested in the
services of this distinguished man, therefore, will find
in these works ample information.

But it is due to " the million," to whom those
volumes are unattainable, to place within their reach
in a clear and impartial form, a record of the deeds

* " Narrative of Services in the Liberation of Chili, Peru,
and Brazil," by Thomas, Earl of Dundonald, G.C.B., 2 vols. ;
Ridgway, 1859.

† " Autobiography of a Seaman," by Thomas, Earl of Dundonald, Vol. I. and II. ; Bentley, 1860.

of one of the **bravest and most ill-used** of British naval heroes.

An autobiographer, **particularly one who has** been engaged in deeds of arms, must ever be **at a great dis**advantage. **He** cannot place **his own** gallant services in a correct point of view without incurring the risk of being charged with egotism, **or** with arrogating to himself **an** undue share of credit.

An autobiographer, moreover, **who** has suffered from unmerited persecution, too often fatigues his readers,—who are ready enough to admire his gallantry—by dwelling too much upon his personal wrongs. Comments which flow freely and unquestioned from the pen of an impartial biographer, would be looked upon as exceedingly out of place when published by the principal party interested.

Lord Cochrane (for by that name he is most familiarly known) particularly laboured under these disadvantages. He performed heroic actions, which he could not specify as such, and suffered grievous wrongs, the remembrance of which were, naturally enough, always uppermost in his thoughts, and colouring his narratives.

It has been the object of the author of this biography to remove these drawbacks as far as possible, and to set his hero before the world in his true light; neither hiding his faults, magnifying the merit of his achievements (for that, indeed, would be difficult), nor overstating his grievances. Like most men of ardent temperament, he was occasionally led away by its impulses, and not unfrequently imputed faults to others which were due, in some measure, to himself.

The great cause of Lord Cochrane's downfall was the charge he brought against Lord Gambier. He, in that case, seemed to forget that the admiral had the charge of an important fleet, and did not make sufficient allowance for the difference of age, rank, and responsibility that existed between himself and his superior officer. It was not his province, as one of Lord Gambier's captains, and still less as a member of Parliament, to question, as he did, the conduct of his commander-in-chief; and **he** found, when too late, that the missile **he had** somewhat heedlessly aimed at his admiral **recoiled** upon himself, and destroyed **his** fortune, if it exalted his fame.

At all times, it **is** well to remind the service of **deeds of** daring, and to show by a statement **of facts, what may be done** by practical skill, perseverance, **and** intrepidity. Those who hesitate to undertake ordinary risks will do **well** to refer **to** the account of the capture of **a large ship by** a brig **of** 158 tons; to read the **account of** the **engagement** under the batteries **of Aix roads, when a** small 12-pounder frigate challenged, **and gallantly engaged,** another frigate more **than a** third superior **in** weight of metal and number of men; **or** to reflect upon the daring valour shown on the 12th April, 1809, when a frigate advanced, single - handed, to the attack of four grounded line-of-battle ships. If other examples are wanting, let them turn **to the storming** and capture of Valdivia; the cutting-out **of** the *Esmeralda*; or the chase of a squadron of thirteen sail by one ship.

The author does not pretend, in the following pages, to do more than furnish a popular account of this noble officer's services. He does not appear either as his panegyrist, his defender, or, still less, as **his** accuser. His object is to give an impartial sketch of the Life of a hero whose deeds the country may well be proud of, and to render the name of COCHRANE, like that of NELSON, a " Household Word."

GREENWICH HOSPITAL,
January, 1861.

CONTENTS.

CONTENTS.

PAGE

LIFE OF THE EARL OF DUNDONALD.

ADMIRAL THE EARL OF DUNDONALD, G.C.B., better known to fame as Thomas Lord Cochrane, K.B., was born at Amisfield, a small town bordering on Lanarkshire, on the 14th December, 1775. He was the eldest of seven children, of whom the second, third, and last died young. Two of his brothers, Basil and William Erskine, entered the army; and his youngest brother, Archibald, the navy, in which he rose to the rank of post-captain. Basil became Lieutenant-Colonel of the 36th regiment, and William a major in the 15th Light Dragoons.

He was descended from a very ancient family, traditionally associated with a celebrated Scandinavian sea-rover who is supposed to have settled on the lands of Renfrew and Ayr. In Crawford's Peerage of Scotland it is stated that the family derives its name from the barony of Cochrane, in Renfrewshire. "Opposite to Johnstoun," runs this authority, in the description of Renfrew, "upon the east side of the river, lye the house and barony of Cochran, the principal manour of the Cochrans, a family of great antiquity in this shire; whose ancestors have possessed these lands well-nigh 500 years, and, without doubt, **have** taken appellation **from their** hereditary lands when fixed surnames came to **be used.**"

Pinkerton, in **the** *Iconographia Scotica,* **or Por-**traits of Illustrious Persons **of** Scotland, relates that one of his ancestors, Robert Cochran, gained distinction, **in** the **reign of James** III. of Scotland, **as** an architect; **and** that he **afterwards** rose to eminence as **a** courtier, **but never lost** his cognomen of "the mason chiel." He was created Earl of Mar; but, unfortunately, the favour of King James brought upon him the jealousy of the Scotch barons, and he was hung over the bridge of Lauder.

In 1669, the first Lord Cochrane was created Earl **of** Dundonald; and the subject of this memoir was the son of Archibald, the ninth earl. Archibald was descended from John, the younger son of the first earl, and on default of issue in the elder branch of the family, the title devolved on his grandfather Thomas, who married the daughter of Archibald Stuart, Esq., of Torrence, 'in Lanarkshire, and had issue one daughter and twelve sons, the most distinguished among whom was Admiral the Honourable Sir Alexander Inglis Cochrane, father of the present Admiral Sir Thomas Cochrane, G.C.B. The mother of Lord Cochrane **was** Anna, daughter of Captain James Gilchrist,* of the royal navy, and a very distinguished officer.

---

* On the 28th March, 1759 (Lord Dundonald, **in his** Autobiography, places the action a year earlier), the *Southampton*, of 32 guns, Captain James Gilchrist, and the 36-gun frigate *Mclampe*, Captain W. Hotham, cruising in **the** North Sea,

Archibald **Cochrane was** for some years in the navy; but having served on the coast of Guinea as an acting lieutenant, conceived a great dislike to the profession, and entered the army. This dislike had the effect of inducing him to do all in his power to prevent his son from joining the sea service.

The Earl of Dundonald was peculiarly given to scientific pursuits and investigations, which appear to have involved him in many pecuniary losses and embarrassments. Among his inventions, was one for preserving the bottoms of ships from the attacks of the *teredo navalis;* but the introduction of copper sheathing about that time, rendered his preventive of little value.

Lord Cochrane lost his mother during his boyhood; and so much had the speculations of his father im-

chased two large ships. The *Melampe* was the first to get into action, and for three quarters **of an** hour engaged the **two** strangers, which proved to **be** large **class** French frigates. The *Melampe,* being much damaged, dropped astern; but the *Southampton,* passing her, brought **the** sternmost frigate to action, when the other made all sail away. After a very sharp contest, **the** *Southampton's* opponent, which was the French 40-gun frigate **Danäe,** observing the *Melampe* to be again approaching, surrendered. **Out** of a crew of 330 men, the *Danäe* lost her first and second captains, and 30 men killed, and a great many wounded. **The** *Melampe* sustained a loss of 8 killed, and **20 wounded.** The *Southampton* had one man killed, and 8 wounded, **but among the** latter **was** her gallant captain, who received so **bad a wound in** the shoulder from **a** pound shot, that he was disabled **from further** employment; and in reward for past services, a pension of £300 a year was settled **upon** him for life.

poverished the family, that it was found impossible to pay for the education of the children. The minister of Culross, Mr. Rolland, kindly offered to supply the place of a tutor gratuitously; but pride, unhappily, stood in the way of the acceptance of this generous offer. To the widow of Captain Gilchrist, their maternal grandmother, they owed much of the education they did receive, that lady having applied her small income to the exigencies of her daughter's children. But even this imperfect education was early put an end to; for the young lord was made his father's companion during a journey which he made to London, in the hope of inducing the Government and ship-owners to adopt his coal-tar composition for ships. He failed to obtain the patronage of the Admiralty; and the ship-builders declared that they had no wish to prevent the ravages of the worms, as they were their best friends.

Lord Cochrane was destined by his father for the army, while the son was bent on becoming a sailor. His uncle, the Hon. Captain Alexander Cochrane, probably aware of the youngster's bias, took the wise precaution of placing Lord Cochrane's name on the books of the ships he severally commanded, so that, unknown to the earl, Lord Cochrane was nominally serving his majesty in the *Vesuvius, Carolina, La Sophie*, and **Hind**.

This, though irregular, was a common practice at that period, so that many a lad who was at school was supposed to be at sea. Though objectionable, inasmuch as the government were paying wages for

services not performed, there is no doubt that benefit
sometimes accrued from the practice, as a lad of eleven
or twelve years of age was much more likely to
become a good officer by remaining at school for a
few years, than by being knocked about at sea without a schoolmaster.

Through the influence of a friend, the young lord
received a nomination to a commission as ensign of
the 104th regiment, and was placed by his father
under the tuition of an old sergeant, who lost no
time in inducting his pupil in the mysteries of the
profession. His hair, cherished with boyish pride,
was brought down to the regimental " crop," and
plastered back with pomatum compounded of candle-
grease and flour, to which was added the cultivation
of a queue. " My neck," wrote his lordship, in his
autobiography, " from childhood open to the lowland
breeze was incased in an inflexible leathern collar or
stock, selected according to my preceptor's notions of
military propriety : these almost verging on strangu-
lation. A blue semi-military tunic, with red collar
and cuffs in imitation of the Windsor uniform, was
provided; and to complete the *tout-ensemble*, my
father, who was a determined Whig partisan, insisted
on my wearing yellow waistcoat and breeches—yellow
being the Whig colour, of which I was admonished
never to be ashamed."

One can imagine how hateful this restraint must
have been to a high-spirited lad, whose stature, being
beyond his years, was calculated to make his mounte-
bank costume more remarkable. " Passing one day,"

said he, "near the Duke of Northumberland's palace at Charing-cross, I was beset by a troop of ragged boys evidently bent on amusing themselves at the expense of my personal appearance, and, in their peculiar slang, indulging in comments thereon far more critical than complimentary. Stung to the quick, I made my escape from them, and rushing home, begged my father to let me go to sea with my uncle in order to save me from the degradation of floured head, pigtail, and yellow breeches." This burst of despair, however, only aroused the indignation of the parent and the Whig; and the result was "a sound cuffing." Remonstrance was useless; but his dislike to everything military became confirmed, and the events of that day certainly cost his Majesty's 104th regiment an officer, notwithstanding that the military training by his tormenter proceeded with redoubled severity.

The Earl of Dundonald having, at this juncture, contracted a second marriage with Mrs. Mayne, the widow of a clergyman, by which he slightly improved his circumstances, Lord Cochrane and his brother Basil were sent to an academy in Kensington-square, London; but this lasted only six months. A lapse of four years and a half succeeded, during which Cochrane did all in his power to improve his education, but grew more than ever determined never to take up his army commission. The Earl,* finding

* In the annual address of the Registrars of the Literary Fund Society in 1823, the following notice appears relative to this unfortunate nobleman:—" A man born in the high class of the

this to be **the** case, at length **gave** his consent, and Captain Cochrane, his uncle, being then in command of the *Hind*, consented to receive him, or rather to allow him to join the ship, on the books **of** which his name already figured. The expense of his outfit was met by a timely advance of £100 on the part of the Earl of Hopetoun, and with the stock **thus purchased and** his father's gold watch as a keepsake—the only patrimony he ever inherited—he started to seek his fortune.

ENTERS THE NAVY.

[1793–4.]

ON the 27th of June, 1793, Lord Cochrane, being then of the mature age of **seventeen** years and **six months,** presented himself **on** board his Majesty's sloop *Hind*, of 28 **guns, lying** in **Sheerness** harbour. He was **accom**panied **by** his uncle the Hon. John

old British peerage has **devoted his** acute and investigating mind solely to the prosecution **of science ; and his** powers have prevailed in the pursuit. **The** discoveries **effected by his** scientific research, with its direction altogether to utility, **have** been, **in many** instances, beneficial to the community, **and in** many **have been the source of** wealth to individuals. To himself alone **they have** been **unprofitable ;** for with a superior disdain, or **(if** you please) a culpable disregard of the goods of fortune, he has scattered around him the produce of his intellect, with a lavish and **wild** hand. If we may **use** the words of an apostle,— 'though poor, he hath made **many** rich ;' and though in the immediate neighbourhood of **wealth, he** has been doomed to suffer through a long **series of** laborious **years** the severities of want." We may add **that this** venerable martyr to **an** inventive genius died at Paris in poverty, on the 1st July, 1831, at the age of eighty-three."

Cochrane, who undertook to introduce him to the first lieutenant. The officer in question was one of, at that time, a numerous and most valuable class in the service. He had been promoted from before the mast, but retained his fondness for the forecastle notwithstanding, and was never more at home nor better pleased than when engaged in teaching those about him their duty by manual labour. Jack Larmour, for that was the generally received name of this rough specimen, was, on this occasion dressed in the garb of a seaman. He was superintending the setting-up of the lower rigging, with a marlin-spike slung round his neck, and a lump of grease in his hand to ease the laniards. Young Cochrane was six feet high and a lord, besides being the nephew of the captain. These circumstances did not, however, appear to make a favourable impression. He probably had the look of what was termed a "K.H.B.," otherwise "King's hard bargain." He might have done for a spare topmast; but no one, to look at him, would have expected him to be useful as a midshipman. Whatever others might have thought, this was unquestionably the first lieutenant's impression.

The presence of the captain's brother for the time prevented any expression of this feeling. On the contrary Jack affected civility, but terminated the introduction by ordering this addition to the ship's complement to get his traps below. Our hero was then left alone in his glory.

Of all the spectres which haunted first lieutenants in those days, and the feeling has even now scarcely died out, a large midshipman's chest was the most appalling. Many unhappy youngsters have had to stand by and see a clumsy ship's carpenter engaged in "docking" the receptacle of all his earthly valuables, and Cochrane was not exempt from this trial. "Does Lord Cochrane think he is going to bring a cabin on board this ship?" asked, or rather ejaculated, the indignant Jack Larmour on viewing the chest which he had just ordered to be taken below; "get it up again on the main deck; send down to Lord Cochrane for the key."

The Newcome complied with the latter request more readily than many would have done, but hearing the sound of a saw at work, and perhaps warned by the hints of his messmates, he followed the bearer of the key just in time to see all his valuables turned out upon the dirty deck.

This sea-ogre, in high glee, was standing over a man who was cutting the chest just beyond the key-hole, and uttering sneering remarks on the folly of midshipmen in general, and lords in particular. Reduced to what Jack was pleased to consider reasonable dimensions, he pointed out the lubberliness of shore-going carpenters in not making keyholes where they could most easily be got at, namely, at the end instead of the middle of a chest.

The young Scotchman bore this with wonderful temper, so that if Lieutenant Larmour was guilty of this act of folly, in order to try the mettle of the midshipman, he at least did not succeed in disturbing his equanimity.

Pride seemed to have been eliminated from the composition of the poor Earl's son. Poverty had sternly schooled him, and it would have been well for him, had he through life maintained the same prudent control over his temper.

From this time, this rough son of Neptune seemed to have conceived an interest in the captain's nephew. We can imagine that the gaunt midshipman was for a term the sport of his messmates, but his steadiness, and determination to acquire a knowledge of his duty, were such, that, assisted by the ability to retort their practical jokes, he was not long in obtaining an easy footing on board the ship.

The first cruise of the *Hind* was to the coast and fiords of Norway, about which French privateers were suspected to be lurking. The interception of an enemy's convoy which was expected from the West Indies, going north about, was also an object in view.

But beyond eliciting much hospitality from the Norse men and Norse ladies, their cruise was unproductive. Captain Cochrane, though a strict disciplinarian at sea, and indeed elsewhere, knew when to relax. He knew that he would be better served by his officers, if he respected their little privileges; and as there was no particular call of duty, the officers and crew spent more of their time on shore than on board. Sleighing, fishing, and shooting, were their every-day sports.

Although Cochrane had made up his mind to avoid everything in **the shape of** transgression, he was one

day caught tripping by his hard-a-weather first lieutenant. **It was his** watch **on deck,** and Cochrane had,
for a few minutes only, quitted his post, when hearing
his name called, he found, to his cost, that his *lâche*
had been discovered. Larmour had hit the unlucky
blot. The ordinary mode of punishment for midshipmen in those days, and for the succeeding half
century, was the absurd and often cruel one of " mast-
heading." **Many old** officers can tell tales of this
ridiculous and objectionable mode of punishment ;
how they have had to endure long hours of hunger and
cold merely **to** gratify the whim, or appease the anger
of some irascible first lieutenant or captain. Some
particularly smart officers have been known to resort
to the absurdity of decorating not only mastheads
but yardarms with midshipmen, and it was not until
a first lieutenant **was tried** by **a** court-martial for
having caused a midshipman, who refused to go to
the masthead for a punishment, to be hauled into the
top, that common sense interfered, and put a stop to
so objectionable a mode of reclaiming offending junior
officers.

Cochrane had no sooner regained his post on deck,
than the curt but ominous and well-understood command, " Masthead, sir," assailed his senses. Remonstrance or excuse **was** utterly out of the question, and
the six-foot middy was, in due course, ensconced
under the **lee** of the maintopmast-head, endeavouring
to shelter himself from the cutting cold wind.

" The thermometer," said Cochrane, " was below
zero ;" but this we take to be a mistake, as the ship

would, under such circumstances, have been **frozen** in, which was not the case. We presume he meant "below the freezing point," and quite **cold enough** even that temperature must have been at the mast-head. The first lieutenant calculated the power **of** endurance in his victim to **five minutes, and** when he thought it probable that frost-biting would **commence,** he prudently called his midshipman **down. This was** the only time the punishment **was** inflicted **upon** Cochrane; but we have no doubt Jack **duly** practised the art of torture upon others who had **less** influence in the captain's cabin. **As a** general rule, **it was** found that those officers **who had** come **from** before the mast, were the most rigorous **in their** discipline.

A laughable incident is recorded connected with this period. The *Hind* was, as a matter of course, thrown open to the **N**orwegians, and the ship had generally a good sprinkling of visitors on board. **The** seamen had **a** pet parrot, which, from constantly hearing the boatswain's whistle and following call, had acquired the sounds to the greatest nicety. Sometimes Poll would "turn the hands up," to the great annoyance of those who were thus imposed upon; and one day **a** party of ladies having arrived alongside to visit the ship, a chair suspended by a single purchase on the main-yard, was duly lowered into the boat to "whip" them over the **side.** One or two ladies had been safely landed on deck, and the chair had been again lowered and **the** whip hauled taut, when Polly mischievously piped "let go." The order was promptly obeyed, and the lady consequently ducked over head and ears. Jack Larmour, fortunately, was out of the ship at the time this happened, or the innocent mischief-maker would have no doubt paid a severe penalty for practising her imitative art.

The *Hind* returned to Sheerness, and her officers and crew were turned over to the 12-pounder 32-gun frigate *Thetis.* The *Hind* was a class of ship just then going out. They were vessels of about 600 tons, armed on the main deck—for they were frigate-built —with twenty-four long 9-pounders, and on the quarter deck and forecastle with four long 6-pounders. The *Thetis* was not much better. She measured about 680 tons, and was armed with twenty-six long 12-pounders on the main deck, four long 6-pounders on the quarter deck, and two of the same description on the forecastle.

As the *Thetis* had to be fitted for sea, Cochrane, instead of going on shore as others in his position would have done, remained by the ship, and assuming the frock of a seaman, turned to with the crew, determining to make himself familiar with this practical portion of a sailor's duty. The bowsprit of the *Thetis* overhung the common highway, and, perched upon this, Jack Larmour might have been seen busily superintending the process of " gammoning," assisted by his six-foot midshipman. At this period intelligent young officers found their advantage in a close attention to the minutest details, and studied to understand everything connected with the ship to which they belonged, from stowing the hold to rigging the top-gallant mast. "The modern practice," said Cochrane, "is to place ships in commission with everything perfect to the hands of the officers and crew, little being required of them beyond keeping the ship in order while at sea. The practice is, to a certain **extent**, praiseworthy; but it has the disadvantage of impressing officers with the belief that handicraft skill on their part is unnecessary; though in the absence of practically-acquired knowledge it **is** impossible even to direct any operation efficiently. Without a certain amount of this skill, as forming an important part of training, no man can become an efficient naval officer."

PROMOTED TO THE RANK **OF** LIEUTENANT.
[1794-9.]

The *Thetis*, at the latter **end of 1794,** being manned and ready for sea, was ordered **to** join the squadron of Vice-Admiral George Murray, fitting out for North America, and designed for the capture of the French islands of St. Pierre and Miquelon. During the voyage some icebergs were fallen in with, **on the** top of one of which was **a** polacre-rigged ship. Being now in his twentieth year, and having, by virtue of the nominal time served in his uncle's ships, become eligible for promotion, Admiral Murray gave Lord Cochrane an acting order as third lieutenant of the *Thetis.*

This unexpected piece of good fortune caused him to redouble his zeal, and having been tolerably well ground up by the first lieutenant, he was, perhaps, far from being **an** inefficient officer. But the speedy promotion was, we are disposed to think, to some extent, the cause of the misfortunes which afterwards attended the career of this gallant man. From a very remote period it has been a rule for those who are intended to become executive officers to betake themselves very early to the sea. The peculiarity about naval discipline is, that it must form a part, as it were, of a young man's growth. Obedience must be instilled into his mind when the will is, to a certain extent, in a plastic state, or discipline will never have its proper effect upon the actions. This practice was carried to far **too** great an extent at one period, for mere children were taken to sea under the idea that they would grow more into the service. Unhappily they took the inclination too much, and were for ever afterwards unable to **divest** themselves of the quarter-deck and its asperities, even in domestic life. There is a mean, no doubt; and **we** agree with the authorities of the day, that fourteen is a good limit of age. Cochrane, as we have seen, did not ship until nearly eighteen, and in less than two years from that time he was a confirmed lieutenant. Midshipmen in those days were hardly considered officers. They were "midshipmen," and had no rank, relative or otherwise. Some years later they were called "quarter-deck petty officers;" they have now the relative rank of ensign.

On the **13th April, 1795, Cochrane was** transferred to the 64-gun ship *Africa,* **commanded** by Captain **Rod**dam Home; **and** on the **6th July** he was confirmed to the rank of lieutenant. While on board this ship Cochrane met with a very disagreeable accident. He had invented a machine for catching porpoises. This consisted of a leaden shot, stuck round with barbed prongs. The surgeon laid him a wager that he could not hurl this missile a certain distance, in the attempt to accomplish which one of the barbed prongs or hooks caught the fore-finger, and very nearly separated it from the hand. The pain attending this wound put Cochrane's philosophy to the rout. He had arrived at the conclusion, by his specious reading, that pain was not an evil, or that pain had no existence. "As the doctor was dressing my hand," said he, "the pain was so intense that my crotchet was sadly scandalized by an involuntary exclamation of agony. 'What!' said the doctor, 'I thought there was no such thing as pain?' Not liking to have a favourite theory so palpably demolished, the ready reply was, that my exclamation was not one of pain, but mental only, arising from the sight of my own blood. He laughed, whilst I writhed on; but the lesson knocked some foolish notions out of my head."

The rough and ready Larmour, who was a lieutenant of twelve years' standing, having obtained promotion to the rank of master and commander,* Captain Cochrane obtained the removal of his nephew to the *Thetis.* On rejoining this ship he was ordered to pass an examination, showing his qualifications for the rank

---

* This title, though for a long time common in the navy, was officially disused in 1797. For a century prior to that date the title was that of "master and commander." Captain Larmour obtained post rank in April, 1800, and died in 1807.

of lieutenant, which, as a matter of course, he was able to do, as the certificates of his uncle were available for the requisite six years' servitude.

Cochrane, by his absence from the *Thetis*, had lost a fine chance. In company with the *Hussar*, that ship had captured a French frigate and corvette, which was the only action in which she participated during her five years' service on the station.

Admiral **Murray** was succeeded by Vice-Admiral George Vandeput; and on the 21st June, 1797, Cochrane was appointed a lieutenant of the flag-ship *Resolution*. Admiral Vandeput was a sea oddity, if we are to judge from the following anecdote:—"Being seated near the admiral at dinner, he inquired what dish was before me. Mentioning its nature, I asked if he would permit me to help him. The uncourteous reply was, that whenever he wished for anything he was in the habit of asking for it. Not knowing what to make of a rebuff of this nature, it was met by an inquiry if he would allow me the honour of taking wine with him. 'I never take wine with any man, my lord,' was the unexpected reply."

Cochrane fancied he had got among the Goths, and that Vandeput was their chief; but he found that it was only a habit which the gallant admiral had acquired. He thought, by showing his worst qualities first, he would improve by acquaintance. In this he was tolerably sure of succeeding, provided he always met with those who could put up with his *brusquerie*, and give him a second trial. Cochrane described him as being a perfect gentleman, and one of the kindest commanders living.

Tired of the quiet monotony of Halifax, the vice-admiral determined on wintering in the Chesapeake, and took up his quarters on shore, inviting his officers in turn to spend a week with **him. The** service was most agreeable. The innkeeper **of the** small town mustered a pack of hounds, which often led their followers into perilous situations in a country so over-grown with wood, the thick forests frequently compelling the riders to lie flat on the backs of their horses to escape being thrown off. Cochrane here met with a curious adventure. It was his turn to spend a week at the admiral's house; and as the admiral was about to give a large dinner **to the** neighbouring gentry, Cochrane officiously determined to add some delicacy to the feast.

He sallied out with this object in view, and **on** reaching the forest, encountered a huge wild-looking sow, with a farrow of young pigs. The idea of a sucking-pig immediately suggested itself to the sportsman; and selecting the most promising of the lot, he levelled his rifle, and, being a good shot, stretched the infant porker on a gory field. But his shot was not paid for. He had aroused the maternal sympathies of Mrs. Pig, and the consequence was a ferocious charge upon the butcher of her tender offspring. Retreat was decidedly advisable. He could not shoot the sow, for his rifle was unloaded. Fortunately a tree interposed its friendly shelter, and now the **gallant lieutenant,** leaving his rifle at its foot, might have been seen perched in the fork of the tree, and watching, with unwonted earnestness, the movements of his wild-looking acquaintance. Maternal duty at length called away his persecutor, and Cochrane was released from his very unpleasant dilemma. It would have occasioned no surprise had the slain sucking - pig been devoured by the bereaved parent and the young brothers and sisters; but such was not the case, for Cochrane found the defunct animal, which he carried back in triumph to the admiral's house, but too late for that day's feast.

Having told his story, Cochrane found that if little piggy had escaped roasting, it was only in order that the operation should be performed upon himself, and the fire was sustained until Cochrane's skin began to scorch.

Another incident is mentioned in his Autobiography, which throws some light upon the character of our hero. Byron has said—

> Man being reasonable must get drunk,
> The best of life is but intoxication;

but wiser men than Byron have declared wine to be a "mocker," and an "equivocator." Cochrane declared that even in his early days, when hard drinking was considered an indispensable qualification for a gentleman, he never indulged in the vice so as to become inebriated. While on the bank of the Chesapeake, however, he was severely tried. The bottle circulated freely, but Cochrane managed to pour the wine into the sleeve of his coat. The evasion was discovered, and he was sentenced to **drink a** bottle as **a** penalty ; but **he** had a desperate **struggle,** and at length escaped from his boon **companions, and** took refuge in a farm-house for **the** night. His longevity, and the freshness and vigour **which continued to the** last, are strong arguments in **favour of temperance.**

Cochrane returned **to England after an absence** of five years, and Lord **Keith** having been **appointed** to succeed Earl St. Vincent, **in command of the** Mediterranean fleet, offered to take him as a **super-**numerary lieutenant on board his flag-ship. He thankfully accepted the offer, as it would place him in the fair way of promotion; **and, on** arriving at Gibraltar, in December, 1798, he was appointed to the *Barfleur,* bearing Lord Keith's flag.

As, however, **Lord** St. **Vincent did not** give up command, but remained at Gibraltar, **Lord** Keith was despatched in command of the fleet employed in the blockade **of Cadiz. For** four months **the** fleet **was** engaged **on** this service, the monotony **being occa-**sionally relieved by **a** stretch across to Tetuan **Bay,** for water and fresh beef.

The first lieutenant of the *Barfleur,* Philip Beaver,[*] was **an** officer of some note, and it was Cochrane's misfortune to have a serious quarrel with this officer, which ended in **a** court-martial. The account given by Lord Cochrane tells very much against himself. His lordship had, it appears, made some **very** strong

* This officer died a post-captain. **A** memoir **of his** services was published in 1829, written **by** the present Vice-Admiral Smyth, **D.C.L.**

remarks with reference to certain commercial speculations with the hides of beasts slaughtered on board the *Barfleur*, which some of the officers of the ship were engaged in, and had thereby incurred their animosity; but this circumstance seems to have had little bearing on the dispute with the first lieutenant. The account given by Cochrane was as follows:—

"One day when at Tetuan, having obtained leave to go on shore and amuse myself with shooting wildfowl, my dress became so covered with mud as to induce me not to come off with other officers in the pinnace, preferring to wait for the launch, in which the filthy state of my apparel would be less apparent. The launch having been delayed longer than I anticipated, my leave of absence expired shortly before my arrival on board—not without attracting the attention of Lieutenant Beaver, who was looking over the gangway.

"Thinking it disrespectful to report myself on the quarter-deck in so dirty a condition, I hastened to put on clean uniform, an operation scarcely completed, when Lieutenant Beaver came into the wardroom, and in a very harsh tone demanded the reason of my not having reported myself. My reply was, that as he saw me come up the side, he must be aware that my dress was not in a fit condition to appear on the quarter-deck, and that it had been necessary to change my clothes before formally reporting myself.

"Lieutenant Beaver replied to this explanation in a manner so offensive, that it was clear he wanted to surprise me into some act of insubordination. As it would have been impossible to be long cool in opposition to marked invective, I respectfully reminded him that by attacking me in the ward-room, he was breaking a rule which he had himself laid down, viz., that 'matters connected with the service were not there to be spoken of.' The remark increased his violence, which at length became so marked as to call forth the reply, 'Lieutenant Beaver, we will, if you please, talk of this in another place.' He then went on deck, and reported to Captain Elphinstone, that in reply to his remarks on a violation of duty, he had received a challenge!"

Although Cochrane seemed to think the interpretation put upon his observation was not justified, we cannot see that it bore any other. Cochrane meant we will talk of this "on shore," or his words had no meaning.

Captain Elphinstone endeavoured to soften the matter down, and suggested that Cochrane should apologize; but as he declined to do this, a court-martial was the necessary result, and Cochrane was "admonished to be more careful in future." The Admiral's secretary, who officiated as judge-advocate, was one of the raw-hide speculators, and, after the business of the Court was over, Lord Keith advised Cochrane privately to "avoid in future all flippancy towards superior officers." The secretary over-hearing the remark, embodied it in the sentence of the court-martial—at least Cochrane was under that impression, but, if correct, it was one of the most extraordinary proceedings on record.

Lord Keith having shifted his flag to the *Queen Charlotte*, Lord Cochrane joined that ship in June, 1799, and **Lord St.** Vincent having quitted the station, Lord Keith became the Commander-in-Chief, thereby putting an end to a series of very questionable proceedings, such as are certain to result from divided authority.

On the 21st **December,*** 1799, Lord Cochrane participated in a gallant affair in the straits of Gibraltar. The hired cutter *Lady Nelson*, of 10 guns, was attacked off Cabreta point, and captured by three French privateers and some gun-boats. The act being observed on board the *Queen Charlotte*, **at anchor in the bay,** Lieutenant **William** Bainbridge **was ordered to take the barge and proceed to recapture the British vessel.** He was accompanied **by** several other boats, **of one of which** Lord Cochrane was in charge. Bainbridge at the head of the barge's crew of sixteen men, gallantly boarded the cutter, and, after a sharp conflict, recaptured her, making seven officers and twenty-seven men prisoners, but at **the expense** of a severe sabre cut in his head. The boat which Cochrane commanded was not so honourably mentioned. Observing two privateers which had been engaged making off, Cochrane dashed alongside, and jumped on board; to his surprise, however, not a man of his boat's crew ventured to follow him. "This," says Cochrane, "was the **only time I** ever saw British seamen betray **symptoms of** hesitation."

* In the "Autobiography of a Seaman" the date of this affair is erroneously given in September.

The French 74-gun ship, *Généreux*, having been captured off Malta by the British squadron on the 18th February, 1800, was despatched to Port Mahon under the charge of Lord Cochrane as prize-master. The crew, hastily made up of invalided men, contributed by the ships of the fleet, were very inefficient, and the ship badly rigged ; but by dint of hard work, in which Cochrane was assisted by his brother Archibald, a volunteer, the ship was eventually navigated to her destination. To this circumstance he owed his escape from probable destruction in the *Queen Charlotte*, that ship having been burnt off Leghorn, when three-fourths of her officers and crew perished.

PROMOTED TO THE RANK OF COMMANDER.
[1800.]

For his conduct as prize-master of the *Généreux*, Lord Keith took the opportunity of recommending Lord Cochrane for promotion to the rank of commander, and his recommendation being successful, he not only gained the step in rank, but was appointed to command the *Speedy*, a brig of 14 guns. The *Speedy*, was a very small vessel, but had just before gained great distinction under the command of Captain Jahleel Brenton, and had been particularly successful among the Spanish gun-boats. Her armament was contemptible according to our present notions, but had, nevertheless, done good service. The guns were long 4-pounders, but at close quarters, and well supplied with grape and canister shot, they proved to be capable of doing much execution. Cochrane treated this little craft with some disdain, for his ambition led him to covet the command of the finest corvette in the navy, the *Bonne Citoyenne*, which vessel had not long before been captured from the French ; but he was forestalled by the secretary, who had got the promise of her for his brother. Little did he think, perhaps, that he would gain more honour in command of a little brig of 158 tons than would have fallen to his lot in a corvette of 511 tons.

The *Speedy* was at least well manned. She was, in fact, crowded with a complement of eighty officers and men, a needlessly large number, except for boarding purposes or manning prizes. Thinking the armament insufficient, Cochrane applied for and obtained an addition of two 12-pounders for bow and stern guns ; but was obliged to return them into store, as there was not space on deck to work them, independent of which the brig's scantling was too slight to bear the weight.

Behold now Lord Cochrane his own master! No longer the object of persecution to a Jack Larmour, nor liable to the strict etiquette of the stiffly starched Philip Beaver. No doubt he felt proud at the time of his command, and he has confessed as much, although his Autobiography abounds with remarks deprecatory of the humble little brig.

She was rather low between decks, and Cochrane said he had to resort to a singular expedient in order to shave with comfort. He caused the skylight over his cabin to be removed, and pushing his head and shoulders through the aperture, made the deck **his** toilet-table. The *Speedy's* mainyard being sprung, the foretop-gallant yard of the *Généreux* was supplied in lieu, and found too square. His cabin had not room enough for a **chair—the** floor being entirely engrossed by a small table surrounded by lockers, serving as seats and store-closets. To one of Cochrane's stature, the height of the cabin must have been inconvenient enough, being only five **feet.**

THE FIRST CRUISE OF THE *SPEEDY*.
[1800].

On the 10th May, **1800,** the *Speedy* sailed from Cagliari for Leghorn, having under convoy a fleet of merchant-ships. At 9 A.M. a strange sail hove in sight, which boarded and took possession of a Danish brig, one of the convoy. The *Speedy* immediately bore up in chase of the marauder; and at 11·30 A.M. recaptured the Danish brig, and captured the assailant, which proved to be the French privateer *Intrépide*, of 6 guns and 48 men.

Four days afterwards, during a calm, five armed boats from Monte Christo were observed making for the convoy. The *Speedy* got out the sweeps, and proceeded towards the vessels under her protection, but was not in time to prevent the boats from taking possession of two of the sternmost ships. A breeze springing up, the *Speedy* was soon alongside the captured vessels, and regained possession of them, together **with** the prize crews; but the armed boats escaped. The convoy arrived safely at Leghorn on May 21st.

Shortly after this, the French under Massena having been starved **into a** treaty with Lord Keith for the surrender of Genoa, the *Speedy* was ordered to cruise **off the** Spanish **coast.** On the **16th June, a** tartan was captured off Elba. On the 22nd, **a** French privateer, with a Sardinian prize in tow, was chased off Bastia, and the prize, laden with oil, recaptured; but the privateer escaped by taking refuge under Caprea. On the 26th, she brought out a Spanish 10-gun letter-of-marque at anchor under a fort near Bastia; and afterwards engaged five gun-boats which came out of **Bastia** with **the** intention of recapturing the **prize. The gun-boats** followed the *Speedy* until midnight, **but** did no considerable damage **to** her. On the 29th, observing a French privateer off Sardinia, the *Speedy* cast off **her** prize **and** endeavoured **to** bring the stranger to **action,** but **was** outsailed. On the **4th** July, anchored in Port Mahon with her prize. Thus, in the space of eighteen days, the *Speedy* had fought three actions and captured three prizes.

On the 9th July she again put to sea, and when off Cape Sebastian, cut out a vessel at anchor under the protection of the forts. Ten days afterwards she captured a small French privateer; on the 27th, made preparations for cutting out three others off Pianosa, but **was** deterred by a large military force; and on the 31st recaptured a prize which had been taken by another privateer. All **these** little incidents took place during a voyage from Port Mahon **to** Leghorn.

It seems scarcely credible that so many services should **have been** accomplished **without** loss or casualty of any sort; **but the** fact indicates the great ability of the *Speedy's* commander, and which his subsequent brilliant achievements developed more fully.

His actions were not, **even in the** dawn of his career, disfigured by rashness. It was not mere bravado and dash **with him,** but discreet courage, and admirable **skill and** forethought. His **patron,** Lord Keith, must **have felt** greatly pleased **with the** success; and, probably imagining that this flush might induce him to overrate his powers, gave **him** a timely caution against attempting too much.

The gaieties of Leghorn, now freed from **the** restraints of the French army, were a welcome relief, no doubt, to the young captain; but his stay was not very prolonged. The *Speedy* sailed again, on the 16th August, for a run down the Spanish coast; and on the 21st **she captured a** French privateer, with which, and a number of prisoners put on board by the *Mutine* and *Salamine,* she returned to Leghorn.

This cruising continued; but, on the 5th October, the *Speedy* again anchored at Minorca, and learnt that several Spanish vessels were on the look-out to capture the little *Speedy.* This induced Lord Cochrane to apply for an increased armament. He was, accordingly, supplied with 6-pounders, but the ports were not large enough, and the old long-fours resumed their position. She put to **sea** again on the 12th, but was unsuccessful; and, moreover, received so much damage in a heavy gale, that she was obliged to return to Port Mahon to repair the injuries sustained, which detained her till the middle of December.

On the 15th December she fell in with several of the enemy's vessels off Majorca, and chased the most promising of the group. A French bombard appeared disposed to defeat the *Speedy's* object, upon which the latter cleared for action, and altered course to meet her opponent. A running action ensued, which ended in the bombard going on the rocks between Dragon Island and the main. But observing three other vessels in the passage, the *Speedy* turned her attention to the strangers, and engaged and captured one of the number, which was a 10-gun privateer bound from Alicant to Marseilles. As the bombard appeared likely to become a wreck, no further attention was paid to her; but an unsuccessful pursuit commenced after the other two vessels. Cochrane was now so crowded with prisoners that he was obliged to land a number. One secret of his great success was the night-work. During the day the crew of the *Speedy* were allowed to sleep ; but no sooner did the night close in, than all hands were on the alert looking out for strangers ; and their watchfulness was seldom unrewarded.

NEARLY CATCHING A TARTAR.
[1800–1].

The information conveyed to Cochrane at Minorca, in October, was correct. The Spaniards had prepared a rod wherewith to chastise the insolence and presumption of the little British brig ; but in making certain of success, they reckoned without their host. Nevertheless, the danger was imminent; and the cruise of the *Speedy* would most assuredly have been cut short, but for the singular adroitness and foresight of **her** commander. There was a Danish man-of-war brig on the station very peculiarly painted; and when Cochrane heard that the Dons were **on the watch** for him, he determined to copy the Danish brig **Clomer,** thinking he might, on a push, be able to personate one of **that** nation. In order to make the deception, should he have to practise it, more complete, he shipped a real Danish quartermaster, and procured a suit of Danish naval uniform. Never was precaution more needed; for on the 21st December, being off Plane Island, the *Speedy* discovered a large ship inshore, having all the appearance of a well-laden merchant-ship. All sail was, of course, made to close the stranger; and before the true character of the chase was discovered, the *Speedy* was completely in her power. The " deep-laden merchant-ship" opened her ports, and disclosed an array of heavy guns, a well-directed broadside from which would have sent **the** little brig to the bottom without more ado.

We can imagine the chagrin of Cochrane at having been fairly caught in the trap laid for him. Fight was out of the question, so he tried the effect of a ruse. Hitherto he had hoisted no colours. **Had** he run down under British colours, the Spaniard would have opened fire without asking a question; but no doubt the imitation of the *Clomer* occasioned the hesitation, which saved the *Speedy* from certain capture. Danish colours were therefore displayed, and the Danish quartermaster **was put in** requisition, ready to answer any questions. **But** anxious to avoid too searching a scrutiny, and in particular to escape being boarded, Cochrane deemed it advisable to resort to another plan. He hoisted the yellow flag at the fore, so that when the Spanish boat came alongside, there would be no difficulty in preventing the officer from boarding. The *Clomer*, which the *Speedy* assumed to be, had, so **it was** said, just left the Barbary **coast, and** the **yellow** or quarantine flag denoted a foul **bill of health. The** boat **from the** Spanish frigate **only came within** hailing distance. The " Danish **officer" stood in** the gangway, **and** answered **the** Spaniard's questions. He **told the** Spanish officer that he had just left Algiers, where the plague was raging; and the information was so much to the point, that, after wishing them a good voyage, the Spanish frigate **made** sail, and parted company. James, in his " Naval History," confounds this frigate with the *Gamo* subsequently captured; **but** Lord Dundonald, in his Autobiography, **has declared this to be erroneous.**

Unbounded praise was due to Lord Cochrane, **for** the admirable finesse displayed throughout; and **so** highly was he commended for it by his gallant uncle and former captain, **Sir** Alexander Cochrane, that the latter wrote to Lord St. Vincent on the occasion, **and** begged his promotion on the score of the ability **he** had displayed.

The *Speedy* resumed her cruise, and was again

successful. On the 24th December she captured a Spanish vessel **off** Carthagena, laden with wine; and engaged two privateers, which had charge of the convoy. On the 25th chased another under a battery, and on the 30th had **a skirmish** with gun-boats. She refitted at Port Mahon; **and on the** 16th January, 1801, again put **to sea, and in less than a** week took three small privateers of ten, eight, **and** one gun respectively. The *Speedy* had now more prisoners than crew, and was obliged to put twenty-five of them into a launch, **and let** them go.

A MASQUERADE BALL.
[1801].

The *Speedy* went to Malta; **and it happened** that the officers of a French Royalist regiment had organized a fancy-dress ball. Cochrane purchased **a** ticket, and selected for his character that of **a British** sailor. So closely **did** he copy a genuine tar, that when he presented himself at the door he was refused admission. A rough, uncouth looking sailor he must **have** appeared. If our readers will picture **to** themselves " Long **Tom Coffin**," in **a** round tarry canvass frock, a tarpaulin hat with a lump of tallow stuck in the fore part, an iron implement, known as a marlinespike, suspended round his neck by a bit of spun yarn, redolent of tar instead of atar of roses, and with the true swagger, they will bring before them Lord Cochrane at the door of the ball-room. **The** dress **was not** admissible, and **Cochrane** grew indignant. The French master of the ceremonies insisted on his

leaving. "Jack Tar" elected to remain. "Some,"
said he, " were in the guise of shepherds, others in
fantastic costumes of various kinds; but the sailor
was too true a resemblance of a veritable Jack to pass
muster." In fact, he was thought not to be an
imitation at all, but the real thing. An altercation
ensued, which reached such a pitch as to render it
necessary to call in the picket from the guard-house.
No sooner had Lord Cochrane declared his name and
rank, than he was released; but the French officer
who had endeavoured to expel his tarry visitor, requested an apology. As Cochrane refused to apologize
to a man for collaring him, a duel was the consequence.
They met the following morning behind the ramparts,
and exchanged shots. The French officer was shot
through the thigh, and Cochrane had a narrow escape
—a ball having perforated his clothes and grazed his
side. And so this piece of folly ended; but Cochrane
declared that the lesson was not lost upon him, and
that he made a vow " never to do anything, even in
frolic, which might give unintentional offence."

ANOTHER CRUISE.
[1801.]

Cochrane's next cruise was to the coast of Tripoli.
Off Tunis Bay a strange sail was observed and chased,
which being a French vessel, ran into the bay to claim
the asylum of a neutral port. The brig mounted four
guns; and Cochrane having ascertained that she was
laden with arms and ammunition for the army in
Egypt, undertook to violate the neutrality of the

D

port. At night he boarded and took quiet possession; and having lifted her anchor, the captured brig was expeditiously moved down close under the *Speedy's* lee, **so** as to prevent any communication **with** the shore. Cochrane then **coolly ordered a** portion of the French ammunition **to be transferred to** the *Speedy's* magazine. As the crew of the French vessel evinced a disposition to **murmur** at this unauthorized **pro-**ceeding, an opportunity was afforded **them to make** their escape. The launch was left in their way; and, taking the hint, they got into the boat, and rowed **out** of the bay. Nothing more was ever heard of **this** affair; and the Tunisian Government either did not or would not know anything **of this** outrage, for such it undoubtedly was, and Cochrane conducted his cleverly but unscrupulously obtained prize to Port Mahon.

On the 18th March, the *Speedy* **had** another narrow escape from capture. A large frigate was observed towards evening in chase, and the *Speedy* made all sail to get away. During the pursuit, the frigate was gaining rapidly; and to add to the danger of being overtaken, the *Speedy* sprung her maintopsail-yard, **and** was under the necessity of lowering it to fish **it.** This added to the loss of ground, and her capture must have followed but for a clever, though not original, expedient. A tub was prepared, properly ballasted, and a lantern with a lighted candle, so placed as to be visible to the chasing ship. Every light on board the *Speedy* was then carefully covered up or extinguished, and the tub, with the light in it, lowered gently over the side. The *Speedy* then altered her course several points, leaving her pursuer to chase the light. The wind having, in the mean while, changed and freshened considerably, the *ruse* was the more likely to be successful, and, indeed, it succeeded admirably, as at daylight the enemy was not in sight.

CAPTURE OF THE *GAMO*.
[1801.]

After being engaged in several other affairs of secondary importance, the *Speedy* now approached the culminating point of her glory. The attempt to rid themselves of this destructive little pest to their trade and small privateers was resumed, and the merchants and others of Barcelona equipped a smart sailing frigate-built ship, which they sent to sea in the hope of effecting her **capture.** The ship was **the** *Gamo*, and although described as a xebec frigate, she appears, from a drawing by Pocock, from which we give an engraving, to have been a square-rigged, polacre ship, with the exception of her mizen-mast, which had a long lateen yard, not much unlike the mizen-yard which was in vogue until towards the close of the **last** century. A number of gunboats were sent as a bait **to** the trap the Spaniards had laid for her, with orders to decoy the *Speedy* well under the land, so as to insure her capture, and also, probably, to endeavour to shoot away some of her spars.

After a running fight of **some duration with** the gunboats, the *Speedy* chased them into port, and after repairing the damages sustained in this encounter, the *Speedy* again stood in-shore.

At daylight, on the morning of the 6th May, a large ship was observed in the offing, bearing E.S.E. steering under all sail for the *Speedy*. Had Cochrane tried his hardest, we doubt whether he could have evaded this foe, for he was hemmed in with the land; and had any effort been made to escape, it would assuredly have marred any chance of victory over so powerful an adversary. The officers and ship's company of the brig, too, were emboldened by their success, never having met a repulse; and, no doubt, reposed implicit confidence in their captain. Some murmurs had also been heard consequent upon the former retreat from a Spanish frigate; so, putting all these considerations together, Cochrane made up his mind to engage the approaching foe.

The proper complement of the *Speedy*, as we have already seen, was eighty officers and men; but of these, no less than twenty-six were absent in prizes. The total force in officers and men, therefore, was only fifty-four. These comprised the commander, Lieutenant Richard W. Parker, Surgeon James Guthrie, Mr. Archibald Cochrane, midshipman, and two warrant officers.

It is to be regretted that scarcely any of the gaps left by historians have been filled up by Cochrane's Autobiography, and that the names of some of his gallant followers and supporters appear to have escaped his memory.

The ship's company having expressed their wish to fight the stranger, every preparation was made calculated to bring the contest to a successful issue. The

Speedy's four-pounders would have stood a poor chance against the heavy metal of the frigate, and Cochrane, like an experienced wrestler, determined **to** cling so closely to his opponent as to **neutralize** his superior strength. The guns of the *Gamo*—for **by** that name we may as well at once call the stranger—were nearly six feet **out** of water, and the top of the *Speedy's* bulwarks not more than five. By getting close to the enemy, therefore, the shot from the *Gamo's* guns would go harmlessly over the *Speedy;* while the small four-pounders of the latter, loaded with round and grape, would produce their full effect.

The danger attending this position was that arising from the enemy's musketry, and from boarding. Cochrane's aim was, therefore, to run alongside **to** leeward, and without **securing or** lashing, **maintain a** close action.

The *Speedy* consequently hauled close to the wind, to hasten the junction, and at 9h. 30m. A.M. the *Gamo* hoisted Spanish colours, and fired **a** gun. The *Speedy* hoisted American colours, and crossed the frigate's bows **on** the starboard tack, passing to windward of her antagonist, in the hope of inducing her to reserve her fire until the brig could get on the other tack ; but the *Gamo* was not to be thus deceived, and discharged a broadside. Fortunately, the guns were ill directed, and the *Speedy* sustained **no** damage of importance. She then hove about, and bearing up, ran close under **the** lee and larboard or port **side of the** *Gamo*, her yards locking in with those of her huge opponent.

Not till then were the guns of the *Speedy* discharged; and the effect was greater than any one could have looked for. The Spanish captain, Don Francisco de Torres, and one of his principal officers —the boatswain — were among the killed by this broadside, the loss of whom must have been severely felt.

The shot of the *Gamo*, **in the mean** while, flew harmlessly over the *Speedy*; but this being discovered, the Spaniards determined to put an end to the contest by boarding. The movement was not unobserved. The helm of the *Speedy* was put a-starboard, and a water space of twenty or more feet quickly interposed. The assembled boarders, exposed also to a murderous fire of musketry and grape-shot, returned to their guns, and the *Speedy* again rubbed sides with her.

This movement **was repeated** with no better result; but, notwithstanding these successful manœuvres, it was clear that the *Speedy* was in **a** position of great danger. Her rigging and sails had been nearly cut to pieces, and if the contest had continued a little longer in this manner, her masts would probably have been shot **away.** Cochrane therefore, as the only chance of victory remaining, determined on boarding; and his plans were very cleverly laid.

The whole crew were to be engaged on this service —one division to board forward, and the other abaft; and both to work their way towards a junction in midships. The party ordered to board at the bow had their faces blackened, so as to look as hideous as possible; and these, headed by Lieutenant Parker, were not **long in** gaining **a** footing on the enemy's deck, notwithstanding the presence of a large body **of** Spaniards. The begrimed faces of the *Speedy's* men, added to their impetuosity, struck **dismay into** the hearts **of** the *Gamo's* defenders, **and they** incontinently gave way.

Cochrane in person had simultaneously headed **the** aftermost division; **and** the enemy, thus unexpectedly assailed forward and aft, were driven a confused mass in the waist. Here a desperate hand-to-hand struggle ensued, which would probably have continued much longer, had not one of the *Speedy's* men, by direction of Lord Cochrane, fought his way **to** the ensign-staff, **and hauled** down the Spanish colours. The effect of this **was the surrender of the Spaniards** — they believing that **the colours** had been hauled **down by** their commanding officer's directions. In order **that** every man should have a share in this boarding expedition, Mr. Guthrie volunteered to take the helm, and performed his task with great dexterity.

The difficulty now was to secure the prisoners **and** the **prize.** Several gunboats were observed coming out of Barcelona, and had they acted with any degree of spirit, and attacked the *Speedy*, she must either have relinquished her hard-earned prize, or have been captured. Cochrane's brother Archibald, a smart young officer, a volunteer **on** the occasion, was placed in charge of the prisoners, who had all been driven **into** the main hold of the *Gamo*, the ladders removed, and guns pointed down upon them, a man standing with a lighted match ready at any moment to repress any attempt to retake the ship.*

The following is a comparative statement of the force of the two ships :—

		Speedy.		*Gamo.*
Broadside guns .... {	No. 7	..	16
	lbs. 28	..	188
Crew	54	..	319
Tonnage	158	..	600

Lord Cochrane's official letter respecting this truly brilliant and cleverly-conducted action, was as modest as the service was commendable. It was dated, " Off Barcelona, 6th May, 1800," and addressed to Captain Manly Dixon, who was the senior officer at Port Mahon, on the *Speedy's* arrival :—

"**I** have the pleasure **to inform you that the sloop** I have the honour **to** command, **after a** mutual chase and warm action, **has** captured **a** Spanish xebec **frigate of 32** guns, **22** long 12-pounders, 8 nines, **and 2 heavy** carronades, **viz., the** *Gamo*, commanded

---

* The difficulty thus experienced, brings to the recollection of the author of this little work a similar one experienced on the coast of Africa, some **thirty years ago, by a** mate—the late Captain Edw. H. Butterfield. **He had** captured a Spanish slaver **full of men,** with a boat's crew ; and as the prisoners were as six to one, he had recourse to a novel mode of keeping them in subjection. The chain cable was ranged along the deck, and each **of** the prisoners shackled to it by one leg. The anchor was at the same time all clear, and a man in charge of the prisoners **was** stationed at the stopper ready to let go. So that, had any attempt been made to re-capture the vessel, the man had nothing to do but drop the anchor.

by Don Francisco de Torres, manned by 319 officers, seamen, and marines.

"The great disparity of force rendered it necessary to adopt some measure that might prove decisive. I resolved to board, and with Lieutenant Parker, the Hon. A. Cochrane, the boatswain, and crew, did so, when, by the impetuosity of the attack, we forced them to strike. I have to lament, in boarding, the loss of one man only; the severe wounds received by Lieutenant Parker, both from musketry and the sword, one wound received by the boatswain, and one seaman.

"I must be permitted to say, that there could not be greater regularity, nor more cool, determined conduct shown by men, than by the crew of the *Speedy*. Lieutenant Parker, whom I beg leave to recommend to their lordships' notice, as well as the Hon. Mr. Cochrane, deserve all the approbation that can be bestowed; and the exertions and good conduct of the boatswain, carpenter, and petty officers, I acknowledge with pleasure, as well as the skill and attention of Mr. Guthrie, the surgeon."

After a delay of a month and three days, Captain Dixon forwarded the above despatch to Mr. Nepean, Secretary of the Admiralty, with a brief covering letter, describing the affair as " a very brilliant and spirited action with a Spanish xebec frigate." Lord Cochrane, however, had meanwhile sent a duplicate copy of the letter to Admiral Lord Keith, who was then with his flag on board the *Foudroyant*, at

Alexandria. **Lord** Keith returned the following **answer, dated June 9th, 1800 :—**

"I have received **your lordship's letter of** the 13th ultimo, enclosing **a copy of your letter to** Captain **Dixon, detailing your engagement with,** and capture of the **Spanish xebec of 32 guns, and cannot** fail to be **extremely** gratified **with the communication of** an event so honourable **to the** naval service and **so** highly creditable **to your lordship's** professional reputation, and to the **intrepidity and** discipline of the *Speedy's* officers and men, **to all of whom I** request your lordship will make **my perfect satisfaction** and approbation known."

The *Speedy*, accompanied by her prize, reached Port Mahon in safety, on the 13th May.

The casualties among the *Speedy's* crew were wonderfully slight in comparison **with the** magnitude of **the achievement.** Two men **were** killed **prior to** the boarding and five **wounded,** but the loss in carrying the enemy was one **man** killed ; Lieutenant Parker severely, both **by musketry** and the sword, the boatswain, and one **seaman,** wounded. The *Gamo* commenced the action with **274** officers and seamen and 45 marines, of whom she had killed, the captain, boatswain, and 13 men, and 41 wounded.

In his gazetted letter, as we have seen, **Lord Cochrane** mentions in fitting terms Lieutenant Parker, the Hon. **Mr. Cochrane,** Mr. Guthrie (surgeon), the boatswain, and carpenter, whom he has failed to name,

SPEEDY AND GAMO GOING INTO PORT MAHON.

Page 42

and the petty officers. Had a similar announcement appeared **half a century later, every** person mentioned would unquestionably **have been promoted to the** date of the transaction; **but in those days,** when heroic deeds were of every-day **occurrence,** Gazette letters descriptive of them were looked upon as chronicles of mere matters of course. The friends of Lord Cochrane, however, vigorously plied the First Lord of the Admiralty, who was then Admiral Earl St. Vincent, with applications, which the earl, not willing to concede any favour to the *protégé* of Lord Keith, chose to treat as demands. The rule of promotion in the navy has never been properly defined. The authorities in this age, if for no more commendable reason, aware **that** any failure **on** their part to reward conspicuous valour, would be warmly taken up in the House of Commons, have made a practice of promoting all officers **whose** names appear in **a** gazetted despatch, or at least the seniors; but we doubt whether any first lord, even now, would concede a promotion, if claimed as a matter of right.

His uncle, Captain **Sir** Alexander Cochrane, wrote two very pressing letters, one relative to the escape of the *Speedy* from the Spanish frigate, and the other on learning the particulars of the capture of the *Gamo.* **The** Earl of Dundonald also wrote a letter on behalf **of** his son, in **which he** expressed his " surprise and disappointment " at finding several masters and commanders **on** the station, who were his son**'s** juniors long before, and for several months after the taking of the *Gamo*, placed before him on the captain's list.

The loss of time in acknowledging Lord Cochrane's great merits was not, however, attributable solely to any disinclination on the part of the first lord. Captain Brenton, in his "Naval History," says that "an illustrious person" had told Lord St. Vincent that he "must promote Cochrane," and that **Lord St.** Vincent replied, "The first lord knows no 'must';" but the delay was mainly owing to the absence of Lord Keith, and to the round-about red-tape system which, from the earliest times, had been the curse of the Admiralty. Had Captain Dixon forwarded the despatches home immediately, the letters might have been laid aside because they had not passed through the office of the commander-in-chief, and no one would have been more likely than Lord St. Vincent to take this exception, for the navy never had a greater stickler for forms and discipline than the noble admiral. The chief reason, therefore, was the absence of Lord Keith in Egypt.

The intelligence thus delayed, reporting the *Gamo's* capture, reached England very nearly at the same time with the news that the *Speedy* had herself been **taken by** the French squadron, and Lord Cochrane's promotion was, therefore, ostensibly withheld on that account. But Lord St. Vincent is justly to be censured by posterity for having allowed petty jealousy, for it could have been nothing else, to interfere with **his** sense of justice and duty to a brother officer. **He** might with propriety have resisted every attempt to claim that as a right which custom had placed in his power **to** give freely, or to withhold for a time ; but when he did concede the boon he ought, as a brave man, to have rightly estimated the gallantry and ability of the young lord, and have had his captain's commission antedated.

We wish that, as the impartial **biographer of** Cochrane, we could acquit him **of** having done anything to widen this breach. In this age we view Lord St. Vincent **as a hard,** implacable commander ; a man for the **times,** however, fitted to crush the demon of **mutiny** with the iron heel of authority. **We view him** as a stern, immovable admiral, ready to carry out Articles of War to the strict letter, without the slightest feeling of compunction **or** hesitation. He was the Judge Jeffreys of his time, and thought nothing of hanging a dozen men suspected of mutiny, or of allowing them to be tortured from ship to ship by the infamous **and** brutal punishment of " going round the fleet."

Yet at times St. Vincent could joke, and even do generous acts ; but his antipathies were insurmountable. Cochrane most unwisely put himself in the power of this officer, although he was doubly armed with the authority **of** an admiral and of First Lord of the Admiralty.

Before quitting the Mediterranean, Cochrane addressed a letter to Earl St. Vincent, requesting him to promote Lieutenant Parker, who had been severely wounded in the action. To this letter no answer had been received on his arrival in England, and he wrote a second letter. This also remaining unanswered, he wrote again; and to this Lord St. Vincent vouchsafed a reply that his "application could not be entertained, as it was unusual to promote two officers **for such a** service;" besides which, **he** said, "**the** small number **of** men killed **on board** the *Speedy* did not warrant the request."

Prudence would **then** have dictated **a** cessation of letter-writing. **The** correspondence had gone far enough to show that Lord St. Vincent was not a man to be dunned into promoting Lieutenant Parker; but the probability is that an early opportunity would have presented itself to reward that gallant officer had the matter been allowed **to** settle down. But Cochrane took the surest means to prevent this. **He** wrote again to Lord St. Vincent in terms **which** were extremely unbecoming, considering the **relative** positions of the correspondents. Lord St. Vincent need not have **stated** any reason for **not** complying with Cochrane's request, **and the** gratuitous observation about the small number killed was most absurd, inasmuch as that circumstance **was** the best feature in the action; but it was not the province of a young captain **to** beard an officer holding the rank and position of Earl **St.** Vincent. By doing so he not only injured **himself, but in** gratifying his spleen ruined his unfortunate lieutenant. **He said** that his (Lord St. Vincent's) reasons for not promoting Lieutenant Parker, because there were only three **men** killed on board the *Speedy*, were in opposition to his lordship's own promotion to an earldom; **for that** in the battle from which his lordship derived his title, there was only one man killed on board his own flag-ship; so that he wrote "there were more casualties in my sloop than in your line-of-battle ship."

The remark was true enough, and this, no doubt, made the arrow enter the deeper; but that accident, for such it was, had no proper bearing. Cochrane might have said that seven ships in the battle off Cape St. Vincent did not lose one man, and that their first lieutenants were promoted notwithstanding; but that remark would have been less personal, and, consequently, not so sarcastic, although more to the point. The result was that poor Parker lost his promotion for five years. Cochrane, having got into Parliament, had influence enough to get him promoted ultimately; but either through ignorance or intention, he was appointed to a ship supposed to be in the West Indies, and went to that station to take up his commission, when he found that no such ship was in the navy.

In the "Autobiography of a Seaman" a great deal is made of this latter circumstance, much more than the fact warrants. Our impression is that it resulted from an oversight. Whenever an officer is promoted, he is appointed to some ship "for rank." This is perfectly understood, and an officer may be appointed to the *Royal William* or to the *Royal Oak*, but without any intention of his repairing on board to take command. It is simply a form; and had Commander Parker consulted the commander-in-chief at the nearest port, or have applied to the Admiralty to order him a passage out to join his ship, he would at once have been undeceived.

A petition was presented to the Admiralty in 1824 from the widow of this officer, setting forth that her husband had sustained **a loss** of a thousand pounds in going to the West Indies on this bootless errand, and claiming **relief on that score ; but nothing** was ever done for her.

THE END OF THE *SPEEDY*.
[1801.]

Subsequently **to the** return of the *Speedy* to Port Mahon, Lord Cochrane **was** ordered to proceed to Algiers for the purpose of remonstrating with the Dey upon the illegality **of his** cruisers in capturing an English vessel. The Dey is reported to have simulated much anger, in the hope of alarming the representative of the British Government, and **re-**marked that **" the** British vessels were the **greatest pirates in the** world **;" to** which compliment Cochrane bowed. The mission was, however, successful, and the British vessel consequently released. The Dey was not far wrong **in** his censure, and Cochrane afforded an instance **in** the fact that he had captured **a Spanish 6-gun priva**teer not long before, and **had given the** command of her to his brother Archibald, **to** cruise as the *Speedy's* tender.

The next, and last, service **of the *Speedy* was** performed in conjunction with Commander Pulling, of the *Kangaroo*. On the 1st June she **fell in** with the *Kangaroo* **off** Barcelona, **and in** consequence of information obtained **from a** Minorquian privateer, it was determined **to go in pursuit of a Spanish** convoy of twelve sail, protected by five armed vessels.

On the morning of **the 9th they** gained **sight of** the object of their search at anchor under **the** battery at Oropeso. Commander **Pulling,** though the **senior** officer, intrusted the conduct **of** the expedition **to Lord** Cochrane, and directed **him to** lead into the **bay.** By noon the two brigs anchored within half gun-shot of the enemy, consisting of a xebec of 20 guns and three gunboats, to **which** were afterwards added a large felucca moun**ting 12** guns, and two other gunboats, and commenced action. These vessels were lying under a large, square tower, mounting 12 guns, which commanded the anchorage, and which kept up a galling fire. At 3 P.M., **two of the** gunboats were sunk by the fire of the *Kangaroo* and the *Speedy;* but the firing was kept up by the **fort and** some vessels in the offing until 5 P.M.

The *Kangaroo* then slipped her cables, and Commander Pulling despatched the boats under the command **of** Lieutenant Thomas Foulerton, **of** the *Kangaroo*, Lieutenant Warburton, of the *Speedy*, assisted by the **Hon. A.** Cochrane and Messrs. Dean and Taylor, midshipmen, which succeeded in bringing off three brigs laden with wine, rice, and bread,—all, **in fact, that** remained afloat. When the strong position of the convoy is taken into consideration, coupled with the paltry fire of two small brigs, the result is not only surprising, but reflects great credit upon all concerned. When the action ceased,

the two vessels had expended nearly all their ammunition.

The *Gamo*, during the absence of the *Speedy* from
Port Mahon, had been sold for half her value to the
Algerines. Cochrane would **have** made a large fortune
in command of such **a vessel; but** the opportunity
was not afforded him.

The last service **upon** which the *Speedy* was engaged
was in convoying a dull sailing-packet from Port
Mahon to Gibraltar. The *Speedy* and her sluggish
charge had reached Alicant, when two vessels were
observed at anchor in a bay close at hand. The *Speedy*
made sail towards them, when, without waiting her
near approach, they cut their cables and ran ashore.
As they could not be got off very easily, the *Speedy's*
boats went in and set them on fire; and as they were
laden with oil, they naturally made a **great** blaze.
This, unfortunately, attracted the **attention of** three
French line-of-battle ships in the offing, and occasioned the *Speedy's* capture.

On the 3rd July, before daylight, these three ships
were seen from the *Speedy*, and at first taken for
galleons; but daylight soon dispelled the illusion.
The *Speedy* having **the** weather-gage, endeavoured,
on discovering the **true** character of the strangers,
and that they were line-of-battle ships, **to** escape by
means of using her sweeps **or** oars. This proving
unavailing, the guns were thrown overboard; and the
brig put before the wind, but **in vain,** for **the** *Dessaix*,
being the **nearest, opened** fire upon her. The chase,
or rather dodging, lasted three hours; and at length,

as a last resource, the *Speedy* being by this time lightened **of nearly all** her stores, endeavoured to get away by suddenly altering her course, and setting studding-sails. But it was too late. **The** *Dessaix* was within musket-shot, and the game being up, the *Speedy* hauled down her colours. There can be no **doubt** that every effort which good seamanship could dictate, was used; and Captain Palliere, of the *Dessaix*, deservedly complimented Lord Cochrane on the skill he had displayed, and treated him, as it was the custom of French officers to do, with great kindness and hospitality.

The Speedy, under Lord Cochrane's command, had **done** good service. **The** prize-money accruing from his numerous captures, had enriched all hands, notwithstanding the extortions of the Malta prize-court, so bitterly complained of. The partiality shown by Lord Keith, in giving the *Speedy* the best cruising-ground, had excited the jealousy of other captains of small vessels, and Cochrane attributed his having been sent to convoy the packet to this circumstance. He **had,** however, made hay while the sun was shining, and had in all captured or retaken no less than fifty vessels, mounting 122 guns.

The *Speedy* was carried into Algeçiras Bay; and shortly afterwards Cochrane had to witness the untoward attack made by the squadron under the command of Sir James Saumarez, which terminated in the grounding and loss of the 74-gun ship *Hannibal*. He **was** not, however, long detained a prisoner of war; for owing to the wonderful celerity with which the

British squadron was refitted at Gibraltar, the disabled ships, reinforced by the *Superb*, got to sea on the 12th July, in time to intercept a squadron of Spanish and French ships in the Straits of Gibraltar, when on their way to Algeçiras, and Cochrane was exchanged for the second captain **of the** *Saint Antoine*, one of the prizes.

A court-martial, as a matter of form, was held upon Lord Cochrane for the loss of the *Speedy*, which resulted in his honourable acquittal; and his promotion **to post** rank was dated 8th August, 1801, just three months **and two days** subsequent to the spirited **capture of** the *Gamo*.

COMMAND OF THE *ARAB*.
[1803-4.]

Lord Cochrane **had now** cause to repent his indiscreet letter to **the** First Lord of the Admiralty. True it was a time **of peace**; but his restless disposition still prompted **him** to seek further work. But Lord **St. V**incent was in power, and had the nomination of captains to ships. Cochrane, therefore, visited Edinburgh, and during his stay there attended the university **college**. He made few acquaintances, and gave **himself up to study**. The peace was of short duration; **for on the 6th May**, 1803, war with France was again formally declared, and Cochrane made his **way to** the Admiralty, and became a candidate for a ship,—**no matter of** what sort, so long as it was a ship. He waited on **the** First **Lord; but** St. Vincent had nothing **whatever open** likely **to suit him**. One ship named was **too large, another** promised, and a third not ready for the pendant. Nettled **at the treat-**ment, he stated **his** intention **of** returning to Edinburgh to study, **with** the **view to** seek **some other** employment.

Lord **St.** Vincent did not intend **this;** he wished, however, to punish him **for the** disrespect **he** had shown him. The torture **he had** in store for him was of a more refined **description** than simple **refusal;** so he appointed him **to one of** the most confirmed laggards of **a ship in** the British navy. A number of worthless north-country-built ships **had** been purchased into the service, with the view to their being employed in charge **of** convoys. The inequality in sailing between the heavy merchant-ships and men-of-war having struck **some clever** individual, who perhaps had ships to sell, the Admiralty were induced **to** purchase a small **fleet of** them, nearly all of which came to an untimely **end.** The *Wolverine*, one of this class, was captured in 1804, in defending **a** con-**voy;** and the *Alert* sunk by a few broadsides from an **enemy's** frigate, and such a fate was **predicted for the** delectable craft, the command of which was conferred upon **Lord Cochrane.**

Lord St. Vincent ordered Cochrane to proceed **to** Plymouth, and on his arrival there, he found himself appointed to command **the** *Arab.* Never was a ship more inappropriately named, — **the** *Tortoise* would have been a fitting designation. Cochrane repaired **to the** dockyard **to** find the craft which was to bear his pendant; and his chagrin may be imagined at finding the *Arab* a barque, under conversion to a man-of-war, which had previously been engaged in a very becoming employment for her,—that of carrying coals from Newcastle. The dockyard people were patching her up with **old converted** timber; and when finished, she was armed with 18-pounder carronades. The *Arab*, in fact, though designated a ship-sloop, was a far less effective man-of-war than **the** little 22-gun *Speedy.*

His commission was dated October, 1803; and he remained in this tub until November, 1804. The *Arab* would not stay **in** a moderate breeze of wind; and **had** she been caught on a lee shore in half a gale of **wind,** must have been lost. Cochrane was enduring the fires of professional purgatory; for, in addition to giving him the most inefficient ship **in the navy, his** tormentor ordered him to cruise to **the** north-east of the Orkney Islands, to protect fisheries,—aware, all the time, that no fishermen visited the locality pointed out. Fortunately for him, Lord St. Vincent's term of office was brief; and when the *Arab* returned from her penal service in November, 1804, Lord Melville was First Lord of the Admiralty.

GOLDEN CRUISE OF THE *PALLAS.*
[1804-5.]

On the 24th November, 1804, Lord Cochrane was transferred from the *Arab* to a **new 32-gun** fir-built frigate of 667 tons, armed **with long** 12-pounders on the main-deck, **and** 24-pounder **carronades** on the quarter-deck **and forecastle.** The *Pallas* had been off the stocks **only four** days, having been launched from Plymouth dockyard on **the** 17th November, on the same day with **the _Hibernia_,** 104, then the largest ship in the navy, and the _Circe_, **32. The** _Pallas_, though classed as a 32-gun frigate, in fact mounted 38 guns. In the same way, owing to the erroneous **mode of** calculation, 38-gun frigates mounted 46 guns; and 44-gun frigates, 50 guns. The _Pallas_, being fir-built, possessed the quality **of** speed, which **was** one in great request; and, after such a tortoise as the _Arab_, this frigate **must have** seemed a hare when under canvas.

Cochrane, however, had hardly effected this, to him, very desirable exchange, when he found himself in-**volved in** a disagreeable controversy. The commander-in-chief at Plymouth **was** Vice-Admiral William Young; and, in order to **claim a** share of the prize-money which the **new _Pallas_** was likely to make, he, so says Lord Dundonald, copied the Admiralty orders, and so constituted the _Pallas_ a ship belong-ing to his squadron. This practice was, we believe, not uncommonly resorted to by port-admirals; and captains **were** only too glad to consent to the arrange-ment, inasmuch **as** it generally secured to them the most lucrative cruising-ground, and often prevented their being employed **in** the monotonous and unpro-fitable service of convoying **a** fleet of merchant-ships to North America or elsewhere. But Cochrane was **an** unwilling party to the arrangement, which proved **a** good one for the admiral. Lord Melville had pro-mised him **a short cruise,** as **a** means of rewarding him for his past neglect; and had he remonstrated against the act, Admiral Young would, most likely, have been ordered to cancel his selfish and un-authorized order. Had he foreseen the success in store for him, he would, no doubt, have done this.

The *Pallas* put to sea, and proceeded to cruise off the Western Islands—a perfect El Dorado, as it turned out. One month was to be the duration of the cruise. On the 6th February, the *Carolina*, a large Spanish ship from Havannah, bound to Cadiz, was fallen in with, captured, and sent to Plymouth. This piece of good fortune was rendered doubly so by the information gained from the prisoners, namely, that the *Carolina* was one of a convoy from which she had not long before parted company.

That day week the *Pallas* fell in with a second, still more valuable; for, in addition to an ordinary cargo, she had on board valuable diamonds and bars of the precious metals. This vessel was also sent to Plymouth; and two days afterwards a third, richer still, fell into his net. This ship having a great many dollars on board, they were trans-shipped to the *Pallas* for better security, and the prize despatched to England. Next day, on the 16th, a fine Spanish letter-of-marque was captured, also having on board a quantity of dollars, but which, owing to the heavy sea running, could not be removed without risk. The treasure was, therefore, left on board, and reached Plymouth in safety. In ten days Cochrane had realized a very respectable fortune. The amount is nowhere stated, but it must have been considerable;

but the drawback was, that the port-admiral claimed a third of the captain's share.*

Fortune, which had thus come so suddenly upon the *Pallas*, seemed about to desert her, for while in the act of securing the fourth prize, a British privateer was observed to take possession of another Spanish vessel, which was in fact more valuable than either of those captured ; and had not the privateer, in her endeavour to prevent the *Pallas* from sharing, made sail away, the probability is the fifth of the convoy would have also found her way to Plymouth. The privateer, in avoiding the *Pallas*, caused her rich prize to fall into the jaws of a French squadron, by which she was recaptured.

We gather from the *Naval Chronicle* for 1805, that the *Fortuna* had on board 450,000 dollars, equal to £132,000, and about the same sum in valuable merchandise ; and as the other three prizes were very

---

* It was a common saying among sailors at this period, that when the pay-clerk went on board ships to pay prize-money, he clambered with his money-bags into the maintop, and showered the money down at random. All which remained upon the splinter netting (a coarse rope netting, spread as a kind of awning) was for the men, and all that went through, for the officers. There was some reason for this saying. The captain of a ship, not under an admiral's flag, received three-eighths of the net proceeds. Lord Cochrane would therefore have enjoyed three-eighths of the proceeds of his four fabulously rich prizes, had not Admiral Young thrown in his claim for one of the eighths, or one-third of Lord Cochrane's share. In the Autobiography, it is said that Admiral Young took "a half ;" but this could not have been so, unless some private arrangement was made prior to the cruise.

valuable, the total net proceeds, at a moderate estimate, could not have been far short of £300,000,
of which Lord Cochrane took one-fourth or £75,000,
and Admiral Young £37,500. But Cochrane was
well-nigh losing a good part of his booty as well as
his liberty. While on the passage home, between
the Azores and the coast of Portugal, a light fog
came on, which, though obscuring the hulls of vessels,
left their mast-heads visible to the look-out men
aloft. Three ships were reported, and it was soon
seen that they were line-of-battle ships. It was a desperate position. The wind freshened to half a gale, and
the *Pallas*, being a crank ship, was sailing with her
hammock-nettings half under water. The escape
appears to have been admirably managed. Finding
that the pursuing ships were gaining in the chase,
Cochrane determined to try what he could effect
by a manœuvre. He ordered everything to be prepared for taking in every stitch of sail together;
and, just as the enemy's ships were expecting to
take possession of their prize, every sail was suddenly clewed up and lowered down, and the three
chasing ships—one being on the weather, another
on the lee beam, and the third nearly astern or on
the weather-quarter, unable to get the canvass off in
time and haul to the wind, shot miles away to leeward.
Meanwhile the *Pallas* wore round and made sail on
the opposite tack. The pursuing ships, however, were
not long in resuming the chase, and were soon again
in the track of the *Pallas*. Night fortunately came
on, and the old trick of a lantern in a cask was put

in practice, while the *Pallas* altered her course and got clear of her pursuers.

The golden *Pallas*, as she was now truly designated, reached Plymouth ; and, as Cochrane had, while manning his ship, partly by pressing, promised to fill men's pockets with Spanish " pewter " and " cobs," he fully redeemed his promise by entering the harbour not only loaded with dollars, but with a **gold** candlestick, five feet in height, at each mast-head.* Cochrane never had occasion after that to send out a press-gang, for men readily presented themselves as volunteers. " Pewter " and " cobs," the nicknames for silver and dollars, superadded to gold candlesticks, never fail to have a strong attraction for sailors.

FIGHTING CRUISE OF THE *PALLAS*.
[1805–6.]

The *Pallas* was next ordered to convoy a fleet of merchant-ships to Quebec. An incident in connection with this voyage is worth recording. When the *Pallas* sighted the American coast, it was found that **she** was no less than 800 miles out in her dead reckoning. The cause of this great deviation proved to be incorrect compasses ; and upon investigation it was found that the binnacles were surrounded by iron instead of copper bolts. Finding this to be

---

* As these fine pieces of workmanship, intended for the cathedral at Madrid, came under the denomination of manufactured articles, the custom-house authorities demanded that **they** should pay duty ; to avoid which they were broken up and passed as old gold.

the case, Lord Cochrane, instead of entering the Gulf of St. Lawrence, proceeded to Halifax ; and although the dockyard authorities for a time demurred to making any change without first communicating with the home authorities, yet as Cochrane refused to lift an anchor until the defect had been remedied, they at last gave in.

The *Pallas* on her return to England in December, was ordered to join Rear-Admiral Thornborough's squadron, intended to cruise off the French and Spanish coasts; and, accordingly, left the Downs on the 23rd January, 1806. Previously to proceeding thither, however, Lord Cochrane cut out a vessel by means of his boats at the mouth of the Somme, and also captured a fast-sailing lugger. The *Pallas* sailed in company with the squadron on the 22nd February ; and on the 24th, being off the Isle Dieu, detained seven French fishing-boats. Having purchased a quantity of fish, Lord Cochrane released the boats ; but not before he had obtained information which enabled him, in the night, to capture a vessel laden with wine. The boat used by the night parties in capturing vessels was a very large galley, the private property of the captain, which rowed eighteen oars, double banked. Her rapidity was such that the French merchant vessels, on observing her approach, invariably endeavoured to run ashore.

Having made several prizes by these and other means, the *Pallas*, being detached from the rest of the squadron, chased a convoy on the 5th April into the Garonne; and learning that some French corvettes were at anchor in the river, Lord Cochrane came to the resolution of attempting to cut out two of the number with the **boats.** **The** *Pallas* accordingly anchored near the Corduan shoal; and just after dark the boats started on this perilous service. With the exception of Lord Cochrane and forty men, who remained in the *Pallas*, the whole crew embarked in the boats, under the command of Lieutenant John Haswell, assisted by **Mr.** James Sutherland, master, and Messrs. Edward Perkyns, John Crawford, and W. A. Thompson, midshipmen. A hard pull of twenty miles **was before** them, as the two corvettes were **at anchor a long** way above the shoals.

It was not until 3 A.M. on the 6th that the boats arrived up with one of the objects of their search—this was the national brig *Tapageuse*, mounting fourteen long 8-pounders, and having a **crew** of ninety-five men. The struggle **was** severe; but the boarding party, having taken her **at** different points, the French were eventually overpowered. The tide ebbing **strongly,** it was found impossible **to** ascend the river **further, to** attack the other vessel; and being, therefore, obliged **to** content themselves with their one prize, the *Tapageuse* was got under sail, and at daybreak was on **her** way to join the *Pallas*. But the consort of the captured brig got under way and opened fire upon the British **prize.** A running action was therefore sustained until the *Tapageuse* reached **an** anchorage outside the river. So ably had this **gallant** and desperate service been conducted, that only **three** British seamen were wounded.

In the mean while the *Pallas* was in no small danger. Three strange sail made their appearance in the offing, standing in for the river. The private signal was made; but as it remained unanswered, Lord Cochrane was convinced that the strangers were enemies. Forty hands were all that remained in the *Pallas*, but Cochrane had recourse to a trick in order to make the enemy believe he had a full complement on board. He sent men aloft to cast loose the gaskets and stop the sails with single rope yarns, and was thus able to let fall the sails together, giving an idea of a numerous crew to those who did not notice the slow process of sheeting home the topsails. The *Pallas* then weighed anchor and made sail for the largest ship; which had scarcely received half a dozen shots when she ran ashore, and was dismasted by the shock. The crew took to the boats; and, fortunately for the *Pallas*, pulled for the shore, for had they been bold enough to board the frigate, they would have encountered a feeble opposition.

The two other ships now appeared standing towards the frigate; and after firing a few broadsides into the grounded ship, to prevent her from being extricated, the *Pallas* again made sail to close the strangers. When within shot of the nearest, the frigate opened fire from the bow guns, when the second vessel, following the example of the corvette, bore up and ran upon the rocks. The shock, as in the former case, caused the masts to fall over the side; and this crew also abandoned their vessel. The third corvette met with a similar fate; for after attempting to enter the

Garonne, the efforts made by the *Pallas* to intercept her occasioned her running on shore. Thus three fine vessels, each a match for the *Pallas* with her reduced crew of forty men, were driven on shore and eventually destroyed.

The following is a copy of Lord Cochrane's letter to Vice-Admiral Thornborough, narrating the particulars of these captures, dated off Chasseron, 8th April, 1806:—

" Having received information, which proved correct, of the situation of the corvettes in the river of Bourdeaux, a little after dark on the evening of the 5th the *Pallas* was anchored close to the shoal of Cordouan ; and it gives me satisfaction to state that about 3 o'clock on the following morning the French national corvette of fourteen long 12-pounders * and ninety-five men, who had the guard, was boarded, carried, and cut out about twenty miles above the shoal, and within range of two heavy batteries, in spite of all the resistance, by the first lieutenant of the *Pallas*, Mr. Haswell; the master, Mr. Sutherland; Messrs. Perkyns, Crawford, and Thompson, together with the quarter-masters, and such of the seamen and crew as were fortunate enough to find places in the boats.

" The tide of flood ran strong at daylight. *La Tapageuse* made sail. A general alarm was given. A sloop of war followed, and an action continued,

---

* This was an error, as no French brig mounted anything heavier than 8-pounders, equal to English long nines.

often within hail, till, by the same bravery by which
the *Tapageuse* was carried, the sloop of war which
before had been saved by the rapidity of the current
alone, was compelled to sheer off, having suffered as
much in the hull as the *Tapageuse* in the rigging.

"The conduct of the officers and men will be justly
appreciated. With confidence I shall now beg leave
to recommend them to the notice of the Lords Commissioners of the Admiralty.

"It is necessary to add that the same morning,
when at anchor, waiting for the boats (which, by the
bye, did not return till this morning), three ships
were observed bearing down towards the *Pallas*,
making many signals, and were soon perceived to be
enemies. In a few minutes the anchor of the *Pallas*
was weighed, and with the remainder of the officers
and crew, we chased, drove on shore, and wrecked one
national 24-gun ship, one of 22 guns, and the *Mali-
cieuse*, a beautiful corvette of 18 guns. Their masts
went by the board, and they were involved in a sheet
of spray.

"All in the ship showed great zeal for his Majesty's
service. The warrant officers and Mr. Tatnall, midshipman, supplied the place of commissioned officers.
The absence of Lieutenant Mapleton is much to be
regretted. He would have gloried in the expedition
with the boats. The assistance rendered by Mr.
Drummond, of the Royal Marines, was such as might
have been expected. Subjoined is a list of the
wounded, together with that of vessels captured and
destroyed since the 26th ult."

The foregoing letter was forwarded to Earl St. Vincent, commander-in-chief of the Channel fleet, by Admiral Thornborough, with a most complimentary letter, in which particular attention was drawn to the high state of discipline of the crew of the *Pallas*, instanced in the humanity displayed by them in the conflict; and Lord St. Vincent forwarded the dispatches to the Admiralty, with a letter concluding with the following paragraph:—"The gallant and successful exertions of the *Pallas* therein detailed reflect very high honour on the captain, officers, and crew, and call for my warmest approbation."

Lord Dundonald, in his autobiography, described the praise bestowed by Lord St. Vincent in this letter as "reluctant," and as intended to act "as a wet blanket on the whole affair." **It** is hard, however, to discover any strong **ground** for this assumption. Cochrane often complained bitterly of the neglect of his first lieutenant, Haswell, who commanded the cutting-out expedition; but it is to be feared that the cause rested in some degree upon the letter of the **8th** of **April**, which we have just reprinted from the **Gazette.** Lord Cochrane, it is true, stated that the boarding was conducted by Lieutenant Haswell; but nowhere **mentioned** that officer's services individually with any praise. He wrote—"the conduct of the officers and **men,**" &c., "will be justly appreciated;" and Lieutenant Haswell was allotted no particular **share** of the credit; in **fact, there was, as** it were, a sinister intention manifested to give to Lieutenant Mapleton, who was not present, the share of praise which belonged to Haswell. What else was meant by the passage " the absence of Lieutenant Mapleton is much to be regretted : he would have gloried in the expedition with the boats " ? Had the " He " been italicized, there would have been no question as to the intention.

Owing, no doubt, chiefly to the " reluctant praise " of Lieutenant Haswell, that officer lost his promotion for a time, and Cochrane subsequently made of this neglect a rod with which to castigate the authorities.

On the 14th, the *Pallas* returned to the scene of her actions with the corvettes, and after silencing a battery which had been thrown up for the protection of one of the grounded vessels, boarded and set her on fire. Attempts were also made to destroy the two other grounded vessels, but without effect, owing to the badness of the weather.

The next service of the *Pallas* was a reconnaissance of the French squadron at anchor under Isle d'Aix, when Cochrane counted one three-decked ship, one of 80, three of 74 guns, five frigates, and three brigs. He wrote a letter to Vice-Admiral Thornborough reporting this service, and after describing the force, added, " The *Calcutta* * is not among them, neither are there any corvettes. They are all very deep, more so than vessels are in general for common voyages. They

---

* This ship, formerly an Indiaman, commanded by Captain D. Woodriff, mounting 54 guns, had been captured by the Rochefort squadron on the 25th September, 1805, not off St. Helena, as stated in the autobiography, but in lat. 49° 30′ N., long. 9° W.

may be easily burned, **or** they may be taken by sending here 8,000 or 10,000 men, as if intended for the Mediterranean. If people at home would hold their tongues about it, possession might thus be gained of the Isle d'Oleron, upon which all the enemy's vessels may be driven by sending fire-ships to the eastward of Isle d'Aix."

This proposition was never entertained; but Lord Cochrane, on many subsequent occasions, referred to the fact of his having offered the very important and feasible suggestion.

The following official despatches are sufficiently explanatory of themselves to show the nature of the service referred to, that of destroying signal-stations. It was addressed to Vice-Admiral Thornborough, and dated St. Martin's Road, **Isle Rhe,** May 10, 1806 :—

"The French trade having been kept in port of late, in a great measure **by** their knowledge of the exact position of His Majesty's cruisers constantly announced at the signal posts, it **appeared** to me to be an object, as there was nothing better **to** do, **to** endeavour to stop this practice.

" Accordingly the two posts at Point de la Roche were demolished; next **that** of Caliola; then two in L'Anse **de** Repos, one **of** which Lieutenant Haswell and Mr. Hillier, the **gunner,** took in a neat style from upwards of **100** militia. **The** marines and boats' crews behaved exceedingly **well.** All the flags have been brought off, and the houses built by government burnt **to** the ground.

" Yesterday, too, the zeal of Lieutenant Norton, of the *Frisk* cutter, and Lieutenant Gregory, of the *Contest* gun-brig, induced them to volunteer to flank the battery on point d'Equillon, whilst we should attack in the rear by land; but it was carried at once, and one of fifty men, who were stationed to three 36-pounders, was made **prisoner,** the **rest** having escaped. The battery is laid in ruins, guns spiked, carriages burnt, barrack and magazine blown up, and all **the** shells thrown into the sea. The convoy got into **a** river beyond **our** reach. Lieutenant Mapleton, Mr. Sutherland, master, and Mr. Hillier, were with me; **and as** they do on all occasions, so they did at this time—whatever was in their power **for** His Majesty's service. The petty officers, seamen, and marines, failed not to justify the opinion that there was before reason to form ; yet it would be inexcusable were not the names of the quartermasters, Barden and Casey, particularly mentioned, as men highly deserving any favour that can be shown in the line to which they **aspire.**"

But the fighting cruize of the *Pallas* was not yet finished. On the 14th May, Lord Cochrane, pursuant to orders, again stood close in towards the Isle d'Aix, to renew the reconnaissance of the French squadron under Allemand. He found that they had moved from their former anchorage, and were then lying at **the** entrance to the Antioche passage. In Cochrane's previous reconnaissance a black frigate and three **brigs had made a feint at** coming out; but could not be drawn **from** under the shelter of the batteries. **On** this occasion, however, the intention of engaging was much more **strongly manifested, and** the gallant contest which ensued is very well described **in Lord** Cochrane's public letter, dated off Oleron, May 15, and addressed, as before, to the Vice-Admiral.

"This morning when close off Isle d'Aix reconnoitring the French squadron, it gave me great joy to find **our** late opponent the black frigate, and her companions the three brigs, getting under sail. **We** formed **high** expectations that the long-wished-for opportunity had **at last arrived.**

"The *Pallas* remained under topsails **by** the wind **to await** them. At 11·30 A.M., a smart point-blank firing commenced **on both sides,** which was severely felt by the enemy. The maintopsail-yard of **one of** the brigs was cut through, and the frigate lost her after-sails. The **batteries on Isle** d'Aix **opened on** the *Pallas*, and a cannonade continued, interrupted on **our** part only by the necessity we were under to **make various** tacks to avoid the shoals, till **one o'clock,** when our endeavour to gain the wind **of the** enemy, and get **between him** and the batteries, proved successful. An effective distance was now chosen, a few broadsides were **poured in,** and the enemy's fire slackened. **I ordered ours to** cease, and directed Mr. Sutherland, the master, **to run** the frigate on board, with intention effectually **to** prevent her **retreat.**

"**The** enemy's side thrust our guns back into the

port, the whole were then discharged, **and** the effect
and crash were dreadful.　Three pistol-shots were the
unequal return.

"With confidence **I** say, **that the frigate** was lost
to France, had not the unequal collision torn away
our foretopmast, jibboom, **fore and** maintopsail-yards,
spritsail-yard, bumpkin, cathead, **chain** plates, fore-
rigging, foresail, and bower-anchor, **with which** last **I**
intended to hook **on** ; but **all** proved insufficient.　She
was yet lost to France, had not the French admiral,
seeing his frigate's foreyard gone, her rigging ruined,
and the danger she was **in,** sent two others to her
assistance.*

"The *Pallas* being nearly **a wreck, we** came out
with what sail could be set; and his Majesty's sloop,
the *Kingfisher*, afterwards **took us in** tow.

"The officers and ship's company behaved as **usual.**
To the names of Lieutenants Haswell and Mapleton,

* "My gallant adversary in that frigate was Captain Collett,
who kept the deck after every one of his crew had been driven
below by our fire, which, as the *Minerve* had taken the ground,
swept her decks.　My gallant opponent, however, kept the
deck, or, rather, stood **on a** gun, with as much *sang-froid* as
though we had been firing a salute.　On our becoming entangled with the *Minerve's* rigging, he raised his hat with **all**
the politeness of **a** Frenchman of the old school, and bowed **to**
me, **a** compliment which **I** returned.　Judge **of** my surprise
when refused admission into the prison **at** Dartmoor, and
prowling about its out-offices, at finding **my gallant** enemy
located in *the stall of a stable*, he having **been** recently made
prisoner. I promised **to use** my **best endeavour to** get him
removed, and **on** my **arrival in** London **did so, I** believe with
effect."—*Autobiography of a Seaman.*

whom I have mentioned on other occasions, I have to add that of Lieutenant Thos. L. Robins, who has just joined."

This very gallant affair was attended with the loss of one marine killed, and Mr. William Andrews, midshipman (very badly), and four seamen, wounded.

It was afterwards ascertained that the "black frigate" was the *Minerve*, a fine ship of 1,100 tons, nearly double the size of the *Pallas*, and mounting long 18-pounders on her main deck, manned with a crew of 330 men and boys, of whom seven were killed and fourteen wounded. The three brigs were the *Lynx, Sylphe*, and *Palinure*.

There was an amount of heroism about this action, scarcely ever equalled in the annals of the British navy, and never surpassed. A cramped-up little ship which the *Pallas* was, of less than 700 tons, deliberately paraded herself before an enemy's squadron, and courted a battle under their own batteries and amidst their own shoals. Twice had Cochrane thus thrown the gauntlet into the teeth of an enemy of such superior magnitude, and when at length he was able to grapple with the foe, nothing but the over eagerness with which the ship was laid on board, and the subsequent advance of two fresh ships to the rescue, prevented him from achieving a triumph never gained during the war, namely, the capture of an 18-pounder by a 12-pounder **frigate**.

Being pretty well mauled by this time, the *Pallas* was ordered to proceed to Plymouth to refit, having

under convoy a fleet of transports, **and** where she
arrived on the 27th.

THE NAVAL M.P.
[1806.]

While the *Pallas* was **refitting** in Plymouth harbour, Cochrane was preparing **for a** campaign of
another sort—an electioneering one. **On** his arrival
home from his **"golden** cruise," he **had** been induced **to**
stand for the **borough of** Honiton; but having failed
to apply **the "palm-oil,"** without which there could **be
no return, he suffered defeat.** Never was there such
a man for expedients. Beaten **though he** was, he
managed **to** make his overthrow the stepping-stone
for a future victory. He **had not** bribed, so he said,
before the election; but when **the** struggle was over,
he set the town-crier to work **to announce that all**
those who **had recorded** their votes in his, Lord Cochrane's, favour, might **receive the** sum of ten **guineas** on
application **to** his agent. **A new** election **was on** foot
just **as the** *Pallas* arrived, and Cochrane, **in a** coach
drawn by six horses, **accompanied by** several carriages-
and-four filled with officers **and** seamen **of** the *Pallas*,
drove into Honiton, thereby making an imposing
display.

Cochrane **was** looked upon as a millionaire. **The**
story of the galleons and golden candlesticks, when
duly magnified by rumour, had a great effect, and his
triumphant return **for** the corrupt borough **of** Honiton
resulted **as a matter of course.**

And now the excited voters crowded round him with **open hands itching for** the customary fee. The candidate who could give ten guineas to those who voted for him when defeated, would not certainly be so shabby as not to at least double the present. Dire **was their** disappointment however. **Cochrane was** returned, and returned by a good majority, and without having bribed, and he coolly told his deluded supporters that he had not the slightest intention of paying them for their venality.

Cochrane was inexorable, and the votes could not **be recalled, but it** was now their turn to cajole. "**Your lordship** wont refuse to give us a public **supper?**" He could not refuse so moderate a request, **and did** not think it necessary to limit the expense. **The** supper **was** given, but it was preceded by a ball, **and shortly** afterwards **the bill was** sent to Lord Cochrane, amounting to the **sum of** £1,200. This he at first refused to pay, but was ultimately obliged to liquidate.

The first use made of his position as a member of **the** House of Commons, was that of applying for the promotion **of** his neglected first lieutenants in the *Speedy* **and** *Pallas*. The application was at first met with **half-promises, but** either the threat or the fear of having the gross injustice instanced in the nonpromotion **of** those officers brought before the House, had the effect of obtaining **that** which ought to have been freely conceded long before.

The neglect of Haswell **might** possibly have resulted **from** the ambiguous and dubious terms in which Lord Cochrane had mentioned his name in his official letter ;

and Parker was the innocent victim of his captain's ill-judged letter-writing.

Lieutenant Haswell was promoted, but his commander's commission was dated eleven **days** later than that of Lieutenant Sibley, who **cut out** the 16-gun brig *César* from Verdon roads **on the 15th** July, succeeding the capture of the *Tapageuse*. **Lord** Cochrane claimed **for the capture of** the *Tapageuse* equal merit with that of the cutting out the *César ;* and when the **two** exploits **are** fairly viewed, he will be thought right. The *César* **was,** it is true, more powerfully protected, and better prepared to resist the assailants ; but the attacking force comprised twelve boats, contributed by a squadron of six sail of the line and **two** frigates. The resistance was most determined, **and** one lieutenant, one mate, and seven seamen **were** killed ; and four lieutenants, one mate, and thirty-four men wounded ; irrespective of which, one midshipman and nineteen men were made prisoners, their boat having been struck by a shot, and sunk. **The** *Tapageuse* was captured by a portion of the ship's company of one small frigate, in a narrow river, defended by batteries, and in the presence **of** another French vessel of **the** same strength as the prize, and only three men were wounded in effecting it. Tested by the standard **of** "killed and wounded," the capture of the *César* was infinitely superior to the cutting out of the *Tapageuse ;* but by that of "common sense" the result is the **reverse.** The object which Cochrane invariably kept steadily in view, was to avoid loss to his own crew ; and this we take to have been his greatest merit. By the exercise of the faculty of foresight, he was able to avoid many defeats and casualties into which mere bull-dog courage might have plunged him and his followers; but an absurd rule existed at the Admiralty, which defined the "butcher's bill" as the criterion of gallantry.

The delay in promoting Lieutenant Haswell entailed upon those who were engaged with him in his perilous exploit in the Garonne, the loss of the naval medal granted in 1846. Never was there a more unrighteous decision than that which denied the medal to those who **served in an** action which was not marked by promotion. Cochrane's actions are direct cases in **point. It** suited the caprice of the Admiralty, in 1806, **to** withhold promotion justly due; and their successors in office **in 1846** punished gallant survivors in consequence, **by** denying them the grant of a silver medal.

No one can be surprised that this studied neglect of his officers and himself should have for ever after rankled in Cochrane's mind. He had performed what no other officer had had the good fortune of doing— cut out with his boats one corvette, and driven on shore and **destroyed three** others; and the Admiralty had taken so little notice of it as to refuse to advance the senior promotable officer. In many cases, ships destroyed under similar circumstances had been paid **for** as captures; but the Admiralty refused even to purchase the handsome little vessel which was the trophy of this victory. Truly Cochrane had good reason to complain of this marked and cruel treatment, the more so, when he saw a similar vessel, which had been captured by the *élite* of a large squadron, added to the British Navy.

Another slight, which was of less importance **to** Cochrane than to the service, was the refusal of the Admiralty **to purchase a** quantity of excellent claret which he had captured, except at the price of small beer. His agents refused to part with it upon such terms, although, from **the** enormous duty levied upon claret at the custom-house, it would scarcely realize a better price elsewhere. The Victualling Office might have taken it duty free; and it would have been **a** treat to our sailors; but, as they offered a sum so ridiculously beneath the proper value, the captors had the bungs of the casks knocked in, and the wine started into the sea, rather than submit to such terms.

A curious **incident is** connected with this wine; and as the late earl attributed most of his after **mis-**fortunes to it, we think it right to advert to it at some length. One of his friends at this period was the late Right Hon. John Wilson Croker, who for very many years held the post of Secretary to the Admiralty. This gentleman, who was on terms of great intimacy, was dining with Lord Cochrane, when some of the claret for which the Victualling Office had offered small-beer price—seven pipes of which had been cleared at the custom-house by Lord Cochrane's brother—was produced. Croker called it " superb," and Cochrane offered him as much as he pleased at the cost of the duty, which offer he appeared disposed to accept thankfully. Croker shortly afterwards became Secretary to the Admiralty, and from that time was a stranger to Lord Cochrane's table; but, meeting him in the street, Cochrane asked him why he had not sent for his wine; to which Croker replied, that his friends had already supplied him more liberally than he required. Other similar observations passed, and the consequence was the dead cut.

Our readers will have some difficulty in placing any other construction upon this story as told than that Croker expected the wine to be presented to him *duty paid*, and was annoyed at the terms upon which Cochrane had offered to supply him. This is certainly not a very charitable construction, neither is it very feasible; for the offer might have been declined without any compromise on either part. **Had** it been known that the Admiralty Secretary accepted presents, there is no doubt he would have **been** well supplied; and one is disposed to look rather upon Croker's accession to office as the real ground of the separation. Cochrane's views differed very widely from those of the cautious official; **and** it is not surprising that he should have availed **himself** of any excuse for declining future intimacy; **but it** is hardly possible to believe that so paltry **a disagreement** should have converted a friend, or even **a** common acquaintance, into the bitter and implacable enemy and persecutor which he is represented to have been afterwards.

The bitter enmity which subsequently manifested **itself** was most likely brought about by Cochrane's unflinching speeches in Parliament. They invariably sat on opposite benches, and what one said the other felt it his duty to contradict. Croker was in possession of Cochrane's confidential opinions upon naval subjects, and was, therefore, all the better able to answer his objections to the then existing abuses.

But Cochrane had **hardly had** time to make himself known in the House **when** he received an appointment to another ship.

THE *IMPÉRIEUSE.*
[1806–7.]

THE *Pallas* having received very severe treatment in her last encounter with the *Minerve*, it was considered desirable to give Lord Cochrane another ship. He was accordingly ordered to turn over with his officers and crew to the 38-gun frigate *Impérieuse.* He accordingly commissioned this fresh ship on the 2nd September.

The ship of which Cochrane now found himself the captain was one worthy of his pendant. She was formerly the Spanish frigate *Medea,* captured by Sir Graham Moore's squadron on the 5th October, 1804, and her name changed **to** *Impérieuse.* She was built in 1798, and measured 1,046 tons. Her armament consisted of twenty-eight long 18-pounders on the main deck, twelve 32-pounder carronades on the quarter deck, and two 32-pounder carronades and two long 9-pounders on the forecastle. Subsequently to the purchase of this ship, however, it was found that extensive repairs were needed, and when these were completed, she was more like a new ship destitute of seagoing fittings than one that had performed **several voyages.**

Before her fittings were nearly completed, or even her rudder hung, the *Impérieuse* was ordered to put to sea; and **so** urgent and peremptory **were the** Admiralty mandates, that when at length, on the 17th November, her rudder was hung and the rigging temporarily set up, she put to sea, she did so with lighters alongside discharging into her provisions, stores, and ammunition. The guns were not secured, and the **carronades** not fixed on their slides; and yet this ship was supposed to be in a condition to encounter an enemy!

This was what was termed "despatch." Possibly there might have been in the case of the *Impérieuse* a dash of the Croker **enmity**. The **ship** had been in commission **over six weeks,** and having a full complement ought not to have been so long getting ready for sea; neither would she, had not the dockyard been greatly overtaxed. A plea of that kind quietly urged in the right quarter would have been certain to cause imperative orders to be issued, and neither captain nor port-admiral would have dared to dispute the direction. **In** vain would it be said that the ship's rudder was not hung, or that the hold was not stowed, or provisions **on board, the** reply would have been, "Then it *ought* to have been hung, the hold *should* have been stowed, and **you must** proceed to sea immediately, stowed or not." **Such** was authoritative logic in 1806, and for many years afterwards.

The *Impérieuse* having got in mid-channel, and

having divested herself of her attendant hoys, commenced restowing the after-hold, and clearing the
decks. But her lower rigging having been only temporarily set up, the motion of the ship had caused it to
stretch so much that, had a gale come on, the ship must
have been dismasted. Fighting would have been out of
the question. Not a cartridge was filled, and hardly
a gun fitted ready for action. While employed in completing work that should have been done in harbour,
or, at any rate, in the Sound, the *Impérieuse* drifted
over to the French coast, and struck on some rocks off
Ushant. Luckily she sustained no injury, and was
extricated without difficulty, when she joined the
Channel fleet lying in Basque Roads, and on the
19th December captured two vessels off the Sables
d'Olonne.

On the 4th January, 1807, the *Impérieuse* chased
several vessels which made for Arcasson, and on the
5th the boats were sent away in chase of two of the
vessels which took shelter in a creek, under a battery
advantageously placed on a small island at its entrance. The frigate having anchored off the Cordouan,
the boats were sent away early on the morning of the
7th to attack the battery. This was successfully
performed. The guns, which comprised four 36-
pounders, two field-pieces, and a 13-inch mortar, were
spiked or destroyed, and the carriages burnt. Several
gun-boats at anchor in the rear of the island, together
with the vessels previously chased, were also burnt.
It was deemed imprudent to remain to get them
afloat, a general alarm having been given along the

coast. The *Impérieuse* was ordered to return to Plymouth shortly after this, at which port she arrived in February.

RETURNED FOR WESTMINSTER.
[1807.]

A dissolution of Parliament having taken place, Lord Cochrane, not wishing to face again his deluded Honiton victims, was induced to aspire to the representation of Westminster. Lord Cochrane's extreme opinions made **him an** acceptable candidate. **He** was an ultra-Whig, **which, in** those days, meant a great deal. Cobbett was of **the** same way of thinking. **Sir** Francis Burdett, who stood with Lord Cochrane, was noted as one of the most unflinching disciples of the Reform school of **politics ;** and he found in Lord Cochrane much congeniality of feeling **upon most** political questions. The candidates, at starting, were Brinsley Sheridan, Mr. Paul, and Lord Cochrane. Sir Francis Burdett was unable to present himself in person, in consequence of a wound which he had received **in** a duel with Mr. Paul; but he was, nevertheless, put **in** nomination. At the close **of** the first day Lord Cochrane was at the head of **the poll,** Mr. **Paul second,** Sir Francis Burdett third, and Sheridan **fourth; but at** the final close Sir Francis and Lord **Cochrane were at** the head, and consequently elected. Cochrane **probably** considered himself fortunate; but had he **been able** to peep into futurity, he would have seen that his return for Westminster was the most untoward event that could have happened to him. His naturally impetuous disposition was stimulated by the strong-minded men whom he met in Parliament. At no period, perhaps, was party feeling stronger or more unscrupulous, and Cochrane soon found, to his cost, that he had made enemies much more to be dreaded than Frenchmen or Spaniards. In the House of Commons he waged war against " venality and corruption," and received more desperate wounds in the contest than he risked in his most perilous action with the open and avowed enemies of England. On the 7th July, he brought forward the following motion :—" That a committee be appointed to inquire into and report upon all offices, posts, places, sinecures, pensions, situations, fees, perquisites, and emoluments, of every description, paid out of, or arising from, the public revenues or fees of any courts of law, equity, admiralty, ecclesiastical, or other courts, held or enjoyed by, or in trust for, any member of this House, his wife, or any of his descendants for him, or either of them, in reversion of any present interest; with an account of the annual amount of such, distinguishing whether the same arises from a certain salary, or from an average amount; that this inquiry extend to the whole of his Majesty's dominions, and that the said committee be empowered to send for persons," &c.

It was not to be expected that a motion of such a character, conveying, as it did, whether justly or not, an insinuation that members of Parliament were acted upon by corrupt influences, would pass muster. Various shifts and evasions were tried, and attempts made to put the motion in another form; but Cochrane insisted upon holding to the original, and pressed it to a division. **The motion was** lost by a majority of 20.

Encouraged rather than daunted at this defeat of his "little go," he determined to bring on his great question of "Naval Abuses." The following extract from Hansard will show with what ill success his motion was attended:—

LORD COCHRANE rose and said,—

"Sir,—A wish to avert part of the impending dangers of my country, has made me resolve to move for certain papers relative to the naval service, not with a retrospective view to blame individuals, but that unnecessary hardships may cease to exist. I am willing to believe that members of this House, whose talents are capable to do justice to the cause, **are** ignorant of circumstances which for years have embittered the lives of seamen employed in his Majesty's service; and that as to the gentlemen of the naval profession who have seats here, I suppose that the diffidence occasioned by the awe which this House at first inspires, has prevented them from performing this important **duty.** I shall be as brief as possible, but **as the nature** of some of the papers for which I am about **to** move is unknown to many members of this House, **it** will be **necessary** that I should give some explanation. **The first motion is,** 'That there **be** laid before this House copies of all letters or representations made by the commanders of H.M's. sloop *Atalante* and schooner *Felix*, addressed to Captain

Keats (commanding off Rochefort), respecting the state and condition of those vessels, and the sick therein.' The object of this motion is to prove that vessels under the present system, are kept at sea in a dangerous state, and that the lives of many officers and men are in constant peril. Lieutenant Cameron, who commanded the *Felix*, and since lost in that vessel, was one of the best and ablest officers I **ever** knew. **He** found it incumbent on him to report that the *Felix* ought to be sent into port to repair. I shall read part of two letters from the surgeon, dated three months before they all perished, and previous to Lieutenant Cameron's being appointed to command that vessel. The other dated eight days before that melancholy event. On the 14th of November, he says,—' Our noble commander has been very active in his endeavours to get confirmed to this vessel, much more than I should be; she sails worse and worse, and I think the chances are against our ever bringing her into an English port.' On the 14th of January, 1807, the surgeon says,—' Every endeavour has been put in force by Cameron and myself to get her into port, but without success. He attacked the commodore with most miserable epistles of distress throughout, and I attacked him with a very formidable sick list, but all, my friend, would not do.'

"I may be told that there is danger in agitating such subjects; but there can be none at any time in bringing to the knowledge of the Legislature, for redress, that which is notorious to those who have a right to claim it. No, Sir, let grievances be redressed in time, and complaints will cease. When the *Impérieuse*, the **ship I** command, was about to leave Rochefort, I was ordered to revictual the *Atalante* for six weeks, though she had then been out eight months—a period sufficient to ruin the health, break the energy, and weary the spirit of all employed in such **a** vessel. The *Atalante* was hauled alongside, the commander and several officers came on board, and informed me of the bad condition of their sloop. They said she was wholly unfit to keep the sea, and that a **gale** of wind would cause her inevitable loss. I think **they said** the foremast, and bowsprit, and fore-yard, were all sprung; besides, the vessel made twenty inches of water per hour. I thought it well to mention the circumstances, thus reported, to the commanding officer off Rochefort—for I well knew that the minds of subordinate officers ordered to survey, were impressed with terror, lest any vessel surveyed should not be found, on arriving in port, quite so bad as represented. Their usual plan therefore is, to say such a vessel can keep the sea a while longer—knowing that if any accident occurs it will **be ascribed** to zeal for the good **of his** Majesty's service! **So much** impressed was I with the bad state **of this** vessel, **that** I said to the builder of Plymouth-yard, in the presence of Admiral Sutton, on my arrival there, **that the first** news we should have from Rochefort, **if there should happen to be a gale** of wind, **would be the loss of the** *Atalante*. Under the harassing system of eight or nine months' cruises, men get tired of their lives, and even indifferent **as to the** choice between a French prison and their present misery. The next document I propose to move for is,—'An abstract of the weekly accounts of H.M's. ships and frigates employed off Brest and Rochefort, from the 1st of March, 1806, until the 1st of March, **1807.'** From this the number **of** men employed, the number of sick, the time the ships have been kept at sea, and the time they have **been** allowed in harbour to refit the vessels and recruit the crews will appear. The *Plantagenet*, for instance, was eight months within four hours' sail of England. **She was** then forced, **by** stress of weather, into Falmouth, where she remained twelve days wind-bound; but an order existed (which **I** shall presently make the subject of a motion), by which neither officer nor man could stretch his legs on the gravel beach within fifty yards of the ship! In order to show how little benefit has been derived from supplies at sea, as a substitute for refreshments and recreation which the crews were formerly suffered to enjoy, I shall next move,— 'That there be laid before this House an account of the quantity of fresh provisions, expressed in days' allowance, received at sea by each of H.M's. ships off Rochefort and Brest, from the 1st of March, 1806, to the 1st of March, 1807.' Formerly when the four months' provisions were expended, the return of a ship to port was a matter of course; but now they are victualled and re-victualled at sea; so that an East-India voyage is performed with more refreshment than a Channel cruise. Lime-juice is the **substitute** for fresh provisions, a debilitating antidote to the scurvy — unfit to re-establish the strength of the body impaired by the constant use of salt provisions. The next motion (which I shall propose) is,—'That there be laid before this House all orders issued and acted on between the 1st of March, 1806, and March, 1807, respecting leave to be granted or withheld from officers or men, distinguishing who was commander-in-chief at the times of issuing such orders.' It is a hard case that in harbour neither officer nor men shall be permitted to go on shore. These orders I do not hesitate to condemn; and the injustice appears the more striking, when it is remembered that the commander-in-chief resided in London, enjoying not only the salary of his office, but claiming the emolument of prize-money gained by the toil of those in active service. **I** shall not be surprised to find the office of commander-in-chief bestowed on some favourite as **a** sinecure by some future minister.

" With respect to the sick, I feel it necessary to say a few words, but I shall first read my motion on **that** subject,—' That there be laid before this House all orders issued and acted on between the 1st **of** March, 1805, and the 1st of March, 1807, by, or by the authority of the commander-in-chief of H.M's. ships and vessels in the Channel, allowing or restraining commanding officers from sending men to the naval hospitals. or restricting their admission to such hospitals.' In consequence **of** regulations established **in** these institutions, men are frequently refused admittance. No **man**, whatever may be his state of health, can be sent to an hospital from any of the ships in the Channel fleet, unless previously examined by the surgeon of the commander-in-chief. Deaths, amputations, and total loss of health, were the consequences of the impossibility of this officer going from ship to ship in bad weather, when opportunity offered to convey the sick to port. So pertinaciously were such regulations adhered to, that although I **sent a** sick lieutenant **and a man** ruptured to the hospital, they **were** not admitted. The disease of the one (who was under salivation) was declared to be **contrary to** the order regulating admission, and he **was** returned through sleet and rain; the other was refused because everything *possible* had not been done to reduce the rupture, as he had not been hung up by the heels, in a rolling sea, which might have proved his death! The system of naval hospitals is thoroughly bad. Mistaken economy has even reduced **the** quantity of lint for the purpose of dressing wounds. **To the** ships there is not half enough allowed. Unworthy savings have been unworthily made, endangering the lives of officers and seamen. Indeed, the grievances of the navy have been, and are so severe, through rigour and mistaken economy, that I can see nothing more meritorious than the patience with which these grievances have been endured."

Sir Samuel Hood, Admiral Harvey, Admiral Markham, the Chancellor of the Exchequer, Mr. Windham, and others, spoke against the motion.

Lord Cochrane rose *in reply*, and said :—" I disclaim, Sir, any **motive** whatever, except a regard for the real interests of my country, though I confess that I cannot **help** feeling, **in** common with others, the treatment received. Improper motives have been imputed **to me, and I might reply to** one of those gentlemen **w**ho has denied facts which I **can** prove, that he **was** one of those who established this abominable system.* What his abilities may be, in matters not connected with the naval service, I know not; but it is a known fact that **his noble patron, the Earl** of St. Vincent, sent the master of the *Ville de Paris* to put his ship **in some** tolerable order. (Here there was a **cry of** order, order, from Admiral Harvey and others.)

With respect to the assertion made by the same gentleman, that the health of the men **is** increased by long cruises at sea, and that of the commander-in-chief is improved by being on shore, he may reconcile that if he can. I shall not **follow the** example of imputing improper motives (looking **at** Captain Sir **Samuel** Hood); but another complaint is, that under this obnoxious system of favouritism, captains have been appointed to large commands of six **and seven sail of** the line, as many frigates, and as many sloops of war, the **right** of admirals who have served, and can serve, their country, and who have bled in its cause. But, perhaps, for such times, their rank did not afford a prospect of their being sufficiently subservient. This House, I believe, need not be told that from this

* This arrow was aimed at Admiral Markham, who was one **of the** Lords of the Admiralty in 1801 and for several years subsequently.

cause **there** are admirals of ability who **have** lingered in neglect. (A cry of order, **order**, from Admiral Harvey and others.)

"Sir, two parts of the **statement of the honourable** knight are especially **worthy of** notice, so far as they were meant as a reply to my **statement.** He said he had a hundred men **killed** and wounded in his ship, and no complaint, no inconvenience arose from want of lint or anything **else.** First, this occurred when surgeons supplied their own necessaries, and next, the wounded men were sent on the day following to Gibraltar Hospital. Now, Sir, with respect to the **blame said to** be attributed **by me to** Lord St. Vincent for the loss of the *Felix* and *Atalante*, I have to say, that it is of the general system **and** its consequences of which I complain—of endless cruises, rendering surveys at sea a substitute for a proper examination of the state of ships in port. The honourable knight is a little unfortunate in the comparison he has made, saying that Lord St. Vincent was no more **to** blame in the case of these vessels than for my getting the *Impérieuse* on shore on the coast of France. Now, since this subject has been touched on, I must state that I made application for a court-martial on my conduct, but **it** was not granted, because the blame would **have** fallen where it ought—on **the** person whose repeated positive commands sent the ship to sea in an unfit condition. The people of the yard had not finished the work—all **was in** confusion. The quarter-deck guns **lay unfitted**; forty tons of ballast, besides **provisions of all kinds**, remained on deck. The **powder** (allowed to be taken on board only **when the ship is** out of harbour) was received when the ship was **in that** condition, **and** the *Impérieuse* was hurried to **sea** without **a** cartridge filled **or** a gun loaded. The order issued was to **quit** the **port** the instant the ship would steer, regardless of every **other** material circumstance. (Another cry of **order,** order, from the same gentlemen. The Speaker said the noble lord must confine himself to the motion before the House.)

" Well, **Sir,** it is asserted that a profusion of oranges is supplied **to the** fleet at Lisbon, in reply to my statement **that** none are allowed in the hospitals at home. I have not heard from any of those who have so zealously spoken on the other side, a defence of the obnoxious order to **keep** all officers and men **on** board. All such grievances **may** seem slight and matter of indifference **to** those who are here at their ease; but I view them in another light; and if no one better qualified will represent subjects of great complaint, I will do so, independent **of** every personal **consideration.**

" **In the** course of the debate it has been asserted that **I said** lime-juice was a bad cure for the scurvy; no, it is **a** cure, and almost a certain cure, but debilitating: **it destroys** the disease, but ruins the constitution. An hon. member (**Mr.** Sheridan) has said that all this should have **been** represented to the Admiralty, that this House is **an im**proper place for **such** discussions, and he has threatened to call for all letters **from me to the Board.** To the first I answer,

that Boards pay **no** attention to the representations
of individuals whom they consider under their command; next, that if the right honourable gentleman
calls for my letters, he will find some that will not
suit his purpose. Sir, besides the public abuses, the
oppression and scandalous persecution of individuals,
often on anonymous information, has been, and is
matter of great complaint. Sir, if the present Admiralty shall increase the sum allowed for the refreshment of crews in **port,** instead of corrupting their
bodies by **salt provisions,** and then drenching them
with lime-juice, they will deserve the gratitude and
thanks of **all** employed. In the **navy,** we have had to
lament the system that makes the Admiralty an
appendage of the minister of the day, and that just
as a Board begin to see, and, perhaps, to plan
reform, they are removed from office. I trust, Sir,
that I shall not be denied the papers moved for,
and that my motion will not be got rid of by a blind
vote of confidence, or the subterfuge of ' the previous
question.' "

The motion was negatived without a division.

Although the government escaped from the effects
of this explosion, they rather desired to avoid any
similar experiments; and with this object in view,
Lord Cochrane was ordered to proceed to sea without
delay. Some latent hope probably existed, that the
electors would thereupon call upon their representative to resign; but so far from this being realized,
they gave him unlimited leave of absence.

SERVICES ON THE COAST OF SPAIN, ETC.
[1807-8.]

The *Impérieuse* arrived at Malta on the **31st** October; and as Lord Collingwood was absent on a cruise, Cochrane sailed **on** the 5th November, to fall in with him. A public letter to the commander-in-chief, dated off Corsica, November 14, details an unfortunate affair which happened during the passage :—

"I am sorry **to inform** your Lordship of a circumstance which has already been fatal to two of our best men, **and I fear** of thirteen others wounded, two will not survive. These wounds they received in an engagement with a set of desperate savages collected in a privateer, said to be the *King George*, of Malta, wherein the only **subjects of** his Majesty were three Maltese boys, one Gibraltar **man,** and a naturalized captain; the others being renegadoes from all countries, and a great part of them belonging to nations **at** war with England.

"**This** vessel was close to the Corsican shore; and on **the** near approach of our boats, a union-jack was hung over the gunwale. One of the three boats, which had **no gun, went** within hail, and told them we were **English. The other** boats then approached, but when close alongside the colours of the stranger were taken in, and a volley **of grape and** musketry discharged in the most **barbarous** manner,—their muskets and blunderbusses being pointed from beneath **the** netting close to the peoples' breasts. The rest of the officers and men then boarded, and carried the vessel in the most gallant manner. The bravery shown, **and** exertion used, were **worthy** of a better cause."

We gather from **the life of the** late Vice-Admiral Sir Jahleel Brenton, that the *King George* is identical with the vessel **which, on the** 14th May previously, beat off the *Spartan's* **boats** with frightful **loss.** On that occasion the British boats, not apprehending any serious opposition to their boarding, ran alongside, when the **pirates opened** a murderous fire upon them, killing the first and second lieutenants, and twenty-six men ; and wounding thirty-five. The boats were suffered to sheer off, and with only seven men able to pull, reached the ship with their melancholy tale. One man only got on board the Polacre,—this was James Bodie, the captain's coxswain,—who escaped by hanging on to the rudder-chains, and who was hauled on board after the boats had left.

Had the boats of the *Impérieuse* approached in an unguarded manner, **the** chances are their crews would have met the same reception. Fortunately for these bloodthirsty villains, the *Spartan* tragedy was not then known. Had the British party slaughtered every **man of the** treacherous crew, no one could have been surprised.

The secret of the opposition to the *Spartan* and *Impérieuse*, however, afterwards transpired. The *King George* was, in fact, a pirate, and £500 had been offered for her capture; but after much litigation she was condemned as a *droit* of Admiralty,

and the promised reward of £500 was never paid.
More **unfortunate** still, the Malta Admiralty Court
condemned **the** captors to pay 500 double sequims
for having seized the vessel. **Tartar** prizes do not
always turn out very profitable; but our sailors had
need be careful how they meddle with Malta prizes.
The supposition was, that certain officials connected
with the Maltese prize-court, had a personal interest
in the band of savages sailing in the *King George*
privateer. The absence of Judge Lynch on such an
occasion, was **a** misfortune.

After landing the wounded men at Malta, Cochrane
was **directed to** proceed to the Archipelago to relieve
the senior officer in command of a small squadron
stationed there. The captain of the squadron, however, not wishing to give up the command, represented Lord Cochrane to **be unfit** for the appointment; and Lord Collingwood upon that representation, was induced to recall him. Cochrane attributed this to his having intercepted off Corfu, a
number of the enemy's vessels, having passes illegally
issued by the captain he was about to supersede.

On **receiving an** unexpected letter of recall, Cochrane, unaware of the cause, at once obeyed the
mandate; and was **for a** long time in ignorance of
the real cause. **At length,** however, it was revealed
to him, and he then related the story of the intercepted passes.* When **an officer** glosses over a

* The name of this officer will probably be no secret to old
Adriatic cruisers; but as it is not mentioned in the autobiography, **we** think it advisable not to hazard any guesses.

neglect of duty, he should endeavour to forget it alto-gether. Cochrane, by covering this fraud for so long a time, made himself a party to it. He did not make Lord Collingwood acquainted with the fact until his doing so had the appearance of revenge.

Rejoining Lord Collingwood in January, 1808, off Corfu, Cochrane was despatched to Malta, and subsequently received instructions to repair to Gibraltar and employ the ship under his command in harassing the French and Spanish coasts as opportunity presented. **On the** 9th February, in pursuance of these orders, he captured two vessels to the eastward of Barcelona; then, running down the coast of Valencia, the *Impérieuse* arrived off Carthagena, near which place she engaged four Russian gun-boats, captured one armed with a long 32-pounder, a brass howitzer, and two smaller guns; and sank two others. The fourth escaped into Carthagena; and as there was a Spanish squadron at anchor in that port, it was not considered prudent to follow her. The *Impérieuse* at the same time captured a brig valuably laden.

The next service in which the boats of the *Impérieuse* were engaged was unhappily accompanied by the loss of a promising young officer, Lieutenant Edward Caulfield. Lord Cochrane, having learnt that a large French ship, mounting 10 guns, laden with military stores, was at anchor in the bay of Almeira, on the coast of Granada, despatched the pinnace and barge, on **the** morning of the 21st February, under the command of that officer, **to cut** her out. The service was gallantly and successfully performed, the

the vessel's **cables cut,** and **sail** made ; and two brigs
laden with stores also captured ; but the leader of the
expedition **was** shot as **soon as** he ascended the side
of the ship.

The *Impérieuse* stood into the bay to the support
of the boats, and to assist in bringing out the prizes ;
but having got becalmed, was for a length of time in
great danger from the fire of the batteries. Fortunately a breeze sprang up, which soon carried the
frigate and her prizes out of their range, or the whole
would **have** been sunk or captured. They had
scarcely **got clear of** the bay, when a Spanish line-of-
battle ship hove **in** sight to seaward ; but the *Impé-*
rieuse and her prizes, consisting of a ship mounting
10 guns, and two brigs laden with cordage, managed
to evade their pursuer, and reached Gibraltar on the
23rd. Lieutenant Caulfield was here landed and
buried with military honours.

After leaving Gibraltar, the *Impérieuse* next paid
a visit to the Balearic Isles, in company with the
Hydra, to reconnoitre the Spanish fleet at anchor in
Port Mahon. Here she had several engagements with
the enemy's batteries. Having obtained a supply of
water **near Cape Blanco,** on the island of Majorca,
the *Impérieuse* returned **to** the main land, and effected
numerous small captures. Lord Cochrane managed
to keep the whole coast in a state of continual alarm.
So erratic were his movements that they never knew
where he would next turn up. The gun-boats and
batteries were continually on the *qui vive*, and it was

surprising with what impunity the ship and her gallant crew escaped.

On the 21st of May, being off Cape Palos, the *Impérieuse* engaged a flotilla of twelve gun-boats, which had been sent **out to** drive her away. During the action the *Impérieuse* **grounded when** in stays, but fortunately got afloat again immediately, or her destruction would have been more than probable. Two of the gun-boats were captured, but subsequently set on fire and abandoned, together with a large vessel, the state of the weather compelling Lord Cochrane to look to the safety of his own ship. The flotilla and convoy thus intercepted consisted of heavily-armed gun-boats, each mounting one long gun in the bow, and two abaft, with a crew of fifty men. The *Impérieuse* returned to Gibraltar on the 31st of May, with several prizes.

Spain having **in** June declared war against France, our former enemies became objects **for our** protection ; and instead of harassing **the** Spaniards, Lord Cochrane received orders from Lord Collingwood, then off Cadiz, to co-operate with them against the common foe. In pursuance of these instructions, the *Impérieuse* sailed from Gibraltar on the 23rd **of** June, and **proceeded** to Carthagena, where Lord Cochrane landed to pay a visit to the Governor. His reception, though at first constrained, soon turned into a hearty welcome ; but it was hardly to be supposed that the captain who had so often defied and annoyed them should be very cordially received.

Cochrane next visited Majorca, at which island he

found two of his midshipmen,—the late Lord Napier and Mr. Harrison—who had been captured in prizes; and on the 5th of July stood over to Barcelona, hoisted Spanish colours, and fired a salute of twenty-one guns. Barcelona was then in possession of the French, who returned the salute with shotted guns, but which did no damage. The *Impérieuse* then ran along the coast of Catalonia, but everywhere, except at Gerona, which was besieged, the French were in possession.

SPANISH CO-OPERATION.
[1808.]

On the 19th July the Spanish government embarked **all the** available **troops** in the island of Minorca, in **six sail of** the line, **for C**atalonia. Lord Cochrane **and the** marines of **his ship** did a great deal towards impeding the advance of **the F**rench towards Gerona, by breaking up the roads. Cochrane had turned engineer and soldier. **General D**uqesme, having **been** compelled to raise the siege of Gerona, divided his **forces, one** portion making for Barcelona, and the other **for** Figueras. Aware that, in **order** to reach Barcelona **with their** heavy siege guns, it would be necessary **that they** should pass the fortress of Mongat, Cochrane determined, in conjunction with the Spanish militia, to endeavour to capture that place by driving out the French who garrisoned it. On the **31st** July, at 8 A.M., the *Impérieuse* got under weigh and stood towards the castle. Observing this, the Spaniards made a desperate attack upon and carried an outpost. Lord Cochrane then landed at the head of his marines, under Lieutenant Hore, and the commandant surrendered, under a promise that he and his garrison should be escorted off to the frigate. The Spaniards would, most probably, have murdered every one of them in cold blood but for this interference, so exasperated were they, and naturally so, at the enormities practised by the French intruders upon their territory. The castle was then blown up. Lord Cochrane wrote the following despatch, dated off Mongat, July 31st, reporting this operation :—

"The castle of Mongat, an important post, completely commanding a pass on the road from Gerona to Barcelona, which the French are now besieging, and the only post between these towns occupied by the enemy, surrendered this morning to His Majesty's ship under my command. Lieutenant Hore, of the marines, took possession of the castle, which is now levelled with the ground; and the pending rocks are blown into the road, which in many other places is also rendered impassable to artillery without a very heavy loss of men, if the French resolve to repair them."

The *Impérieuse* then proceeded to St. Philou, to water; and here Lord Cochrane landed, and, putting himself in communication with the Catalans, gave them instructions as to the best mode of strengthening their position. From St. Philou he proceeded to the Gulf of Rosas, where he found Captain West* in the

* Sir John West, now Admiral of the Fleet.

Excellent, on board which ship was the late Spanish governor of the fortress of Figueras, taking refuge from his countrymen, who were exasperated at his pusillanimous surrender of that important stronghold.

There being no further services to be done on the coast of Catalonia, Lord Cochrane passed into the Gulf of Lyons, determined to see what could be effected on the French coast. On the 15th August the *Impérieuse* anchored off the mouth of the Rhone. A gun-boat tender was then sent in chase of a small vessel, which was captured and burnt; and it then occurred to Lord Cochrane that much facility would be afforded him in his cruising if he could destroy the telegraph-stations by means of which his approach was announced along the coast. The design was no sooner conceived than acted upon. The first destroyed was at the mouth of the Rhone. On the 17th he attacked the station at Boni. A party, numbering ninety, was landed, and, after securing the signal-flags, the station was blown up. Not many hours afterwards another station was observed at Montpelier, which was destroyed with difficulty, the approaches to it being across two small rivers. The stations of La Pinede and Dumet were next doomed, and at the latter place four houses connected with the station were burnt.

On the 21st, while at anchor in the Gulf of Dumet, the boats were sent away at 3 A.M. to destroy the custom-house. After burning that building, the party were about to destroy another signal-station, when a large body of troops were observed from the frigate to be approaching, and the boats were recalled.

Two signal stations in the Bay of Perpignan,—one called Canet, the other at St. Maguire,—were next destroyed. The latter service was most skilfully executed. The boats landed, under the command of Lord Cochrane in person, at 4·30 A.M. on the 24th, it being still dark. Two heavy gu**ns** were discharged at them, but without doing any damage. " Fearing an ambuscade," wrote his lordship, " we pulled **out of** reach of musketry ; but, calculating that the French would not venture **far in the** dark,—my favourite time for attacks of any kind,—instead of returning to the ship, **we** made direct for the signal-station, and blew it up amidst a dropping fire of musketry, which, as we could not be distinguished, did no harm. Having completed this work, we marched along the beach towards a battery observed on the previous evening. On storming the battery, with the usual British cheer, the enemy rushed out in an opposite direction, firing as they **went,** but without effect. We then took possession **of** two brass twenty-four pounders ; but, while making preparation for getting them off, were alarmed by recall guns from the frigate, from the masthead of which, as day was now beginning to break, a force of cavalry had been seen making for us over the crest of a **hill.**"

The storming party had had a very narrow escape. On taking possession of the battery it was found that preparations had been made for blowing it up, including, of course, the British storming party. The match, however, owing to the sudden approach of the British, had not been ignited. The train was now made useful, and before Cochrane and his daring companions evacuated it, the match was lighted, and they were barely out of **reach** of the explosion when **the** magazine **and battery** were in fragments. The **only** casualty **attending** this hazardous service was the **burning** of the seaman who fired the train. He had **incautiously** kept his cartouch - box buckled around him while lighting the match, and, the fire having communicated with the ammunition, he was blown up.

The following characteristic anecdote, with reference to one of these exploits, appeared many years ago in **the** *Naval Chronicle :* " This brave man, after having for some time kept the coast of France in a state of constant alarm, sent the boats to destroy a battery then in view from his ship. They soon afterwards returned, the object being declared impracticable. Lord Cochrane, on being informed that the boats were alongside, came to the gangway, and, addressing the coxwain of the cutter (a gallant fellow who had always accompanied his lordship on the most desperate occasions), said : ' Well, Jack, **do** *you* think it impossible to blow up the battery ? ' ' No, my lord,' answered the **coxwain**, and twenty other voices, ' 'tis not impossible ; **we can** do it if *you* will go.' His lordship instantly sprang into the cutter, and at the head of his brave **party** carried the battery in a moment. Jack, the coxwain, attended with a small barrel of powder on his shoulder, and the signal-station was blown to pieces."

Having thus carried out his orders, Cochrane joined

Lord Collingwood off Toulon; but he had done his work so well hitherto that the commander-in-chief considered he could not be better engaged than in continuing his operations.

The spirited co-operation of a single frigate had inspired the Catalans with such confidence, that the French, though in great force about Figueras and Rosas, hesitated to advance into their country.

On the morning of the 3rd September, being close in with Ciotat, a town lying between Toulon and Marseilles, Cochrane despatched his boats to cut off a gunboat which had separated from a flotilla lying under the land. Observing, however, that a heavy fire was being opened upon them from a battery, the boats were recalled. A squadron of six sail of the line was at this time seen coming out of Toulon; but as the ships were to leeward, their distant presence did not prevent Cochrane from making an attack upon the town and mole of Ciotat.

An hour before noon the *Impérieuse* anchored under a small island which sheltered her from the fire of the battery, upon which the enemy threw shells at her, but without effect. The boats were then again sent away, provided with rockets, and succeeded in twice setting fire to the town. The ship then got underway, and standing closer in, commenced firing with effect upon the fort. Cochrane persevered in his attack as long as possible, but was at length obliged to consult his own safety, and make sail, as the advanced frigate of the Toulon squadron was within a few miles.

On the 6th the *Impérieuse* anchored in the Bay of Marseilles, to the evident consternation of the inhabitants, and next day **was** joined by the *Spartan*, under the command of Captain Jahleel Brenton. The latter being the senior officer, Cochrane put himself under his orders, and the two ships on the following day stood into the gulf of Foz. This service having been ably described in the memoirs of that distinguished officer—the late Vice-Admiral Sir Jahleel Brenton, Bart.—to which we have already adverted, it is due to Lord Cochrane to give that version of it :—

" In the beginning of September, the *Spartan* was ordered to cruise in the Gulf of Rosas, to prevent the **enemy's** vessels from collecting on the coast between Cape Creux and Cape Couronne. On the 7th, Captain Brenton fell in with the *Impérieuse*, commanded by Lord Cochrane, and joined him in **an** attack he was making upon some merchant-vessels near Cape Mejean ; one of which they burnt, and captured two ; which, not being worth sending into port for adjudication, they destroyed. The *Impérieuse* had **one** man killed upon this occasion, and the *Spartan* one wounded.

" On the 8th, the boats of the two ships landed and destroyed the signal-post and telegraph in the Bay of Saintes Maries ; from thence they proceeded to attack three batteries upon the isthmus of Leucate, where a number of vessels were lying hauled up on the beach. **Lord** Cochrane had reconnoitred this part of the coast **some** days previously, and had landed and spiked one of the guns on the southern battery. On the 10th, at

daylight, the boats landed and completed the destruction of that battery, whilst the ships protected them
by their fire from the troops which were assembled.
At 1 P.M. the boats were formed in two divisions,
the first of which made a feint* of landing near the
village of Caunet, by which means the troops were all
drawn to that point, and the ships, **running** in, attacked
the centre battery near the village of Lauren. The
second division of boats, in the mean while, proceeded
under cover **of** the *Impérieuse* and carried the north-
ernmost battery."

The biographer of Sir Jahleel has seized this oppor-
tunity of paying a well-merited tribute to the great
professional skill of Lord Cochrane.

"**A** beautiful instance," he writes, " of ready seamanship was displayed by Lord Cochrane on this
occasion. Having already reconnoitred the coast, he
requested he might be permitted to lead upon this
occasion. The *Spartan* was following the *Impérieuse*,
at less than a cable's length distance, the ships going
about three knots; when the *Impérieuse* was observed
suddenly to swing round with much more rapidity
than any action of **the helm** could have produced.
The fact was, that Lord Cochrane from the mast-head
saw a squadron of the enemy's cavalry galloping
towards a gorge on the coast, which, had they
passed, would have cut off the retreat of our people,

---

* In his autobiography Lord Dundonald states that both
Spartan and *Impérieuse* manned their small boats and the rocket-
boats with ship's boys, dressed **in** marines' scarlet jackets, in
order to make the feint more effective.

who were employed in spiking the guns. His lordship immediately ordered the anchor to be let go; and the swinging round brought the frigate's starboard broadside to enfilade this gorge, by which means the cavalry were instantly turned. The boats were then again despatched, when one vessel was blown up and another burnt, the others considerably injured by the fire from the frigates; but the enemy having collected in considerable force, with field-pieces, the boats were recalled to the *Spartan*."

Further on, the editor of that work pays a general tribute to **the** character of Cochrane, and states that he has "frequently heard Sir Jahleel Brenton mention that he admired nothing more in Lord Cochrane than the care he took of the preservation of his people. Bold and adventurous as he was, no unnecessary exposure of life was ever permitted under his command. Every circumstance was anticipated, every precaution against surprise was taken, every provision for success was made; and in this way he was enabled to accomplish the most daring enterprises with comparatively little danger, and still less of actual loss. The public, who heard of his unceasing activity and dauntless courage, regarded him as one only ambitious of the character of a successful commander; and little knew that he never risked an attack of which he had not calculated all the probable contingencies, and compared most zealously the loss he might himself sustain with the injury to be done to the enemy."

We have frequently had occasion to draw the attention of our readers to this important feature of Lord

Cochrane's character, and are particularly happy in having the testimony of so deservedly distinguished an officer as the late Sir Jahleel Brenton in support of our view.

On the 11th the two ships anchored off Cette, and endeavoured to burn the shipping in the harbour by means of congreve rockets, but without effect, owing to the faulty construction of the missiles. Next day, the boats were again sent away, and the crews having landed, they burnt a custom-house, near Mont Julien, two pontoons on the canal, and some guard-houses, bringing away a quantity of small arms.

The joint cruise was most effective, for on the 13th the frigates chased nine sail of merchant-ships off Point de Tigne, and captured six of them, comprising one ship, three brigs, a xebec, and a bombard. These vessels had run on shore, and the frigates having anchored near them, had succeeded in getting them all, with the exception of one brig, afloat, when it came on to blow directly on shore. This detained them at their anchors till the 16th, every day expecting that the enemy would bring down guns and attack them, as they were within range of the beach.

Captain Brenton, in his official letter reporting these operations, states that the conduct of Lord Cochrane was above all praise; and that it was throughout an animating example of intrepidity, zeal, and professional skill and resources, which he trusted would be treasured up in the memory of all who witnessed it.

The gallant captains parted company next day, we

may fancy with some regret, **as** there was much
kindred feeling betwen them, the *Spartan* making sail
to rejoin Lord Collingwood, and the *Impérieuse* for
Rosas, with one of the prize brigs in **tow,** where she
anchored on the 18th. The brig **had** received much
damage **on** the rocks, but having been patched **up,**
was despatched to Gibraltar, under charge of the first
lieutenant.

The *Impérieuse* then returned to the Gulf of Foz,
and completely destroyed another signal-station, in
the presence of **a** body of troops assembled for its
protection. The troops were kept at bay by the fire
of the frigate.

The following official despatches from Lord Col-
lingwood, addressed to the Hon. Wellesley Pole,
Secretary of the Admiralty, dated 19th Oct., 1808,
relate to the foregoing services :—

" I enclose a letter which **I** have just received **from**
the Right Hon. Lord Cochrane, captain of the *Impé-*
rieuse, stating the services in which he has been
employed on the coast of Languedoc. Nothing can
excel **the** zeal and activity with which his lordship
pursues **the** enemy. The success which attends his
enterprises **clearly** indicates with what skill and ability
they are **conducted;** besides keeping the coast **in**
constant alarm, **causing a** general suspension of the
trade, and harassing **a body of** troops employed in
opposing him. He has probably **prevented** these troops,
which were intended for Figueras **from** advancing
into Spain, by giving them employment in the defence
of their **own** coasts."

The letter enclosed was dated 28th Sept., 1808 :—

" With varying opposition, but with unvaried success, the newly-constructed semaphoric telegraphs, which are of the utmost consequence to the safety of the numerous convoys that pass along the coast of France, at Bourdique, La Pinede, St. Maguire, Frontignan, Canet, and Fay, **have** been blown up, and completely demolished, together with their telegraph-houses, fourteen barracks of *gendarmes*, one battery, and the strong tower on the Lake of Frontignan.

" Mr. David Mapleton, first lieutenant, had command of these expeditions. Lieutenant Urry Johnson **had** charge of the field-pieces, and Lieutenant Hore, of the Royal Marines. To them and to Mr. George Gilbert, assistant-surgeon, Mr. Burney, gunner, Messrs. Houston Stewart* and Stovin, midshipmen, is due whatever credit may arise from such mischief, and for having, with so small a force, drawn about 2,000 troops from the important fortress of Figueras, in Spain, for the defence of their own coasts. The conduct of Lieutenants Mapleton, Johnson, and Hore, deserves my praise, as well as that of the other officers, Royal Marines, and seamen."

The casualties attending these exploits are returned as " one man singed in blowing up the battery."

* The present Vice-Admiral Sir Houston Stewart, K.C.B.

OPERATIONS ON THE COAST OF CATALONIA.
[1808-9.]

The *Impérieuse*, standing in need of some repairs, proceeded to Gibraltar to refit; but the 12th of November found her again off Barcelona, which place was still in the occupation of the French. Cochrane then recommenced his harassing system, the effect of which was soon observable, every battery being constantly in a state of excitement. The *Impérieuse*, accompanied by the *Cambrian*, frequently engaged the batteries, but fortunately escaped loss. A singular accident was mentioned by Lord Cochrane. One of the enemy's shot entered the muzzle of a brass 32-pounder on the forecastle of the *Impérieuse*, which was at the instant in the act of being discharged. The shots met, and the gun burst in the middle. This harassing work gave the Spanish patriots many advantages; but the French were still too strong for them.

Information now reached Lord Cochrane that the French had invested Rosas; and in furtherance of Lord Collingwood's general instructions he considered it his duty to repair thither without delay. He therefore left the *Cambrian* at Barcelona, and on the 20th of November anchored in the bay. A heavy cannonade was then going on between the citadel and some French batteries thrown up on the cliff above Fort Trinidad. To ascertain how he could most effectually take part in the defence, Lord Cochrane landed at the town, and communicated with the

Spanish **troops.** **He then got** the frigate as close in as he could with safety, in a position to enfilade the besiegers. On the 22nd he again went on shore to the citadel, into which **the** French were continually throwing shells ; **but owing** to the construction of the place they did little **damage.** **Having** ascertained the position **of the enemy's entrenchments,** he was able **to** give **directions for** the more effectual attacks upon them. His co-operation soon drew upon the frigate rather **too** much notice, for the attention of the besiegers of the citadel was drawn to this new annoyance. The result was a combined fire of shot and **shell,** which made **it** necessary for her to withdraw **out of** range.

Fort Trinidad, up to this time, had been garrisoned by the marines of the *Fame ;* but as the place had been breached, Captain Bennett, deeming it imprudent to keep **his** men there any longer, withdrew. Cochrane, however, unwilling **to** leave the Spaniards to themselves, earnestly requested the governor not to abandon the place until he had tried what he could do, and that he would himself land and assist the garrison. The governor, having reluctantly consented, Cochrane disembarked **and** took command of the damaged **fort.** **Among** the volunteers who accompanied **Lord Cochrane** in this hazardous service was the late Captain Frederick Marryat, then a midshipman of the *Impérieuse,* but who subsequently made his name immortal by his naval **romances.** Under the *nom de plume* of " Frank Mildmay," he has given one of the most lucid, and possibly truthful, narratives of this particular service **extant;** and as our volume would be incomplete without this **well** told story, we **republish the chapter as "an Episode."** The sober account given by his lordship, differs in no essential **particular** from the sketch **of** the lively author **from whose** work we are **about** to quote; but **it is neces-**sary that two or three preliminary facts **should be** correctly laid down.

The castle of Trinidad stood on the side **of a steep** hill, but was commanded by precipitous cliffs which would have rendered its occupation impossible, had it not been **for the** peculiar construction of the fastness. The walls were of immense thickness. Next to the **sea was a** fort, the walls of which were fifty feet in height; and in the rear of this was a tower, rising thirty feet above it, with its back to the cliff. The defensive character **of these** three fortifications **was** very great, but unfortunately **they** had very little offensive power.

The French had managed to effect a partial breach **in the** tower, just over a bomb-proof interior arch, **which arch** was fifty feet high, and was easily con-verted **into a serious** obstacle to a storming party, by simply **breaking in** the crown of it, and thereby forming a **deep chasm** inside the outer wall. In this tower Cochrane and **his band of** heroes were located, and holding out **against the French** besiegers. Here it was that Lord Cochrane **placed** his cleverly-con-structed man-trap. Let **us, however,** now turn to **Frank** Mildmay's account.

AN EPISODE.

> The shout
> Of battle now began, and rushing sound
> Of onset .   .   .   .   .
> 'Twixt host and host but narrow space was left.
>
> MILTON.

From the deservedly high character borne by the captain of the frigate which I was ordered to join, he was employed by Lord Collingwood on the most confidential services; and we were sent to assist the Spaniards in **their** defence of the important fortress of Rosas, in Catalonia. It has already been observed, that the French general, St. Cyr, had entered that country, and, having taken Figueras and Gerona, was looking with a wistful eye on the castle of Trinity, on the south-east side, the capture of which would be a certain prelude to the fall of Rosas.

My captain determined to defend it, although it had just been abandoned by another British naval officer as untenable. I volunteered, though a supernumerary, to be one of the party, and was sent: nor can I but acknowledge that the officer who had abandoned the place had shown more than a sound discretion. Every part of the castle was in ruins. Heaps of crumbling stones and rubbish, broken gun-carriages, and split guns, presented to my mind a very unfavourable field of battle. The only advantage we appeared to have over the assailants was, that the breach which they had effected in the walls was steep in its ascent, and the loose stones either fell down upon them, or gave way under their feet, while we plied them with every **kind of** missile: this was our only defence, and all we **had** to prevent the enemy marching into the works, if works they could **be** called.

There was another and a very serious disadvantage attending our locality. The castle was situated very near the summit of **a** steep hill, the upper part of which was in possession of the enemy, who were, by this means, nearly on a level with the top of the castle, and, on that eminence, three hundred Swiss sharpshooters had effected a lodgment, and thrown up works within fifty yards of us, keeping up a constant fire at the castle. If a head was seen above the walls, twenty rifle bullets whizzed at it in a moment, and the same unremitted attention was paid to our boats as they landed.

On another hill, much to the northward, and consequently farther inland, the French had erected a battery of six 24-pounders; this agreeable neighbour was only 300 yards from us; and allowing short in**tervals for** the guns to cool, this battery kept up a constant **fire** upon us from daylight till dark. I never could have supposed, in my boyish days, that the time would arrive when I should envy a cock upon Shrove-Tuesday; yet such was my case when in this infernal castle. It was certainly not giving us fair play; we had no chance against such a force; but my captain **was** a knight errant, and as I had volunteered, I had **no** right to complain. Such was the precision of the enemy's fire, that we could tell the stone that would be hit by the next shot, merely from seeing where the last had struck, and our men were frequently wounded by the splinters of granite, with which the walls were built, and others picked off like partridges, by the Swiss corps on the hill close to us.

Our force in the castle consisted of 130 English seamen and marines, one company of Spanish, and another of Swiss troops in Spanish pay. Never were troops worse paid and fed, or better fired at. We all pigged in together; dirty straw and fleas for our beds; our food on the same scale of luxury; from the captain downwards there was no distinction. Fighting is sometimes a very agreeable pastime, but excess "palls on the sense:" and here we had enough of it, without what I always thought an indispensable accompaniment, namely, a good belly-full; nor did I conceive how a man could perform his duty without it; but here I was forced, with many others, to make the experiment, and when the boats could not land, which was often the case, we piped to dinner *pro formâ*, as our captain liked regularity, and drank cold water to fill our stomachs.

I have often heard my poor old uncle say that no man knows what he can do till he tries; and the enemy gave us plenty of opportunities of displaying our ingenuity, industry, watchfulness, and abstinence. When poor Penelope wove her web, the poet says—

The night unravell'd what the day began.

With us it was precisely the reverse: the day destroyed all the labours of the night. The hours of darkness were employed by us in filling sand-bags, and laying them in **the** breach, clearing away rubbish, and preparing to receive the enemy's fire, which was **sure to** recommence **at** daylight. **These** avocations, **together** with a constant and most vigilant watch **against** surprise, took up **so much** of our time, that little **was** left for repose, and **our meals required still less.**

There was some originality in one of our modes of defence, and which, not being *secundum artem*, might have provoked the **smile of an** engineer. The captain contrived **to make a** shoot of smooth deal boards, which **he received from** the ship; these he placed in a **slanting** direction in the breach, and caused them to **be well** greased with cook's slush; so that the enemies, who wished to come into **our** hold, must have jumped down upon them, **and would in** an instant be precipitated into the ditch below, a very considerable depth, where they might either **have remained** till the doctor came to them, or, if they were able, begin their labours *de novo*. This was a very good bug-trap; for, **at that time,** I thought just as little of killing a Frenchman **as** I did of destroying the filthy little nightly depredator just mentioned.

Besides **this slippery** trick, which we played them with great **success, we** served them another. We happened to have on board **the frigate** a large quantity of fish-hooks: these **we planted not only** on the greasy **boards,** but in every part **where the** intruders were **likely to** place their hands or feet. The breach itself was mined, and loaded with shells and hand-grenades;

masked guns, charged up to the muzzle with musket-
balls, enfiladed the spot in every direction. Such were
our defences; and, considering that we had been three
weeks in the castle, opposed to such mighty odds, it
is surprising that we only lost twenty men. The crisis
was now approaching.

One morning, very early, I happened to have the
look-out. The streak **of fog** which **during** the night
hangs between the hills in that country, **and** presses
down into the valleys, had just begun to rise, and the
stars **to** grow more dim above our heads, when I was
looking over the castle walls towards the breach. The
captain came out and asked me what I was looking
at. I told him I hardly knew; but there did appear
something unusual in the valley, immediately below
the breach. He listened a moment, looked attentively
with his night-glass, and exclaimed, in his firm voice,
but in an undertoned manner, " To arms!—they are
coming ! "

In three minutes every man was at his post; and
though all were quick, there was no time to spare, for
by this time the black column of the enemy was distinctly visible, curling along the valley like a great
centipede; and, with the daring enterprise so common
among the troops **of** Napoleon, had begun in silence
to mount the breach. It was an awful and eventful
moment; but the coolness and determination of the
little garrison was equal to the occasion.

The word was given to take good aim, and a volley
from the masked guns and musketry was poured
into the thick of them. They paused—deep groans

ascended! They retreated a few paces in confusion, then rallied, and again advanced to the attack; and now the fire on both sides was kept up without inter-mission. The great guns from the hill fort, and the Swiss sharpshooters still nearer, poured copious vollies upon us, and with loud shouts cheered on their comrades to the assault. As they approached and covered our mine, the train was fired, and up they went in the air, and down they fell buried in the ruins! Groans, screams, confusion, French yells, British hurras, rent the sky! The hills resounded with the shouts of victory! We sent them hand-grenades in abundance, and broke their skins in glorious style! I must say that the French behaved nobly, though many a tall grenadier and pioneer fell by the symbol in front of his warlike cap. I cried with rage and excitement; and we all fought like bull-dogs, for we knew there was no quarter to be given.

Ten minutes had elapsed since the firing began, and in that time many a brave fellow had bit the dust. The head of their attacking column had been de-stroyed by the explosion of our mine. Still they had re-formed, and were again half-way up the breach when the day began to dawn; and we saw a chosen body of one thousand men, led on by their colonel, and advan-cing over the dead which had just fallen.

The gallant leader appeared to be as cool and com-posed as if he were at breakfast; with his drawn sword he pointed to the breach, and we heard him exclaim, " *Suivez-moi!* " I felt jealous of this brave fellow—jealous of his being a Frenchman; and I threw a lighted hand-grenade between his feet—he picked up, and threw it from him to a considerable distance.

" Cool chap enough that," said the captain, who stood close to me; " I'll give him another;" which he did, but this the officer kicked away with equal *sang froid* and dignity. " Nothing will cure that fellow," resumed the captain, "but an ounce of lead on an empty stomach. It's a pity, too, to kill so fine a fellow—but there is no help for it."

So saying, he took a musket out of my hand, which I had just loaded — aimed, fired — the colonel staggered, clapped his hand to his breast, and fell back into the arms of some of his men, who threw down their muskets, and took him on their shoulders, either unconscious or perfectly regardless of the death-work which was going on around them. The firing redoubled from our musketry on this little group, every man of whom was either killed or wounded. The colonel, again left to himself, tottered a few paces farther, till he reached a small bush, not ten yards from the spot where he received his mortal wound. Here he fell; his sword, which he still grasped in his right hand, resting on the boughs, and pointed upwards to the sky, as if directing the road to the spirit of its gallant master.*

* Lord Dundonald gives a different version of this affair :— " They were gallantly led, two of the officers attracting my especial attention. The first was dropped by a shot, which precipitated him from the walls ; but whether he was killed, or

With the life of the colonel, ended the hopes of the French for that day. The officers, we could perceive, did their duty—cheered, encouraged, and drove **on** their men, but **all in vain!** We saw them pass their swords through **the** bodies of the fugitives; but the **men did not** even mind that—they would only be killed **in** their own way—they had had fighting enough for one breakfast. The first impulse, **the fiery onset,** had been checked by the fall of **their brave** leader, and *sauve qui peut*, whether coming from the officers or drummers, no matter which, terminated the affair, and we were **left** a little **time** to breathe, and to count the number **of our dead.**

The moment the French perceived from their batteries that the attempt had failed, and that the leader of the enterprise was dead, **they** poured in an angry fire upon us. I stuck **my hat** on the **bayonet of** my musket, and just showed it above the wall. **A dozen of** bullets were through it in a minute: **very** fortunately my head was not in it.

only wounded, I do not know, probably wounded only, as his body **was not seen** by us among the dead. The other was the last **man to quit** the walls, and before he **could do** so, I had covered **him with my** musket. Finding escape impossible, he stood **like a hero to receive the** bullet, without condescending to lower his **sword in token of** surrender. I never saw a better or a prouder man. **Lowering my** musket, I paid him the compliment **of remarking that so fine a** fellow was not born **to** be shot down like **a** dog, and **that so far as I was concerned he** was at liberty to make **the best of his** way **down the** ladder; **upon** which intimation **he** bowed, **as** politely as though on **parade,** and retired just as leisurely."—*Autobiography of a Seaman,* **vol. i. p. 311.**

The fire of the batteries having **ceased, which it** generally did at stated periods, we had **an opportu-**dity of examining the point of attack.   Scaling ladders **and** dead bodies lay **in profusion.**   All the wounded had been removed; but what magnificent "food for powder " were the bodies **which lay** before us !—all, it would seem, **picked men ;** not one **less** than six feet, and some more; **they** were clad **in** their grey capots, to render their appearance more *sombre*, and less discernible in the twilight of the morning; and as the weather was cold during the nights, I secretly determined to **have one** of these great coats as a *chère* **amie to keep** me warm in night-watches.   **I** **also** resolved to have the colonel's sword to present to my captain; and as soon as it was dark, I walked down the breach, brought up one of the scaling ladders, which I deposited in the castle ; **and,** having done so much for the king, I set out to do something for myself.

It was pitch-dark.   I stumbled on; the **wind** blew **a** hurricane, and the dust and mortar almost blinded me ; but I knew my way pretty well.   Yet there was something very jackal-like, in wandering among dead bodies in the night-time, and I really felt a horror at my situation.   **There** was a dreadful stillness between the **blasts, which** the pitch-darkness made peculiarly awful to an unfortified mind.   It is for **this** reason that I would ever discourage night-attacks, unless **you** can rely on your men. **They** generally fail : because the man of common bravery, who would acquit himself **fairly in broad** daylight, will hang back during the night. Fear and Darkness have always been firm allies, **and** are inseparably playing into each other's hands. Darkness conceals Fear, and therefore Fear loves Darkness, because it saves the coward from shame; and when the fear of shame is the only stimulus to fight, daylight is essentially necessary.

I crept cautiously along, feeling for the dead bodies. The first I laid my hand on made my blood curdle. It was the lacerated thigh of a grenadier, whose flesh had been torn off by a hand-grenade. "Friend," said I, "if I may judge from the nature of your wound, your great-coat is not worth having." The next subject **I** handled had been better killed. A musket-ball through his head had settled all his tradesmen's bills; and I hesitated not in becoming residuary legatee, as I was sure the assets would more than discharge the undertaker's bill; but the body **was** cold and stiff, and did not readily yield its garment.

I, however, succeeded in obtaining **my** object, in which I arrayed myself, and went on **in** search of the colonel's sword; but here I had been anticipated by a Frenchman. The colonel, indeed, lay there stiff enough, but **his** sword was gone. I was preparing to return, when I encountered, not a dead, but a living enemy.

" *Qui vive?* " said a low voice.

" *Anglais, bête!* " answered **I**, in a low tone; and added, " *mais les corsairs* **ne se** *battent pas.*"

" *C'est vrai*," said he; and growling " *Bon soir*," he **was** soon out of sight. I scrambled back **to** the castle, gave the countersign to the sentinel, and showed my new great-coat with a vast deal of glee and satisfaction. Some of my comrades went on the same sort of expedition, and were rewarded with more or less success.

In a few days the dead bodies on the beach were nearly denuded by nightly visitors; but that of the colonel lay respected and untouched. The heat of the day had blackened it, and it was now deprived of all its manly beauty, and nothing remained but a loathsome corpse. The rules of war, as well as of humanity, demanded the honourable interment of the remains of this hero; and our captain, who was the very flower of chivalry, desired me to stick a white handkerchief on a pike, as a flag of truce, and bury the bodies, if the enemy would permit us.

I went out accordingly with a spade and a pickaxe; but the tirailleurs on the hill began with their rifles, and wounded one of my men. I looked at the captain, as much as to say, "Am I to proceed?" He motioned with his hand to go on, and then I began digging a hole by the side of a dead body, and the enemy, seeing my intention, desisted from firing. I had buried several, when the captain came out and joined me, with a view of reconnoitring the position of the enemy. He was seen from the fort, and recognized; and his intention pretty accurately guessed at.

We were near the body of the colonel, which we were going to inter, when the captain, observing a diamond ring on the finger of the corpse, said to one of the sailors, " You may just as well take that off; it can be of no use to him now." The man tried to get off, **but the** rigidity of the muscle after death prevented **his moving it.** "He won't feel your knife, poor **fellow,**" said the captain; "**and a finger more or less is no** great matter **to him now:** off with **it.**"

The sailor began to saw the finger-joint with his knife, when down came a twenty-four **pound shot, and** with such a good direction, that it took the shoe off the man's foot and the **shovel out of** the hand **of** another **man.**

"In **with him, and cover him up!**" said the captain.

We did so; when another shot, not quite so well **directed as** the first, threw the dirt in our faces and ploughed the ground at our feet. The captain then ordered his men to **run into the** castle, **which they** instantly obeyed; **while he** himself walked leisurely along through a shower **of** musket-balls from those cursed Swiss dogs, whom I **most fervently** wished at **the** devil, because, as an aide-de-camp, **I felt** bound in honour as well as duty to walk by the **side** of my captain, **fully** expecting every moment that a rifle-ball would **have hit me** where I should have been ashamed to show the **scar.** I thought this funeral pace, after the funeral was over, confounded nonsense; but my fire-eating captain **never had run** away from a Frenchman, and did not intend to begin then.

I was behind him, making these **reflections**; and as **the shot** began to fly very **thick, I** stepped up alongside of him, and, **by degrees, brought him between me** and the fire. "Sir," said I, "as I am only a midshipman, I don't care so much about honour as you do; and, therefore, if it makes no difference to you, I'll take the liberty of getting under your lee." He laughed, and said, "I did not know you were here, for I meant you should have gone with the others; but, since you are out of your station, Mr. Mildmay, I will make that use of you which you so ingeniously proposed to make of me. My life may be of some importance here, but yours very little, and another midshipman can be had from the ship only for asking; so just drop astern, if you please, and do duty as a breastwork for me!"

"Certainly, sir," said I; "by all means." And I took my station accordingly.

"Now," said the captain, "if you are '*doubled up*' I will take you on my shoulders!"

I expressed myself exceedingly obliged, not only for the honour he had conferred on me, but also for that which he intended; but hoped I should have no occasion to trouble him.

Whether the enemy took pity on my youth and *innocence*, or whether they purposely missed us, I cannot say; I only know I was very happy when I found myself inside the castle with a whole skin, and should very readily have reconciled myself to any measure which would have restored me even to the comforts and conveniences of a man-of-war's cockpit. All human enjoyment is comparative; and nothing ever convinced me of it so much and so forcibly as what took place at this memorable siege.

Fortune, and the well-known cowardice of the Spaniards, released me from this jeopardy. They surrendered the citadel; after which the castle was of **no use,** and we ran down to our boats as fast as we **could ; and** notwithstanding the very assiduous fire of the watchful tirailleurs on the hill, we all got on board without accident.

In addition to their other lines, the French had thrown up a battery on the cliff, by means of which the breach was **soon** considerably widened. The garrison did all in their power to repair the damages, and the stone dislodged by the enemy's guns rendered this more **easy.** These splinters of stone, however, were dangerous—a fact of which Lord Cochrane had personal proof. He was struck in the face, and his nose driven back into the roof of his mouth. The agony caused by this wound was intolerable; but by the great skill of his surgeon, Dr. Guthrie, the injury was, after a time, repaired, and the nose rendered serviceable.

The French, having gained possession of the town of Rosas, redoubled their fire upon the fortress, and on the **30th had** effected what they considered a practicable **breach.**

The following singular presentiment is related by Lord Cochrane. " The dawn of the 30th might have been our last but from the interposition of what some persons may call presentiment. Long before daylight I was awoke with an impression that the enemy were in possession of the castle, though the stillness which prevailed showed this to be a delusion. Still I could not recompose myself to sleep; and after lying for some time tossing about, I left my couch, and hastily went on the esplanade of the fortress. All was perfectly still, and I felt half ashamed of having given way to such fancies.

"A loaded mortar, **however,** stood before me, pointed during the day **in** such a direction that the shell should **fall** on the path over the hill which the French must necessarily take whenever they might make an attempt to storm. Without other object than that of **divesting my mind of** what had taken possession of it, I fired the **mortar.** Before the echo had **died** away, a volley of musketry from the advancing column of the enemy showed that the shell had fallen amongst them just as they were on the point of storming."

Finding that nothing more could be done, Lord Cochrane determined **on** evacuating the fortress, and leaving the Spaniards to their fate, having had three **of his** men killed and five **wounded.**

The following is a copy of his official letter to Lord Collingwood, dated Bay of Rosas, 5th December, 1808:—

"The **fortress of** Rosas being attacked **by an** army of Italians in the service of France, in pursuance of discretionary orders to assist the Spaniards whenever it could be done with effect, I hastened here. The citadel, on the 22nd ult., was already half invested, and the enemy was making his approaches towards the S.W. bastion, which was blown down last war by the explosion of a magazine, and tumbled into the ditch. A few thin planks, and dry stones, had been put up by the Spanish engineers, perhaps to hide the defect. All things were in a most deplorable state without and within; even measures for their powder, and saws for their fuses, were not to be had, and mats and axes supplied their place. The castle of Trinity, situated on an eminence, but commanded by heights, was also invested. Three 24-pounders battered in breach, to which a fourth was afterwards added, and a passage through the wall to the lower bomb-proof being nearly effected on the 23rd, the marines of the *Fame* were withdrawn.

"I went to examine the state of the castle; and as the senior officer in the bay had not officially altered the orders I received from your lordship, I thought this a good opportunity, by occupying a post on which the acknowledged safety of the citadel depended, to render them an effectual service; the remaining garrison, consisting of about eighty Spaniards, who were on the point of surrendering when I threw myself into the fort with fifty seamen and thirty marines of the *Impérieuse*.

"The arrangements I made need not be detailed to your lordship: suffice it to say that about a thousand bags made of old sails, besides palisades and barrels, supplied the place of walls and ditches; and that the enemy, who assaulted the castle on the 30th with 1,000 picked men, were repulsed, with the loss of their commanding officer, storming equipage, and

all who **had attempted to** mount the breach. **The**
Spanish garrison, having been changed, gave good
assistance. As to the officers, seamen, and marines
of this ship, the fatigues they underwent, and the
gallant manner in which they behaved, deserve every
praise. I must, however, particularly mention Lieutenant [Urry] Johnson, **R.N.**; Lieutenant [James R.]
Hore, R.M.; Mr. Burney, gunner; **Mr.** Lodowick,
carpenter; and Messrs. [Houston] Stewart, Slovin,
and [Frederick] Marryat, midshipmen.

"Captain [Robert] Hall, of the *Lucifer*, at all
times, and in every way, gave his zealous assistance;
and I feel also indebted to Captain [James] Collins,
of the *Meteor*, for his aid.

"The citadel of Rosas capitulated at twelve o'clock
this day; and seeing further resistance in the Castle
of Trinity useless and impracticable against the whole
army, the attention of which had been naturally
turned to its reduction, we embarked in the boats of
the *Magnificent*, *Impérieuse*, and *Fame*, after firing
the trains for exploding the magazines."

Lord Collingwood, upon the receipt of the despatch,
wrote **to** Mr. **Wellesley** Pole, Secretary of the Admiralty, as follows :—

" Captain Lord Cochrane has maintained himself
in the possession of Trinity Castle with great ability
and heroism. Although the fort is laid open by the
breach in its works, he has sustained and repelled
several assaults, **having** formed a sort of rampart

within the breach **with** his ship's hammock-cloths, awnings, &c., filled with sand and rubbish. The zeal and energy with which he has maintained that fortress excites the highest admiration. **His** resources for every exigency have no end."

Writing again to the Admiralty, dated January 7, 1809, Lord Collingwood said: "The heroic spirit and ability which have been evinced by Lord Cochrane in defending this castle, although so shattered in its works, against the repeated attacks of the enemy, is an admirable instance of his lordship's zeal; and the distinguished conduct of Lieutenants Johnson* and Hore, and the officers and men employed in this affair under his lordship, will doubtless be very gratifying to my Lords Commissioners of the Admiralty."

The Spanish press, also, were loud in the praises of their heroic defender. The following is a concluding paragraph of a high-flown eulogium :—

" **It is** sufficient to mention that in the defence of the **castle** of Trinidad, when the Spanish flag hoisted on the **wall fell** into the ditch under a most dreadful fire from **the enemy, his** lordship was the only person who, regardless **of the shower** of bullets flying about him, descended into the ditch, returned with the flag, **and** happily succeeded in placing it where it was."

* This officer was made a commander 6th September, 1809; but it does not appear that the promotion was given as an especial reward for his gallantry on this occasion.

From all but one side Cochrane was justly applauded. His commander-in-chief, his equals, and his subordinates, were unanimous in his praise ; but he was the Whig Radical Member for Westminster, which, in the **eyes of the** reigning party, was enough to render all his **noble** deeds valueless. For all the fighting, which we **have only** briefly recorded, not a promotion, and consequently not even a silver medal, has ever been awarded. **Can** we wonder that a warm-blooded, high-spirited man felt indignant at such treatment, **and** that he carried with him to the grave the remembrance of the injuries he then, as well as before and subsequently, **received ?**

Once more he had **to write a despatch,** reporting a service off Barcelona. His letter **bore date** Carthagena, 2nd January, 1809 :—

"Having **received** information **of two French** vessels **of war** and a convoy of victuallers **for** Barcelona being in this port, I have the **honour to inform your** lordship that they are all, amounting to thirteen sail, in **our** possession. **The names of** the prizes were, *La Gauloise,** cutter, **7 guns, 46** men, commanded by M. Avanet, a member of the Legion of Honour ; *La Julie,* lugger, **5 guns, 4 swivels, 44** men, and eleven victuallers."

---

* This vessel was placed in charge **of** Lieutenant Harrison, **who was** ordered to proceed to Gibraltar ; **but** when off Tarragona he went on shore in a boat, with two **hands,** not knowing that it was in the possession of the French, **and** was taken prisoner. The cutter, however, made her escape, and proceeded to Minorca.

This service was not accomplished without difficulty. Having anchored in Caldagues bay, the *Impérieuse* opened fire on the vessels of war, two of which sank, the crews escaping to the shore. The frigate then warped close in shore for the purpose of silencing the fire of a battery, and at the same time despatched the boats in two directions to attack the enemy in flank and rear. Observing this movement, the French, afraid of being cut off from the main body, threw some of the guns over the cliff. The remaining guns, four brass 18-pounders, were captured and brought off; and the magazine blown up. The cutter and lugger were raised, and some other brass guns recovered.

On the 9th January he destroyed another battery, near Silva, throwing the guns into the sea. The arrival of large reinforcements, however, induced the French to regain possession of the coast; but finding their two batteries destroyed, and their guns gone, they opened a heavy fire of musketry, and also commenced a smart fire from a battery lower down the cliff, by which two men on board the *Impérieuse* were wounded. After some further active co-operation, the *Impérieuse* proceded to Minorca, and on the 30th January joined the fleet under the command of Vice-Admiral Thornborough.

Lord Cochrane, being anxious to bring under the consideration of the House of Commons the extortionate system pursued in the Admiralty Court at Malta with respect to the prizes sent thither for adjudication, applied for leave of absence. He also wished to put on record the marked neglect shown to his officers who had so gallantly assisted him in his laborious and hazardous exertions on the enemy's coasts, as well as to revive his plan for seizing some of the islands in the Bay of Biscay. Permission to return to England having been **accorded, he** quitted the Mediterranean in the *Impérieuse,* and **arrived** at Plymouth in the month of March.

THE AFFAIR IN BASQUE ROADS.
[1809.]

We now approach the last of Lord Cochrane's services in the British navy. Hitherto he had worked harder **than any officer** of his standing during the most exciting period of the war. He had been, we may say, constantly under fire, and had gained **a** name for professional dash, combined with prudence, which gave promise of his attaining the highest naval honours. True, he had been grievously neglected and persecuted; but so transcendent **had** been the skill evinced by him, that a little more would have placed him far above the reach of the machinations of his enemies. Shortly after his return to England, he received a letter couched in the most complimentary terms, **from the second** sea Lord of the Admiralty,—Captain **W. Johnstone** Hope,—acquainting him that an undertaking of great moment was in contemplation against Rochefort, and that **the** Board were of opinion **his** local knowledge **might be** of the utmost consequence. This letter **was** quickly followed by a telegraphic **summons to** attend the Admiralty. Lord

Cochrane lost no time in obeying the mandate. There will be no doubt in the minds of many readers, that this seeming compliment was only a means resorted to in order to deter him from again agitating the House of Commons with his intended motions on the navy.

On reaching the Admiralty, he was sent for by Lord Mulgrave, the first lord, by whom he was confidentially consulted as to the practicability of destroying the French squadron lying in the Aix roads, then blockaded by Admiral Lord Gambier, the commander-in-chief of the Channel fleet. Great fears were entertained that by some accident the French squadron would effect its escape, and do considerable damage among our West-India islands, whither the squadron was bound.

The proposition in agitation was, the possibility of destroying these ships by means of fire-vessels; but which operation Lord Gambier appeared desirous to set aside, deeming it "hazardous if not desperate." Much conversation ensued on the occasion, and Lord Cochrane demurred for a time to undertake a service which the commander-in-chief had pronounced against. It ended, however in Lord Mulgrave's giving him Lord Gambier's letter to read, containing the following paragraph :—" The enemy's ships lie much exposed to the operation of fire-ships: it is a horrible mode of warfare, and the attempt hazardous, if not desperate; but we should have plenty of volunteers for the service."

Lord Mulgrave then observed that Lord Gambier

had thus thrown the onus of failure upon the Admiralty, and again, in effect, proposed to his lordship to accept the unenviable risk of becoming the scape-goat. Lord Gambier had said in his private letter, that the advanced work, between the isles of Aix and Oleron, had been injured in its foundation, and that consequently there would be no difficulty in bombarding the French ships; but was evidently averse from the fire-ship proposition. Cochrane did not at the time see the drift of all this. He concurred with Lord Gambier, that fire-ships alone would probably fail; but he thought that fire-ships and his explosion vessels, seconded by the fleet, would be sure to succeed. The interview ended in Lord Mulgrave's requesting him to put his plans in execution, to which he at length assented.

On the 25th March, a letter was addressed to Lord Gambier by the Board of Admiralty, acquainting the admiral that they had thought fit to select Lord Cochrane for the purpose of conducting, under his orders, the squadron of fire-ships, intended to be employed on this important service.

Let us now take a survey of the position of the French ships, which numbered ten sail of the line, a 54-gun store-ship, and three frigates. To render this clearer, we give a wood engraving taken from the most correct French chart then extant, in which the position of the ships is shown by dots, and also the soundings and intricacies of the navigation. The line of battle-ships were moored in a double line, so arranged that the broadsides of the inner ships could

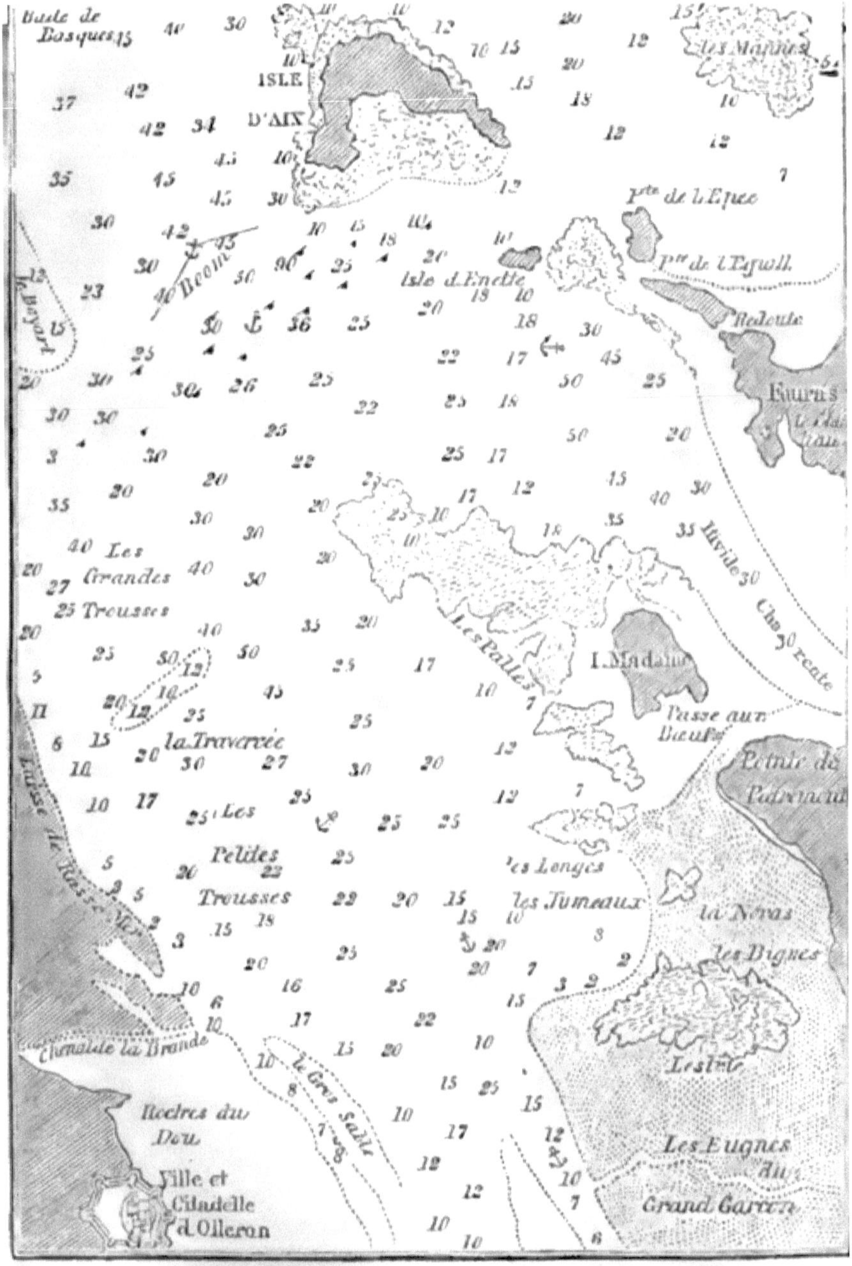

SOUNDINGS IN FEET AT LOW WATER SPRINGS.

0 1 2 3 4 5

Scale of Nautical Miles.

Page 136.

fire clear of the outer ships; and each ship had the power, by means of a spring on the outer anchor, to present a clear broadside force sufficient to sink the British fleet, had it attempted to force an entrance.

The following will **show** the positions occupied by the French ships:—

Indienne.   Hortense.   Pallas.

Foudroyant. Varsovie. Océan. Régulus. Cassard. Calcutta.

Tonnerre. **Patriote.** Jemmappes. Aquilon. Tourville. Elbe.

As a protection against the advance of fire-ships, a boom, half a mile in length, had been laid down, composed of spars, and cables of the largest dimensions,* secured by 5-ton anchors. This boom, forming an obtuse angle, occupied the deep-water channel between the Isle d'Aix and the Boyart shoal. **This** obstruction was something new, and one which would have proved effectual against the passage of fire-ships; but not, as it was proved, to Cochrane's explosion-vessels.

He had had two explosion vessels constructed, the largest containing 1,500 barrels of powder, contained in puncheons placed on end, and secured together by stout hawsers, and formed into a solid mass by wedges and wet sand rammed hard between the

---

* Mr. James (vol. v. p. **150**) **states that** the cables were 31½ English inches in *diameter*, **but he has in this, we** imagine, substituted " diameter " for " circumference," by which rope is **always** measured. A cable 31½ inches in *diameter* would be termed **a 94-***inch cable!*

casks. On the top of this mass of gunpowder nearly 400 live shells, with short fuses, and some hundreds of hand grenades and rockets were deposited. Twelve fire-ships were assembled, but it does not appear that these were placed entirely under Lord Cochrane's control.

The *Impérieuse* arrived in Basque Roads on the 3rd of April; and **Cochrane** immediately reported himself to Lord Gambier. His reception was **civil, and the** admiral put **him** in possession of the order he **had** received from the **Admiralty.** Not so, **however, his** reception by others; **the** appointment of a junior officer to conduct the **service** was viewed, not unnaturally, as a slur upon the captains and junior flag-officers of the fleet. The captain of the flag-ship, Sir Harry Neale, and Rear-Admiral Stopford appear to have been exceptions to this rule. Rear-Admiral Eliab Harvey, who, in the *Téméraire*, so gloriously seconded Lord Nelson at Trafalgar, was especially indignant, and remonstrated in terms so vehement and insubordinate **as to lead** to a court-martial, which dismissed him the service. Of all this, however, Cochrane was innocent. He had not sought the responsible position, and had only obeyed orders **in** the matter. There is not, **we** think, ground **for** concluding that this feeling operated to any great extent against Lord Cochrane. All differences of such **a** nature are pretty sure **to** vanish before the smell of powder; and **we are** inclined to think more stress has been placed **upon** the fact that **his** appointment was unpopular among the captains than the results **warranted.**

The fire-ships arrived on the 10th of April, and the admiral, Allemand, who commanded the French fleet, made every disposition calculated to defeat the operation which he then must have clearly seen was **intended.** The launches and other boats of the fleet, manned and armed to the number of seventy-three, were assembled and formed into five divisions, and stationed each night at the boom, ready to board any fire-ships that might approach, and to engage any British boats by which **they** were accompanied. The line-of-battle ships got their topgallant-masts on deck, struck topmasts **and** unbent sails. The three frigates were alone kept ready for making sail. All the available troops were put on shore to man the batteries on the Isle d'Aix.

The strength of the defences on Isle d'Aix have been variously estimated. Lord Cochrane considered that they were of **no** importance; while Lord Gambier's report was that they were very strong. There can be no doubt that the French were alive to the danger of their position, and that they had done their **best** to strengthen their defences. Additional works were observed in progress on the Boyart **shoal** some days previous to the arrival of the *Impérieuse*, which Captain Irby, in the *Amelia* frigate, had been ordered to attack, and which, by means of his boats, he succeeded in destroying. The strength of the Aix batteries has been variously estimated at from 13 to 50 guns. The truth probably lies **in** the mean ; but as these guns were all long 32-pounders, placed low down, and as the forts were, in addition, furnished with the heaviest mortars, they were not to be despised. The troops by which they were garrisoned numbered 2,000 ; but it has been said they were chiefly conscripts. Three and a half miles to the eastward of Aix were the Oleron gun and mortar batteries.

Time was too precious to be lost. The fire-ships were ready, and *one* mortar vessel, the *Etna*, out of five that had been promised, had arrived. The night of the 11th was, accordingly, fixed for the operation. The *Impérieuse* anchored in deep water, close to the inner end of the Boyart shoal. The frigates *Aigle*, *Unicorn*, and *Pallas*, anchored in line to the northward of the *Impérieuse*, in order to receive the crews of the fire-ships, and to support the boats of the fleet; and the *Etna* was anchored off the north-east point of the Isle d'Aix, covered by the *Emerald* frigate, and *Beagle*, *Doterel*, *Conflict*, and *Growler*, gun brigs. The *Redpole* and *Lyra*, with screened lights hoisted, were the pointers, one being close to the southern end of the Boyart, and the other just out of range of the Aix batteries. The fire-ships were to pass between these two light-vessels, and then shape a course for the boom. The wind was blowing strong from north-west, which was about two points free to the ships running for the boom.

Cochrane, accompanied by Lieutenant William Bissell, embarked on board the largest of the explosion vessels at 8·30 P.M., and started on his perilous undertaking. The *Mediator* and other fire-ships followed him. He was accompanied by a boat's crew of four volunteers only, besides Lieutenant Bissell. Having **arrived as near to** the boom as he thought necessary, he ordered Lieutenant Bissell and the men to get into the boat while he ignited the port-fires. The fuses had been calculated to burn fifteen minutes, by **which** time it was expected the boat would have been well out of the range of the grenades; but the boat had not left more than five minutes ere the explosion took place. The escape of the party was almost a miracle. A mountain wave was thrown up, while the grenades and **rockets** were darting round them on **all** sides. The ignition of the powder had been instantaneous, **and** the flight of shells and missiles of every description perfectly frightful.

Had the explosion-vessel reached the boom, however? Upon this point a great deal rested. Mr. Fairfax, the master of the fleet, who was on board the *Lyra,* a stout Gambier partisan, stated that the vessel exploded a mile from the boom; but, from the position laid down on his manufactured chart, it is evident the explosion must have taken place within a very short distance, if not when in actual contact. **The** *Mediator,* an old Indiaman of 800 tons, was **the first** to enter the opening which the explosion-vessel had caused, and Commander James Wooldridge was awarded the merit of having directed his ship with the effect necessary to accomplish this **feat.** The momentum with which a ship of 800 tons would strike a floating obstruction, moored by enormous anchors, would, however, have been insufficient for such a purpose. The boom, as we have already stated, formed an obtuse angle, its apex being towards the Basque Roads. A ship striking it would, therefore, have been morally certain to glance off, whereas it would have succumbed to the enormous shock produced by the explosion of 1,500 barrels of powder. It was, undoubtedly, the concussion of the exploding mass of gunpowder which displaced the spars and cleared away the obstruction.

Great credit was due to Commander Wooldridge, for he remained at his post after the vessel was in flames, and was blown out of the ship, together with the gunner (who was killed), Lieutenants Clements and Pearl, and one seaman. Six other fire-ships were also **well** directed, and by their approach produced the most terrible alarm. The captain of the French frigate *Indienne,* which ship was at anchor just inside the boom, was in a position to verify Lord Cochrane's assertion, and to deny that of Mr. Fairfax. According to the account kept on board that ship, the explosion vessel blew up only about 120 yards distant from that frigate, and covered her with a sheet of flame.

By the time the *Mediator* broke the boom, which was at 9h. 45m., **the** frigates were under way. The *Régulus,* 74, and *Océan,* 120, were soon afterwards grappled by fire-ships. The *Océan* was in imminent peril, and was obliged to cut her cables, so as **to** bring the fire-ship to leeward. In doing this she fouled the *Tonnerre* and *Patriote,* and their escape from destruction was miraculous. The *Océan* took the ground on the Palles shoal, and had another narrow escape from a second fire-ship running down upon her; and, had not the three-decker shot away the mainmast of the blazing ship, she must **have been fouled** and destroyed. She lost fifty **men in** freeing herself from her first assailant.

The crews of the French ships became panic-stricken, and **all** hands did their best to quit so dangerous **a** roadstead. The darkness of the night rendered the effect of the burning masses and repeated explosions still more **awful.** The sky was illumined by the **red** glare of the fire-ships, and, added to the flashes of guns from the forts and the incessant flight of shells and **rockets, the** scene was awfully sublime. The strength of the wind, however, was such that the fleet lying **in** Basque roads could not hear the reports of the guns, or even of the explosion vessel.

Daylight on the 12th revealed the results of the night's operation. The *Océan* flag-ship was in the mud, half a mile to the eastward of her former anchorage. Owing to the quantity of provisions on board for the supply of the colony whither she was bound, the *Océan* drew 28 feet water. She was consequently aground, not on the shoal, but in what may be termed the edge of the roadstead of Aix. About 500 yards to the south-west of the *Océan*, upon a patch of rocks called the Charenton, **the** *Varsovie* and *Aquilon* were on shore; and close to these ships, but upon more even ground, were the *Régulus* and *Jemmappes.* The *Tonnerre,* with her head to the south-east, lay on a hard shoal, 200 yards to the eastward **of** the Pontra rock, near **the Isle** Madame. The latter ship was bilged, and had **cut away** her mainmast, and thrown the principal part of her guns overboard. Some distance south-west of the *Tonnerre*, on the extremity of the Palles shoal, lay the *Calcutta*. The *Patriote* and *Tourville* were in the mud, off Isle Madame, at no great distance from the channel of the Charente. The four frigates were also on shore: the *Elbe* and *Hortense* upon the Fontenelles, the *Pallas* upon the mud off the Fort of Barques, and the *Indienne* three-quarters of a mile to the eastward of the *Océan*. All the ships, but particularly the six on the hard part of the Palles, were somewhat upon the heel, and most were in a very dangerous position.

The explosion-vessel and fire-ships had therefore not been employed in vain; for, although no ships except the *Océan* and *Régulus* had been actually in contact with them, the effect in so confined an anchorage had been almost as detrimental as if each had been grappled. The *Impérieuse* being nearest to the scene of destruction, was the first to notify to the admiral the position of the enemy.

It may be as well to remark here, that hardly two ships' logs agree precisely as to the time at which any particular signal was made. According to the log of the *Caledonia*, Lord Gambier's flag-ship, the *Impérieuse*, made the first signal—"Half the fleet can destroy the enemy "—at 5h. 48m. A.M.; but Lord Cochrane states it was "six o'clock;" and as the *Impérieuse* made the signal, the latter time should be adopted. According to the latter authority, therefore, we find that at 7h. A.M., Cochrane again signalled—"All the enemy's ships, except two, are on shore." An hour and a half later, **not** observing any movement on board the fleet in Basque Roads, Cochrane signalled—" Half the fleet can destroy the enemy;" and, subsequently—" The frigates alone can destroy the enemy." Lord Cochrane's impatience was natural: and had the commander-in-chief really taken no other notice of his important intimations than by hoisting the affirmative pendant, there would have been good ground for dissatisfaction. Lord Gambier, however, says that, on learning the position of the French ships, he ordered the fleet to be immediately unmoored; but that as the wind was strong from the north-west, and the tide at the last quarter ebb, which rendered his getting the fleet under way a useless proceeding, he annulled the signal. " Between nine and ten o'clock," says Lord Gambier in his defence (but the average time of the logs gives it an hour later), " which was much before the flood had sufficiently made to enable the fleet to get into action," the ships weighed and made sail, until within three miles of the Isle d'Aix, when the *Caledonia* and most of the ships brought up. The 74-gun ships *Valiant, Bellona*, and *Revenge*, with the frigates, were, however, directed to anchor as near as possible to the Boyart shoal, to be in readiness to proceed to the attack when the **depth** of water was sufficient for them to go in.

It must be obvious, that **as the** French ships had gone on shore just before high-tide, they were, for the most part, in a position to float as soon as there was water for the attacking ships to go in. In other words, the water which would render the approach of the British line-of-battle ships safe, would suffice to float off most of the grounded ships. Lord Gambier, however, committed an inexcusable error in summoning a council of war, to give him countenance in this extremity. The bugbear responsibility evidently weighed him down, and, in order to escape the incubus, he made a signal for all captains to attend on board the *Caledonia*, to hold a conference with him. The facts were plain enough; all but two of the French line-of-battle ships were on shore. An attack upon the Aix batteries, close to which was deep water, and the near approach of four or five sail of the line, with the frigates, at half-flood, would in all human probability have had the effect of completing the panic which the fire-ships had originated. On the other hand, the anchoring of the fleet three miles from the Aix batteries, was most injudicious, for it reassured the stranded enemy, and gave their officers and crews an opportunity to warp their ships off the shoals. The risk of losing two or three British ships, which was, at the greatest, only a remote one, was set against the moral certainty of the destruction of eleven sail of the line; but Lord Gambier hesitated, and, to give an excuse for his hesitation, summoned a council of war!

The result of this conference was just what might have been expected. Lord Gambier thought, and, as a matter of course, his opinion found his backers in the majority, that, as the enemy were on shore, it was unnecessary to run any risk, the object of their destruction having been already obtained. As a proof, however, of the effect which would have been produced by a more determined front, it may be stated that the *Foudroyant* and *Cassard*, who had been many hours in getting up their topmasts and top-gallant masts, deeming an attack probable, weighed anchor at about three-quarter flood, and made for the Charente.

Ever since daylight, the *Océan* had been making great preparations for hauling off. Provisions and stores were thrown overboard; water started, and anchors laid out. The other ships had followed the Admiral's example, and by 2 P.M. the *Patriote*, *Régulus*, and *Jemmappes* had extricated themselves, but only to ground again in the mud off the Charente. The *Océan* floated a little before high water, and warped about 700 yards from her former position, when she again grounded. Observing the impunity with which these attempts at extrication were attended, the *Calcutta*, *Aquilon*, and *Varsovie*, were resorting to the same expedients, and there seems no reasonable ground for doubt, that had not Lord Cochrane shamed the fleet by his example, every ship, with the exception of the bilged *Tonnerre*, would have quietly made their exit from the scene of their night's overthrow.

Noon had passed away unimproved; one o'clock saw no change, except that the one mortar vessel, the *Etna*, had run down for the purpose of throwing a few harmless shells. Cochrane's patience was at an end, and without waiting for those instructions which he felt assured would never issue, he ordered the anchor of the *Impérieuse* to be tripped, and so dropped down towards the enemy with the flowing tide. He avoided making sail, fearing to be recalled; but at 1h. 30m. grew bolder, and ordering the top-sails to be set, steered for the group of ships aground on the Palles. He then made the signal, "the enemy's ships are getting under sail," and ten minutes afterwards, "enemy superior to chasing ship." As this brought no immediate assistance, he resorted to the expedient of making the signal that the ship was in distress, and requiring assistance. Not until two o'clock, however, could Lord Gambier be aroused to action. He then signalled the frigate *Indefatigable*, to weigh, and proceed to the assistance of the *Impérieuse;* but the wind having dropped considerably the *Indefatigable*, though under a crowd of sail, was nearly an hour in arriving near the ship presumed to be in distress. The *Valiant* and *Revenge*, got under way at 2h. 30m.; and the other frigates and smaller vessels, one by one, followed Cochrane's noble example.

In the mean while, however, the *Impérieuse* had not been idle. The signal of distress had been thrown out by way of spur, and not that the ship was in any great danger. Her bow-guns were discharged with effect into the stern of the *Varsovie*, but her broadside was principally directed against the *Calcutta;* and on the near approach of the other frigates, the colours of that ship were hauled down. The tide had now reached its height, and all the British frigates, as well as the two line-of-battle ships, were actively engaged. At 3h. 20m., observing that the crew of the *Calcutta* were abandoning the ship, Lord Cochrane sent a mid-shipman and boat's crew to take possession; but for a time the boat was unable to approach, owing to the fire still kept up by other ships, who appeared ignorant of the fact of her having surrendered. The prize was at length boarded; and the young officer, not knowing what else to do with the now abandoned ship, set her on fire.

The *Varsovie* and *Aquilon*, at 5h. 30m., each showed a union-jack, to denote their surrender; for just at that time the 74-gun ship *Theseus* arrived, and anchored between the *Revenge* and *Valiant*, which, it may be presumed, destroyed any hopes those ships might previously have entertained of escape. The *Tonnerre* was also shortly afterwards abandoned, and set on fire by her own crew. The destruction of the *Varsovie* and *Aquilon*, was subsequently accomplished under the orders of Captain Bligh, so that the result of the night and day's work may be stated as follows:—

84-gun ship *Varsovie*, and 74-gun ships *Aquilon* and *Tonnerre*, 50-gun ship *Calcutta*, *armée en flûte*, taken and destroyed.

The only ship beside the *Impérieuse* that sustained any loss, was the *Revenge*, which ship had three men killed, and Lieutenant James Garland and fourteen men wounded. The *Revenge* also sustained much damage to her hull, all, however, from the batteries of the Isle d'Aix, which Cochrane wrongly considered as unimportant defences. The *Impérieuse* had three seamen killed; Mr. George Gilbert, assistant surgeon,

Mr. Mark Marsden, purser, seven seamen, and two marines, wounded. This loss was occasioned principally by the fire of the *Calcutta*. The *Indefatigable* and *Beagle*, received some damage to their spars, rigging, and sails, but had no one injured.

The French loss, in killed and wounded, was never ascertained. The *Calcutta* had only 230 men on board, of whom twelve were badly wounded by the fire of the *Impérieuse*, and the hull of the ship was riddled by shot. The captain of the *Aquilon* was killed in the boat of the *Impérieuse* by the side of Lord Cochrane, by a shot from the burning *Tonnerre*. Her crew suffered very little ; but the *Varsovie* had upwards of a hundred killed and wounded.

Five sail of the line were still aground and assailable, although from the want of bomb-vessels, and ships of a light draught of water, the difficulty in producing any effect was great. The *Océan*, *Cassard*, *Régulus*, *Jemmappes*, *Tourville*, and frigate *Indienne*, were all aground off the entrance to the Charente ; but, inasmuch as our line-of-battle ships drew more water than the French ships,—the latter having been lightened of provisions, water, and stores,—the difficulty was to get at them.

Rear-Admiral Stopford, in the *Cæsar*, who was intrusted with this inshore service, caused three transports to be hastily fitted as fire-ships, and, accompanied by the launches of the fleet, fitted to throw congreve rockets, stood close in towards Aix Roads, to further the exertions of the squadron already engaged. The batteries on the Isle d'Aix, and also upon Oleron, opened fire upon this force; but by keeping close to the Boyart shoal the shot did not reach. In endeavouring to avoid these opposite dangers, however, the *Cæsar* took the ground near the extremity of the shoal, and did not float off until the flood **had** made strong. The *Valiant* and *Theseus* had taken the ground at 7 P.M., the former on the edge of the Palles, but the *Revenge* remained afloat. The *Indefatigable* and *Impérieuse* also grounded for a short time, but sustained no damage.

At midnight **the** fire-ships were ready; **but** the wind having shifted **to** the south-west, rendered their **employment out** of the question; and the *Cæsar*, **taking** advantage of the fair wind out, weighed anchor and proceeded to Little Basque Roads. Captain Bligh, in the *Valiant*, being thus left senior officer, removed the prisoners from the *Varsovie* and *Aquilon*, and at 3 A.M. these ships were set on fire.

The effect of this w**as to** revive the panic among the French ships. The burning line-of-battle ships, though stationary, were taken for more fire-ships, and treated accordingly by the *Océan*, *Tourville*, *Indienne*, and some **others**, who opened a fire upon the flaming masses. **The** captain and crew of the *Tourville*, moreover, were so alarmed that they took to their boats in a state of the greatest trepidation, and landed at Pointe des Barques; but observing at daylight that the *Tourville* was unharmed by the supposed fire-ships, **he** returned with his crew, and resumed the command. **In** the mean while, however, his ship, though not in danger from a *brûlot*, was very nearly being made a prize of by a British boat; and but for the presence of mind of a French quarter-master, who had been left on board by accident, the *Tourville* would most probably have been boarded and captured.

The morning of the 13th April found Cochrane with the *Impérieuse*, *Pallas*, and the gun-brigs, in the inner road, but the frigates and line-of-battle ships had all taken their departure. The *Pallas* would have gone out with the others, but that Captain Seymour, having ascertained Lord Cochrane's intention to remain, nobly decided on giving him all the assistance in his power. Lord Cochrane had previously endeavoured to induce Captain Rodd, of the *Indefatigable*, to join with him in an attack upon the *Océan*; but the invitation was declined, Captain Rodd giving as a reason that the *Indefatigable* drew too much water, and had a wounded topmast; and, further, that he could not do so in the presence of superior officers.

At 8 A.M. Lord Cochrane despatched the brigs and mortar - vessel to attack the French ships still aground. The *Beagle* most gallantly anchored in sixteen-feet water upon the *Océan's* quarter, and engaged her for five hours, receiving in return the fire from the French ship's 36-pounder poop-carronades. The brig escaped without loss of men, and with very little damage. The *Etna*, which vessel might have rendered valuable service at this juncture, was disabled, having split her mortar. The *Océan* received very little injury from the fire of the gun-brigs, and at the top of the tide made some further progress towards the river. Had the *Impérieuse* and *Pallas* been able to take part in the attack, much more might have been done. But owing to the strong wind and tide, it was deemed unsafe to lift the anchor.

At noon the *Doterel, Foxhound, Redpole*, and two more rocket-vessels joined the *Impérieuse.* By one of these vessels Lord Cochrane received two letters, one public and the other private. The first contained directions for him to attack the *Océan*, but gave it as his opinion that no good would result from it; but the private one was of a most complimentary description. The latter was as follows:—

" *Caledonia*, 13*th April*, 1809.

"My DEAR LORD,—You have done your part so admirably, that I will not suffer you to tarnish it by attempting impossibilities, which I think, as well as those captains who have come from you, any further effort to destroy those ships would be. You must, therefore, join as soon as you can, with the bombs, &c., as I wish for some information which you allude to before I close my despatches.

"Yours, my dear Lord, most sincerely,

"GAMBIER."

The public letter was comprised in a "P.S":—"I have ordered three brigs and two rocket-vessels to join you, with which and the bomb you may make an attempt on the ship that is aground on the Palles, or towards Isle Madame; but I do not think you will succeed, and I am anxious that you should come to me, as I wish to send you to England as soon as possible. You must, therefore, come as soon as the tide turns."

But Cochrane was impervious to hints. He professed to treat the letter as one leaving him an option; and he therefore replied, " We *can* destroy the ships that are on shore, which I hope your lordship will approve **of.**" The *Impérieuse* accordingly remained until the 14th, and at daylight observed the French ships as nearly as possible in the same position; but surrounded by *chasse marées*, which were receiving on board the stores and guns of the line-of-battle ships. Lord Cochrane felt convinced that it was not even then too late to have destroyed more, if not all, of the grounded ships, had the admiral permitted him to follow them up, and given him the assistance of the frigates. This, however, Lord Gambier would not permit, and finding that Cochrane would not leave the spot so long as the shadow of discretionary authority remained, he resorted to the step of superseding him in the command of the fire-ships. The following letter of recall was, therefore, addressed to him, signals having been disregarded: " My dear Lord,— It is necessary I should have some communication with you before I close my despatches to the Admiralty. I have, therefore, ordered Captain Wolfe to relieve you in the service you are engaged in. I wish you to join me as soon as possible, that you may convey Sir Harry Neale to England, who will be charged with my despatches; or you may return to carry on the service where you are. I expect two bombs to arrive every moment; they will be useful in it."

As further delay would have been direct disobedience of orders, the *Impérieuse* got under way, and proceeded to Basque Roads. His interview with Lord Gambier was anything but agreeable, and Lord Gambier insinuated that in complaining of what had been done, he was desirous to take all the merit of the service to himself. They parted on unfriendly terms, and the *Impérieuse* sailed for England with Sir Harry Neale, the bearer of the despatches.

THE COURT-MARTIAL.

THE affair in Basque Roads was doomed to be more than a nine days' wonder. Lord Cochrane took his seat in Parliament, and it having become known to him that a vote of thanks was about to be proposed, he waited on the First Lord of the Admiralty, Lord Mulgrave, and informed him that, as one of the Members for Westminster, it was his intention to oppose the motion. Lord Mulgrave advised him to desist from any such course, and gave him full credit for his important share in the operations; but his advice, and the arguments by which it was supported, failed in inducing Cochrane to change his mind. But he endeavoured to draw the nice distinction, that he should not oppose the vote of thanks as the captain of the *Impérieuse*, but in his senatorial capacity. Lord Mulgrave then tempted him with the offer to command a squadron of three frigates in the Mediterranean, with a *carte blanche;* but this he resisted. He stood upon the loftier ground of duty to those who had sent him to represent them in Parliament, and steadily refused to accept anything as a bribe for holding his tongue. And dearly he paid for his patriotism.

Lord Mulgrave had now no option but to acquaint Lord Gambier with Cochrane's determination, and at the same time Lord Gambier was directed to write a revised report of the operation, altogether ignoring Cochrane's services. This was dated 10th May, 1809, and written in London. In his first letter, which was published in the *London Gazette*, Lord Gambier had written : " I cannot speak in sufficient terms of admiration and applause of the vigorous and gallant attack made by Lord Cochrane upon the French line-of-battle ships which were on shore, as well as of his judicious manner of approaching them, and placing his ship in a position most advantageous to annoy the enemy, and preserve his own ship; which could not be exceeded by any feat of valour achieved by the British navy."

Personally Cochrane had only to complain of the inadvertence, as it might have been, of giving Commander Wooldridge the credit of breaking the boom, and of leading the fire-ships. The fact that the explosion vessel in advance of the *Mediator* dislodged the boom, for which we were indebted to the French officers, was not known to Lord Gambier; and his lordship was probably misled by the master of the fleet, Mr. Fairfax, who asserted that the explosion took place a mile distant from the boom. This misrepresentation Lord Gambier would no doubt gladly have corrected had Cochrane afforded him the necessary data; but he had put this out of the admiral's power.

Lord Cochrane was now called upon to prefer charges against his late commander-in-chief. The request was conveyed to him in a letter dated May 22nd, from Mr. Wellesley Pole, the Admiralty secretary. After quoting Lord Mulgrave's statement to the Board, he goes on to say " I am commanded by their lordships to signify their directions that you state fully to me, for their information, the grounds on which your lordship objects to the vote of thanks being moved to Lord Gambier, to the end that their lordships may be enabled to judge how far your lordship's objections may be of a nature to justify the suspension of the intended motion in Parliament, or to call for further investigation."

Cochrane's reply was dated May 30th, in which he said :—" I have to request, Sir, that you will submit to their lordships that I shall at all times entertain a due sense of the honour they will confer by any directions they may be pleased to give me, that in pursuing the object of those directions my exertions will always go hand-in-hand with my duty, and that, to satisfy their lordships' mind in the present instance on the point of information regarding the late services in Basque Roads, I beg leave to state that the log and signal books of the fleet there employed at the period alluded to contain the particulars of that service, and furnish premises whence accurate conclusions may be readily drawn," &c.

The court-martial assembled on board the *Gladiator*, in Portsmouth harbour, on Wednesday, the 26th of July. **The** following **admirals and** captains composed the tribunal :—

Admiral Sir Roger Curtis, **Bart.**

Admiral William Young.	Vice-Admiral **Sir J. T.** Duckworth.
Vice-Admiral Sir **H.** Stanhope.	Vice-Admiral Billy Douglas.
Vice-Admiral Geo. Campbell.	Rear-Admiral John Sutton.
Captain John Irwin.	**Captain** Robert Hall.
Captain E. S. Dickson.	Captain R. D. Dunn.

M. Greetham, Esq., Jun., *Judge-Advocate.*

The charge, if such it may be termed, **was** contained in the Admiralty order for summoning the court-martial as follows :—

" **And** whereas, by the log-books **and** minutes of signals of the *Caledonia*, *Impérieuse*, and other ships employed in that service, it appears to us that the said Admiral Lord Gambier, on the 12th day of the said month of April, the enemy's ships being then on shore, and the signal having been made that they could be destroyed, did for a considerable time neglect or delay taking effectual measures for destroying them ; " and " we do hereby direct you to try the said Admiral Lord Gambier for his conduct in the instance hereinbefore mentioned ; and also to inquire into his whole conduct as commander-in-chief of the Channel fleet employed in Basque Roads between the 17th of March and 29th of April, 1809."

Having given in the foregoing pages a close and impartial account of what was really done, it is not necessary to enter into further detail. The master of the *Impérieuse*, Mr. Spurling, satisfactorily answered several questions relative to certain alterations in the log of that ship made subsequent to the original entries, and Lord Cochrane stated his case with great clearness.

The only other witnesses called in support of the charge were Rear-Admiral the Hon. R. Stopford and Captain Wolfe, whose evidence merely went to show what steps had been actually taken, unaccompanied by any opinion.

Lord Gambier was then called upon for his defence, which, although very laboured, contained some strong arguments tending to exculpate him as commander-in-chief.

The following is a summary of his argument:—

"It now only remains for me to request the attention of the Court to some conclusions which I think may be drawn from the whole of the statements I have submitted to the consideration of you, sir, and the rest of the members of this honourable Court, and by which, with the additional evidence I have to adduce, it will, I flatter myself, distinctly appear:—

"First, that during the whole of this service the most unwearied attention was applied by me to its main object, the destruction of the enemy's fleet.

"Secondly, that in no part of the service was more zeal and exertion shown than during the 12th of April, when I had necessarily in view two objects,—the destruction of the enemy's fleet, and also the preservation of that under my command; for the extreme difficulties in approaching an enemy closely surrounded by shoals, and strongly defended by batteries, rendered caution in my proceeding peculiarly necessary.

"Thirdly, that three out of the seven of the enemy's ships aground on the Palles were, from their first being on shore, totally out of reach of the guns of any ships of the fleet that might have been sent in, and that at no time whatever, either sooner or later, could they have been attacked.

"Fourthly, that the other four of the eleven ships of which the enemy's fleet consisted, were never in a situation to be assailed after the fire-ships had failed in their main object.

"These are the points on which I rest my justification, trusting that it will appear to the Court, upon their review of my whole case, that I did take the most effectual measures for destroying the enemy's fleet; that neither neglect nor unnecessary delay did take place in the execution of this service; and on the contrary, that it was owing to the time chosen by me for sending a force in to make the attack, that the service was accomplished with so very inconsiderable a loss. Had I pursued any of the measures deemed practicable and proper in the judgment of Lord Cochrane, I am firmly pursuaded the success attending this achievement would have proved more dearly bought than any yet recorded in our naval annals, and, far from accomplishing the hopes of my country or the expectations of the Admiralty, must have disappointed both. If such, too, were the foundation of his lordship's prospects, it is just they should vanish before the superior considerations attending a service involving the naval character and most important interests of the nation.

"I conclude by observing, that the service actually performed has been of great importance, as well in its immediate effects as in its ultimate consequences; for the Brest fleet is so reduced as to be no longer effective. It was upon this fleet the enemy relied for the succour and protection of their West-India colonies; and the destruction of their ships was effected in their own harbour, in sight of thousands of the French; and I congratulate myself and my country that this important service has been effected, under Providence, with the loss only of 10 men killed, 35 wounded, and 1 missing; and not even one of the smallest of our vessels employed has been disabled from proceeding on any service that might have become necessary. The extent of difficulties and prospect of danger in this enterprise were extreme, and the gallantry and determined spirit of those engaged most conspicuous. These merits and those difficulties ought not to be depreciated on account of the inconsiderable loss sustained on the occasion. I by no means seek to arrogate to myself any merit by these observations; but I make them as a tribute of praise due to the zealous services of the brave officers and men under my command, and with a view of pointing out how justly they are entitled to the gratitude of their country."

The reading of the defence having been finished, Mr. Edward Fairfax, **master of the fleet,** gave the **following opinions.**

Being asked if any ships of the line had been sent into Aix Roads, towards the entrance of the Charente, any **time of the morning of the 12th** of April, **to** attack the enemy's ships that were aground, at what time was it possible for them to return under the circumstances of wind and tide?—he answered, "They could not have shifted their situation till four o'olock P.M. **As** for returning, I should think it impossible. They would have been within range of shells and shot from the enemy's batteries while they remained there. With the wind as it blew the whole of the day of the 12th **of** April, the ships must have taken advantage of the ebb-tide to work out, to have got **out at all. If** the wind had continued **as** it did the whole of that **day, and** if those ships had been **crippled,** or lost a mast, they must have remained under the fire of the enemy's batteries until the wind should shift. The probable fate **of** those ships would have been destruction."

In **reply to the** question, had the fleet been un-**moored at the time** Lord Cochrane made the signal on the morning of the 12th, would it have tended to promote the destruction of those two ships that were left at anchor near the Isle **of Aix**?—he answered, "It could not make any difference."

Mr. Stokes, master of the *Caledonia,* described the

situation of the French fleet **on** the morning of the 12th of April, and stated that, **with** the wind as it blew the whole day, **had, any** ships of the line been sent into Aix Roads towards the entrance of the Charente, **it would not have** been **possible** for them to return that night. They would have been within half-range of shell and point-blank of shot.

Captain Bligh, of the *Valiant,* expressed his opinion that had any of the line-of-battle ships been sent in, they could never have returned, but must inevitably have been destroyed.

Being **further** examined, he **said** he did not observe that any of the fortifications on the Isle d'Aix **bad** been blown up and destroyed. Lord Gambier having asked him if he heard Lord Cochrane express to Captain Beresford, in Aix Roads, the probability of three or four of our line-of-battle ships being **lost** in attacking the enemy, **and what** passed on that subject, he answered, " When Captain Beresford asked Lord Cochrane his reason for making the telegraphic signal **that** half the fleet could destroy the enemy in the morning, he said he calculated on our losing three or four of **the ships, if** the commander-in-chief had sent the squadron in." He thought that nothing further could have **been** practicable, and that there had been no neglect or delay on the part of Lord Gambier.

Captain Beresford, of **the** *Theseus,* thought that if two of our ships had been placed as the two French ships—*Cassard* and *Foudroyant*—afloat were, we could have defied an enemy's approach, for the approaching ships must have been end on. His opinion as to the impracticability of the return of line-of-battle ships, if crippled, was similar to that of Mr. Fairfax, Mr. Stokes, and Captain Bligh, and he thought that no blame attached to the conduct of Lord Gambier.

Captain Kerr, of the *Revenge*, gave it as his firm belief, that had any of the line-of-battle ships gone in sooner than they did, they would have been crippled; by which means the French ships would have discovered the strength of their position, and of course remained instead of going up the river, and have prevented the four ships that were afterward destroyed from being so.

Captain Douglas, of the *Bellona*, and Captain Godfrey, of the *Etna*, deposed to the same effect.

Mr. Wilkinson (Secretary to Lord Gambier) stated, that when Lord Cochrane came on board the *Caledonia*, on the evening of the 14th of April, he told the admiral, that if he had sent the ships agreeably to the signal, he calculated upon three or four of them being lost. He alluded to the signal; "Half the fleet can destroy the enemy."

Captain Hardiman, of the *Unicorn*, deposed that there had been no neglect or delay on the part of the commander-in-chief.

Captain Seymour, of the *Pallas*, thought that everything practicable had been done for effecting the destruction of the enemy's ships. When the general question was put, as to neglect, misconduct, or inattention, his answer was in substance as follows:—" I conceive myself a very incompetent judge of the commander-in-chief's conduct; but I know no instance of conduct to which any of those terms can be applied. From the knowledge I have subsequently gained of the proceedings of the ships on the 12th, I think the line-of-battle ships might have floated in the last half of the flood tide. This would have been at eleven o'clock. The line-of-battle ships went in soon after two. This opinion was formed from the depth of water we found on going in, and from seeing the *Revenge* going out at a corresponding time of tide on the following day. Two ships of the line were anchored in a situation to annoy ships going in. At the time I possessed no information of the strength of Isle d'Aix, or the depth of the water, to allow me to form a judgment. I have my doubts whether line-of-battle ships would have succeeded in doing good by going in. There was water sufficient for the line-of-battle ships to have gone in at eleven o'clock. It was a point where the discretion of the commander-in-chief might be fairly used. I confine myself to the depth of water."

Captain Newcombe, of the *Beagle*, corroborated the testimony of the former witnesses, and upon being asked by the Court, whether he could state any one instance of neglect or misconduct in the commander-in-chief?—he replied, none; save and except had the commander-in-chief thought it proper in his situation to have sent the vessels in earlier than they went, although there might have been great risk in so doing, there was a possibility of annoying the enemy more than they were annoyed; however, our ships must have been subjected not only to the fire of the enemy's ships that remained at anchor, but also to that of the batteries of the Isle d'**Aix**. The risk, as the wind and **tide** were, was rather **too** great; and we had **not** a perfect knowledge of the anchorage further **to** the southward, between the Palles and Oleron. He thought that everything had been done that was practicable **to** destroy the enemy's ships, considering all the circumstances stated. Being re-examined, he stated, that in **his way** out of Aix **Roads,** to join the squadron in Basque Roads, his ship was struck by the batteries from the Isle d'Aix, on the morning of the 13th, the shells from **Oleron passing** over her **at** the same time. On the 12th, the bowsprit was severely wounded, great part of the running rigging and sails cut to pieces, five planks of the quarter-deck cut through, and its beam completely carried away, and a number of shots in different parts of the hull; three men killed and fifteen wounded. two of whom afterwards died. The damages in **the hull**, and killed **and wounded, were** from the batteries of Isle d'Aix entirely, part of the running rigging from the *Aquilon* and *Varsovie.*

Captain Pulteney Malcolm said:—" Had it appeared to me that there was no other chance of destroying the enemy's ships but by an attack from line-of-battle ships at noon, I certainly think it ought to have been made ; but it was understood that they must all again ground at the mouth of the Charente, where it was the received opinion they could be attacked by gun-vessels, bombs, and fire-vessels again, without any risk; and had we had a reserve of fire-

ships ready that morning, I think some of them would
have been destroyed **on the** flood tide of the 12th.
Had the French ships which **got** on shore upon the
Palles, on the night of **the 11th** of April, been attacked
by the British ships, they could not have been warped
off, as it was necessary, in order so to do, to **lay out**
anchors. Those that were not aground, had always
the option of running farther up the Charente. If
our ships had risked against them in the attack,
there is no doubt they could not have warped off. The
moment that the two French ships quitted their
defensive position, the risk was small, and I would
have sent in. It was between the hours of one and
two; soon after that time the bombs and brigs were
sent in; the *Impérieuse* and *Beagle* very soon followed, and in about twenty minutes all the frigates."
Being further questioned **as to** the actual delay which
took place, Captain Malcolm replied, — " Certainly
there was not more than half-an-hour, or three-quarters
of an hour, from the time the two ships quitted the
defensive till ships were sent in by signal. This was
the **only** time that can possibly be called the delay.
Every practicable effort was made **to** destroy **the**
ships of the enemy that got into the entrance of the
Charente."

Captain Burlton, Captain Ball, and Captain New-
man, were not aware of any blame attaching to Lord
Gambier.

Captain Broughton, of the *Illustrious*, stated that
he was on board the *Amelia* when she was ordered to
dislodge the enemy from the Boyart shoal; and being

above the enemy, on the Isle d'Aix, he observed the fortifications. They appeared in a very different state from what he had observed them in two or three years before, **when** he was with Sir Richard Keats. He thought they were repairing the works they were throwing up. **He counted** on a semi-circular battery, which commanded the road where the enemy lay, between fourteen and twenty guns. There was a small battery lower down, nearer the sea. He did not know the exact number of guns there—there might be six or nine. What he had before **taken for** the block-house, above the semicircular battery, seemed to have no guns whatever. It appeared to be a barrack ; and he thought, from this observation, that the fortifications of the island in that part were not so strong as was supposed, and he reported his opinion to Lord Gambier. He thought it would **have** been more advantageous if the line-of-battle ships, frigates, and small vessels **had** gone in at **half** flood, between 11 and 12 o'clock. They would **have been** exposed to the fire **of the** two ships that remained at anchor, **the** French admiral's ship and the batteries of the Isle d'Aix, at the same time ; but they were partly panic-struck, and on the appearance of **a force coming in,** might have cut their cables, and tried **to make** their escape up the river. In the event of their proving not to have been so panic-struck, the British ships must have suffered; **but** ships, he thought, might have been placed against the batteries of Isle d'Aix, so as to take off their fire and silence them. **He** thought, **as** the wind was N.W., they might have found safe anchorage in what is called in the French chart, **Le Grand** Trousse, where there is thirty or forty feet water, out of the range of shot and shells in every direction. In reply **to** the question,—How many ships **of** the line he thought would be sufficient to silence the batteries of **the** Isle d'Aix? —he said,'two would be quite sufficient; and that five sail of the line, of the least draught of water, should have been sent in **to** attack the line-of-battle ships. He thought some ships might have been disabled by the batteries, but that the discomfited French squadron would have made very little resistance.

Captain Kerr was then recalled by Lord Gambier, and asked,—What from his experience of the effect of the batteries on the Isle d'Aix, would have been the **fate** of the *Revenge*, and any other 74-gun ships, had they been placed within two or three cables' length of those batteries, with a view of silencing them? He replied,—"I should certainly have expected, from the heavy fire they kept up, both in coming in and going out, that ships stationed there must have been completely dismasted, and must have suffered a severe loss of men. If dismasted, with the wind blowing from **the** north, as it did on the 12th, they must have been lost. The battery on the Isle d'Aix was low enough **to** admit of its being destroyed by the guns of ships on the south side, not on the south-west side."

At ten o'clock on Friday morning (the ninth day of the trial) the Court met, when the President, Sir Roger Curtis, Bart., stated his having received a letter from Lord Cochrane, purporting his wish to be examined on several points, particularly relating to the conversation with Lord Gambier, after the action; but that the Court did not think proper to accede to his request.

The Court was then cleared; and after the re-admission of strangers, the following sentence was pronounced:—

"The Court agreed, that the charge 'That Admiral the Right Honourable Lord Gambier, on the 12th of April, the enemy's ships being then on shore, and the signal having been made that they could be destroyed, did, for a considerable time, neglect or delay taking effectual measures for destroying them,' had not been proved against the said Right Honourable Lord Gambier; but that his lordship's conduct on that occasion, as well as his general conduct and proceedings as commander-in-chief of the Channel fleet, employed in Basque Roads, between the said 17th day of March, and the 29th day of April, 1809, was marked by zeal, judgment, and ability, and an anxious attention to the welfare of his Majesty's service; and did adjudge him to be most honourably acquitted; and the said Admiral the **Right** Honourable Lord Gambier is hereby most honourably acquitted accordingly."

Sir Roger Curtis then desired Lord Gambier's sword to be handed to him, which he returned to his lordship, with the following address:—

"Admiral Lord Gambier, I have peculiar pleasure in receiving the command of the Court to return you your sword, in the fullest conviction that, as you have

hitherto done, you will on all future occasions use it
for the honour and advantage of your country, and to
your own personal honour.   Having so far obeyed the
command of the Court, I beg you will permit me, in
my individual capacity, to express to **you** the high
gratification I have upon this occasion."

Lord Gambier answered :—

" I cannot sufficiently express the sense I feel of
the indulgence of the Court, and beg to return
thanks to you, sir, for the obliging manner in which
you have conveyed the sense of the Court."

Thus ended this solemn farce.   In those days few
naval officers of subordinate rank would venture to
declare their convictions upon a subject of so much
importance, and which admitted of so much latitude,
—and no wonder.   Lord Cochrane is an example of
the sad effects of having questioned the conduct of
his superior.   Gifted in an extraordinary degree with
professional talent, he was, from the day of his announcing to Lord Mulgrave his intention to oppose
the vote of thanks, virtually a crushed and ruined
man.   We have given all the opinions of the officers
examined upon the court-martial without reference to
Lord Cochrane's views, the object being to publish to
the world an unbiassed and wholly disinterested view
of this important controversy.

With the exception of Captains Pulteney Malcolm,
and Broughton, the evidence, as we have seen, went
to acquit Lord Gambier of all blame; and Captain
Malcolm charged him with the delay of half an hour

only on the 12th April; but can any one, notwithstanding this weight of testimony in Lord Gambier's
favour, arrive at the conclusion that he was blame-
less? We think not. There is the strong stubborn
fact to be overcome of his having anchored the bulk
of his fleet "three miles" from the enemy's batteries
when there was water close to them; and the equally
damaging one of his having delayed **for** half an hour
sending in the **two** line-of-battle **ships**, and the
frigates, to second **Lord** Cochrane in his noble attack
upon the grounded ships. If the French had not **been
panic stricken,** they **never would** have deserted their
ships, **as it is proved some of them** did, for the odds
were in their favour. They were **in a** state of great
consternation; and had Lord Gambier, with the bulk
of his fleet, moved down and attacked the batteries on
the Isle d'Aix at noon, or a little after, instead of
remaining three miles away from **those defences,** the
probability is, Admiral Allemand **would** have saved
him any further trouble by burning every one of his
ships. It was not the **interest of** any one to declare
this at the court-martial. **An** officer of high rank and
great political influence was on his trial; and our
French neighbours **were** ready to join in the outcry
against the **English** for want of energy. Policy induced every **one** to make it appear **the** navy had
gained **a** great victory at Basque Roads; and Cochrane
was sacrificed, because he abided **by** and openly
asserted the plain, the naked **truth.** Lord Gambier
did not do, what might have been done—destroy the
French ships; and although " most honourably ac-

quitted" by the court-martial, posterity will never affirm the verdict. There is one very remarkable fact connected with **this affair.** Although Lord Cochrane had been in **command of** the *Impérieuse* in so many brilliant **actions, the** only one for which he **gained a bar to** his *Speedy* **medal,** was for his participation **in the** Basque Roads affair.

PROFESSIONAL RUIN.
[1809–10.]

Just as **the** court-martial had ended, a joint naval and military expedition was projected for Walcheren. Sir Richard Strachan was placed in command of the fleet, **and the** Earl **of Chatham** in command of the forces. Badly treated **as** Cochrane had been, his ardour was unabated, and **he** made a proposition to the Government to **destroy the** French fleet then in the Scheldt, by means **of** explosion-vessels. His proposal was coldly declined. Pending the court-martial, the *Impérieuse* had been placed **in** command of the Hon. Captain H. Duncan, and had been sent to the Scheldt; **and when** the court-martial was over, Cochrane **wished to** resume command while on that service, but this was **refused.** He then asked to be allowed to attend as **a spectator at the** siege of Flushing; but he received in **reply a** laconic note from Lord Mulgrave, acquainting **him the** Board of Admiralty had **decreed** that " his request could not be complied with." The Admiralty had, in **fact, done** with him; for he **had** committed what in their eyes was a heinous offence, **in questioning** Lord Gambier's conduct. His craving after further service, therefore, was unappeased, and all that was left him was the bitter cud of Admiralty wrath.

In the meanwhile the vote of thanks was brought forward. The Chancellor of the Exchequer moved the thanks of the House to Lord Gambier, " for his eminent services in destroying the French fleet in *Basque Roads !*" to **this** was added, **as** if in mockery, **the** following paragraph, " particularly marked by the brilliant and unexampled success of the difficult and perilous mode of attack by fire-ships, under the immediate direction of Captain Lord Cochrane." After an animated debate, the vote was carried by a large majority—161 to 39.

In the House of Lords the vote was moved by Lord Mulgrave ; but no mention whatever was made of Lord Cochrane, except in terms of implied censure. The officer who might have had command of a frigate squadron, and an opportunity of realising a large fortune, only for holding his tongue, was shut out from particular notice by Lord Mulgrave, because he had been so imprudent as to drag truth to light.

But Lord Cochrane had not been wholly overlooked. The king had conferred upon him the highest honour he could bestow upon an officer of his rank—the Knighthood of the Bath. His Majesty had granted him the same decoration as that given to Nelson for his services in the battle of St. Vincent. But the Admiralty had resolved that he should never again hoist his pendant as a captain, and the resolve was kept.

Lord Cochrane now turned his attention to defeat the system of corruption on shore, and endeavoured, in particular, to correct naval abuses. On the 11th May, 1810, Mr. Croker brought forward a vote for navy estimates; and Lord Cochrane took this opportunity of moving an address for certain returns relative to pensions on the civil list, contrasting them with pensions to naval officers.

In the course of his speech, he drew the following somewhat humorous parallels. " A worn-out admiral is superannuated at £410 a year, a captain at £210, while a clerk of the ticket-office retires on £700 a year. Four daughters of the gallant Captain Courtenay (killed in action with the enemy when commanding the *Boston*) have £12. 10s. each. The daughter of Admiral Sir A. Mitchell and of Admiral Epworth have each £25; Admiral Keppel's daughter, £24; the daughter of Captain Mann, who was killed in action, £25; and four children of Admiral Moriarty, £25 each. Thus, thirteen daughters of admirals and captains, several of whose fathers fell in the service of their country, receive from the gratitude of the nation a sum in the aggregate less than Dame Mary Saxton, the widow of a commissioner."

The pension-list presented the following features. " Captain Johnstone received £45. 12s. for the loss of an arm; Lieutenants Arden and Ellison, £91. 5s. each for a similar loss; Lieutenant Campbell £40 for the loss of a leg; and Lieutenant Chambers, R.M., £80 for the loss of both legs; whilst Sir A. Hamond retires on a pension of £1,500 per annum."

His lordship also showed that 32 flag-officers, 22 captains, 50 lieutenants, 180 masters, 36 surgeons, 23 pursers, 390 warrant officers, and **41** cooks, cost the country £4,028 less than the sinecures of Lords Arden, Camden, and Buckingham; and that all the superannuated admirals, captains, and lieutenants put together, cost the country only £1,012 a year more than the Earl Camden's sinecure! "Should," his lordship pertinently asked, "31 commissioners, commissioners' wives, and clerks, have £3,389 more than all the wounded officers of the navy of England? I find," he continued, "that the Wellesleys receive from the public £34,730, a sum equal to 426 pairs of lieutenants' legs, calculated **at** the rate of allowance of Lieutenant Chambers's legs. Calculating for the pension of Captain Johnstone's arm, Lord Arden's sinecure is equal to 1,022 captains' arms; while the Marquis of Buckingham's sinecure would maintain the whole ordinary establishment of the Victualling department at Chatham, Dover, Gibraltar, Sheerness, Downs, Heligoland, Cork, **Malta**, Mediterranean, Cape of Good Hope, and **Rio** de Janeiro, and leave £5,460 in the Treasury."

Mr. Wellesley Pole denied the accuracy of Lord Cochrane's figures, being evidently very much averse to this inconvenient line of argument. He hinted, that if his lordship would desist from adopting "the wild theories of others," he might still have an opportunity of adhering "to the pursuits of his profession," of which he was "so great an ornament." Had Cochrane consented **to** forsake his party, it was plain that the road was still open to him to return to the service. As, however, he declined to avail himself of this hint, he received an intimation that he was unjustifiably absenting himself from the *Impérieuse*, which ship had in the meanwhile returned to England, and that he must join "within a week."

Mr. Yorke, who had succeeded Lord Mulgrave as First Lord of the Admiralty, requested to know "on what day next week" it was his intention to rejoin his ship. Lord Cochrane replied in a long letter, in which several foreign topics were introduced; but Mr. Yorke cut the matter short, by stating that it was "neither his public duty nor his inclination to be drawn into any official controversy" with his lordship, "either in his capacity of captain of a frigate or of a member of Parliament," and requesting to be informed whether or not it was his wish to join the *Impérieuse*, "then under orders for foreign service, and nearly ready for sea." Mr. Yorke added that, should he receive an answer in the negative, he should consider it tantamount to a wish to be superseded.

Lord Cochrane replied in a long and rambling letter, concluding with the following:—"But as the *Impérieuse* is to proceed immediately, I fear it is impossible for me to be in readiness to join her within the time specified." There can be no question, therefore, that Lord Cochrane's letter of the 14th June, 1810, was equivalent to a resignation of the command of the *Impérieuse*. Had he asked for more time, and his request been denied, he might have complained of sharp practice; but after reading his correspondence with the First Lord of the Admiralty, we cannot arrive at any other conclusion than that he, in effect, resigned the command of his old frigate ; and that, although Lord Mulgrave might have been, Mr. Yorke's board was not to blame for his non-employment.

THE MALTA PRIZE COURT.
[1811.]

In "The Autobiography of a Seaman," a very amusing account is given of Lord Cochrane's proceedings at Malta, in 1811, whither he had gone, in a yacht, with the intention of prosecuting some disputed, or delayed prize claims. He entered the court when no business was going on, to search for a table of fees, which ought to have been hung up in the court-house for the information of parties having causes. Not finding the document in its proper place, he passed from one room to another, and at length discovered the table in the judge's closet. He took it away with him, and gave it to the captain of a ship **in** harbour on the point of sailing for Sicily. Lord Cochrane was observed leaving the court, and the paper being missed, it was concluded that he had taken it. The court determined to prosecute him for contempt, and after some delay eventually arrested him. He was put in prison, but managed to live upon the fat of the land, and kept a sort of open house for the captains of the ships in port. At length, however, he thought he had carried the joke far enough, and made his escape by cutting away the bars of his prison and lowering himself down from a three-story window.

He was assisted in his escape by the captain of the *Eagle;* and embarking **on board** the packet, then on **the** point of leaving **for** Naples, he proceeded thither. The whole affair, however, was pointless **as** it was profitless, and apparently conceived in a wild spirit.

NAVAL DEBATES.
[1812-13.]

On his **return from** his yacht cruize and crusade against **the Maltese** pirates, Lord Cochrane entered again with **spirit** on his parliamentary duties and brought under consideration their shameful and extortionate practices. He created a great sensation **by** producing the copy of a proctor's bill, " long enough to reach from **one** end of the **house** to **the** other," **and** complained **of** the infamous charges contained in it. No result, however, followed. **He also** brought under consideration his arrest and imprisonment at Malta, but the motion founded thereon was " negatived without a division."

We cannot undertake to follow Lord Cochrane in his parliamentary career. He was an unflinching supporter of extreme Whig opinions, and a staunch ally of Sir Francis Burdett, Mr. S. Whitbread, and others, who had raised the standard of opposition to parliamentary and governmental abuses. He was, in fact, a radical reformer. The following debate, however, is so purely professional **that** we cannot avoid giving it at some length. On the **5th of July,** 1813, he made the following speech, the object of which was to increase the wages **and** limit the service of seamen in the royal **navy**.

"I think it is **my** duty to **lay** before the House, the reasons why **our** seamen **prefer** the merchant foreign service to **that** of their **own** country, to enter **which** they discover a very **great reluctance**. The facts **by** which I mean to prove this, **I** have compressed into one resolution, as I am anxious that when the members of the **House** retire from their parliamentary duties, **they may** consider these facts **at their** leisure, and **satisfy themselves** of the correctness of the statement, in **order that** when they meet again, they may **have no hesitation in** adopting some propositions, the object of **which would** be **the redress** of those grievances which were **the** subject **of it**. As I do **not conceive** that any objection can **be made** to the mode **of** proceeding I have adopted, **I will** not **occupy the** time of the House **any longer** than **by** reading the resolution." **The noble lord** then read the following resolution :—

" That the honour **of His** Majesty's crown, the glory and safety of the country, do, in a great degree, depend on the **main**tenance, especially in time of war, of an efficient naval establishment.

" That during the late and present war with France, splendid victories have been gained by His Majesty's fleets and vessels of war over a vast superiority in the number of guns and men, and the weight of metal.

" That these victories, thus obtained, were acquired

by the skill and intrepidity of the officers, and by the energy, zeal, **and valour of the crews.**

" That during **the present war with** the United States of America, His Majesty's **naval service** has, in several **instances,** experienced defeat **in a manner, and to a degree, unexpected** by **this House, by the** Admiralty, and by the country at large.

" That the cause of this lamentable **effect is not** any superiority possessed by the enemy either in skill or **valour, nor the** well-known difference in the weight **of metal, which** heretofore has been deemed **unimportant ; but** arises chiefly from the decayed and **heartless state** of the crews of His Majesty's ships of **war,** compared with their former energy and zeal, and compared, on the other hand, with the freshness and **vigour** of the crews of the enemy.

" That it is an indisputable fact, **that long and** unlimited confinement **to a** ship, **as well as to any** other particular spot, and especially when accompanied with the diet necessarily **that of** ships of war, **and a** deprivation of the usual recreations of man, **seldom** fails to produce a rapid decay of the physical powers, **the** natural parent, in such cases, of despondency **of mind.**

" That the late and present war against France (including a short interval of peace, in which the navy was not paid off), have lasted upwards of twenty years, and that a new naval **war** has recently commenced.

" **That** the duration **of the term of service** in His Majesty's navy is absolutely without any limitation ;

and that there is no mode provided for by law, for the fair and impartial discharging of men therefrom; and that, according to the present practice, decay, disease, incurable wounds, or death, can alone procure the release of any seaman, of whatever age or whatever length of service.

" That seamen, who have become wholly unfit for active service, are in place of being discharged and rewarded according to their merits and their sufferings, tranferred to ships on harbour - duty, where they **are** placed under officers wholly unacquainted with their character and former conduct, who have no other means to estimate them but by the scale of their remaining activity and bodily strength; where there is no distiction made between the former petty officers and the common seamen; between youth and age; and where those worn-out and wounded seamen, who have spent the best part of their lives, or have lost their health in the service of their country, have to perform a duty more laborious than that of the convict felons in the dockyards, and with this remarkable distinction, that the labours of the latter have a known termination.

" That, though **the** seamen thus transferred and thus employed have **all** been invalided, they are permitted to re-enter ships of war on actual service; and that such is the nature of the harbour-duty, that many, in order to escape from it, do so re-enter, there being no limitation as to the number of times of their being invalided, or that of their re-entering.

" That to obtain a discharge from the navy by

purchase, the sum of £80 sterling is required by the Admiralty, which, together with other expenses, amounts to twenty times the original bounty, and is equal to all that a seaman can save, with the most rigid economy, during the average period in which he is capable of service ; that this sum is demanded alike from men of all ages, and of all lengths of servitude, from those pensioned for wounds, and also from those invalided for harbour-duty ; thus converting the funds of Greenwich, and the reward of former services, into a means of recruiting the navy.

" That such is the horror which seamen have of this useless prolongation of their captivity, that those who are able, in order to escape from it, actually return into the hands of Government all those fruits of their toil which, formerly, they looked to as the means of some little comfort in their old age.

" That, besides these capital grievances, tending to perpetuate the impress service, there are others worthy the serious attention of this House : that the petty-officers and seamen on board of his Majesty's ships and vessels of war, though absent on foreign stations for **many** years, receive no wages until their return home, and **are, of** course, deprived of the comforts which those wages, paid at short intervals, would procure them : that it is now more severely felt, owing to the recent practice of postponing declarations of war until long after the war has been actually begun ; by **which** means the navy is deprived, under the name of droits, of the first-fruits and greatest proportion of the prize-money to which they have heretofore been entitled ; and thus, and by the exactions of the Courts of Admiralty, the proportion of captures which at last devolves to the navy is much too small to produce those effects which formerly were so beneficial to the country.

"That while their **wages** are withheld from them abroad, when paid at home, which, to prevent desertion, usually takes place on the day before they sail out again, having no opportunity to go on shore, they are compelled to buy slops of Jews on board, or to **receive** them from Government at 15 per cent. higher than their acknowledged value; and, being paid in **bank-notes,** they are naturally induced to exchange them for money in other countries, and which it is notorious they do at an enormous loss.

" That the recovery of the pay and prize-money by the widows, children, or relatives of seamen, is rendered as difficult as possible; and, finally, the regulations with regard to passing of the examination requisite, previous to an admission **to** the benefits of Greenwich Hospital, subject the disabled seaman to so many difficulties, and to such long delays, that, in numerous cases, he **is** compelled to beg his way in the pursuit of a boon, the amount of which, even in the event of the loss **of** both eyes or both arms, does not equal that of the common board-wages of a footman.

" That one of the best and strongest motives to meritorious conduct in military and naval men is the prospect of promotion, while such promotion is, at the same time, free of additional expense to the nation; but that, in the British naval service, this powerful and honourable incitement has ceased to exist, seeing that **the** means of rewarding merit has been almost **wholly** withdrawn from naval commanders-in-chief, under whose inspection services are performed; in fact, it **is** a matter of perfect notoriety that it has become next to impossible for a meritorious subordinate petty-officer or seaman to rise to the rank of lieutenant; that, in scarcely any instance, **promotion** or employment is now to be obtained in the navy through any other means than what is called Parliamentary interest,—that is to say, the corrupt interest of boroughs.

"That, owing to these causes chiefly, the crews of his Majesty's ships of **war have, in** general, become in **a** very considerable degree worn-out and disheartened, and inadequate to the performance, with their wonted energy and effect, of those arduous duties which belong to the naval service; and that hence has arisen, by slow and imperceptible degrees, **the** enormous augmentation of our ships and men, while the naval force of **our enemies** is actually much less than in former years.

"That, as **a** remedy for this alarming national evil, it is absolutely **necessary** that the grievances of the navy, some of which only have been recited above, should be redressed; **that a** limitation of the duration of service should be adopted, accompanied with the certainty of a suitable reward, not subject to any of the effects of partiality; and that measures should be taken to cause the comfortable situations in the ordinary, of the dockyards, the places of porters, messengers, &c., &c., in and about the offices belonging to the sea-service, the under-wardens of the naval forests, &c., to be bestowed on meritorious decayed petty-officers and seamen, instead of being, as they now generally are, the wages of corruption in borough elections.

"That this House, convinced that a decrease of energy of character cannot be compensated by an augmentation of the number of ships, guns, and men, which is, at the same time, a grievous pecuniary burden to the country, will, at an early period next session, institute an inquiry by special committee, or otherwise, into the matters above stated, and particularly with a view to dispensing suitable rewards to seamen; that they will investigate the state of the funds of Greenwich Hospital, and ascertain whether it is necessary to apply the droits of the Admiralty and the droits of the Crown as the natural first means of compensation to those who have acquired them by their valour, their privations, and their sufferings."

Sir Francis Burdett seconded the resolution.

Mr. Croker opposed it in a long and angry speech. The noble lord had stated that seamen were obliged to purchase their discharge by no less a sum than £80, no matter what was the condition of the individual. Now, he had to state most positively that this was not the case. The sum specified might, indeed, be *required from able seamen*, who wished for their discharge; but the sum of £40 only was required from ordinary seamen; from ordinary seamen transferred to harbour-duty only £30; from persons who were originally landsmen, not more than £20. And he had to state further that many persons transferred to harbour-duty, and considered unfit for service, were discharged without any consideration whatsoever. The noble lord had stated formerly in the House the case of a harbour-duty man, who had been obliged to pay £80 for his discharge.

When the noble lord had thought proper to make that statement, he had answered in his place that he could not take upon him to vouch for the individual case. He had, however, subsequently been at considerable pains to discover the particular case alluded to by the noble lord, and had examined every document in which he thought it could be traced, but in vain—he could find nothing of the kind; he had then applied to the member for Bedford to procure for him the name of the man from the noble lord, but this had not been done, and he had never had the pleasure of seeing the noble lord since. Now, he thought that under such circumstances the noble lord should have abstained from receiving the statement, unless he was disposed to give the name of the individual, and thus supply the means of confuting it.

The noble lord's resolution asserted that there was no fair system of promotion in the navy,—that everything was conducted upon a principle of corruption. Was, then, the commission of the noble lord himself given him upon such a principle? Did he obtain the red ribbon, which was, before him, never

given to an individual of his rank, through corruption?
Was it through corruption that a relative of the
noble lord's had made his way to the top of his profession, and had been appointed governor of Guada-
loupe? Was it through corruption that the influence
of the noble lord had had considerable weight in
effecting the promotion of those persons on whose
behalf he had used it? He was aware that an answer
to this last question in the affirmative might be
grounded upon the assumption that the naval acquaintances of the noble lord were persons of little
worth, and such as could owe their promotion to
nothing but corruption. But he who well knew the
reverse would not allow him even this miserable
refuge. Was the promotion of Captain Duncan the
effect of corruption? Were the honours which that
gallant officer's father had obtained the result of corruption? The friends of the noble lord had felt the
benefit of his interference, and much was it to be
wished that it had been confined to promote their
wishes, and through them the interest of the country,
and had never been mischievously exercised on such
occasions as the present. Did not the noble lord
recollect, when he had left his ship, that he had been
consulted as to who was the fittest to succeed him,
and that his recommendation had been acted upon?
If, indeed, he had never left that ship, it would have
been well for his own reputation, as it would have
been well for the interests of his country. Most
heartily did he wish the noble lord had stayed in her
to be serviceable to the public instead of coming here

to be the reverse. The noble lord loved to deal in generals. He talked loud about corruption, but he wished him to state who paid, and who received, the wages of corruption.

" I must express my sanguine hope that the House will not, by adopting such motions as those moved by the noble lord, sanction the gross libels which they contain against the navy, against Parliament, and against the country. I wish to lay aside all little considerations to suppose that the resolutions are not meant to apply more to the persons now engaged in the management of our naval affairs than their predecessors; but if it be otherwise, still I wish to sink any feeling that might be supposed to arise in my mind in consequence, and to answer the noble lord only as defender of that gallant body of men who have stood so long forward as our firmest bulwark against the vileness of our foe, and who are well entitled to the warmest feelings of gratitude we can cherish toward them. I hope, therefore, that if the noble lord does dare to push the House to a division, that he will be left in a minority, such as will not merely mark their sense, but also their indignation."

Sir F. Burdett said that the honourable secretary had indulged in a warmth and a severity of animadversion which the occasion by no means justified. His noble friend had asserted much, and the honourable gentleman had denied much, and that on a very important subject; but it remained to be seen who was in the error. The honourable member had taxed his noble friend with exaggeration; but it was impossible to conceive anything more exaggerated than the whole of the honourable gentleman's speech. He had stated his noble friend to have described our seamen as having wholly lost the energy and valour which had once distinguished them. Now, his noble friend had never so described them: he had stated that their spirits were depressed by long confinement and various other hardships, but he had never stated that their hearts were subdued, or that, when brought into action, they did not forget everything but that they had their own character and the character of their country to support.

Lord Cochrane replied. He said he was not displeased at the warmth with which his proposition had been met. It certainly would be injurious to no one, except to the feelings of certain members of that House. The honourable secretary had met his statements with individual instances of gallantry. The existence of these he did not deny; but he asserted that the physical power of our seamen was decreasing, partly from the length of the war, and partly the system of harbour-duty, established in 1803, from which service decayed seamen re-entered **the navy**. He had heard that the system was about to be changed, and he should be happy to learn from the honourable secretary that such was the fact. The honourable secretary had challenged him to show an instance of a petty officer having purchased his discharge from such service. He would name a William Ford, who had served with him in the *Impérieuse*, who had done so; Lord Nelson's coxswain, a person of the name of Farley, who had been returned to him, **and** died on board, completely worn out in the service. These were facts which he **was** prepared to prove at the bar, as he was all those which had been **denied** with so much warmth by the honourable secretary. To show further that the **crews of** British ships of war were unequal to themselves heretofore, he would relate what was the opinion of a person not at all likely to be disaffected to the order of things ; he was the son of a bishop, who had taken an American privateer, the crew of which consisted of only 130 men, and he had declared publicly that he would rather have them than the whole of his own crew, consisting of 240. If the honourable secretary doubted this fact he might inquire, and he would easily verify it. With respect to parliamentary influence, the honourable secretary **had** asked whether he **had found** it of service to himself in his profession ? He certainly had not, because he had never prostituted his vote for that purpose ; but he **knew** others who had found that influence of great avail. **When** he again brought forward the subject, he should prove all the facts he had adduced, and he hoped so **much** ignorance of important facts would not then be found to prevail. He had chosen the present form of his motion in order to put his sentiments on record in **a way not** susceptible of misrepresentation.

The resolution was negatived without a division.

Being much dissatisfied with this unpropitious re-

sult, Lord Cochrane sought opportunity to return to
the charge, and his colleague, **Sir Francis** Burdett,
accordingly gave him the opportunity he wished for,
by moving, on the 8th July following, for **a** return
respecting seamen's wages and prize-money.   Mr.
Croker, according to his **usual tactics**, endeavoured to
show that Sir Francis had not made out a case to call
for the return.   Then turning his fire upon Lord
Cochrane, he told **him** he could now " flatly contradict " his assertions with regard to the sums paid **by**
Ford and others for their discharge from the service,
and charged his lordship with having falsified the
books of the *Impérieuse* in discharging a number of
men for their incapacity, **as** he stated **he** had done.
Mr. Croker concluded by asserting, that in his resolutions of the previous debate, he had libelled the
heroic Broke, who commanded the *Shannon* **at** the
capture of the *Chesapeake*.

Lord Cochrane replied, admitting all **that** could be
said **of** the gallantry of our seamen, **but** maintained
that a great and rapid decay **had** been produced in
their physical powers **by the** causes to which he had
felt it his duty **to call the** attention of the House.
He said, he **was pleased** that he had done so **in the**
form **of a resolution,** which could neither be misrepresented **or** misquoted without detection. **It was** in the
recollection of the House that he **had** not cast the
slightest reflection, either on **officers or** men, collec-
tively or individually, although **the** honourable secretary (Mr. Croker) had chosen to defend them in both
cases.   Such a line **of** conduct might be best calcu-

lated to excite a feeling **of disapprobation** towards him (Lord Cochrane) **in the minds of** those who had **not** attended **to the subject, but it** was **not an honour-able or candid mode of proceeding to** put words in his mouth and then argue to refute them. He had **never** mentioned the **name of** Captain **Broke,** or alluded **to him in** the slightest degree, although the secretary **had** spared no pains **to** defend **him.** Captain Broke had done his **duty, his** men **proved** adequate to the task imposed **upon them ;** but, if **his** (Lord Coch-rane's) **information was** correct, the *Shannon* was the only frigate **on the** American station in which a captain would have been justified in trusting to the physical strength of his crew. The honourable secretary seemed to flatter himself, **from the** exulting manner in **which** he had delivered **his** speech, that he had also refuted those facts **which he (Lord** Cochrane) did **state.** " Ford," says **he,** " **did not** pay £80 for his discharge, or any other sum." **But** does not the honourable secretary know that this **man** raised four substitutes, and that he, William Ford, could not procure **them** otherwise than by money ? Was not the difficulty **of** getting seamen such, that the Admiralty demanded **four men for** the discharge of one ? **Under** such circumstances, **it** was obvious that the navy was manned, not by the national bounty or the prospect of reward from the service, but out **of** the funds of those who had long served their country. He pledged himself to establish at the bar of the House every circumstance stated in the resolutions which he had moved on a former evening. Ford, he repeated, paid

£90 for his discharge; a sum equal to all that he could have saved during his eighteen years' service! No man of feeling could justify the continuance of such a practice. As to the case of Farley, the honourable secretary assured the House that he was not invalided for harbour-duty, neither did he die in the service; facts which will not be deemed important when it is known (and it can be proved) that this respectable petty-officer, who had been in thirteen general actions, and thirty-two years in the navy, was not invalided until within a few days of his death; and that, unable to return to his friends, he died on board the *Impérieuse*. Ought not seamen to be entitled to their discharge before they are reduced to this state? Can ships be efficient whilst men so debilitated form part of their crews? It is impossible. The honourable secretary laid particular emphasis on the case of Milton as above all the most unfounded of his (Lord Cochrane's) unfounded assertions. He had discovered that Milton had received his pension through Gawler,—perhaps this was the easiest way; but he (Lord Cochrane) knew that Milton deserved that pension, having been wounded under his command: he was the first man who boarded the *Tapageuse*, in the river Bordeaux, when that ship-corvette was captured by the boats of the *Pallas* alone. He pledged himself to prove to the House the material fact that Milton had served seventeen years, and had paid nearly £100 for his discharge. Surely such length of service should entitle seamen to some deduction from so oppressive an expense. This was not **the case,** however; neither was there any period **fixed to** which they could look forward as the termination **of** their compulsory confinement. He (Lord Cochrane) did not accuse the present Admiralty of originating these abuses; possibly **they** were even ignorant of their existence. Boards never listened to individuals, and, therefore, he had adopted the present mode of calling the attention of Parliament, and of the country, to the state of the navy. Could any person have believed that the Admiralty, **instead** of decreasing the sum to be paid by meritorious seamen after long service, actually increased the amount! Lord Cochrane then read an extract from a letter which, he said, he had received that morning from a seaman's wife, the mother of a family, and whose husband was compelled to pay £60 for a discharge, which left their children without bread. She owed £7 to **her** doctor, who had written to Mr. Croker, stating her extraordinary exertions for her family's support as the cause of her illness. The husband, after long service, had but £17 remaining, and he was obliged to go down to Plymouth before he could **get his** discharge. Was this a situation in which **a British** sailor should be placed? **He was** in the judgment of the whole navy, and he would prove his facts at the bar. If the honourable secretary had any feelings, they ought to wring his breast, and prevent him from daring to defend such abuses. **He** would not detain the House longer than to say, **that the** army was now a model on which to form the navy, **so** much had circumstances changed. Their service was limited, and officers who did gallant acts were rewarded by promotion and brevet. He named Lieutenant Johnson, **who** served under his command in Basque Roads, as an instance to prove the unwillingness of the Admiralty to do justice unless by favour.

Mr. Croker returned to the charge. He said he would not permit the noble lord to lead the House away by stating that **his** material facts **had not been** disproved. He (Mr. C.) had contradicted his main assertions. The noble **lord** had not got rid of that; **and if he** would give him further opportunities, he would give him an equally satisfactory answer. With respect to Lieutenant Johnson, nothing irregular, except in his promotion, had taken place. He left the insinuations of personal enmity in the Admiralty against the noble lord to what he thought it deserved—the contempt **of** the House.

Lord Cochrane admitted that **the honourable secretary had** " contradicted " his assertions, **but** he defied him **to** disprove them, **or one word** contained in his resolution. As the **feelings of** his brother officers might be excited by **the** statement of the honourable secretary, **who had stood** forward in their defence though **they had not been** attacked, he would **add** again, **that he** had not even thought **disrespectfully** of any individual to whom the **honourable** secretary had alluded. He admired the **gallant conduct** of Captain Broke, and asserted **that, if the** Admiralty did their duty, no 38-gun **frigate of** ours need shrink from **a contest** with the Americans. He repelled, with contempt, the accusation made against him of endeavouring **to excite** dissatisfaction in the navy.

Sir Francis **Burdett then rose, and complimented his noble friend on his** exertions **to benefit a** service **of which he was so bright an** ornament. What **he** had **stated** of abuses **in** the navy, **he said, was done** with the hope that **they** would be corrected. The seamen could not have a more proper advocate ; and if his noble friend's advice **was** attended to, instead of dissatisfaction, the result would be advantageous to the navy. What improper motive could possibly be assigned to his noble friend ? Every man must feel and acknowledge the importance of the services of Captain Broke, particularly under the present circumstances ; but, **where** all concurred in the **same** feeling, it was not **necessary** for every person **to** take up the time of **the House in** praising undisputed merit. When it was found that, after long service, the seaman forgot everything but his duty to his country, a strong reason was afforded for looking into his situation. **It** was inconsistent with the justice **of** the country **to** dole out such miserable pittances to brave men. **There** might be unmerited pensions and sinecures, the retaining **of** which prevented the just discharge of well-founded obligations. It might **be** impossible to reward the deserving while a corrupt borough influence prevailed. **Let** that be stopped, and some enlargement made **for** the sake of justice, and the nation would reap the benefit.

Sir Francis Burdett's motion met with the same

fate as Lord Cochrane's resolutions, and fell to the ground without a division.

DISGRACED AND DEGRADED.
[1814.]

In the year 1814, official corruption had reached a height scarcely surpassed in any modern age. Unblushing jobbery prevailed in every department of Church and State. The country was defrauded on all sides by contractors, and there is only too much reason to fear that purity did not thrive any more at Whitehall than in less aristocratic regions. Promotion and lucrative appointments openly awaited those who could best help their party, no matter by what means. In later times, favouritism and parliamentary interest have gone a long way; but we believe that at no recent period had anything at all approaching to the intrigue prevalent in 1814 been suffered to exist. Lord Cochrane had made himself particularly **obnoxious**, by stirring up strife among, and spoiling the bargains of his political opponents; and he found in Mr. Croker an unscrupulous and unrelenting foe. The part actually taken **by** Mr. Croker in persecuting and ruining his *quondam* friend, will never, perhaps, come fully to light; but the presumption is strong, that he indirectly aided the conspiracy against Lord Cochrane. We append a narrative of the circumstances attending this hitherto unparelleled scheme for blasting the reputation **of one of** the most heroic and talented of British officers. There is, however, nothing in the explanation afforded, at all equal to the solemn assertion contained in the Autobiography of the deceased venerable peer. "But when," he wrote, "an alleged offence was laid to my charge in 1814, in which, *on the honour of a man now on the brink of the grave, I had not the slightest participation, and from which I never benefited, nor thought to benefit one farthing*, and when this allegation was, by political rancour and legal chicanery, consummated in an unmerited conviction, and an outrageous sentence, my heart for the first time sank within me, as conscious of a blow, the effect of which it has required all my energies to sustain."

This solemn asseveration ought, of itself, to be accepted as a proof of noncomplicity in the fraud committed; but since the Biography of the Earl of Dundonald would be very incomplete without a full narrative drawn from the pen of the victim, we give the statement of the principal facts upon which it is believed our late sailor-king, William IV., was pleased to reinstate the sufferer in his naval rank.

"The crime to which I was accused of being a party, occurred almost immediately after my appointment **to** the command of the *Tonnant*, **in** which I expected shortly **to** proceed to join the British fleet in America. While the ship was fitting out at Chatham, I obtained leave to come to town to settle my private affairs, and, among others, to complete the specification to a patent for an improved lamp—of which I may here observe, that the light was so brilliant, that had it not been for the introduction of gas, which took place about that period, it would, I have every reason to believe, have been very generally adopted **as** a street light, as well as for other uses; and **I** anticipated that it would prove **a discovery of** great public utility, as well as creditable and profitable to myself. **I** had also adopted the principle of this invention to the manufacture of ship-lanterns and signal-lamps for use at sea, far superior to any theretofore used, and I was anxious to take a supply with me for the use of the *Tonnant*, and for conducting the convoy which was to sail under her charge, and also to take out a set for especial service in America; and during my leave of absence **from** the ship, I was daily employed in superintending the construction of those **lamps,** at the manufactory near Snow-hill, and was so engaged on the 21st of February, when the visit of De Berenger led to consequences which blasted all my prospects.

"Independent of that visit, and the circumstances which attended it (which were truly and fully narrated **by myself,** but foully and **falsely** misrepresented by **my** prosecutors), the chief and indeed only fact of any importance alleged against me, was my having at that period a time-speculation in the funds, and that the stock which **I held** was sold at a profit on that day. This was **alleged** to have been my first speculation, and **to have** been made with a view **to** that particular day; but it was proved that **in the** course of the four preceding months I had, **by** instructions **to a** broker, made many purchases **and** sales of stock for time in the funds, and usually at a profit; for having had a favourable opinion of the state of public affairs at that period, and of the success of the military measures then in progress, I was convinced that I had no more to **do than** to continue to hold such purchases for a short time to become a gainer without **injury to any one; and** during that period of four months, I had gained upwards of £4,000, by what was admitted to be fair speculation. I had, therefore, a sufficient inducement to renew **my** account in **an** honest way, without any temptation to adopt any dishonourable or dangerous expedient. Besides, it so happened, that the amount of stock which I held at the time **of** the fraud, instead of being larger than on former occasions, was considerably smaller than it had frequently been before, which would surely not have been the case had I risked the commission of a fraud with a view to excessive gain ; and the sale of the stock on the day of the fraud, took place under the general order which **I** had from the commencement of those speculations given to the broker, to sell out (without waiting for further directions) whenever a profit of one per cent. could be **made.** It could not, therefore, be otherwise than that my stock should be sold **on that day,** when the prices enabled the broker to **act on the** standing order I had long before given. Had **I** anticipated any extraordinary rise on that particular day, and had stooped to a fraud to effect that rise, I should either have had a larger amount for sale, or have aimed **at** more than one per cent. profit; and much more **was obtained** on that **day** by many speculators who never were charged with a knowledge of the fraud. It was proved that I

did not myself attend the Stock-Exchange on that
day, and that the whole of my stock **was sold** in the
morning at a gain on an average of one and **a** quarter
per cent., which was less than half the profit it might
have made, had it been held a few hours longer. I
have frequently been told by persons who best knew
me, that I stood fully acquitted in their opinion, not
only on the ground of their believing me incapable of
a base transaction, but because they felt confident,
that were it possible for me so to degrade myself, it
must have been with a large prize in view, and that
I should have been found to be the largest holder and
seller on that day, instead of being so to a compara-
tively small extent. The weight of this argument in
my favour—the improbability of my suddenly becoming a fraudulent knave for so small an object, was felt
at the trial—and the judge had recourse to a singular
expedient to obviate it. He directed my amount of
stock, and the respective amounts of two others of the
accused parties, one of whom had held nearly three
times, and the other nearly four times the amount
that I held, to be **added** together, and directed the
omnium to be reduced into Consols, to increase the
numerical sum-total, and then exclaimed, ' Of that
amount **of** stock *they* were holders on that day!'
Thus assuming that there was a partnership, an actual
and equal partnership between me and **two** other
persons, and that I had an equal interest and responsibility with them in their large accounts; than which
a more unproved, unfounded, or injurious assumption
was never made in a court of justice.

" It is, moreover, a fact, and a proved one (so far as motives can be proved by conduct), that I never anticipated the sale of my stock taking place on the 21st of February, in preference to any other day between that day and the final settling-day, which was **then at three** weeks' distance.

" The rise in the price of the funds, on the 21st of February, 1814, was attributed partly to the agency of the individual who, in the scarlet uniform of an aide-de-camp, presented himself at the Ship Inn, Dover, about one o'clock in the morning, under the assumed name of Colonel Du Bourg, and in the false character of the bearer of despatches from the allied armies, with intelligence of a great victory; and who, after forwarding a letter with the false news to the Port-Admiral at Deal, ordered **a** post-chaise and four, and proceeded to London; **and** partly to the agency of three other persons (of whom **I** had never heard till charged with being their co-conspirator), who arrived in a Dartford chaise about noon, and made a sort of triumphal entry into the city, announcing, or by such display insinuating, similar false intelligence. The former individual, the pretended Du Bourg, who was afterwards **proved to** be De Berenger, arrived at the Marsh Gate, **Lambeth**, about nine o'clock in the morning, and immediately took a hackney coach, and came to my house in Green-street, Grosvenor-square. I had only recently become acquainted with him, but **under** circumstances (stated hereafter) which afforded him a pretence for coming to my house, and rendered his visit to **me** perfectly natural, and in no way calculated to excite my suspicion that he had been engaged in so nefarious a transaction, of which at that time I neither knew nor suspected him to **be** capable. He had taken care to **divest himself of his** scarlet uniform before he came **to me** (though it was most falsely alleged and sworn that he **came** to my door in a red coat), and by means of **his** portmanteau had substituted a green one.

" Not expecting any such visitor, I was not at home when he arrived, but was engaged, as I daily was, at the lamp-manufactory near Snow-hill, as before-mentioned. On his finding that I was absent, and being informed by my servant that I was probably at such manufactory, he hastily wrote and sent a note to me there, soliciting an interview. From whom the note came I did not know, my servant, who brought it, saying that he had never before seen the person who sent it, and the signature was so indistinct that I could not make it out ; but it requested me to return home, and stated to the effect **that the** writer had something to communicate **of an** affecting nature. This circumstance, and the servant's informing me that the writer appeared to be an army officer, having a sword, and wearing a military great coat, and military cap, **led** me to fear that he was an officer from Spain, with intelligence of the death of my brother, Major Cochrane, whom I knew from a letter received only three days before was dangerously ill.

" Under this painful impression I hastened home, and was agreeably surprised to find, instead of a messenger of ill news from Spain, a person whom I knew as Captain Berenger, who had been recommended to Admiral Sir Alexander Cochrane and myself as a person skilled in pyrotechnics, and qualified **to assist in** the minor preparations for the execution of my then recently-discovered method of attacking forts or fleets in a peculiar and irresistible manner,— a method which Sir Alexander intended to adopt under my superintendence in America. With this view he had applied for permission to take De Berenger to America, but on account of his being **a** foreigner the application had been refused. De Berenger was also reputed a master of the rifle, having been adjutant to the Duke of Cumberland's rifle corps, commanded by Lord Yarmouth; and it was partly and ostensibly for the purpose of employing him as **a** teacher of sharpshooting, **but** principally for **the** secret and **more important** object above-mentioned, that Sir Alexander had applied **for him.** And though **De Berenger** himself was not aware **of** the principal **motive for** the application, yet he well **knew** that Sir **Alexander had** requested leave to embark **him as a** rifle-officer, **and he** came to me on the said 21st **of** February **in a** sharpshooter's dress, and besought me to take **him with me to** America, and permit him to go immediately **on board the** *Tonnant*, to instruct **the** marines in the **rifle exercise.** He represented himself as involved in **debt, as having no** hope **of paying** his creditors while **he remained in** England; **that he had** left his lodgings **in the rules of the** King's Bench, **had equipped** himself as well as he could, **had** brought the sword with him that had been his father's, and that to that and to Sir Alexander Cochrane he would trust for obtaining an honourable appointment.

"But although I felt compassion at his tale of distress, and although it was infinitely more agreeable to see before me, instead of the expected messenger of the news of a brother's death, the very individual who had been recommended as peculiarly qualified to assist in the preparations for executing my new plan of war; and though he came expressly to solicit me to take him where I hoped shortly to be employed in carrying that plan into execution, and thereby to render an essential service to my country, and acquire honourable distinction for myself, yet I refused his request, unless he could first obtain the sanction of the Board of Admiralty; and I contend that this refusal does of itself refute the imputation that he came to me as his accomplice in a crime. If I could, by one and the same act, have afforded an asylum to an agent in an infamous transaction, and thereby have screened both myself and him from its penal and degrading consequences, and have secured the assistance of the man, so as aforesaid recommended as competent to facilitate the preparations for the peculiar service I had in view in America, was it possible that I should have been so scrupulous as to refuse to take him for want of formal authority? There was also another proof that there was no criminal acquaintance between him and me, for, on my refusing him permission to go on board, he urged, as a claim to my favourable consideration, the certificates* to his good conduct which he had formerly shown me from Lord Yarmouth and others, which he surely would not have thought it necessary or relevant to do, had he been my agent in a fraud.

" This circumstance, however, led to another (my giving **him a** coat and hat) which was turned to my disadvantage at the trial, though most unjustly, seeing that I myself had divulged it, which I need not have done, and certainly should not have done, had it been criminal. On his reminding me of the certificates, I advised him to apply to Lord Yarmouth, and those who had given him such certificates, or any other friends, to exert their influence, in procuring him leave from the Admiralty, for that I had none; on which he observed that he could not go to Lord Yarmouth, or any other of his friends, in that dress, nor return to his lodgings, where it would excite suspicion; meaning, as I understood, suspicion that he had absented himself from the rules without leave, or that he was preparing to make a final escape; and he added that he must take a great liberty and request me to **lend him a** hat to wear instead of his military cap. **I gave** him a hat, and on his buttoning up his great coat, and observing that the collar of his green uniform appeared **above** that of his great coat, I offered him a cast-off black coat which lay on a chair,

* Two of these certificates were **from Lord** Yarmouth and **General** Jenkinson, and had been obtained by De Berenger only **one** month previous, for the express purpose of recommending himself to Sir Alexander Cochrane and me as a fit person to be employed under our command in the war with America.

which he accepted; and having put up his green coat in a towel he went away, taking also with him a small portmanteau which he had brought, and in which I have no doubt he had concealed the scarlet coat in which he had made his fraudulent appearance at Dover that morning.

" Besides the obvious improbability of this man's exposing himself to be traced and detected by proceeding at once without any intermediate concealment to the residence of an accomplice, there was also the moral *impossibility* (supposing me to be sane) that I should have voluntarily published his name and all that occurred at the interview, the change of dress included, had I been a partner in his guilt. Yet I was not only the first to publish the name of my visitor, together with all that passed between us (which none but he or I could have published), but I did so with the least possible delay after hearing the report that the pretended Colonel Du Bourg had been at my house. I did so fully and on oath, omitting only the circumstance that the principal motive for the application made in his behalf by Sir Alexander Cochrane was his supposed capacity to be useful in the preparations for carrying into effect my new method of maritime warfare, conceiving that it would be unnecessary and imprudent to make any public allusion to that important secret. With this exception, I told all I knew. I made no secret of the change of dress, because, as far at least as I was concerned, it was an innocent transaction. I was perfectly ignorant, at the time of my interview with De Berenger, that he had

appeared that morning at Dover in a false character;
I neither knew nor suspected that **he** had come any
further than from his own lodgings, and had no knowledge whatever **that any** fraud on the funds had been
committed or contemplated. And **on the** 11th of
March following, when **I** made the affidavit (which I
could not have made sooner, as has been fully proved
in **former** and **more** detailed statements), publishing
the name of my visitor and the circumstances of his
visit,—in **consequence of** which he was found out and
brought **to trial,—I** was still in ignorance that he was
the perpetrator **of** the fraud, and had no other reasons
for **suspecting him to be so** than the report that the
pretended Colonel **Du Bourg** had proceeded to my
house, and my having **had no** recollection of seeing
any other officer than **De** Berenger, or person appearing **to be an** officer, **on the** day in question;
while, on the other **hand, his app**earing before me,
not in a scarlet coat under **a** brown great-coat, as had
been described, but in a green **coat** under a gray
great-coat, strongly inclined me **to believe** that he
was not the person who had personated **Du** Bourg;
and **such belief was** further strengthened **on its being**
reported **to me, previous** to the trial, that he **would**
plead and prove **an** *alibi*. And it is a positive fact
(involving a **monstrous** injustice) that I had neither
knowledge nor belief **of the identity** of Du Bourg
with De Berenger, until **that identity** was proved in
court at that very trial **in which** I was convicted as
his accomplice!

" **When it** is considered that there was only one witness to swear that **De Berenger entered** my house in a scarlet coat, and that he only professed to see it underneath his great coat, which **he** described as brown, though, in fact, it was gray; and when it is considered that this single, and, at best, inaccurate witness, was the brutal hackney-coachman before mentioned, who expected the whole, or a large part of the advertised reward, and that even he deposed to the important fact that De Berenger had with him a small portmanteau, "**big** enough to wrap a coat up in;" and when it is considered how easily he might, by means of that portmanteau, have changed his scarlet **coat for** his green one, either **in** the post-chaise that brought him to the Marsh Gate, Lambeth, or in the hackney-coach which brought him thence to my house in Green-street, Grosvenor-square; and when it is considered that two persons, householders, residing near the Marsh Gate, voluntarily **came** forward (though, unfortunately, not until **after the trial) and** deposed that they saw the **person stated** to have brought the good news pass **from** the chaise to the coach in a green coat under a gray great coat; and when it is further considered that I afterwards succeeded in ascertaining and proving that De Berenger's first arrival **at Dover** was not in the scarlet uniform in which he personated Du Bourg, but **in a** green coat, and that he did not leave that green coat behind him at Dover, but brought it back with him to London, I think I have furnished as much corroborative evidence as any reasonable **man can** desire of the truth of my oath to the fact that he appeared before me, not in a scarlet coat, but a green **one**. And though I may not have been able to show with certainty why he remarked that he could not go to Lord Yarmouth, or return to his lodgings in that dress, yet I conceive that my answer to the question that was asked why he **could call** on me in a dress in which he could not **call on** Lord Yarmouth, was perfectly satisfactory; for he came to me to solicit permission to go immediately on board my ship to instruct the marines in the rifle exercise, for which the dress he wore (a plain green uniform) was perfectly suitable; but as it was neither the usual garb of a gentleman, nor the uniform of Lord Yarmouth's rifle-corps, which, as that nobleman deposed, was a green waistcoat with a crimson collar; and as his military cap was totally different from the cap of that corps, it could not have been a proper dress for **an** officer of that corps **to** wear on a visit to his **colonel**. It does not need to be proved, for it is obvious, that, **if I** did not know what De Berenger had been about, there was nothing **in his** exception to his dress that could reveal to me that **he had** been engaged in a crime.

" One **thing is** certain and conclusive, that it was I, and I alone, **who voluntarily**, and with no other necessity than that **which** truth imposes on a conscientious mind, divulged the fact of a change of dress; it was a private transaction between De Berenger and myself, no other person being present, **and it** was optional **with** me either to relate it or conceal **it**. **I** could have had no motive for telling it but the obligation to truth. Had it been a guilty transaction, and in any respect other than such as **I described** it, I must have felt both the facility and the necessity of not divulging it at all. **It** was monstrous to hold, yet it was held at the trial, that I had disclosed the truth as to the change, and sworn **falsely to** the colour; or, in other words, that I had **committed** perjury, not in my own defence, but to afford **a** handle to my prosecutors to convict me at once **both of perjury and** fraud. How far it was legal to put in my own affidavit as evidence **against me, and to direct** the jury to credit that part which, taken separately, would admit of a criminative inference, and to discredit that part which stood in connection with **it, and** was destructive of such inference, I do not presume to decide; **but I** do know that such *over-sharp practice* may be productive of the most dreadful injustice, and was so in my case.

"Of a piece with this injustice was **the conduct of** the court in compelling my counsel **to enter on the defence at** a late hour of the night, when they declared themselves exhausted, and **in delivering** a charge to the jury, unexampled in point of partiality since the days of Judge **Jeffreys**; and in refusing to **hear** me in application **for** a new trial (under the frivolous pretext before mentioned) until they **were** about to pass their infamous sentence, and in **rejecting** the testimony which I then offered under **pretence** of its legal inadmissibility. Had **there** not been a pre-determination to make sure **of the** power to degrade and punish by means of **the** verdict obtained, why refuse a new trial, which **is so** frequently granted in cases of far less importance? The result could only have been **a confirmation of my guilt,** if guilty **I** had **been,** and a justification **of all the** previous **proceedings.** It was not **that the evidence I then offered was not sufficient to justify the granting a new trial,** but the apprehension that it might prove effectual to the rescuing my character **and person out of their** merciless hands—it **was this which caused** the court to refuse what I, if guilty, could **have had** no inducement to ask, and which **they, if just, could** have had none to deny.

"It is **a remarkable** fact, that no evidence was produced **at the trial of** De Berenger and his alleged accomplices **of** his outward journey to Dover; but **the** persons with whom he **lodged in** the rules of the King's Bench (Launcelot Davidson **and his wife),** **were** brought forward **to** swear that **he left their** house a little before eleven o'clock on Sunday **morning, the 20th of February, which** was sufficiently early to admit of his arriving at Dover before **the time at** which the pretended Du Bourg presented himself with **his false** news at the 'Ship Inn' there, at one in the morning of Monday the 21st. Their evidence, however, was *false;* **for,** in fact, as some friends of mine afterwards ascertained, he set off from London by the heavy Dover **coach on** Saturday night (the 19th), arrived at the 'Royal Oak Inn' there at ten o'clock on Sunday morning, dressed in a *green* coat, and **having** with him a portmanteau, considerably larger than that with which he returned to London. I was advised to indict Launcelot Davidson for perjury, and I did so, not with any ill-feeling towards him, whom

I never saw, but for the purpose of proving in a court of law the important fact (important as corroborative of my veracity and innocence), that De Berenger had with him, on his journey to Dover, and on his return, the same description of dress as that which I had sworn he appeared in before me; and in this object I completely succeeded; for the people of the 'Royal Oak' deposed that he arrived there on Sunday morning in a green coat, and that in the course of the morning he changed it (by means of his portmanteau) for a black coat, so that, so far from not having the means of shifting himself, as alleged by the judge at my trial, he had more than one change of dress. The witnesses also proved that he passed the whole day at Dover, and that he inquired his way to the residence of an inhabitant of that town, and went out as if to visit that individual--and that he returned, and finally left the 'Oak Inn' at ten or eleven o'clock at night (two or three hours before his appearance at the 'Ship Inn' in his fraudulent character as Colonel Du Bourg). They also proved that he left a portmanteau at the 'Oak Inn,' which was afterwards applied for and delivered up to the port-collector of Dover, who must have been authorized to demand it by superior authority, and such as would not have concealed its contents had they been unfavourable to me—and, therefore, the fact that he did not leave his green coat behind him in that portmanteau is certain; because if he had, it would unquestionably have been alleged and proved that he did so, in refutation of my assertion that he wore it when he appeared before me. Consequently, it was the smaller portmanteau, ' big enough to wrap a coat up in ' (which he was proved to have had with him on his return to London), which contained that green coat, until he exchanged its contents during the last stage of his journey, for the purpose of concealing his scarlet uniform and appearing before me in his green one. Now, whether those who conducted the prosecution in 1814 did, or did not, ascertain how or when De Berenger went to Dover (though the probability is that they did ascertain it, and that it was at their instigation that the portmanteau, left at the ' Oak Inn,' was demanded by the port-collector), it is quite clear that it must have been as easy for them to have traced his outward journey, previous to the trial, as it was for me or my friends to find it out at a later period ; and, therefore, it is difficult to conceive any other reason for their substituting the false evidence of Davidson and his wife for the true evidence of the Dover witnesses, than their desire to suppress the evidence of the green coat. And it has been pertinently asked, ' If they availed themselves of false evidence for the purpose of suppressing the green coat at one end of the journey, what was to hinder them from also having recourse to false evidence as to the colour of the coat in which he appeared at the other end of his journey ?' It is true that Davidson was acquitted of the perjury, because the judge declared that he might have mistaken one Sunday for another—though that was perfectly impossible, as has been clearly demonstrated in an examination of the case formerly published. The conduct of the judge in charging for an acquittal, was, however, less atrocious than his attempt to deprive me of the benefit of the evidence adduced. He said, ' It is to my mind a very extraordinary state of things which is now presented to you. We must assume that this prosecution is set on foot by some one or more of the persons who were defendants on that occasion, and yet the evidence which they now allege and prove to be false, was evidence, though not absolutely irrelevant, certainly much more favourable to them upon that occasion, than the evidence which has now been given to prove that the former evidence was false.' His lordship did not choose to see that evidence corroborative of the guilt of one of the defendants might tend to prove the innocence of another. The new evidence would certainly have been stronger against De Berenger than that false evidence which was substituted for it at the former trial; but it was also evidence that the dress which that individual wore on his arrival at Dover, was similar to that which I had sworn that he wore when I saw him at my house ; and the question of my guilt or innocence turned entirely on the colour of the dress in which I saw him. It has been well observed, that ' The whole world may be defied to produce a more extraordinary instance of the power of prejudice than was exhibited at the trial of David-son, when the judge himself persisted in linking Lord Cochrane's case to that of De Berenger, after hearing evidence, the object and effect of which was to separate them, and which, **if adduced at the** former trial, must have severed **them for ever.' "**

ACCOUNT OF THE TRIAL.
[1814.]

The following is a brief report of this momentous trial, extracted from **the** *Annual Register* for 1814 :—

" No trial in the present year so much interested the public, as that **of** the persons concerned in the fraud upon **the Stock** Exchange. The report of the trial **itself** occupies a bulky volume : and we can only **allot for it a** space sufficient for a very summary **view of** the principal **points of** the evidence, and the **result** of the whole.

"**The persons tried were** Charles Random de **Be-renger, Sir** Thomas Cochrane, commonly called **Lord** Cochrane, the Hon. **Andrew** Cochrane Johnstone, Richard Gathorne Butt, **Ralph Sandon,** Alexander McRae, John Peter Holloway, **and** Henry Lyte. **The crime** charged was a conspiracy **for** raising the **funds, and** thereby injuring those who should become purchasers **in** them. The Court was **the King's** Bench, Guildhall, before Lord Ellenborough, **on** June 8th **and 9th. The** case for the prosecution having been stated by **Mr. Gurney, the** first witness called was John Marsh, **master of the** ' Packet Boat ' public-house at Dover. **His evidence** went chiefly to prove the fact of **a gentleman, dressed in** a grey great-coat and a red uniform under **it,** with a star, knocking **at the door** of the ' Ship Inn,' early in the morning of February the 21st, whom he assisted to get into the inn, and who said that he was the bearer of very important despatches from France. He was fully satisfied that Berenger was this person.

" This evidence was confirmed by that of Gourley, a hatter, who was at that time in Marsh's house.

"Mr. St. John, who was then at the 'Ship Inn,' as a traveller, deposed in like manner to the arrival of a person who asked for a post-chaise, to his dress, and to the identity of Berenger as this person.

" Admiral Foley was then called to prove the receipt of a letter, despatched to him as port-admiral at Deal, by express from Dover, from a person at the 'Ship Inn,' who signed himself R. Du Bourg, lieutenant-colonel, and aide-de-camp to Lord Cathcart, and which was proved to be the handwriting of Berenger. The purport of the letter was to acquaint the admiral that he was just arrived from Calais, with the news of a great victory obtained by the allies over Buonaparte, who was slain in his flight by the Cossacks, and that the allied sovereigns were in Paris, where the white cockade was universal.

" A post-chaise boy was then examined, who drove a gentleman on that night from Dover to Canterbury, and another from Canterbury to Sittingbourne, and a third from thence to Rochester. They deposed to the receiving of napoleons from him; and the latter boy to his dress agreeing with the former descriptions.

" Mr. Wright, of the 'Crown Inn,' at Rochester, brother to Wright, of the 'Ship,' at Dover (who was prevented from appearing by illness), next gave evidence to the person's coming to his house, of his dress in the great-coat, red uniform, star, and military cap, and of his conversation relative to the news he brought; and was positive that Berenger was the man.

"Other innkeepers and drivers continued the chain of evidence, to that of a Dartford chaise-driver, Thomas Milling, who gave a very circumstantial account of carrying Berenger to the Marsh Gate, Lambeth, and there seeing him into a hackney-coach.

"The driver of this coach, William Crane, then deposed to the carrying him to No. 13, Green-street, Grosvenor-square, and there leaving him; also of the circumstance of his red uniform under a great coat, and to his taking with him into the house a small portmanteau. And thus was completed the process of tracking Berenger from Dover to Lord Cochrane's house in London.

"The next circumstance brought forward for the prosecution, was that of fishing up by a waterman on the Thames, of a bundle containing a coat cut to pieces, a star, embroidery, &c., which was recognized by a military-accoutrement maker, to be the same that he sold on February the 19th, to a person who mentioned its being wanted for one who was to perform the character of a foreign officer, and who also purchased a military regimental coat, and a military cap.

"The person with whom Berenger lodged, deposed that on the 20th he went out in a new great-coat.

"With the main plot in which Berenger was the chief actor, another was stated to be connected, involving McRae, Sandon, Lyte, and Holloway. With respect to this, the first witness called was Thomas Vince, an accountant, who deposed to having been applied to by McRae for the purpose of engaging to assist in a hoax upon the Stock-Exchange, by personating a French officer along with him, which he refused to do. A female witness, a fellow-lodger with McRae and his wife, deposed that McRae brought home, on February 20, a parcel with two coats, and two opera-hats, the coats being like those of officers, with some white ribbon for cockades ; that he said they were for the purpose of deceiving the flats, and that he must go down to Gravesend ; that on the next day she met him in London, apparently much tired ; and that he brought back a bundle containing one of the coats and hats and the cockades ; and that he said he was to have £50 for what he had done.

"Mr. Foxall, master of the 'Rose Inn,' at Dartford, then deposed as to receiving a note from Mr. Sandon, dated from Northfleet, on Monday, February 21, desiring him to send a chaise-and-pair, and to have ready four good horses to go to London with all expedition ; that, in consequence, his chaise brought from Northfleet Mr. Sandon and two gentlemen with white cockades in their hats, who immediately proceeded for London with the four horses. A driver deposed to carrying these persons, the horses being decked with laurels, over London Bridge, through Lombard-street and Cheapside, and thence to Marsh Gate, Lambeth, where they got out, having taken off their military hats and put on round ones. It was then proved by

Mr. Francis Bailey that Holloway confessed, before the committee of the Stock-Exchange, that he was a contriver of this plot, **and** that Lyte confessed himself and McRae to have been the persons who accompanied **Sandon in the** post-chaise.

"**The** next body of evidence produced related to the stock concerns of Mr. Butt, Mr. Cochrane Johnstone, and Lord Cochrane. The most material points went to the close connection between these three persons, to the vast amount of omnium which they held on the morning of the day in which the fraud took place, to the sale of the whole on that day, and to the circumstance of Mr. C. Johnstone's having taken a new office in a court adjoining the side-door of the Stock-Exchange against that day for Mr. Fearn, their principal broker, without having previously acquainted him with his intention. **An** affidavit by Lord **Cochrane** was then read, which admitted the coming of Berenger to his house on the 21st February, but stated that he was in a green uniform, which he put **off,** putting on a black coat which **his** lordship gave **him for the** purpose of waiting on **Lord Yarmouth.** The **affidavit further** averred that Lord Cochrane **had** no knowledge **whatever** of the imposition, and stated that he had **given** instructions to his broker to sell out the whole **of his omnium at** a rise of 1 per cent.

"Mr. Le Marchant **was next exam**ined with respect **to a** conversation **held with Berenger;** and he deposed, that having asked **him how he** could go to America under the command of Lord Cochrane (as he said his intention was) with the embarrassments he lay

under, Berenger replied that he was easy on that score, because, for the services he had rendered Lord Cochrane and Mr. C. Johnstone, whereby **a** large sum might be realized in the funds or stocks, Lord Cochrane was his friend, **and** had told him he had kept a private purse for him. The Hon. Alexander Murray, a prisoner in the King's Bench, also deposed to a great intimacy between Berenger and **Mr.** Cochrane Johnstone.

"Another examination of witnesses to a considerable length was consequent upon the capture of Berenger, who had absconded, at Leith, when there was found in his possession certain papers and bank-notes, which last he was urgent to have restored to him, but which were detained, others of corresponding value being given to him. From an entry in his memorandum-book he appeared to have received a sum of £540, part of which he had expended, and the **remainder, in** notes, was **in** his possession. All these notes, as well as most of those he had paid away, **were wi**th great industry traced to Lord **Cochrane, Mr. C.** Johnstone, and Mr. Butt. This closed the case for the prosecution.

"The business **on the** following day commenced with the evidence **for** the defendants. Letters were first adduced which passed between Le Marchant and **Lord** Cochrane, and which went to contradict the evidence he had given.

"Lord Melville was then called for the purpose of proving that Admiral Sir A. Cochrane had made application to be allowed the service of Berenger in his command on the North-American station. Colonel Torrens, secretary to the commander-in-chief, was examined to the same point, **as was Henry** Goldburn, Esq. The intention, in these examinations, **was to** confirm Lord Cochrane's statement, and to show **a** connection between the parties, independently of any other transactions. King, a **tin-plate** worker, next deposed to Lord Cochrane's being **at** his manufactory in Cock-lane on the morning of the 21st, whence he was called by a note brought to him by his servant. Dewman, a servant of Lord Cochrane's, deposed to a gentleman coming to their house in a hackney-coach, and writing the note which he brought to his lordship.

"Mr. Janourdin, solicitor to Berenger, was called to prove that Mr. Cochrane Johnstone had employed Berenger to make a **plan for** a projected building in some premises belonging **to him,** and had paid him money for it. Two receipts **were** produced for such payment, signed by Berenger; **the** last for £200, **dated** February 26th, 1814. This witness also absolutely **denied** the letter sent to Admiral Foley, at Deal, **to be the** handwriting of Berenger. The Earl of Yarmouth **spoke to** Berenger's having been **adjutant** of the **corps of** Cumberland sharpshooters, and thought the letter to Admiral Foley very unlike his usual writing. **Two** other persons also deposed to their belief that this letter was **not of** his writing.

"A series of evidence was then brought to prove an *alibi* with respect to Berenger. The first of the witnesses **were** W. Smith, and his wife, who were his servants, and who swore to his sleeping at home on the night of February 20th.   Then followed an ostler, of some livery stables at Chelsea, who swore to Berenger's being there on the evening of the 20th. Other depositions were made to the same effect, which it is not material to enumerate, since, from the rank and character of the persons, no regard seems to have been paid to their testimony.   Here the case for the defendants terminated.

" Lord Ellenborough summed up the evidence with a great minuteness, making various observations on different parts.   He particularly dwelt upon the evidence of the identity of the person taking a chaise from Dover, and traced to Lord Cochrane's house, with Berenger; and of the disguise he wore, and the colour of his uniform,—which he seemed to think proved in such a manner that no doubt could remain ; and from these circumstances, and his subsequent change of apparel, he drew a strong inference of Lord Cochrane's privity to the plot.

"The jury retired at ten minutes after six in the evening, and returned at twenty minutes before nine with a verdict, finding all the defendants *Guilty*.

"Subsequent proceedings were taken relative to Lord Cochrane's application for a new trial, and a motion on his behalf was made in arrest of judgment.   It is sufficient here to mention that these attempts were void of effect, and that on June 21 all the persons charged, with the exception of Mr. Cochrane Johnstone, who had absconded, were called up to receive sentence.   This was pronounced by Mr. Justice Le Blanc, and **was** to the following effect:—Lord Cochrane and **R.** Garthorne Butt were condemned to pay the king **a** fine **of a** thousand pounds each, **and J. P.** Holloway **of** five **hundred:** and **these** three, together with De Berenger, **Sandon, and Lyte, were** sentenced to imprisonment in **the** Marshalsea for twelve calendar months. Further, Lord Cochrane, De Berenger, and Butt **were** to stand in the pillory for one hour before the Royal Exchange once during their imprisonment. This last part **of** their **punishment was** afterwards remitted."

IN THE KING'S BENCH PRISON.
[1814–16.]

His enemies had **triumphed**: Lord Cochrane was **condemned to lose the knightly spurs he** had **so** richly **earned,** to have his name erased from the **Navy** List, **to** undergo **a** period **of** servitude in a common jail, to forfeit £1,000, and to stand in the pillory! **He** who had so often fought his country's battles, **and** upheld the honour of the British flag, had fallen under **the feet** of rancorous foes, who rejoiced in trampling **upon** their victim! Nothing but a feeling of conscious **rectitude** could have saved him from the withering effects **of this blow.** But he was not without sympathizers. **The** men of Westminster, who had returned him in his **prosperity** as their representative, scorned to take **advantage** of his downfall. Though expelled the House **of** Commons by a considerable majority—144 to 40—he was again elected by the same large constituency. The civil law, however, was paramount, and Cochrane, the brave and noble, was compelled to suffer within the walls of a prison.

The portion of the sentence which condemned him to stand in the pillory was cancelled; but in all other respects it was carried into full effect. The penalty of a thousand pounds was paid with a bank-note of that amount, endorsed with the following words:—

" My health having suffered by long and close confinement, and my oppressors being resolved to deprive me of property or life, I submit to robbery to protect myself from murder, in the hope that I shall live to bring the delinquents to justice.

" COCHRANE."

"KING'S BENCH PRISON, *July 3rd*, 1815."

This note is, we believe, still preserved in the Bank of England.

There is no rational ground for believing that Lord Cochrane was a guilty participator in the offence for which he thus suffered degradation, fine, and imprisonment. The general belief is, that the real culprit was Mr. Cochrane Johnstone, his cousin, who escaped to the continent; and that Lord Cochrane was artfully and unwittingly drawn into the snare, from which his political foes took care he should not extricate himself. The visit of De Berenger to his house, and the change of raiment with which he furnished that swindling impostor, though given, no doubt, from the purest motives, were facts which no argument could satisfactorily explain away. They identified him with the transaction, just as **an** innocent person who harboured **a** murderer and supplied him with a change of garments would **be** held in law an accessory after the fact. **He was made** the scapegoat **for** the transgressions of a stock-jobbing relative, and of one who had not the common honesty to avow that he was the principal, and that the clutches of the law had fastened on the wrong person.

SERVICES IN CHILI AND PERU.
[1817–19.]

Nearly two years had elapsed from the time of the release of Lord Cochrane from the incarceration to which he had been so **cruelly** sentenced, ere a favourable opportunity **offered to** give him employment. He was now in **his forty-second year, healthy, vigorous,** daring, and craving **for** active service. The **royal navy** was barred against **him,** and his persecutors in **full power; but there were other** lands besides **the one for which he** had fought and bled; **and as the exploits of Cochrane** had made him known from **pole** to pole, his sword was not likely to rust **in its** scabbard. Chili and Peru had thrown off their allegiance to Spain and were making noble efforts to **free themselves** from their hard task-masters; **and, in the summer of 1817, Don** Jose Alvarez, the accredited **agent of the** government of Chili, applied **to Lord** Cochrane to undertake the organization **of a naval** force in that **country.** He accepted **the** invitation, and agreed to superintend the **building and** equipment of a war-steamer then on **the stocks in the** Thames, and **to** take her to Valparaiso when finished.

Subsequently, however, Alvarez **received** orders from his Government to hasten the **departure** of Lord Cochrane, the position of Chili **being** critical, as the Spaniards were threatening **Valparaiso** by sea, and still in possession of the **continent** from Conception to Chiloe. Information, **on** which reliance could be placed, had also been **received** relative to certain efforts making by **the Spanish** Government at Madrid **to recover its lost** possessions **by a powerful reinforcement of** its Pacific squadron.

The **result was** the speedy departure **of Lord Cochrane** in the *Rose* merchant **ship; and towards the end of** November, 1818, he reached Valparaiso. To the " **Life** of General Miller," who was the constant companion of Cochrane during this portion of **his** eventful **life, we** are indebted for many interesting **facts. The** author of that work describes Lord **Cochrane's reception,** both from the authorities and the **people, as** having been most enthusiastic. General **O'**Higgins, the Supreme Director, arrived from the seat of Government **at Santiago,** to welcome him. The governor **of** Valparaiso gave a grand dinner on the occasion, **which, on St.** Andrew's day, Lord Cochrane returned, presiding **in the** full costume of a Scottish chief. The knowledge of his brilliant though unfortunate career had preceded **his** arrival, and all, **except the** old Spanish party, appeared filled with **delight at his** coming.

These **scenes** were re-enacted at the capital, whither General **O'Higgins,** the Supreme Director, insisted on taking **his lordship** and Lady Cochrane; and he was at length obliged **to** remind his excellency, that their purpose was fighting, **and** not feasting.

The Chilian squadron **had just** returned from a **successful** cruise, under the command of Admiral Blanco Encalada, having captured the Spanish 50-gun frigate *Maria Isabel*, in the bay of Talcahuano.

The squadron now placed **under the** flag of Lord Cochrane was as follows :—

Guns.

O'Higgins	50	.. { Vice-Admiral **Lord** Cochrane. { Captain Forster.
San Martin	56	.... Captain Wilkinson.
Lautaro	48	.... Captain Guise.
Chacabuco	20	.... Captain Carter.

The *O'Higgins* **had been** the *Maria Isabel;* **the** *San Martin* **and** *Lautaro* were old Indiamen. In addition to the above-named ships, the Chileno **navy** consisted of the *Galvarino*, 18, recently the British sloop of war *Hecate;* and **the** *Aracauno*, **16** guns.

A commission had been issued, conferring upon Lord Cochrane the title of " Vice-Admiral of Chili, Admiral and Commander-in-Chief of the Naval Forces of the Republic." Admiral Blanco, with patriotic liberality, relinquished his position **in** Cochrane's favour; paying him also the compliment **of personally** acquainting officers and crews **of the sq**uadron with the change which had **been effected.**

There was, however, **a dark side** to this picture, as well as a bright one. The captains of the squadron regarded their **new admiral** with jealousy, the more so, as **he** had **brought** with him from England **some** officers **upon** whom he could place reliance. Two of the **Chilian** commanders, Guise and **Spry,** had **shortly** before arrived from England with **the** *Hecate,* **which** had been sold out of the British **navy, and** bought by them on speculation. **The** Buenos Ayrean Government having **declined to** purchase her, they had proceeded to Chili, where she was not only purchased, but her former owners were taken into its service. These officers, **together** with Captain Worcester, **a** North American, **got** up a cabal, the object of which was **to** bring about a divided command. But as Admiral Blanco would not listen to this, they induced others—whose jealousy was more easily aroused—to entertain the notion that it was dangerous to **a** republican Government to allow a foreigner to command its navy. This unhappy schism was the cause of much mischief; and but for the patriotic disinterestedness of Admiral Blanco, who consented to serve as second in command, the effect would have been most alarming, if not fatal, to the cause.

The four ships just enumerated sailed from Valparaiso on the 14th January, 1819.

The squadron had hardly got out of port, when it was considered desirable to send back the *Chacabuco* to Valparaiso, in consequence of the disorganized state of her crew. Having apparently quieted the malcontents, the *Chacabuco* again put to sea, shortly after which **the crew,** headed by the boatswain, took possession **of the** ship. The officers were kept in close confinement **for** several days; but at length, owing principally to **the** gallant efforts of Lieutenant Morgell, of the Marines, they regained possession, but not until the boatswain **and** two other mutineers had been shot. Six of **the** ringleaders were afterwards tried and executed at Coquimbo.

Before leaving port, Lord Cochrane received a volunteer, **in** the person of his son—a noble little fellow then five years of age*—who, mounted on the shoulders of the flag lieutenant, waving his cap, **and** crying "*Viva la Patria !*" had made his escape from his mother. The child was not to be pacified otherwise than by accompanying his father, and he from thenceforth spent the chief part of his time on board the *O'Higgins*.

Hearing that the Spanish line-of-battle ship, *Antonio* had left Callao for Cadiz, with **a** considerable amount of treasure on board, the squadron cruised just out of sight of **the port** till the 21st of February, **in the** hope of intercepting her. As she did not make her appearance, preparations were made to put **in** execution an attack upon the Spanish shipping. Cochrane had previously ascertained that the naval force in **the** harbour consisted of the frigates *Esmeralda* and *Venganza*, a corvette, three brigs of war, **a** schooner, **a large** flotilla of gun-boats, **and six** armed merchant-ships; the whole being **moored** close in **under the** batteries, which **mounted upwards** of 160 guns, whilst the aggregate force of the shipping was 350 guns. A direct **attack** with so small a force seemed, therefore, **too** hazardous a thing to **be** attempted; **but, in its place,** Cochrane had formed the design **to cut out** the frigates during the carnival.

Knowing that two United States ships **of war** were daily expected at Callao, it was **arranged** to take in the *O'Higgins* and *Lautaro*, under American colours, leaving the *San Martin* behind San Lorenzo, and if the *ruse* were successful, to **make a** feint of sending a

* The present Earl of Dundonald.

boat ashore with despatches, and in the mean time to dash at the frigates, and cut them out. The execution of this desperate design was frustrated by one of those thick **fogs, so** common on the Peruvian coast, in consequence of which the *Lautaro* parted company, **and did** not rejoin the flag-ship for four days afterwards, when, the carnival being at an end, the plan was rendered abortive.

The fog lasted till the 29th, on which day heavy firing was heard, and imagining that one of the ships was engaged with the enemy, Lord Cochrane stood into the **bay.** The other ships also simultaneously steered in the direction of the firing, and when the fog cleared for a moment, they discovered each other, as well as a strange sail, which proved to be a Spanish gun-boat, with a lieutenant and twenty men. A boat from the *O'Higgins* took possession of this prize, and the fog again coming on, suggested to the admiral the possibility of a direct attack, which, if not successful, would at least inspire the Spaniards with respect for the Chilian squadron.

Maintaining their Yankee disguise, **the** *O'Higgins* and *Lautaro* stood towards the batteries, but narrowly escaped going **ashore** in the fog.

The viceroy, **who was** at the time inspecting the squadron (the guns **fired** in honour of which occasion first drew attention **to the** spot), having no doubt witnessed the capture of **the** gun-boat, provided for their reception, the garrison being at their guns, and the crews of the ships of war at quarters. Notwithstanding the great odds, the admiral determined to persist in an attack. The wind fell light, which prevented Cochrane from laying the flag-ship and the *Lautaro* alongside the Spanish frigates, as at first intended, but they anchored, with springs on their cables, abreast of the shipping. The Spanish squadron was formed in two lines, the rear ships being judiciously disposed so as to cover the intervals of the ships in the front line. A dead calm succeeding, the *O'Higgins* and *Lautaro* became exposed, for two hours, to a heavy fire from the batteries, in addition to that from the two frigates, the brigs *Pezuela* and *Maypeu*, and seven or eight gun-boats. Notwithstanding these fearful odds, the northern angle of one of the principal forts was silenced by their fire.

A breeze springing up, the two ships weighed, and ran down in front of the batteries, returning their fire. Captain Guise was severely wounded, when the *Lautaro* sheered off, and stood out of range of shot. As neither the *San Martin* nor *Chacabuco* had been able to reach the scene of action, and the *Lautaro* had withdrawn, the flag-ship was left alone to continue the action. Under such circumstances, Cochrane was compelled to relinquish the attack, and withdraw to San Lorenzo, about three miles distant from the forts, which the Spaniards allowed him to do unmolested.

The Spanish naval force present on this occasion, were the *Esmeralda*, 44 ; *Venganza*, 42 ; *Sebastiana*, 28 ; *Maypeu*, 18 ; *Pezuela*, 22 ; *Potrilla*, 18 ; and another of 18 guns ; making, with a schooner and the armed merchant-ships, a total of fourteen vessels, ten of which **were** ready for sea, and twenty-seven gun-boats.

When the firing commenced, Lord Cochrane had **placed** his boy-volunteer in the after-cabin, locking **the door upon him**; but not liking the confinement, the **child** contrived to get out of the quarter-gallery window, and joined his father on **deck**. He was permitted **to** remain, and, attired in a miniature midshipman's uniform, which the seamen had made for him, endeavoured to make himself useful by handing powder **to the** men at the guns.

Whilst **thus** employed, a round-shot took off the head of a marine close to him, scattering the unlucky **man's** brains in his face. Instantly recovering his **self**-possession, to his father's great relief, he ran up **to** his agonized parent, who made sure the boy was killed, exclaiming, **"I am not** hurt, papa ; the shot did not touch me. **Jack** says the ball is not made that can kill mamma's boy."

The Chilian loss in this affair **was** trifling, considering **that the** *O'Higgins* and *Lautaro* had been under **the fire of more** than two hundred guns : the ships, however, **had been** so admirably placed, that the enemy's **frigates lay** between them and the fortress, so that the **shot of the** latter only told upon their rigging, which was **considerably** damaged. The action having been commenced in a **fog**, the Spaniards imagined that all the Chilian vessels were engaged, and **were** not a little surprised, **as** it again cleared, to find that the flag-ship, *O'Higgins*, was their only opponent. This attack so dispirited the Spaniards, that they dismantled their ships of war, their topmasts and spars being formed into a double boom across the anchorage so as to prevent approach.

The Spaniards were previously unaware of the presence of their old foe and friend Lord Cochrane; but when made acquainted with the fact, bestowed upon him the not very complimentary title of "El Diablo," by which *nom de guerre* he was generally known afterwards.

Our readers will not fail to remark in this rencontre a parallel to the daring conduct evinced by Lord Cochrane when in command of the *Pallas* and engaging the *Minerve* in 1806—the same intrepidity and skill which marked his conduct under the batteries of the Isle d'Aix was observable in the harbour of Callao. On the latter occasion, however, he laboured under much greater disadvantages. When in the *Pallas*, he was surrounded by a devoted band of officers and men; but at Callao he knew that he was associated with some who would only be too glad at his failure. The mind was, however, superior to all these disadvantages; and he acted as if he had been confident of the cordial co-operation of every one serving under his flag.

Having repaired damages, the *O'Higgins* and *Lautaro* went in next day and commenced a destructive fire upon the Spanish gunboats, the neutral vessels in the harbour removing out of the line of fire; but as the gun-boats withdrew to a position closer under the batteries, where they could make little impression upon them without getting severely punished by the fire **of** the fortress, Cochrane contented himself with **the** demonstration he had made.

On **the 1st of March,** Captain Foster was **sent** away with the gun-boat captured from the Spaniards, **and the launches of the** *O'Higgins* **and** *Lautaro*, **to** take **possession of the** island of San Lorenzo, when **an instance of** Spanish cruelty presented itself in the **spectacle of** thirty-seven Chilian soldiers taken **prisoners eight** years before. The unhappy men had **ever** since **been forced to** work in chains under the supervision **of a military** guard, their sleeping-place during the **whole of** the period being a **filthy** shed, in which they **were every** night chained **by** the leg to an iron **bar.** The **joy of** the **poor** wretches at their deliverance, after **all hope had** fled, is not to be **described.**

From the liberated patriots and the Spanish prisoners Lord **Cochrane learned** that in Lima there were a number **of Chilian** officers and seamen taken on board the **Maypeu,** whose condition was even more deplorable than **their own, the** fetters on **their legs** having worn their **ancles to** the bone; whilst **their** commander, by a refinement **of cruelty,** had for **more than a year** been lying under sentence of death **as a rebel.** Upon this, the admiral sent a **flag** of truce **to the** viceroy, requesting him to permit **the** prisoners **to return to their** families, in exchange **for the** Spanish prisoners **on board the** squadron and **others** in Chili. The request **was rudely** refused, the **viceroy** concluding his reply with **an** expression of **surprise** that a British nobleman should command the maritime forces of a government "unacknowledged by all the powers of the globe." To this latter observation, Lord Cochrane replied that a **British nobleman** was a free **man, and,** therefore, had **a right to** adopt any country which was endeavouring to re-establish the rights of aggrieved humanity; and that he had adopted the cause of Chili **with the** same freedom of judgment that he had previously exercised when refusing the offer of an admiral's rank in Spain, made to him not long **before by the** Spanish ambassador **in** London, in the name **of** Ferdinand VII.

Cochrane, finding his original plan of attack impracticable with **his** slender means, **resolved** to fit out fire-ships. **A** laboratory **was** formed **on** San Lorenzo, under the superintendence of Major Miller. On **the 19th of** March an accidental **explosion** took place, which scorched the major and ten men **in a** dreadful manner. The former lost **the** nails from both hands; and the injury **was so severe** that his **face was** swelled to twice **its natural** dimensions: scarcely a feature was discernible; he was obliged to be fed through a **sort** of plaster mask; he was blind and delirious for **some** days, and was confined to his cabin for **six weeks.** His fellow-sufferers **on** this occasion **evinced** 'an extraordinary **degree** of attachment, **for** in the midst of their sufferings they refused to have their own burns dressed until they were assured by the surgeon **that** their officer had been attended to.

Three months were busily employed by Lord Cochrane in the manufacture of rockets, and making other preparations for a renewed attack upon the shipping under the walls of Callao.

Leaving Admiral Blanco at Huacho with the *San Martin* and **Puyrredon,** on the 4th of April Lord Cochrane sailed for Supe, with the *O'Higgins* and *Galvarino*, having previously ascertained that **a** sum of money, destined for the payment of Spanish troops, was on its way from Lima to Guambucho. On **the** following day, a party of marines landed, and captured the treasure, amounting **to 70,000** dollars, together with **a** quantity of military stores. On the 7th, having received further information that the Philippine Company had placed other treasure on board a French brig at Guambucho, he sailed for that place, and, on the 10th, the seamen of the **O'Higgins** examined her, and brought off an additional sum of 60,000 dollars.

The secret of his obtaining possession of these and other convoys of Spanish **money** along the coast was, that Lord Cochrane paid the inhabitants for information relative to its transmission. As the Chilian **ministry** refused to allow him "secret service money," these **disbu**rsements were actually made **at** his own expense.

His object **was to** make friends with the Peruvians, by adopting towards them a conciliatory course, and by strict care that none but Spanish property should **be** taken. Confidence was **thus** inspired, and the **uni**versal dissatisfaction with **Spanish** colonial rule speedily became changed into an earnest desire to be freed from **its** shackles. Had it not been for this good understanding with the inhabitants, Cochrane would not have ventured to detach marines and seamen for operations at a distance into the country, as he frequently did.

On the 13th April, the squadron arrived at Paita, where the Spaniards had established a garrison. A party of marines and seamen was again landed, on which the enemy fled from the fort, and a quantity of brass ordnance, spirits, and military stores was captured.

Contrary to strict orders, some marines stole a number of valuable church ornaments; but, on the complaint of the authorities, the admiral caused them to be restored, punishing the offenders, and at the same time presenting the priests with a thousand dollars to repair the damage done in their churches. This latter act, though it failed in conciliating the priests, added much to Cochrane's popularity amongst the inhabitants.

On the 5th of May, the admiral, with the *O' Higgins*, proceeded to reconnoitre Callao, having learned that two of his ships had been chased off the port by Spanish frigates. Finding that these were again moored under shelter of the batteries, Cochrane returned to Supe, convinced that his previous visit to Callao had proved sufficient to deter them from putting to sea for the protection of their own coasts. This had been his chief reason for persisting in attacks which could answer no other purpose; but this alone was an advantage gained, as it enabled him to communicate freely with the inhabitants on the coast and ascertain their sentiments.

On the 8th, he returned **to Supe,** and having learned that a Spanish force was in the vicinity, a detachment of marines and seamen was, after dark, landed through **a heavy surf, in the hope of** taking them by surprise. **But the enemy** was on the alert, and on the following morning the little party fell into an ambuscade, which would have proved serious had not Major Miller, **who** commanded the marines, promptly formed his men, who, attacking in turn, soon put the enemy to flight at the point of the bayonet, capturing their colours and the **greater** portion of their arms. On the 13th, a detachment **of** Spanish troops arrived under Major Camba, who, notwithstanding his superiority of numbers, did not venture to attack **Lord** Cochrane's party, which withdrew to the ships with several head of **cattle** taken from the Spaniards. Major Camba, **in** writing to the viceroy, gave a glowing description **of** his having " driven the enemy into the sea," and, in consequence of his valour, was immediately promoted.

Being unable to purchase supplies from the natives, Cochrane determined to return to Valparaiso, for the **purpose of** victualling, and also of organizing a more effective **force.** He reached that port **in** the middle of June, where **he** found Admiral Blanco **with the** *San Martin* and *Chacabuco.*

Complimentary addresses from the Chilian people were presented to the **admiral in** profusion, and a public panegyric was pronounced **at the** National Institute of the capital upon **the service he** had rendered. **The** people were not a little delighted with the facts that had come to their knowledge, and to find that, whereas only a few months before theirs had been the blockaded port, they were now able to beard the enemy in his stronghold, till then believed, both by Spaniards and Chilians, to be impregnable.

The manufacture of rockets was carried on under the superintendence of Mr. Goldsack, an experienced artist, who had been engaged in England for the purpose; but from a mistaken notion of parsimony, the labour of constructing and filling them had been allotted to a number of Spanish prisoners. In these and other preparations two months were spent, in the course of which an American-built corvette was added to the squadron, and named by the Supreme Director the *Independencia*.

In order to show the position which the admiral occupied, it is only necessary to mention the following cowardly attack made upon Lady Cochrane.

During his lordship's absence, Lady Cochrane resided principally at Valparaiso, doing all in her power to promote objects essential to the welfare of the squadron; but after a time she removed to a delightful country residence at Quillota. It was here that a ruffian in the interest of the Spanish faction, having gained admission to her private apartment, threatened her with instant death if she did not divulge the secret orders which had been given to his lordship. On her declaring firmly that she would not divulge anything, a struggle took place for a paper which she picked off a table, and before her attendants could come to her assistance, she received a wound from a stiletto. The assassin was secured, condemned, and ordered for execution, without the last offices of the Catholic religion.

On the night preceding the day fixed for his execution, **Lady** Cochrane was awoke by loud lamentations beneath her window, uttered by the wretched wife of **the criminal,** and imploring her ladyship's intercession on behalf of her husband. Moved **by** her importunity, Lady Cochrane, on the following morning, used all her influence with the authorities, and at length wrung from them a reluctant consent to commute his punishment to banishment for life.

SECOND ATTACK ON CALLAO.
[1819.]

Although foiled in his first attack upon the shipping at Callao, Cochrane was not disheartened, and resolved to make up for it in a manner which should astonish his Chilian friends. His heroic ally, Major Miller,* though still suffering from his wounds, was well enough to accompany the **new** expedition; and **we are** happy to be able to furnish a detailed account **of the** operations, including also the grand feat at Valdivia, **given by** the author of the biography of that officer, **and based** upon his description.

On the 12th **of** September, the under-mentioned men-of-war sailed from Valparaiso :—

---

* This heroic gentleman, whose name will be repeatedly mentioned in these pages, was living **in** 1860, and a Field-Marshal in **the** Chilian army. For many years he **has** held the appointment **of** Commissioner and Consul-General at Woahoo, Sandwich Islands, but was recently at Callao in very bad health.

	Guns.	
O'Higgins	50	Vice-Admiral Lord Cochrane.
San Martin	56	{ Rear-Admiral **Blanco.** { Captain Wilkinson.
Lautaro	48	Captain Guise.
Independencia	28	Captain Forster.
Puyrredon	14	Captain **Prunier.**

Also **the** *Vitoria* and *Zerezana* to be filled up as
fire-ships. The following joined subsequently:—

	Guns.	
Galvarino	18	Captain Spry.
Aracauno	16	Captain Crosbie.

Four hundred soldiers were embarked to act as
marines. The portion distributed in the Chileno
vessels was above double the usual complement of
marines employed in ships of the same class in the
British navy. The Chileno soldiers so embarked did
the duty of seamen, as well as marines. Lieutenant-
Colonel Charles, who had the superintendence **of the**
rocket department, was the commanding officer.
Major Miller re-embarked **as second in** command of
the troops.

On the 25th, **the** squadron entered the Bay of
Cequimbo, and received some marines on **board.**
Coquimbo is **the** principal city of the province **of the**
same name. The town is situated **twenty miles**
from the port, and at that time **contained a** popu-
lation of ten thousand souls. The inhabitants, with
a few foreign merchants, **showed how** highly they
appreciated the services of the marines embarked,
by raising, in a few hours, a subscription of four

hundred dollars, to be laid out by Miller in the purchase of what he considered they stood most in need of.

On the 27th of September, the squadron sailed for Callao, and on the 28th, the respective captains repaired on board the flag-ship to learn the plan of attack.

The *O'Higgins* was to lead; the *San Martin* and *Lautaro* to follow; and all three were to anchor in line parallel with the enemy's shipping. Miller, on a raft with one mortar, was to take his station in advance, on the extreme left, towards Boca Negra, the mouth of the Rimac. Captain Hind, on a raft with rockets, was to place himself between the mortar-raft and the *O'Higgins*. Charles, on another raft with rockets, on the right of the *Lautaro*. The *Galvarino* and *Aracauno*, with the two fire-ships, were to anchor off the north-east point of San Lorenzo. The brigs were to weigh anchor on the attack commencing, and, with the *Independencia*, to remove to the outside of the patriot line, in order to be in readiness to intercept any vessels that might attempt to escape.

On the 30th the squadron stood into the Bay of Callao. The *O'Higgins* hoisted a flag of truce, and Cochrane sent a boat ashore with a letter to the viceroy, challenging him to send out as many ships as he chose, and the admiral would fight them, ship for ship, and gun for gun. This proposal, of very questionable propriety, met with the laconic answer which might have been expected. The equally useless measure of sending a rocket in the boat to exhibit to the royalists, made an impression very different from what was intended.

The squadron manœuvred for several hours in the bay, and then came to anchor off San Lorenzo, with the exception of the *Independencia,* which continued to cruise off the bay.

On the 1st and following day of October the rafts were put together. Charles reconnoitred in a boat, and tried some rockets, which were not found to answer expectation.

A partial attack took place on the night of the 2nd. The *Galvarino* led the van, towing Miller's mortar-raft, and, under a heavy fire, placed it within 800 yards of the enemy's batteries. The *Puyrredon* followed, with the shells and magazine upon another raft. The *Aracauno,* having Hind's rocket-raft in tow, followed next. Charles, in the last raft, was towed by the *Independencia.* The rest of the squadron remained at anchor.

The persons employed upon the rafts were provided with life-preservers, made of tin, in the shape of the front-piece of a cuirass, and filled with air. The rafts were formed of two tiers of large logs of timber, of the dimensions of sleepers used in laying down platforms in batteries. The upper tier was about a foot above the surface of the water. Not more than one rocket in six went off properly. Some burst from the badness of the cylinders; some took a wrong direction in consequence of the sticks being made of knotty wood; and most of them fell short. The shells sunk a gun-boat, and did some execution in the forts and among the shipping; but the lashings of the mortar-bed gave **way,** and it was with difficulty that the logs of which the raft was composed could be kept together. A great **deal of time was** lost in repairing the defective state of the fastening. Daylight began to appear; and the rockets having completely failed, the rafts were ordered to retire, and were towed off by boats left in attendance for that purpose, to their respective protecting vessels, which again took them in charge and towed them out of **range.**

Thus failed an attack from which so much had been expected. The disappointment was extreme; but the loss of only about twenty in killed and wounded, was considered small under the heavy fire. About forty shot struck the *Galvarino*. Red-hot shot were fired from the batteries, but without much effect. These red balls had an alarming appearance, for they were distinctly visible from the moment they issued from the gun until they hissed in the water. All the men employed were volunteers; yet such was the effect of the **heavy** fire, that one man jumped from the raft into the **water** from fear. Lieutenant Bayley, a very brave young **man,** and a most active officer, was cut in two by a 24-pounder shot, which also **took** off the head of a marine **on** the same mortar-raft. Twelve men were much burnt by the bursting of some rockets. Hind and several of the **men** were thrown into the sea, but were prevented from sinking by the life-preservers.

In the **night of** the 4th, much amusement was

excited in the patriot squadron by the alarm on shore caused by a tar-barrel being set .on fire, and carried by the tide towards the Spanish shipping. A tremendous fire opened upon it, which was kept up for above an hour.

Disappointed by the total failure of the rocket attack, the admiral determined to try what could be done by means of fire-ships. Accordingly, one of the explosion vessels being completed, Lieutenant Morgell and a few men got her under way at 8 P.M. on the 5th, and stood in gallant. style towards the Spanish shipping; but the wind dying away, the vessel was shot through and through like a sieve. The water gaining fast, the train was fired, and the vessel abandoned. She exploded at too great a distance from the shipping to do any serious mischief. The rocket-raft was again employed; but the rockets did as little execution as on the previous occasion. The other fire-ship, in charge of Lieutenant Cobbett, was kept in reserve for a future service.

The *Aracauno*, which had been sent on the 4th to cruise outside the bay, returned on the 6th, and reported that she had seen a strange sail six miles to windward of Chorillos, which Captain Crosbie had no doubt was a frigate. The squadron got under way, and soon caught sight of the stranger; but Cochrane mistaking her for a North-American whaler, returned to his former anchorage on the 7th. It was afterwards ascertained that the strange ship was the *Prueba*, Spanish frigate, of 50 guns, from Cadiz, bound to Lima; but seeing the patriot squadron, she made off, and escaped to Guayaquil. In the almost momentary absence of the blockading squadron, a Spanish ship, with a cargo valued at half a million of dollars, entered Callao in safety.

The admiral, considering that the Spanish shipping could not be destroyed without risking the existence of the patriot squadron, decided upon a different plan of operations. On the evening of the 7th of October the squadron weighed, with the intention of going to Arica; but some of the ships were such dull sailers, that, after beating for three weeks to windward and against the current, Cochrane determined upon landing the marines at Pisco for the purpose of procuring brandy for the use of the squadron. Three hundred and fifty soldiers were distributed on board the *Lautaro*, *Galvarino*, and a transport (late fire-ship). Cochrane then proceeded to the **north** with the *O'Higgins*, *San Martin*, *Aracauno*, and *Puyrredon*, leaving Captain Guise in command to proceed to Pisco.

It was known that a strong detachment of regular **troops** had been stationed at this place, at the request **of the** royalist merchants and landowners, to protect their **property** in depôt there. The patriots intended to land **in the night** and take the garrison **by surprise**; but, **the wind** failing, the ships could not get near enough **to disembark** the troops until broad daylight on the 7th **of** November. On landing, information was given **that** the Spanish garrison amounted to 1,000 men. It might, therefore, have been prudent for the patriots to have re-embarked, especially as two-thirds of the marines were mere recruits, who had not even been taught the platoon exercise; but the remembrance of the disappointments before Callao produced an unanimous desire to attack.

The Spanish force, consisting of 600 infantry, 160 cavalry, and four field-pieces, under the command of Lieutenant-General Gonzalez, were drawn up to receive the assailants. The field artillery, supported by their cavalry, occupied on their left a piece of rising ground, which commanded the entrance of the town, in the square of which the infantry was formed. Their right was supported by a fort on the seashore.

Charles, with twenty-five men, filed off to his right to reconnoitre the enemy's left, whilst Miller pushed on to the town with the rest of the marines. Hind, with a rocket party, composed of seamen, occupied the attention of the fort. The Spaniards kept up a brisk fire from the field-pieces and from the artillery in the fort, as well as from the infantry posted behind walls, on the tops of houses, and on the tower of the church. Not a musket was fired, not a word spoken in the patriot column, which marched with the coolness and steadiness of veterans, in spite of the loss it sustained at every step. The silence, rapidity, and good order with which they advanced, struck a panic into the Spaniards, who fled when the patriots approached within fifteen yards of the bayonet.

The royalists were completely routed. The gallant Charles was mortally wounded whilst charging four times his own numbers outside the town. The last volley of the Spaniards in the square brought down Miller. A musket-ball **wounded him in** the right **arm ;** another permanently disabled his left hand ; **a** third ball entered **his chest,** and, fracturing a rib, **passed out at** the back. His recovery was despaired **of. Charles** and Miller were conveyed **on** board the *Lautaro*. The two friends, both apparently on **the** brink of the grave, took leave of each other in the most affectionate manner, as Charles was conveyed aft through the fore-cabin, in which Miller was already placed by **the** kindness of Captain Guise. In **a** few hours, Charles expired. Cool and collected to the **last** moment, the manner in which he died would **have** done honour to any hero of ancient or modern times. He was brave **and** talented ; and his gentle-**ness and** suavity **of** manners had acquired for him universal love and respect.

Captain Sowersby, who succeeded to the command of the marines, remained **on** shore for four days unmolested, in which time **all** that was required **for the** ships was embarked. Two hundred thousand **dollars' worth** of brandy, private property, lying upon the **beach, was** wantonly destroyed **by a** party of seamen.

No despatch **of the** affair of Pisco was ever pub-blished. This was **an act of** injustice towards the marines, especially as **room was** found in the gazettes **for the** elaborate corespondence **between** Cochrane and Pezuela relative to prisoners **of** war, and for very minute details of naval operations before Callao.

On the **16th,** the *Lautaro* and her consort with the

transport joined Lord Cochrane off Santa, of which
a gallant young officer, Ensign Vidal, who had
remained with the marines not employed at Pisco,
had taken possession after defeating three times his
own number of Spaniards.

The whole squadron, having procured provisions and
water, now put to sea. On the 21st of November, the
O'Higgins, Lautaro, Galvarino, and **Puyrredon**, stood
to the northward. A sort of brain fever, called the cha-
valonga, broke out, and carried off five or six men
daily. The *San Martin* and *Independencia,* being in
a most sickly state, were ordered to make the best of
their way to Valparaiso. Rear-Admiral Blanco went
on board the *Lautaro* to offer Major Miller a passage
to Chili ; but, in his precarious condition, it was
considered dangerous then to remove him. On the
27th November, Cochrane entered the river Guayaquil, and, notwithstanding the danger of the navigation, on account of shifting sand-banks, he continued
to crowd all sail during the night, and captured next
morning, before the crews had time to run them
ashore, two ships, of 800 tons and twenty-eight guns
each, laden with planks. The Spanish frigate *Prueba,*
which so narrowly escaped from Callao, had been
hauled up the river five days before, and, being lightened of her guns, was moved into shallow water
under the protection of the batteries.

On the 13th December Major Miller was removed
in his cot from the *Lautaro* to the *O'Higgins,* which
sailed from the river with the *Lautaro* and two prizes
in company. Each ship was ordered to make the

best of her way to Valparaiso. The *Galvarino* and *Puyrredon* were left behind to cruise.

STORMING OF VALDIVIA.
[1820.]

Lord Cochrane having conceived the daring plan of carrying Valdivia by a *coup-de-main*, employed all his eloquence to induce Freyre to grant a small reinforcement. The governor gave 250 men, commanded by Major Beauchef. They embarked in the *O'Higgins*, the *Montezuma* **schooner, and** the brig-of-war *Intrepido*, belonging to Buenos Ayres. All got under **way on the 25th** January, at 5 P.M., with a light **contrary** wind; at night it fell calm. The officer of **the watch** leaving the deck, gave the *O'Higgins* in **charge to** a midshipman, who, falling asleep, neglected to report when a breeze sprung up. Upon passing the island of Quiriquina, the ship struck on the sharp edge of a rock, and **was suspen**ded amidship on her keel. She shook in a manner **to** produce the greatest **alarm;** for had the swell increased, she must have **gone to pieces.** Cochrane, preserving his customary *sang* **froid,** **ordered** out the kedges, **superintended** everything himself, and at length got the ship **off.** His skill and **presence** of mind on this occasion made a deep impression **on all** who beheld it. When the ship was out of danger, **some of the** officers suggested that she should be examined; **a stern** negative was **the** answer of the admiral, **who,** turning round to **Miller,** said, " Well, Major, Valdivia we must take; **sooner than put** back, it would be better that we all went to the bottom." In fact, his lordship felt keenly his disappointments before Callao. He was aware that his enemies in Chili would raise a clamour if he returned without doing something decisive; and he had made up his mind to run every risk, in order to grasp one redeeming laurel.

" Cool calculation," he observed to Miller, " would make it appear that the attempt to take Valdivia is madness. This is one reason why the Spaniards will hardly believe us in earnest, even when we commence; and you will see that a bold onset, and a little perseverance afterwards, will give a complete triumph; for operations unexpected by the enemy, are, when well executed, almost certain to succeed, whatever may be the odds; and success will preserve the enterprise from the imputation of rashness."

The officers participated in the same adventurous spirit, and hailed with eager satisfaction a determination likely to retrieve the credit of the navy, and make former discomfitures forgotten. The admiral was so resolutely bent on pursuing his course that it was not until sunset on the 26th, that he would receive the first report of " five feet water in the hold." The ship was then thirty miles from land. The pumps were found to be so much out of order that they could not be worked. At eight o'clock " seven feet " was reported. The carpenter, who was a very indifferent mechanic, failed in his efforts to put the pumps in order. The water, though bailed out with buckets, still continued to gain on them. The powder-magazine was inundated, and the ammunition of every description rendered totally unserviceable, excepting the cartridges in the cartouch-boxes of the soldiers.

Notwithstanding it was a dead calm, the swell was considerable, and the brig and schooner were out of sight. **Of 600** men on board the frigate, not more than 160 could have escaped in the boats. The inhospitable coast of Arauco was forty miles distant, and to land there would have been worse than death. The vindictive character of the Arauconians was well known ; and to those who saw no hope of keeping the ship afloat till morning, the alternative was terrific. Alarm and despair were depicted in the countenances of most on board. But Cochrane, still undismayed, pulled off his coat, tucked up his shirt sleeves, and succeeded by midnight in putting two of the pumps **into** a serviceable state. By his indefatigable activity **and** skill, the frigate was prevented from sinking ; and by the serenity and firmness of his conduct, he checked a general disposition to abandon the ship. The leak was happily prevented from gaining. The schooner **and brig** rejoined in the morning, and the vessels arrived **in** the latitude of Valdivia **on** the 2nd of February.

When **about** thirty miles from land, the troops in the frigate **were** removed in a high sea to the schooner *Montezuma*, and the **brig** *Intrepido*. Miller attempted to climb up the schooner's **side,** and caught hold of the main chains, but not possessing sufficient strength **to** lift himself, or, when the **boat** sank in the trough of the sea, to sustain himself, he was on the point of letting go his hold, when Lord Cochrane caught him and prevented his falling under the counter of the vessel.

The admiral, having shifted his flag to the schooner, left the frigate to stand off and on out of sight of land, to avoid exciting the suspicions of the Spaniards on shore. There was, however, so little wind that all hopes of effecting a landing that night vanished. The brig and the schooner made what way they could for the port, in hope of taking the royalists by surprise.

The noble harbour of Valdivia forms a capacious basin, bordered by a lofty and impenetrable forest, extending to the water-edge. It is encircled by a chain of forts, which are so placed as not only to defend the entrance but enfilade every part of the harbour. These forts are Niebla, on the east, and Armagos, on the west, completely commanding the entrance, which is only three-fourths of a mile in width; Corral, Chorocomayo, San Carlos, and El Yngles, on the west side; Manzanera, on an island near the southern extremity or bottom of the harbour, and El Piogo and Carbonero are on the east side.

These different forts were mounted with 118 pieces of ordnance 18 and 24-pounders; each fort with a deep ditch and a rampart, where they were not washed by the sea, excepting El Yngles, which had merely a rampart faced with palisades. They were manned by a force which, according to the muster-rolls of the preceding month, consisted of 780 regulars, and 829 militia. The greater part of the latter were stationed

0   1
VALDIVIA
AND ITS FORTIFICATIONS
Rock
Aguada Yugles
F! S Carlos
Yugles F!
Mill pt
Charin
Mill
Niebla Cas
Amargos F
& Bay
Hill P!
Battery
Chorocomayc
Calvary pt
Corral Water
Plate pt
Corral
Castle
Proys P! & F!
Manzanera F!
Carbonero Bat.
Manzanera I.
P! S! Rosa
Goat I.
I de Lobos
Trinity P!
I de Toros
S! Johns Hill
P! S! Julian
St Johns Bay
St Johns R.
Llanos R.

Page 256.

at Osorno, thirty leagues towards the Straits of Magellan, and the remainder at the town of Valdivia, fourteen miles up the river.

So impervious was the forest, owing to the ravines by which it was intersected, and from its entangled underwood, that there was no land communication between the forts, excepting by a narrow rugged path, which, winding between the rocky beach and the forest, scarcely at any point admitted of the passage of more than one man at a time. Even this path, in crossing a deep ravine between Fort Chorocomayo and Corral, was enfiladed by three guns, situated on the crest of the opposite acclivity.

About a quarter of a mile beyond the fort of San Carlos, and outside of the harbour, is situated the exterior fort of Yngles, and half a mile westward of the fort is the *caleta*, or inlet, which forms a landing-place, both of which communicate with each other, and with San Carlos, by a path equally narrow, rugged, and serpentine as between the other forts.

The schooner and brig, having hoisted Spanish colours, anchored, on the 3rd of February, at 3 P.M., under the guns of the fort of Yngles, opposite the *caleta*, the only landing-place, and between the two. When hailed from the shore, Captain Basques, a Spaniard by birth, who had embarked at Talcahuano as a volunteer, was directed to answer, that they had sailed from Cadiz under convoy of *St. Elmo*, of 74 guns; that they had parted in a gale of wind off Cape Horn; and to request a pilot might be sent off. At this time the swell was so great as to render an immediate disembarkation impracticable, as the launches would have drifted under the fort. Cochrane's object, therefore was to wait until the evening, when the wind would have been abated, and **the** swell subsided. The Spaniards, who had already begun to entertain suspicions, ordered the vessels to send a boat ashore; to which it was answered, they had lost them in the severe gales they had encountered. This, however, did not satisfy the garrison, which immediately **fired** alarm guns, and expresses were depatched **to** the governor at Valdivia. **The** garrisons of all the western forts united at Fort **Yngles.** Fifty **or** sixty men were posted on the rampart commanding the approach from the *caleta*. The rest, about 300, formed on a small esplanade at the rear of the fort.

Whilst this was passing, the vessels remained unmolested; **but** at four o'clock one of the launches, which **had** been carefully concealed **from** those on shore, **by** being kept close under the **off** side of the vessel unfortunately drifted astern. Before it could **be** hauled out of sight **again,** it was perceived by the garrison, **which, having** no longer any doubts as to the hostile **nature of** the visit, immediately opened a fire upon **the vessels,** and sent a party of 75 men to defend the landing-place. This detachment was accurately counted by those on board as **it** proceeded one by one along the narrow and difficult path to the *caleta*. The first shots fired **from the** fort having passed through the sides of the brig and killed two men, the troops were ordered up from below and to land without further **delay.** But the two launches which constituted the only means of disembarkation appeared very inadequate **to** the effectual performance of such an attempt. Miller, with 44 marines, pushed off **in the** first launch. After overcoming the diffi**culties of** the heavy swell, an accumulation **of** seaweed in comparatively smooth water loaded the **oars** at every stroke and impeded the progress of the assailants, who now began to suffer from the effects of a brisk fire from the party stationed at the landingplace. The launch was perforated with musket-balls and the water rushed in. Four or five men were wounded and two of the foreign seamen were daunted and ceased to row, under pretence that it was impossible to make way through the seaweed. One of the soldiers previously named to keep a watch upon them in anticipation of some such occurrence, knocked one of these fellows off his seat with the butt end of his musket. No further difficulty was made.

Quarter-master Thompson of the *O'Higgins,* who acted as coxwain, was shot through the shoulder, **upon which** Miller took the helm. He seated himself on a **spare oar,** but finding the seat inconvenient, he had the oar **removed,** by which he somewhat lowered his position. **He** had scarcely done so when a ball passed through **his hat,** grazing the crown of his head. He ordered **a few of** his party to fire, and soon afterwards jumped **on** shore with his marines, dislodged the royalists at the inlet, and made good his footing; but he was still so feeble that he was unable **to** clamber over the rough rocks without assistance. So soon as the landing was perceived to have been effected, the party in the second launch pushed off from the brig, and in less than an hour 350 patriot soldiers were disembarked. Shortly after sunset they advanced in single files along the rocky track leading to Fort Yngles, rendered slippery by the spray of the surf, which dashed with deafening noise upon the shore, which was rather favourable than otherwise to the adventurous party. The royalist detachment after being driven from the landing-place, retreated along this path and entered Fort Yngles by a ladder which was drawn up, and consequently the patriots found nobody on the outside to oppose their approach. The men advanced gallantly to the attack, but from the nature of the track in very extended order. The leading files were soldiers whose courage had been before proved, and who, enjoying among their comrades a degree of deference and respect, claimed the foremost post in danger. They advanced with firm but noiseless step, while those who next followed cheered with cries of *adelante* (onwards). Others still farther behind raised clamorous shouts of *Viva la patria!* and many of them fired in the air. The path led to the salient angle of the fort, which on one side was washed with the sea and on the other flanked by the forest, the boughs and branches of which overhung a considerable space on the ramparts.

Favoured by the darkness of the night, by the intermingling roar of artillery and musketry, by the lashings of the surge, and by the clamour of the garrison itself, a few men, **under the** gallant Ensign Vidal, crept from the **inland flank of the** fort, and whilst the fire of **the garrison was solely** directed to **the vociferous patriots in** the rear, those in advance **contrived, without** being heard or **perceived, to tear up some** loosened palisades, with which they **con**structed a rude scaling-ladder, **one** end **of which** they placed against the rampart, and the other upon **a** mound of earth which favoured the design. By the assistance of **this** ladder Ensign Vidal and his party mounted the rampart, got unperceived into the fort, and formed under cover of the branches of the trees which overhung that flank. The fifty or sixty men who composed the garrison were occupied in firing upon those of the assailants still approaching in single files. A volley from **Vidal's** party, which had thus taken the Spaniards **in flank,** followed by a rush, and accompanied by the terrific Indian yell, echoed by the reverberating valleys of the mountains around, produced terror and immediate flight. The panic was communicated to the column of **three** hundred men, **formed on** an arena behind the fort, **and the** whole body, **with the** exception of those who were bayoneted, made the **best of** their way along the path that led to the other forts, but which, in their confusion, they did not attempt to occupy **or** defend. Upon arriving at the gorge of a ravine, **between** Fort Chorocomayo and the castle of Corral, about **one** hundred men escaped in boats lying there, and rowed **to** Valdivia. The remainder, about two hundred men, neglecting the three guns on the height, which, if properly defended, would have effectually checked the advance of their pursuers, retreated into the Corral. This castle, however, was almost immediately stormed by the victorious patriots, who, favoured by a part of the rampart, which had crumbled down and partly filled up the ditch, rushed forward, and thus obtained possession of all the western side of the harbour. The royalists could retreat no farther, for there the land communication ended. One hundred Spaniards were bayoneted, and about the same number, exclusive of officers, were made prisoners. Miller was unable to climb the ladder placed against Fort Yngles without assistance, and became so exhausted in the subsequent pursuit, that he could not keep pace with the troops until he made two of his men carry him in their arms. Such was the rapidity with which the patriots followed up their success, that the royalists had not time to destroy their military stores, or even to spike a gun. Daylight of the 4th found the independents in possession of the five forts, el Yngles, San Carlos, Amargos, Chorocomayo, and Corral. So completely was attention absorbed during the night by the rapid succession of exciting events, that till an officer remarked the next morning that Miller's hair was clotted with blood, he did not recollect the scratch he had received previous to landing.

Amongst the prisoners taken in the castle of Corral was Colonel Hoyos, commanding the regiment of Cantrabia, who, in an agony of mind, produced by reflecting on the loss of the forts, had drunk a quantity of rum, and, when Miller appeared, broke out into terms of outrageous abuse. It was with the utmost

difficulty that the victorious soldiers could be restrained
from killing the colonel. The next morning Hoyos
said to Miller, " I thank **you** for having preserved **my**
life; but, after what has happened, death would have
been a **mercy.**" He added, " It is singular that I
should **owe** my life to you, whom I was in some measure instrumental in saving, by supporting the efforts
of Loriga in your favour at Talcahuano." About the
time Fort Yngles was carried Cochrane left the
Montezuma, and caused himself to be rowed as near
the scene of action as the surf would permit a boat to
approach. The patriot troops mistaking the boat for
an enemy's, fired upon it from Fort San Carlos, and
obliged it to sheer off.

On the morning of the 4th, the schooner and brig
entered the harbour, **and** anchored under the castle
of Corral, after receiving **a** few shots from the forts
on the eastern side, **still in** the possession of the
Spaniards. In order **to dislodge** them, two hundred
men embarked in the brig and schooner: the latter
ran aground in crossing the harbour, but soon got off
again. The Spaniards, however, alarmed at the movement, **aband**oned the castle of Niebla, Fort Carbonero
Piojo, **and** Manzanera. The patriots, not less surprised than pleased, found themselves, without further
opposition, masters of what may be called the Gibraltar
of South America. In the evening the *O'Higgins*
entered the port almost **water-logged,** and to keep her
from sinking, she was run aground on a muddy bank
for the purpose of undergoing a repair.

The following **are** extracts from Major Miller's

official report to the admiral, written at the castle of Corral on the morning of the 4th :—

" Having disembarked with little opposition, at the Aguada Yngles, on the north-west shore of the bay, with the marines under my command, I continued my march, united to the detachment of infantry under the orders of Major Beauchef, to attack the enemy on that side. In his formidable position he considered himself perfectly secure from any attack that could be made ; and, indeed, if due weight be given to the obstacles we had to contend with through narrow and almost impenetrable tracks, it is not surprising that such confidence should have existed on his part. But the valour and intrepidity of our officers and soldiers were irresistible, and the most complete success crowned, if not one of the most arduous under-takings ever attempted by such a handful of men, one at least that will add new laurels to the gallant sons of South America.

" It is impossible for me to give your lordship an adequate idea of the valour and determined perse-verance of our small but enthusiastic force. No veterans could have surpassed them : few could have done so much."

On the 5th, Majors Beauchef and Miller proceeded up the river with Lord Cochrane, who took posses-sion of the town of Valdivia, at the head of two hun-dred of the troops. The enemy, five hundred in number, had abandoned it in the morning, and had fled toward Osorno to cross the water to Chiloe. On deserting the town, the Spaniards plundered and committed great disorders. The **governor,** Colonel Montoya, was the first to make his escape. His age and infirmities must **have** incapacitated him for **command,** or he ought to have made a stand against such an inferior **force. The** admiral issued a proclamation, which **induced many of** the inhabitants, who had **fled** from the town on the approach of the patriots, **to** return to their homes.

Amongst the public property taken at Valdivia, were some silver ornaments and vessels, of which General Sanchez had stripped the churches of Conception. There was, besides, a *custodia* inlaid with gold and set with gems. A ship, called the *Dolores,* anchored off the Corral, and taken by the soldiers in the night of the **3rd,** was sold by the prize agent at Valparaiso. **A** quantity of sugar, spirits, and other articles **were taken** and disposed of in like manner.

The fortifications **were so** numerous, that at first it was Lord Cochrane's intention **to** destroy them and embark the artillery, as the Spaniards who had escaped to **Chiloe—w**here another Spanish **regiment** was stationed—**might** return after his departure and recover them, the **force** which could be spared to garrison them being **insignificant** when distributed amongst fifteen forts; **but, on further** reflection, he could not make up his mind to **destroy** fortresses, the erection of which had cost upwards **of a** million of dollars, and **which** Chili would have been **unable** to replace. He therefore determined on leaving them intact, with their artillery and ammunition, intending, before his return to Valparaiso, to render **the** rout of the Spaniards who had escaped, yet more complete.

The booty which fell into the hands of the captors, exclusive of the value of the forts and public buildings, was considerable, Valdivia being the chief military depôt in the southern part of the continent. Amongst the military stores, were upwards of 1,000 cwt. of gunpowder, 10,000 shot, 170,000 **ball** cartridges, a large quantity of small arms, 128 guns, of which 53 were brass. The *Dolores*, afterwards sold at Valparaiso for 20,000 dollars; public stores also sold for the like amount; and the plate, of which Sanchez had previously stripped the churches of Conception, realized 16,000 dollars.

From correspondence found in the archives of Valdivia, it was plain that Quintanilla, the Governor of Chiloe, had serious apprehensions of **a** revolt at San Carlos, **so** that the admiral resolved **to** see what could be effected there. The loss **of the** *Intrepido* was a serious drawback to his means of transporting troops, and the flag-ship would **no** longer float; as, however, he had possession of the *Dolores*, it was resolved to crowd **into her** and the *Montezuma* all **the** troops **that could be** spared, leaving Major Beauchef **the whole of** those brought from Conception.

The news reached Valparaiso by **means** of a small *piragua*, despatched by the admiral, **and** gave rise to such an outburst of popular enthusiasm as had never before been witnessed in Chili. **N**othing could have been more opportune than the arrival of these despatches, for just about the same time Captain Guise reached with the intention of magnifying the failure at Callao, which he and his party attributed to the admiral's want of skill in the use of the rockets; the inference desired to be established being his want of capability to command a squadron.

In consequence of this alleged want of professional skill on the part of Lord Cochrane, Zenteno, the minister of marine, had drawn up an elaborate accusation against him of disobedience to orders, in not having returned according to his instructions; the whole party felicitating themselves on his probable dismissal with disgrace. On hearing the news of the victory, however, all this was immediately hushed up —the ministers, to retrieve their own credit, joined in the popular enthusiasm, which it would have been unavailing to thwart—and poor Goldsack was overwhelmed with reproach **for the** failure of his rockets, though, in point of fact, the **whole** blame rested with the Government contractor, for having employed Spanish prisoners as his workmen.

After providing for the safety of the city and province **of** Valdivia, by establishing a provisional government, and **leaving** Major Beauchef with his own troops to maintain order, the admiral sailed on the 15th of February, **with** the *Montezuma*, and his prize the *Dolores*, for the island **of** Chiloe, taking with him **two** hundred men, under the **command** of Major Miller, his object being to wrest Chiloe **from** Spain, as he had done Valdivia. Unfortunately, the *O'Higgins* was not sea-worthy without tedious repairs, for which there was no time, as success depended on attacking Chiloe before the governor had leisure to prepare for defence. Neither vessel being armed for **fighting, Lord** Cochrane depended altogether upon Major Miller and his handful of soldiers to oppose a thousand regular troops, besides a numerous militia ; **but** having been informed that the garrison was in **a** mutinous state, he calculated that by judicious management, they **might** be induced to join **the patriot cause.**

Unluckily, his design had got abroad, and the Spanish Governor, Quintanilla, a judicious officer, had managed to conciliate his garrison.   On coming to **an** anchor on the 17th, at Huechucucay, Cochrane found a body of infantry and cavalry, with a field-piece, ready to dispute the landing ; but drawing off their attention by a feint upon a distant spot, and thus dividing them into two parties, Major Miller got on shore, and soon routed them, capturing their field-piece.

A night attack being decided upon, the troops, 170 in number, moved on under the direction of a guide, who, wilfully or treacherously, misled them, the men thus wandering about in **the** dark throughout the whole night.   **At dawn,** they found their way to Fort Corona, **which, with a** detached battery, was taken without loss.   Halting for a short time to refresh the men, Major Miller, bravely, but too precipitately, moved on Fort Aguy, in broad daylight.   This fort was the stronghold of the enemy, mounting twelve guns, with others flanking the only accessible path by which entrance could be gained, and was garrisoned by three companies of regulars, two companies of militia, and a full proportion of artillerymen. The fort stood on a hill, washed on one side by the sea, and having on the other an impenetrable forest, the only access being by a narrow path, whilst the means of retreat for the garrison was by the same path, so that the attack became for the latter a matter of life and death, since, in case of defeat, there was no mode of escape, as at Valdivia.

Notwithstanding these odds, and the spectacle of two friars on the ramparts, urging on the garrison to resist to the death the handful of aggressors, Miller, instead of remaining in the forts he had taken till night fall, when he would have been comparatively safe by attacking in the dark, determined to advance. Choosing out of his small band a forlorn hope of sixty men, he perilled his own safety, upon which so much depended, by leading them in person ; every gun and musket of the enemy being concentrated on a particular angle of the path which he must needs pass.

As the detachment reached the spot, a shower of grape and musketry mowed down the whole, twenty out of the sixty being killed outright, whilst nearly all the rest were mortally wounded. Seeing their gallant commander fall, the marines, who were waiting to follow, dashed through the fire, and brought him off, with a grape-shot through his thigh, and the bones of his right foot crushed by a round shot. Another dash by the force which remained brought off the whole of the wounded, though adding fearfully to their numbers. This having been accomplished, Captain Erescano, who succeeded to the command, **ordered** a retreat. **The** Spaniards, animated by success, and urged on by the friars, followed just within musket-shot and making three separate attacks, which were on each occasion repelled, though, from the killed and wounded, the pursuers were now fully six times their number. Nevertheless one-half of the diminished band kept the enemy at bay, whilst the other half spiked the guns, broke **up** the gun-carriages, and destroyed the military **stores** in the forts captured in the morning, when they resumed their march to the beach, followed **by** the Spaniards as before.

The marines **who,** with affectionate fidelity, had **borne** off Major Miller, had been careful to protect him from fire, though two out of the three **who** carried him were wounded in the act; and when, on arriving at the beach, they were invited by him to enter the boat, one of them, a gallant fellow named Roxas, honourably mentioned **in Lord** Cochrane's despatches from Valdivia, on account **of** his distinguished bravery, refused, **saying,** "No, sir, I was the first to land, and I mean **to** be the last to go on board." The marine kept his word; for on his commander **being placed in** safety, he hastened back to the little **band, now** nearly cut up, and took his share **in** the retreat, being the last to get into the boats. Such were the Chilenos. This same gallant fellow was at the side of Lord Cochrane at the capture of the *Esmeralda.*

His forces being now seriously diminished, Cochrane decided on returning to Valdivia, where, finding that the Spaniards who had been dispersed in the neighbourhood were committing **excesses,** he despatched Major Beauchef with 100 men **to** Osorno to secure that town, the relief being accepted with great joy **even by** the Indians. The Spaniards being thus driven from Osorno, the flag of Chili was, on the 26th of February, hoisted on the castle by Major Beauchef, who then returned to Valdivia.

There being nothing further to require the admiral's presence at Valdivia, Lord Cochrane placed the *O'Higgins* under the orders of his secretary, **to** superintend her repairs, and embarked in the *Montezuma,* for Valparaiso.

RECEPTION **AT** VALPARAISO.
[1820.]

On the 27th of February the *Montezuma*, bearing Lord Cochrane's **flag, arrived at** Valparaiso. The populace were most lively **in** their demonstrations, and warm expressions of gratitude emanated from the Supreme Director. But his reception by the ministers **was wholly** different. Zenteno, whose orders Lord Cochrane had disregarded, declared that the conquest of Valdivia **was the** act of a madman : that the admiral deserved to **have lost** his life in the attempt; and ought to lose **his head for** daring to attack such a place without instructions, **and** for exposing the patriot troops to such **hazard.** He afterwards set on foot a series of intrigues, having **for** their object the depreciation of the service which had been rendered ; so that the admiral found himself exposed to the greatest possible annoyance, and the eminent services of his officers and men treated with official coldness.

The congratulatory addresses which poured in on both the Supreme Director and the admiral from all parts, in which the people declared their opinion, contrary to the assertions of Zenteno, that he had acted from a conviction of national utility, and that by its accomplishment the valour of the Chilenos had been gloriously displayed, tended only to increase the chagrin of Zenteno and his party.

In deference to the popular voice, the Government was compelled to award medals to the captors, the decree for this stating that the capture of Valdivia was the happy result of the devising of an admirably arranged plan, and of the most daring and valorous execution. The decree further conferred on Lord Cochrane an estate of 4,000 quadras from the confiscated lands of Conception, which he refused, as no vote of thanks had been given by the Legislature. This vote he, however, finally obtained, as an indemnification to himself for having exceeded his orders; which form was necessary after Zenteno's expressions of ill-will towards him.

The resources of the province of Valdivia, together with those of Conception, had contributed the means whereby the Spaniards maintained their hold upon the Chilian territory. Not only were they deprived of these resources—now added to those of Chili—but a great saving was effected by relieving the Republic from the necessity of maintaining a military force in the southern provinces, as a check upon both

Spaniards and Indians, **who, at** the moment of the conquest of Valdivia, **were being let loose** in all directions against the Chilian patriots.

Had it not **been for** this capture, **the** Spanish power in **Chili, aided by the** Indians, would have **found** it easy to **maintain** itself in such **a** country **for a pro-**tracted period, despite any military **force** Chili **was in** a condition to bring against it; so **that** no effective co-operation with the people of Peru could have been undertaken. A further advantage was the successful negotiation in England of a loan **of** one million **ster-**ling, which was accomplished solely on account of what had been achieved, every attempt at this having failed so long as the Spaniards were in possession of the most important **harbour** and fortress in the country, from which, **as a** basis, they might organize future attempts to **recover** the revolted provinces.

Notwithstanding **these adv**antages, no reward, either for this or any previous service, was paid to Lord Cochrane, the officers, **or** seamen, the Government having appropriated the money **arising from** the **sale of the** *Dolores*, and the stores **with** which she was **loaded, to** other purposes. The guns **and ammu-**nition left **in the** forts at Valdivia, although taken by the Government, were never paid for; while the men who performed **this** achievement were in rags, and destitute. The gallant **admiral,** who had risked his own life in leading his **men on** this desperate enterprise, was treated with **much scorn, and** every encouragement held out to his officers to disobey his orders.

Two whom he had marked for punishment, for the following act of deliberate murder, were actually promoted. Ensign Vidal having captured two Spanish officers in Fort Yngles, they surrendered their swords, receiving the gallant youth's pledge of safety; but Captain Erescano coming up, immediately butchered them. Ensign Latapia, who had been left in command of the castle of Corral, after Lord Cochrane's departure to Chiloe, ordered two of his prisoners to be shot; and four officers would have met the same fate, had not Mr. Bennet, the admiral's secretary, taken them on board the *O'Higgins*. Latapia was placed under arrest, the necessary declarations made out for a court-martial, and he was conveyed as a prisoner to Valparaiso. In place of being punished, both Latapia and Erascano were taken into the liberating army of General San Martin, and given superior rank!

The seamen, thus deprived of what they considered their just due, were now becoming mutinous. They could obtain neither pay nor prize-money. Promises were no sooner made than they were withdrawn or broken; and nothing but the admiral's assurance that they should be paid prevented an outbreak. Lord Cochrane, therefore, addressed a letter of expostulation to the supreme director, recounting their zealous services, and the ill-merited harshness to which they were exposed at the hands of the ministers in return, notwithstanding that, in addition to their labours afloat, they had aided the Government in the construction of wharfs and other conveniences necessary for the embarkation of troops and stores for Peru.

The truth was, however, the proceeds of the captures had been pocketed by the Government, and, to avoid repayment, they declared that the conquest of Valdivia was a restoration, although the place had never been in possession of Chili! On Lord Cochrane's refusal to allow the stores he had brought from thence to be disembarked, unless as a compensation to the seamen, it was alleged, that even if Valdivia had not belonged to the Republic, Chili did not make war on every section of America. It was, therefore, put to his liberality and honourable character whether he would not give up to the Government all that the squadron had acquired.

Finding that he would surrender nothing, it was next debated in the Council whether he ought not to be brought to a court-martial for having delayed and diverted the naval forces of Chili to the reduction of Valdivia without the orders of Government!

As nothing in the shape of justice could be obtained for the squadron, Lord Cochrane tendered the resignation of his commission, stating that, by retaining it, he felt that he should only bo instrumental in promoting the ruin which must follow the conduct of the Supreme Director's advisers. Lord Cochrane also told his excellency the Supreme Director that he, Lord Cochrane, had not accepted the command to have his motives misconstrued, and his services degraded, as they had been, for reasons which he was unable to divine.

This course was more than had been anticipated. The ministers were brought for a time to their senses, the justice of his complaints were acknowledged, and every assurance given that for the future the Government would observe good faith towards the squadron. An estate had been offered him as a reward for his services, which he had declined in the absence of a vote. The offer was renewed, but again declined, as nothing but promises were forthcoming to the service, and the only hold upon the seamen was his personal influence with them. In place, therefore, of accepting the offer, he returned the document conveying the grant, with a request that the estate might be sold, and the proceeds applied to the payment of the squadron.

Shamed by this offer, General San Martin, who had been appointed to command the military portion of the expedition to Peru, arrived at Valparaiso in June, and on the 13th of July the men were paid wages in part. But the admiral insisted on the whole being liquidated, and this was done on the 16th; but still no prize-money. The admiral's share alone of the captures made at and previous to the capture of Valdivia was 67,000 dollars, and for this he received the assurance of the Supreme Director that it should be paid at the earliest possible moment. This done, he accepted the estate which continued to be pressed upon him, the grant expressing the purpose for which it was given, adding, as a reason, that " his name should never cease from the land." *

* This estate, situated at Rio Clara, was, after Lord Coch-

A new source of annoyance now arose; this was the appointment of Captain Spry as the admiral's flag-captain on board the *O'Higgins*, which ship had been repaired at Valdivia, and had returned to Valparaiso. An order to this effect was sent to Lord Cochrane, which he firmly refused to obey, adding that Captain Spry should never tread the quarter-deck as his flag-captain, and that if his privilege as an admiral were not admitted, the Government might consider his command at an end. The point was conceded, and Captain Crosbie appointed flag-captain.

Encouraged by the annoyance given by Zenteno and his party, one or two of the captains thought themselves at liberty to manifest a disregard to authority, which Cochrane, as their admiral, did not choose to tolerate. The foremost of these was Guise, who, having been guilty of several acts of direct disobedience and neglect of duty, was put under arrest, and a demand made that the Government should institute a court-martial for the investigation of his conduct. This act greatly irritated Zenteno, who desired to support the recreant captain, and refused consent to the inquiry; thereby establishing a precedent for the captain of any ship to consider himself independent of the admiral.

This open violation of discipline Cochrane con-

rane's departure, forcibly resumed possession of by the succeeding government; and the bailiff, whom he had placed upon it for the purpose of seeing how it could be improved by culture and the introduction of valuable European seeds, was forcibly expelled from its supervision.

sidered a personal insult, and he once more transmitted to the Government his resignation, at the same time demanding his passport to enable him to quit the country, notifying to the officers of the squadron that on the receipt of the same he should cease to command. A meeting was immediately held amongst the officers, and on the same day he received —not a valedictory address, as might have been expected—but two letters, one signed by five captains, and the other by twenty-three commissioned officers, containing resolutions of abandoning the service also, at the same time handing in their commissions. To this proof of attachment, he replied, by requesting they would not sacrifice their own positions on his account, and recommended them not to make their resolutions public till they had further considered the matter.

Pending the settlement of this question, the equipment of the squadron proceeded with alacrity. His lordship, however, withheld the commissions which had been enclosed to him by the officers of the squadron, lest the measure should excite popular dissatisfaction, and thus cause danger, for which the Government was unprepared.

The only captains who did not sign the resolutions were Guise and Spry, the former being under arrest, and the latter offended on account of Cochrane's refusal to accept him as flag-captain. It is supposed that Guise communicated to Zenteno the resolutions of the officers, for on the 20th the admiral received from him a letter, dated July 20th, begging him, in the most abject and fulsome terms, **not** to take a course which would involve the future operations **of the** arms of liberty in the New **World** in certain **ruin**; and, ultimately, replace in Chili, "his adopted home," that **tyranny** which his lordship abhorred, and to the annihilation of which his heroism had so greatly contributed. He added, "The Supreme Director commands me to inform your lordship, that should you persist in resigning the command of the squadron which has been honoured by bearing your flag—the cause of terror and dismay to our enemies, and of glory to all true Americans—or should the Government unwisely **admit it,** it would indeed be a day of universal mourning in the New World." "The Government, therefore," he continued, "**in** the name of the nation, returns you your commission, soliciting your re-acceptance of it, for **the** furtherance of that sacred cause to which your whole soul is devoted."

With regard to Captain Guise, whom the admiral had placed under arrest, the Supreme Director requested that his trial might be postponed to the first opportunity which did not interfere with the service **of the** squadron.

In addition **to t**his communication from Don Jose Ignacio Zenteno, **the** Minister of Marine, the admiral received private letters from the Supreme Director and General San Martin, begging him to continue in command of the naval forces, and assuring him that there should be no further cause for complaint.

On receipt of these letters Cochrane withdrew his resignation, and returned to the officers of the squa-

dron their commissions, at the same time releasing
Captain Guise from his arrest, and reinstating him in
the command of his ship.

Lord Cochrane considered that he owed some of
his annoyance to General San Martin, and he accused
him of having **assisted his enemies.** He replied,
that **he only** wanted **to see how far** the Supreme
Director would allow a party spirit **to oppose the**
welfare of the expedition; **and** added, " **N**ever mind,
my lord ; I am general **of the army, and** you shall be
admiral of the squadron." **His allusion** to the com-
plicity **of the Supreme Director** Cochrane knew to **be**
false, **as his excellency was anxious to do all** in his power
both for the squadron **and** his country, **had** not the
senate, on which he conferred such extraordinary
powers, thwarted all his endeavours.

CAPTURE OF THE *ESMERALDA*.
[1820.]

The equipment of the squadron **and troops** destined
for the liberation of Peru **had been beset** with difficulties, the Government **being without** credit, whilst
its treasury had **been completely** exhausted by efforts
to organize **an army—a loan** having been refused.
By Lord **Cochrane's** influence with the British **merchants, he succeeded in** obtaining considerable quan-
tities **of stores,** and a subscription was **set on** foot, in
place of a forced loan, upon which **the** Government
hesitated to venture.

But the great difficulty was **with** regard to the
foreign seamen, who, **disgusted at** the bad faith shown

them, refused to re-enter. **Upon this** the Government requested the admiral to resort to impressment, which he declined, telling them, moreover, that the captain of the British frigate then in port would not permit his countrymen to be impressed. The alternative **which he** proposed was, that he should use **his** influence with the men, by issuing a proclamation, dictated by himself, which would render them dependent for their pay and prize-money upon General San Martin, and on the success of the expedition; it being evident **that** they would not place further confidence in the promises of the Government.

A joint proclamation **was** therefore issued by San Martin and the admiral, the signature of the latter being added as a guarantee of good faith. The proclamation contained a direct promise to pay to all foreign seamen who voluntarily enlisted into the **Chilian** service the whole arrears of their pay, and one year's pay over and above **the** arrears, as a premium or reward for their services, if they continued to fulfil their duty to the day of the **surrender** of the city of **Lima, and** its occupation by the liberating forces.

The **result was,** that the crews of the ships were immediately **com**pleted.

The Chilian **force** amounted to 4,200 men, General San Martin being **nomi**nated Captain-General.

On the 21st of **August,** the squadron sailed from Valparaiso amidst **the enthusiastic** plaudits of the people; and on the **25th, hove to** off Coquimbo, taking on board another battalion of troops. On the 26th they again sailed, when General San Martin made known to the admiral his intention of proceeding with the main body of the army to Truxillo, a place four degrees to leeward of Lima.

By representing to General San Martin that this course would cause great dissatisfaction amongst the Chileno officers and men, who expected to be landed and led at once against Lima, for the immediate conquest of which they were amply sufficient, he consented to give up his plan of proceeding to Truxillo, but firmly refused to disembark his men in the vicinity of Lima. Cochrane's plan was to land the force at Chilca, the nearest point to Callao, and forthwith to obtain possession of the capital; an object by no means difficult of execution.

The admiral finding all his arguments unavailing, sailed for Pisco, where the expedition arrived on the 7th of September, and on the 8th, to his great chagrin, the troops were disembarked, and for fifty days remained in total inaction, with the exception of despatching Colonel Arenales into the interior with a detachment, which defeated a body of Spaniards, and took up a position to the eastward of Lima.

In the mean time, the squadron was necessarily kept in inaction, having done nothing beyond capturing a few merchantmen along the coast, and fruitlessly chasing the *Prueba* and *Venganza*, Spanish frigates, which he did not follow up, as involving risk to the transports during his absence. This delay was productive of the worst disasters which could have befallen the expedition. The people, not calculating on such tardiness on the part of San Martin, were everywhere declaring in the favour of the liberators ; but being unsupported, were fined, imprisoned, and subjected to corporal punishment by **the** viceroy.

The fruits of the demonstration early became manifest even amidst inaction. A vessel arrived on the 4th of October from Guayaquil with the intelligence that on receiving news of the sailing of the expedition, that province had declared itself independent. Upon the arrival of this welcome news, Lord Cochrane prevailed upon San Martin to re-embark the troops, and on the 28th the expedition sailed from Pisco, and on the following day anchored before Callao.

After having reconnoitered the fortifications, Cochrane again urged **on** San Martin an immediate disembarcation of the force, but to this he again strenuously objected, insisting on going to Ancon, a place to the northward of Callao. **Having** no control over the disposition of the troops, the admiral was obliged to **su**bmit ; and on the 30th, detached the *San Martin*, *Galvarino*, and *Araucano*, to convoy the transports to **Ancon**, retaining the *O'Higgins*, *Independencia*, and *Lautaro*, **as if for** the purpose of blockade.

Annoyed, **in** common with the whole expedition, at this irresolution on the part of the general, Cochrane determined **that** the means of Chili, furnished with great **difficulty, should not** be wholly wasted, and accordingly **formed a** plan of attack **with** the three ships which **he had** previously kept **back.** This design was **to** cut out the *Esmeralda* frigate from under the fortifications, and also to get possession of another ship, on board of which it was stated that a million of dollars had been embarked ready for flight.

The enterprise was hazardous, for since the former visit of Lord Cochrane the enemy's position had been much strengthened, no less than 300 pieces of artillery being mounted on shore, whilst the *Esmeralda* was crowded with the best sailors and marines that could be procured, these sleeping every night at quarters. The frigate was, moreover, defended by a strong boom with chain moorings, and by armed blockships; the whole being surrounded by twenty-seven gun-boats, so that no ship could possibly get at her.

Three days were occupied in preparations, still keeping secret the purpose for which they were intended. On the evening of the 5th of November, however, the admiral issued the following proclamation :—

"To-morrow you will present yourselves proudly before Callao, and all your comrades will envy your good fortune. One hour of courage and resolution is all that is required of you to triumph. Remember, that you have conquered in Valdivia, and be not afraid of those who have hitherto fled from you. The value of all the vessels captured in Callao will be yours, and the same reward in money will be distributed amongst you as has been offered by the Spaniards in Lima to those who should capture any of the Chilian squadron. The moment of glory is approaching, and I hope that the Chilenos will fight as they have been accustomed to do, and that the English will act as they have ever done at home and abroad."

The proclamation would have done little, however, had not **Lord Cochrane stated** his intention to lead **the attack in** person, the result being that the whole of the marines and seamen on board the three ships offered to accompany him. A hundred and sixty seamen and eighty marines were selected, and in the evening placed in fourteen boats alongside the **flagship**, each man armed with cutlass and pistol, being, for distinction's sake, dressed in white, with a blue band **on** the left arm. Cochrane expected the **Spaniards** would be **off** their guard, **as,** by way of *ruse*, the **other ships had** been sent **out** of the bay **under** the **charge** of Captain Foster, as though **in pursuit of** some **vessels in the** offing—so that the Spaniards would naturally **consider** themselves safe from attack for that night.

At ten o'clock all was in readiness, and the boats **formed in** two divisions, the **first** commanded by **Captain** Crosbie, and the second **by** Captain Guise, Cochrane's **boat** leading. The strictest **silence and** the **exclusive use of** cutlasses were enjoined ; the oars **were muffled and** the night dark : so that the enemy had not **the least** suspicion of the impending attack.

About midnight the **boats neared** the small opening **left in the** boom, their **plan being** well-nigh frustrated **by the** vigilance of **a** guard-boat, but with which **Cochrane in the** launch fortunately fell in. The challenge was given, upon which, in an under-tone, Cochrane threatened the crew of the boat with instant death if they made the least alarm. No reply was made to the threat, and in a few minutes the heroic fellows were alongside the frigate in line, boarding at several points simultaneously.

With the exception of the sentries, all hands were asleep at their quarters—and great was the havoc made amongst them by the Chileno cutlasses. Retreating to the forecastle, they made a gallant stand, and it was not until the third charge that they gave way. The fight was renewed on the quarter-deck, where the Spanish marines fell to a man, the rest of the enemy leaping overboard, or into the hold, to escape slaughter.

Cochrane boarded at the main chains, but was knocked back by a blow from the butt end of the sentry's musket, and falling on a thole pin of the boat, it entered his back near the spine, inflicting a severe injury. Regaining his footing, he reascended the side, and, when on deck, was shot through the thigh, but binding a handkerchief tightly round the wound, he managed, though with great difficulty, to direct the contest to its close.

The affair occupied a quarter of an hour, the Chilian loss being eleven killed and thirty wounded, whilst that of the Spaniards was 160, many of whom fell under the cutlasses of the boarders before they could stand to their arms. Greater bravery was never displayed. Before boarding, the duties of all had been appointed, and a party was told off to take possession of the tops. They had not been on deck a minute, when Lord Cochrane hailed the foretop, and **was** instantly answered **by the** men he had stationed there, an equally prompt answer being returned from **the maintop.**

The garrison, being by this time alarmed, opened fire **on** their own frigate, taking it for granted that she had been captured and not caring that their own men would be the sufferers as well as the captors. Captain Coig, of the *Esmeralda*, in fact, received **a** severe contusion by **a shot** from his own party.

The *Esmeralda* would, in all probability, have been sunk **but for** one **of** Cochrane's clever expedients. **There** were two foreign **ships** of war present during **the** contest—the *Macedonian* and *Hyperion;* and these ships—as previously agreed on with the Spanish authorities **in** case of **a night** attack—hoisted coloured lights as signals, **to prevent** being fired upon. As soon as the fortress commenced its fire on the *Esmeralda*, Cochrane ordered lights similar to those on **board** the British and United States frigates to be **hoisted, so** that the garrison became **puzzled** which vessel **to fire at.** The *Hyperion* **and** *Macedonian* were **consequently** several times struck while the *Esmeralda* **was com**paratively unharmed. To avoid these awkward mistakes, the neutral frigates cut their cables and moved **away; whilst** Captain Guise, contrary to orders, cut **the *Esmeralda's*** cables also, so **that** there was nothing **to be done** but to loose her top-sails **and** follow, the fortress then ceasing its fire.

Cochrane's orders were to endeavour, after taking the frigate, to capture the *Maypu*, a brig of war previously taken from Chili, and then to attack and cut adrift every ship near, there being plenty of time in which to accomplish this; but on Cochrane being disabled by his wounds, Guise, on whom the command of the prize devolved, interposed his own judgment in the matter. Cochrane considered this to have been a great mistake, arguing, that if they could capture the *Esmeralda*, with her picked and well-appointed crew, there would have been little or no difficulty in cutting the other ships adrift in succession.

In the cutting of the *Esmeralda's* cables not one of these objects was effected.

The prize was ready for sea, with three months' provisions on board, and with stores sufficient for two years, and was, no doubt, intended to convoy the treasure-ship.

The commander of the *Macedonian* evinced much sympathy towards Cochrane's gallant band. He ordered his sentinels not to hail the boats—the officers in an under-tone wishing them success.

Captain Basil Hall, who commanded the *Conway*, then in the Pacific, gave the following interesting account of this affair:—

" The inner harbour was guarded by an extensive system of batteries, admirably constructed, and bearing the general name of the ' Castles of Callao.' The merchant-ships, as well as the men-of-war, consisting of the *Esmeralda*, a large 40-gun frigate, and two sloops-of-war, were moored under the guns of the castle, within a semicircle of fourteen gun-boats, and a boom made of spars chained together.

"Lord Cochrane, having previously reconnoitred these **formidable defences in person,** undertook the desperate enterprise of cutting out the Spanish frigate, although she was known to be fully prepared for an attack. His lordship proceeded in fourteen boats, containing 240 men—all volunteers from the different ships of the squadron—in two divisions, one under the orders of Captain Crosbie, and the other under Captain Guise, both officers commanding the Chileno squadron.

"At midnight, the boats having forced their way across the boom, Lord Cochrane, who was leading, rowed alongside the first gun-boat, and taking the officer by surprise, proposed **to** him, with a pistol at **his** head, the alternative of silence or death. No reply being made, **the** boats pushed on unobserved, and Lord Cochrane, mounting the *Esmeralda's* side, was the first to give the alarm. The sentinel on the gangway levelled his piece and fired, but was instantly **cut down** by the coxswain, and **his** lordship, though wounded in the thigh, at the same moment stepped on the deck, **the** frigate being boarded with no less gallantry on **the** opposite side by Captain Guise, who met Lord Cochrane midway on the quarter-deck, as also Captain Crosbie, **and the** after-part of the ship was soon carried, sword **in hand.** The Spaniards rallied on the forecastle, where **they made** a desperate resistance, till overpowered by a fresh party of seamen and marines, headed by Lord Cochrane. A gallant stand was again made on the main deck, but **before** one o'clock the ship was captured, her cables cut, and she was steered triumphantly **out** of the harbour.

" This loss was a death-blow to the Spanish naval force in that quarter of the world; for although there were still two Spanish frigates and some smaller vessels in the Pacific, they never afterwards ventured to show themselves, but left Lord Cochrane undisputed master of the coast."

On the morning of the 6th, the market-boat of the United States frigate was, as usual, sent for provisions, when the mob took it into their heads that the *Esmeralda* could not have been cut out without the assistance of the *Macedonian*, and murdered the whole boat's crew.

The wounded amongst the *Esmeralda's* crew were sent on shore under a flag of truce, with a letter to the viceroy, proposing an exchange of prisoners. The proposal was this time civilly acceded to, and the whole sent on shore; the Chilian prisoners, who had long languished in the dungeons of the fortress, being returned, and ordered to join the army of General San Martin.

On transmitting **the** intelligence of his success to San Martin, Lord Cochrane received an acknowledgment.

" All those who participated in the risks and glory of the deed," wrote the general, "also deserve well of their countrymen, and I have the satisfaction to be the medium of transmitting the sentiments of admiration

which such transcendent success has excited in the
chiefs of the army under my command. Permit me
to express them to **you, in** order that they may be
communicated to **the** meritorious officers, seamen,
and marines **of** the squadron, to whom will be religiously fulfilled *the promises you made.*"

San Martin's expression of "religiously fulfilling
the promises" was an allusion to the proclamation
signed by himself, previous to the departure of the
squadron from Valparaiso. With the preceding letter
the general voluntarily sent another promise to the
captors, **of 50,000** dollars, to be paid on gaining
possession of Lima. Neither the one promise nor the
other were ever fulfilled, nor did they ever obtain any
prize-money.

General San Martin wrote to the Administration
in Chili, stating **it was** impossible for him to eulogize
in proper language **the** daring enterprise of the 5th
of November, by which Lord Cochrane had decided the
superiority of their naval forces—augmented the splen-
dour and power of Chili—and secured the success of
the campaign.

Shortly after his departure for Peru, Lady Cochrane
undertook **a journey** across the Cordillera, to Men-
doza, the passes being, at that season, often blocked
up with snow. **Having** been intrusted with some
despatches of **importance, she** pushed on rapidly, and
on the 12th of October **arrived at** the celebrated
Ponte del Inca, 15,000 feet above the level of the
sea. Whilst proceeding on her mule up a precipitous
path in the vicinity, a royalist, who had intruded

himself on the party, rode up in an opposite direction
and disputed the path with her, at a place where the
slightest false step would have precipitated her into
the abyss below. One of her attendants, a tried and
devoted soldier, named Pedro Flores, seeing the movement, and guessing the man's intention, galloped up
to him at a critical moment, striking him a violent
blow across the face, and thus arresting his murderous
design. The ruffian, finding himself vigorously attacked, made off, without resenting the blow, and
so, no doubt, another premeditated attempt on Lady
Cochrane's life was averted.

Lord Cochrane and his nobly-earned prize proceeded to Ancon, where he arrived on the 8th of
November, and was hailed with great enthusiasm by
the army. The Spanish naval force, it was considered,
had received the *coup de grâce;* and the army made
certain that it would be at once led against Lima,
before the authorities had time to recover from their
consternation. But they reckoned without their
host; San Martin had no such intention; and in
defiance of all argument, ordered the troops to re-
embark on board the transports and return to Huacho.
The *O'Higgins* and *Esmeralda,* abandoning the blockade, were instructed to convoy them. San Martin
was playing a very deep and selfish game, which was
soon made apparent.

By the 12th, the army was again landed at
Huacho, amidst evident signs of dissatisfaction on
the part of the officers, who were naturally jealous
of the achievements of the squadron, from being

themselves restrained **from** enterprise of any kind.
To allay this feeling, San Martin had recourse to
an almost incredible violation **of** truth, intended to
impress upon the Chilian people, that the army, and
not the squadron, had captured the *Esmeralda!* and
declaring that the whole affair was the result **of his**
own plans, to which Lord Cochrane had agreed!

The people of Chili were then told that the army
captured the frigate, and subsequently released the
prisoners. This announcement excited the astonishment of the troops; but as it contributed to their
self-love, they accepted it, whilst Cochrane thought
it beneath his dignity to refute a falsehood palpable to
the whole expedition.

PROVES **HIS** FIDELITY.
[1820-2.]

On the 15th November, the blockade of Callao was
resumed, beyond which nothing could be done; though
even this was of importance, as, by cutting off supplies
from the capital, the inhabitants were subjected to
privations, which caused great uneasiness **to** the Vice-
regal Government.

Several attempts were made to entice the remaining
Spanish naval force **from** their shelter under the batteries, by placing **the** *Esmeralda* apparently within
reach, and the **flag-ship in situations** of some danger.
One day Lord Cochrane **carried the** *O'Higgins* through
an intricate strait called the Boqueron, in which nothing beyond a 50-ton schooner had ever been seen.
The Spaniards, expecting every moment that the ship

would strike, manned their gun-boats, ready to attack as soon as she was aground, of which, however, there was little danger, as Cochrane had previously found, and buoyed off with small bits of wood invisible to the enemy, a channel through which the ship could pass without great difficulty.

These successes caused **great** depression amongst the Spanish troops; **and in** December, the battalion of Numantia, numbering 650 disciplined men, deserted, and joined the Chilian forces. On the 8th, forty Spanish officers followed their example; and every day afterwards, **officers, privates,** and civilians of respectability, **joined** the patriot army, which thus became considerably **reinforced; the** defection of so large a portion of his troops being a severe loss to his **viceroy.**

Notwithstanding this succession **of** favourable events, San Martin still declined to march on Lima, remaining inactive at Huacho, though, **owing to the** unhealthy situation of the place, **nearly** one-third of his troops died of intermittent **fever** during the many months they remained there. **In** place of securing the capital, where the army would have been welcomed, he proposed **to send** half to Guayaquil, in order to annex **that** province, this being the first manifestation **on the** part of San Martin **to** found a dominion **of** his own; for to nothing less did he afterwards aspire.

Determined not to be idle, Cochrane prevailed upon San Martin to give him a division of 600 troops, under the command of Lieutenant-Colonel Miller. On the 13th of March, 1821, the expedition sailed for Pisco, of which, on its previous abandonment by the army, the enemy had again taken possession. On the 20th it was retaken, when it was found that the Spaniards had severely punished the alleged defection of the inhabitants for contributing to the supplies of the **patriot force** during its stay. Not expecting their return, the Spanish proprietors of estates had brought back their cattle, of which Cochrane captured about 500 head, besides 300 horses for the use of the Chilian forces, the squadron thus supplying their wants instead of remaining in total inaction.

By way of conciliating the admiral, San Martin proposed to name the captured frigate the *Cochrane*, as two vessels before had been named the *San Martin* **and** *O'Higgins;* **but to** this he demurred, upon which San Martin suggested *Valdivia*, to which the admiral saw no **objection.** The *Esmeralda* consequently became the *Valdivia*.

The command of the prize had been conferred upon Captain Guise; and after her change of name, his officers wrote a letter deprecating it, and alleging, **that** as they had had nothing **to** do with the conquest **of** Valdivia, it ought to be withdrawn, and one more consonant **with** their feelings substituted. This letter was **followed by** marked personal disrespect towards the admiral, from the officers who had signed it, who made it no secret that the name of " *Guise* " was the one sought to be **substituted.**

As the remarks made by these officers to others of **the** squadron were of a derogatory nature as regarded his character and authority, and likely to lead to serious disorganization, Lord Cochrane brought the whole of those who had signed the letter to a court-martial, two of whom were **dismissed the service,** and the remainder dismissed the ship, with a recommendation to General San Martin for other appointments.

During the time these officers were under arrest Cochrane had made up his mind to attack the fortifications of Callao, intending to carry them by a *coup de main*, similar to that which had succeeded at Valdivia, and **was** convinced **of** the feasibility of the plan.

On the 20th March, he notified this intention by **an order,** stating that on the following day he should make the attack with the boats of the squadron and the *San Martin*, the crew of which received the order with cheers, volunteers for the boats eagerly pressing forward from all quarters. But in place of preparing to second **the** operations, Guise sent him **a note** refusing to serve with any other but the officers under arrest—stating that unless they were restored, he would resign his command. The admiral's reply was, that he would neither restore them nor accept his resignation, without some better reason for it than the one alleged. Guise answered, **that** his refusal to restore **his officers** was a sufficient reason for his resignation, whereupon the admiral ordered him to weigh and proceed on a service of importance; but **the order was** disobeyed on the ground that he could no longer act, having given over the command of the ship to Lieutenant Shepherd.

Seeing that a mutiny was being excited, and

knowing that Captains Guise and Spry were at the bottom of the mischief, Lord Cochrane ordered the latter to proceed with the *Galvarino* to Chorillos, when that officer **also** requested leave to resign, as his friend Captain Guise had been compelled to do so. Such was the state of mutiny on board the *Galvarino*, that the admiral deputed his flag-captain to restore order, when Spry affected to consider himself superseded, and claimed exemption from martial law; upon which the admiral tried him by court-martial, and he was dismissed from the ship.

The **two** captains immediately made their way to head-quarters, and San Martin at once made Spry his naval *aide-de-camp*, thus promoting him in the most public manner for his disobedience to orders, and in defiance of the sentence of the court-martial.

Leaving the *O'Higgins* and *Valdivia* at Pisco to protect the troops, Cochrane shifted his flag to the *San Martin*, and sailed for Callao, where he arrived on the 2nd of April. On the 6th, he again attacked the enemy's shipping under the batteries, and did them considerable damage, but made no further attempt to gain possession of them, the object being to deter them from quitting their shelter. The *San Martin* then returned to Pisco.

The general having given Cochrane discretionary power to do what he pleased with the few troops placed at his disposal, he determined on attacking Arica. Abandoning Pisco, therefore, he re-embarked the troops, and sailed on the 21st. On the 1st of May he arrived off Arica, and sent a summons to the

Governor to surrender, promising to respect persons and personal property. This not being complied with, an immediate bombardment took place, but without any great effect.

After a careful survey, the *San Martin* was on the 6th May hauled nearer in shore, and some shells were thrown over the town. As this had not the desired effect, a portion of the troops landed at Sama, to the northward of the town, being followed by Colonel Miller with the remainder, and Captain Wilkinson with the marines of the *San Martin*; when the enemy fled, and the patriot flag was hoisted on the batteries. A considerable quantity of stores, and four Spanish brigs, besides the guns of the fort and other artillery, was found here, besides a quantity of European goods, belonging to the Spaniards at Lima, all of which was seized and brought on board the *San Martin*.

On the 14th Colonel Miller, with the troops and marines, advanced to Tacna, and by the admiral's directions took possession of the town, without opposition, two companies of infantry deserting the royalist cause and joining the patriots. These were ordered to form the nucleus of a new regiment, to be called the "Tacna Independents."

Learning that the Spanish General Ramirez had ordered three detachments from Arequipa, Puno, and La Paz, to form a junction at Tacna, to carry into effect the usual Spanish order—to drive the insurgents into the sea—Miller determined on attacking them in detail. The Arequipa detachment, under

Colonel Hera, was fallen in with at Maribe, and immediately routed, the result being that nearly the whole were killed or taken prisoners, together with four hundred mules and their baggage. In this affair the patriots lost a Mr. Welsh, an assistant surgeon, who had volunteered to accompany the detachment.

Before this fight was over, the other detachments from Puno and La Paz appeared in sight, and the patriots had to face a fresh enemy. With his usual promptness, Miller despatched Captain Hind, with a rocket party, to oppose their passage of a river; when, finding **that** the Arequipa detachment had been defeated, they decamped.

The result of this and of the successive operations **was** the complete submission of the Spaniards from the sea to the Cordilleras, Arica forming the key to the **whole country.**

General Ramirez **was** now actively engaged in drawing men from distant garrisons to act against this small force, which was suffering severely from **ague;** but just at this juncture the governor of Arequipa informed the admiral that an armistice **had** been ratified **on** the 23rd of May, for twenty days, between San **Martin** and the viceroy Lacerna.

Being thus reduced to inaction, the admiral dropped down to Mollendo, where **he** found a neutral vessel shipping corn for Lima, **which** city had been reduced to great straits owing to the **rigorous** blockade. Lima **was, in** fact, on the point of being starved, whilst the inhabitants foresaw that, although San Martin's army was inactive, Cochrane's little band in the south

would speedily overrun the provinces, which were
in favour of independence. On ascertaining this,
Cochrane wrote to the governor of **Arequipa, expressing** surprise that neutrals should **be** allowed **to em-**
bark provisions during an armistice. He received for
reply that the most positive orders should be given to
put a stop to it, upon which the admiral retired from
Mollendo, leaving an officer to watch. As the **em-**
barkation was continued, the admiral returned and
shipped all the wheat he could find on shore. **In**
consequence of which, Colonel La Hera, with 1,000
royalists, took possession of Moquega, on pretence
that the admiral had broken the armistice.

Convinced that there was something wrong at head-
quarters, Cochrane determined to proceed to Callao
for the purpose of learning the truth, leaving Colonel
Miller to return to Arica.

During Lord Cochrane's absence **Lady Cochrane**
had sailed for England, partly for the sake of her
health, but more for the purpose **of** obtaining justice
for her husband, who, in addition **to** the persecution
he had undergone, was **now** made subject to a
" Foreign Enlistment **Bill**," the enactments of which
were especially aimed **at** those who had engaged **in a**
service which had **for** its object the expulsion of Spain,
then in alliance with England, from her colonies in
the Pacific.

The interest excited in the welfare of this devoted
wife and heroic woman is thus recorded in the
" Memoirs of General Miller ":—
... " On the 25th, 600 infantry and 60 cavalry, all

picked men, were placed under the command of Lieutenant-Colonel Miller, who received directions to embark on a secret service under the orders of Lord Cochrane, and proceed to Huacho. On the day after his arrival there, and whilst he was inspecting the detachments in the Plaza, Lady Cochrance galloped on to the parade to speak to him. The sudden appearance of youth and beauty on a fiery horse, managed with skill and elegance, absolutely electrified the men, who had never before seen an English lady. ' *Que hermosa! Que graciosa! Que linda! Que airosa! Es un angel del cielo!*' were exclamations which escaped from one end of the line to the other. Colonel Miller, not displeased at this involuntary homage to the beauty of his countrywoman, said to the men, 'This is our *generala;*' on which her ladyship, turning to the line, bowed to the troops, who no longer confining their expressions of admiration to suppressed interjections, loud *vivas* burst from officers and men, to which Lady Cochraue, smiling her acknowledgments, cantered off the ground like a fairy."

The *San Martin* arrived at Callao on the 2nd of July, when, learning that Lima was no longer tenable from want of provisions, and that an intention existed on the part of the viceroy to abandon the city, the admiral withdrew to a distance from the port, awaiting the result.

But having learnt on the 5th that an attempt was being made by the viceroy to obtain a prolongation of the armistice, he again entered the bay with the *San Martin.*

On the 6th the viceroy quitted the city, retaining, however, the fortresses at Callao, the garrison of which was reinforced from the troops which had evacuated Lima.

To the astonishment of all, no movement was made by the liberating army to take possession of the evacuated capital; and as the Spanish troops were withdrawn and no government existed, serious disorders were anticipated. Under these circumstances, application was made to Capt. Basil Hall, then in command of the *Conway*, for assistance to maintain tranquillity and protect public and private property, who immediately sent on shore a party of marines for that purpose.

San Martin knew that the viceroy intended to abandon the capital, and had entered the harbour in the Schooner *Sacramento*, but gave no orders for its occupation. On the 7th a detachment of cavalry, without orders, entered Lima, and on the 8th were followed by another detachment of infantry.

The forts at Callao being still in possession of the enemy, Cochrane made preparations to attack them, and destroy the shipping sheltered under them. Aware of those intentions, the garrison, on the 11th, sank the *San Sebastian*, the only frigate left in the harbour. On the following day, the *O'Higgins*, *Lautaro*, *Puyrredon*, and *Potrillo* arrived, so that the squadron was again complete.

The wheat which the admiral had shipped at Mollendo being still on board the *San Martin*, and the city in a state of famine, the general directed that it should be landed at the Chorillos. As the ship was deeply laden, the admiral objected to this from the dangerous nature **of** the anchorage. His objection was, however, overruled, and the ship, as he had anticipated, went ashore and became a total **wreck.**

On the 17th, Lord Cochrane received an invitation from the *Cabildo* to visit the city, and on landing he found that preparations had been made to give the visit the character of a public entry. Finding this to be the case, he declined, especially as San Martin had entered privately. He, however, held a levee at the palace, where the compliments of the established authorities and principal inhabitants were tendered **him.** San Martin declined to attend this complimentary manifestation.

On the 24th July Captain Crosbie, in obedience to the admiral's orders, proceeded to Callao with the boats; and on the following **day** brought out two large merchantmen, and the sloop of war *Resolucion*, together with several launches; burning, moreover, **two** vessels within musket-shot of the batteries.

On **the 27th,** Cochrane received a written invitation from the **Cabildo, to** be present at the proclamation of the independence **of** Peru, couched in the following terms:—" Lima is about to solemnize the most august act which has been performed for three centuries, or **since** her foundation; this **is the** proclamation of her independence, and absolute exclusion from the Spanish Government, as well as from that of any other foreign potentate, and this *Cabildo*, wishing the ceremony to be conducted with all possible decorum and solemnity, considers it necessary that your excellency, who has so gloriously co-operated in bringing about this highly-desired object, will deign to assist at the act with your illustrious officers, on Saturday, the 28th instant."

Feeling, as he had an undoubted right to feel, that himself and his officers had been mainly instrumental in establishing the independence of Peru—for the captain-general had been deaf to every entreaty made to him to move—Cochrane's surprise and indignation may be imagined when, at the ceremony, medals were distributed, ascribing to *General San Martin and the army* the whole credit of having accomplished that which the squadron had achieved.

The inscription on the medals was as follows:— " Lima secured its independence on the 28th of July, 1821, under the protection of General San Martin and the liberating army." Ingratitude more base can hardly be conceived, and the invitation addressed to Cochrane and his officers under the circumstances was little better than a mockery.

The delight of the inhabitants of Lima at this termination of centuries of Spanish misrule, and on finding their independence fully recognized, as had been stipulated, by Chili, was beyond description. As a mark of gratitude, a deputation from the *Cabildo*, waited on San Martin, offering him, in the name of the inhabitants of the capital, the first presidency of their now independent state; but, to their surprise, they were curtly told that the general had already taken the command, and intended to keep it as long as he thought proper, whilst he would allow no assemblies for the discussion of public matters. Thus the **first act of the** freedom and independence so ostentatiously **paraded** on the previous day was the **formation of a** despotic government.

Lord Cochrane knew nothing of this assumption of power, neither did he coincide in it; but finding that San Martin had dubbed himself Protector, he thought it right to call upon him to redeem the promises he **had** made to pay the squadron twelve months' wages and 50,000 dollars on his entering Lima.

The admiral accordingly landed on the 4th August, and requested the general to devise means for liquidating these debts.

San Martin answered, that "he would never pay the Chilian **squadron unless it** was sold to Peru, and then **the payment should be** considered part of the purchase-money." Lord Cochrane replied, that "by such a transaction the squadron of Chili would be transferred to Peru **by** merely paying what **was due** to the officers and crews for services done to that state." San Martin now turned **round to the** admiral, and **said,** "Are you aware, my lord, that **I** am Protector **of** Peru?"—"No," said his lordship. "**I** ordered my secretaries to inform you of it," returned San Martin. "**That** is now unnecessary, for you have personally **informed me,**" said Cochrane. " I hope that the friendship **which has** existed between San Martin and myself will continue to exist between the Protector of Peru and myself." San Martin then, rubbing his hands, said, "I have only to say, that I am Protector of Peru!"

The manner in which this last sentence was expressed roused the admiral, who said : " Then it becomes me, as senior officer of Chili, and, consequently, the representative of the nation, to request the fulfilment of all the promises made to Chili and the squadron; but first—and principally—the squadron." San Martin returned—" Chili! Chili! I will never pay a single *real* to Chili! As to the squadron, you may take it where you please, and go where you choose ; a couple of schooners are quite enough for me."

San Martin paced the room for a short time, and, turning to his lordship, said, " Forget, my lord, what is past." The **ad**miral replied, "I will, when I can," and immediately left the palace.*

General San Martin, following him to the staircase, had the temerity to propose to the admiral to imitate his example, break faith with the Chilian Government, and accept the higher grade of " First Admiral of Peru." A proposition so base was declined in fitting terms, when, in a tone of irritation, San Martin declared that he would neither **give** the seamen their arrears of pay, nor the gratuity **he** had promised.

On arriving **on board** the flagship, Cochrane found an official communication, requesting **him** to fire a salute in honour of San Martin's elevation to the protectorate.

The request was complied with, in the hope that quiet remonstrance might recall San Martin to a sense

* Stevenson's "Twenty Years' Residence in South America."

of duty to the Chilian Government, and on the 7th of August Cochrane addressed him a letter couched in friendly terms, and advising him to adopt a dignified course of action, instead of usurping a power which **he could only wield at the** expense of good **faith.**

To this letter, General San Martin replied eva**sively on** the 9th. He endeavoured therein to make it appear that he had never guaranteed the payment of any reward to the navy, except twelve months' pay, and that he was employed in providing the means, and also in endeavouring to collect the reward of 50,000 dollars which he, Lord Cochrane, offered to the seamen who should capture the *Esmeralda*, and that he **was** not **only** disposed **to** pay these sums, but to recompense valour displayed in the cause of the country.

"But," said he, "you know, my lord, that the wages of the crews do not come under these circumstances, and that I, never having engaged to pay the amount, am not obliged to do so! That debt is due from Chili, whose government engaged the seamen."

In this letter, San Martin attributed his usurpation to a singular current of success, omitting to state that he neither struck one blow nor devised one plan which had led to **it. He** also repudiated all connection with Chili, though he had sworn fidelity to the republic **as** its captain-general.

In the mean while **the** squadron was in a state of destitution. The provisions necessary for the subsistence of the men were withheld, although the Protector had abundant means of supplying them. His object, which soon became more apparent, was to starve both officers and men into desertion, and thus effect the dismemberment of the squadron which Cochrane had refused to give up to his ambitious views.

Concealing his resentment, and reflecting that the forts of Callao were still in the hands of the Spaniards, San Martin endeavoured to explain away the interview with Lord Cochrane on the 4th of August, and repeated, that the arrears due to the squadron should be liquidated, as well as the rewards which had been promised; but as nothing of the kind was forthcoming, the squadron began to show symptoms of mutiny.

On the 11th of August, Cochrane again wrote to San Martin, apprising him of the increasing discontent of the seamen, again requesting payment. To this communication the Protector replied, on the 13th of August, hinting that Lord Cochrane might *reconsider* his refusal to accept the command of the contemplated Peruvian navy, and asserting that he was unable to satisfy the claims of the seamen. This subterfuge was too palpable, for it was well known he had money derived from the spoliation of the Spaniards.

Finding the admiral immovable, and determined not to acknowledge his self-constituted authority, and still less inclined to agree to measures which would have robbed Chili of the navy, the " Protector " issued a proclamation, again promising the payment of arrears to the seamen, and a pension for life to the officers who acknowledged themselves to be officers of

Peru—a direct invitation to the latter to desert from the Chilian service.

But though he promised, not a penny of the arrears and other emoluments was paid to the squadron.

The affairs of the squadron becoming every day worse, and a mutinous spirit being excited from actual destitution, Lord Cochrane endeavoured to obtain possession of the castles of Callao by negotiation, offering the Spanish commandant permission to depart with two-thirds of the property contained in the fort, on condition that the remainder, together with the forts, should be given up to the Chilian squadron. His object was to supply the crews with necessaries, which the Protector continued to withhold. Large sums of money and a vast amount of plate had been deposited in the forts for security. A third of this would have relieved the squadron from their embarrassments. The vessels were in want of stores of every kind, their crews unsupplied with animal food, clothing, or spirits, and their only means of subsistence was upon money obtained from the Spanish fugitives, whom the admiral permitted to ransom themselves by surrendering a third of their property. This appropriation, however, though absolutely necessary, was afterwards trumped up as a charge against him.

As soon as this proposal to the Spanish commandant became known to San Martin, he offered unlimited and unconditional protection, both as to persons and property, on purchase of letters of citizenship! The commandant, therefore, rejected Cochrane's proposal; and the hope of obtaining a sufficient sum for the payment of the seamen and for refitting the ships was at an end.

The Spanish army at Janja, in the beginning of September, spread an alarm in Lima. It appeared that they were determined to attack the capital; and on the 5th of September a proclamation was issued at head-quarters by the self-elected Protector, calling upon the inhabitants of Lima to support his cause.

On the morning of the 10th, Lord Cochrane received a letter from San Martin, informing him that the enemy was approaching Lima, and requesting his lordship to send the army every kind of portable arms then on board the squadron, as well as the marines and all volunteers, he, the Protector, being "determined to bring the enemy to an action, and either conquer or remain buried in the ruins of what was Lima." This high-flown epistle was, however, accompanied by a private one from Monteagudo, containing a request that the boats of the vessels of war might be kept in readiness to embark this Bobabil, and a look-out for him to be placed on the beach of Boca Negra.

Lord Cochrane immediately landed, and pressed forward to San Martin's camp, where, being recognized, a murmur of congratulation was heard. General Las Heras, acting as general-in-chief, saluting the admiral, begged him to endeavour to persuade the Protector to bring the enemy to action. His lordship, on this, rode up to San Martin, and taking him by the hand, in the most earnest manner entreated him to attack the enemy without losing a single moment.

The clamour of the officers at length roused San Martin, who called **for his** horse and mounted. In a moment all was bustle, and the anticipated glow of victory shone in every countenance. The order to **arms was given,** and instantly obeyed by the whole army, amounting to about 12,000 men, including guerillas, all anxious to begin the fight.

At this moment a peasant approached San Martin on horseback, the general with most unparalleled composure lending an attentive ear to his communications as **to where the** enemy was the day before! The admiral, exasperated at so unnecessary a waste of time, bade the peasant "begone," adding, "The general's time is too important to be employed in listening to your fooleries." At this interruption, San Martin frowned on the adm**iral, and turning his** horse, rode up **to** the door of the house, where he alighted and went in.

Lord Cochrane then requested a private conference with San Martin—which was the last time he ever **spoke** to him—and assured him that it was not even then **too** late to attack the enemy, begging and entreating **that** the opportunity might not be lost, and offering himself to lead the cavalry. But to this **he** received the reply, "I alone am responsible for **the** liberties of Peru."

On this the Protector retired to an inner apartment of the house to **enjoy his** customary *siesta*, which was disturbed by **General Las** Heras, who came to receive orders, and recalled to the attention of the **Protector** that the force was still under arms, when San Martin ordered that the troops should receive their rations!

Thus General Cantarac, with 3,200 men, passed to the southward of Lima—within half-musket-shot of the protecting army of Peru, composed of 12,000—entered the castles of Callao with a convoy of cattle and provisions, where he refreshed and rested his troops for six days, and then retired on the 15th, taking with him the *whole of the vast treasure deposited therein by the Limenos*, and leisurely retreating on the north side of Lima.

Had not the Protector prevented the Spanish commandant, La Mar, from accepting Lord Cochrane's offer, a sum of not less than ten millions of dollars would have been added to the resources of the republic.

Having failed in his endeavours to relieve the necessities of the squadron, it was impossible to keep the men any longer from mutiny; for even the officers began to desert to the Protectoral Government.

Some short time previously Lord Cochrane had on board the flag-ship a portion of the money captured at Arica, but as the Chilian Government, trusting to Peru to supply the wants of the squadron, neither sent funds nor provisions, he had been compelled to expend the uncondemned portion of the prize-money belonging to the seamen—a necessity, which, no less than their want of pay or reward, irritated them beyond measure. In addition, he had been obliged to disburse the uncondemned portion of other sums taken on the coast, so that he was now destitute of funds.

On the 2nd of September, Captain Delano, of the *Lautaro*, wrote as follows :—

" The officers as well **as** the men are dissatisfied, having been a long time on the cruise, and at present without any kind of meat or spirits, and without pay, so that they are not able to provide for themselves any longer, though, *until starved*, they have borne it without a murmur. The ship's company have now absolutely refused duty on account of short allowance. The last *charqui* (jerked beef) they got was rotten and full of vermin. They are wholly destitute of clothing, and persist in their resolution not to do duty till beef and spirits are supplied, alleging that they have served their time, with **nothing but** promises so frequently broken that they will no longer be put off.

" The greater portion have gone ashore, so that, under existing circumstances, and with the dissatisfaction of the officers and the remainder of the ship's company, I do not hold myself responsible for any accident **that** may happen to the ship."

On Captain Delano sending his first lieutenant on shore to persuade the men to return to the ship, that officer was **arrested** by order of the Government and put in prison, the Protector's object being to get all the men to desert, **thus** furthering his views towards the appropriation of the squadron.

The *Galvarino* being **in a still** worse condition, the admiral addressed a letter to the ship's company, begging them to continue at their duty till he could devise means for their relief; notwithstanding which, **they persisted in their** demands, **and** expressed their determination not to proceed to sea.

On **the 19th, the** foreign seamen of the flag-ship mutinied in a body, and wrote letters to Captain Crosbie, expressing their determination not to lift an anchor until their claims were settled.

Fortunately for Chili, **an** occurrence took place which averted the threatened evil; this was no other **than the** shipment of large sums of money by the Protector in his yacht *Sacramento*. This vessel had discharged her ballast in order to enable her to stow **the** silver. A merchant vessel in the harbour was also similarly freighted, although the *Lautaro* frigate was lying at the anchorage. This money had been sent to Ancon, ostensibly for the purpose of placing it in safety from any attack by the Spanish forces, but, in fact, to secure it for the further purposes of the Protector. The squadron having thus plain proof that funds were in hand for the payment of the arrears, **the** admiral, in order that the squadron should be no longer defrauded and starved, proceeded to Ancon, and seized the treasure **in the** presence of witnesses. All that professed to belong to private individuals, and also the **whole of** that contained in the Protector's yacht, considering it his private property, was re-spected, although it could have been none other than **plunder** wrested from the Limeños. Besides the silver, there were on board seven sacks of uncoined gold, brought down on account by the Legate San Martin. The admiral immediately made proclamation, that all private individuals, having the customary documents, might receive their property upon application, and considerable **sums** were thus given up. Having returned all the money for which dockets were produced, there remained 285,000 dollars, which was applied to the payment of one year's arrears to every individual **of** the squadron. Relying on the justice of the Chilian Government, Cochrane took no part for himself, but reserved the small surplus that remained for the more pressing exigencies and re-equipment of the squadron.

Accounts of the whole money seized were forwarded to the minister of marine at Valparaiso, as well as vouchers for its disbursement, and in due course, Cochrane received **the** approbation of the Chilian Government for the step he had taken.

San Martin entreated, **in vain,** for the restoration of the treasure, promising the faithful fulfilment of all his former engagements. Letter after letter was sent, begging Lord Cochrane **to** save the credit of the Government, and pretending that the money seized **was all the** Government possessed **for** necessary daily expenses. **To this** Cochrane replied, that had **he** been aware the treasure spared in the *Sacramento* was the property **of Go**vernment, and not that of the **pro**tector, he would **have** seized it also, and retained **it till** the debts due to **the** squadron had been liquidated. Finding his arguments **unavailing, San** Martin had the assurance to address **a proclamation to** the squadron, confirming the distrib**ution** which was going on **by** the admiral's orders, and writing to him that he might employ the money as he thought proper. Subsequently, however, San Martin accused Lord Cochrane to the Chilian Government of seizing the whole of the treasure, that in his yacht included; and asserted, that he had retained the whole belonging to private individuals, all which charges he knew to be most false.

Prior to distributing the money to the squadron, Cochrane requested that a commissary of the Government might be sent on board, to take part in the payment of the crews; but this was not complied with, under the expectation that his lordship would, in case of refusal, place the money in his hands on shore, when it doubtless would have been seized.

Annoyed beyond measure at his having taken such steps to restore order in the squadron, the Protector, on the 26th of September, sent on board the ships of the squadron his two *aides-de-camp*, Paroissien and Spry, with papers for distribution, stating that "the squadron of Chili was under the command of the Protector of Peru, and not under that of the admiral, who was an inferior officer in the service; and that it was consequently the duty of the captains and commanders to obey the orders of the Protector." One of these papers was immediately brought to the admiral by Captain Simpson, of the *Araucano*, to whose ship's company it had been delivered. These emissaries offered, in the name of the Protector, commissions, honours, titles, and estates to all such officers as might accept service under the Government of Peru.

The envoys next proceeded to the *Valdivia*, where similar papers were given to the men, and Captain Cobbett was reminded of the preference which an officer, for his own interests, ought to give to the service of a rich state like Peru. Captain Cobbett pertinently asked Spry whether, if his disobedience to the admiral subjected him to a court-martial, the Protector's authority would ensure him an acquittal?

Unfortunately for the emissaries, Captain Crosbie was on board the *Valdivia* at this time, and on learning their errand, he pushed off to the flag-ship with the intelligence. Observing this movement, the envoys followed him, judging it more prudent to visit Lord Cochrane voluntarily than to risk being compelled. It is needless to say that the offers of the emissaries made no impression upon the admiral, except to confirm him in his resistance to San Martin's pretensions; and that they retired, not a little pleased at having escaped with liberty.

This, and other efforts, however, proved in the end but too successful; nearly all the officers abandoning the Chilian service, together with the whole of the foreign seamen, who were either driven by want, or allured by promises of a year's additional pay, to quit the ships, so that the squadron was half unmanned.

It was now Lord Cochrane's turn to mutiny. An order was sent him to proceed to Chili; but, as the Protector had openly thrown off his allegiance to that state, he felt he had no right to interfere with the Chilian squadron. He was also instigated to the act by the circumstance that the Spanish frigates remained at large, which rendered **the** object of his mission incomplete.

Before going in quest of the latter, it was **essential** to repair and provision the ships, none of which purposes could be effected in Peru, the Protector not only having refused supplies, but having also issued orders on the coast to withhold necessaries of all kinds, even to wood and water. From want of stores, none of the ships, the *Valdivia* not excepted, were fit for sea; and, to complete her inefficiency, the Protector refused to give up the anchors which had been cut away from her bows at the time **of her** capture.

Many of the officers had gone over to the service of Peru, and the foreign seamen had been kept on shore in such numbers, that there were not sufficient left to perform the duties of navigating. **The admiral** therefore resolved on sending part of the squadron to Chili, and with the remainder proceed to Guayaquil, to repair and refit.

The ships reached Guayaquil on the 18th of October, and were well received by the authorities. The work of refitting occupied six weeks, the expenses, which were **heavy, being** defrayed out of **the** uncondemned **prize-money; and** to inspire the seamen with the expectation that the Chilian Government would reimburse them for their liberality, Lord Cochrane added money of his own, on which **they** willingly consented to the appropriation of that due to the squadron.

Before quitting the anchorage, Lord Cochrane was

honoured with a public address, to which he replied in a long letter, urging the patriots to persevere in the good cause.

The necessity for pursuing the enemy's frigates, precluded more than a temporary repair of the ships. Nothing **had been** done to remedy the leak in the hull **of the** *O'Higgins*, as, from the rotten state of her masts, it would have been unsafe to heave her down, so that when she got in a sea-way she made six feet of water a day. The patched-up ships quitted Guayaquil on the 3rd **of** December, and coasted along the shore. On the 11th they reached Cocos Island, where Lord Cochrane captured an English pirate, and on the following day a felucca, the crew of which **had** deserted from Callao. From the **crew** of the latter Cochrane learned that, after his departure, San Martin had refused to fulfil the promises by which he had induced the foreign seamen to leave the Chilian squadron, and that they had consequently been compelled to seek their own living. As these men, though clearly pirates, had committed no depredations, Lord **Cochrane** suffered them to escape.

On the 14th the squadron made the coast **of** Mexico, **and** on the 19th the *O'Higgins* anchored in Fonseca Bay with five feet of water in the hold, the chain pumps **being so** worn as to be useless. There being no artificers **on** board to. repair the pumps, **the ship** was only kept afloat by the greatest exertions, and Lord Cochrane's manual skill in smith's work was called into requisition to put the pumps in order.

After three days' constant baling at the hatchways, two pumps were obtained from the *Valdivia*; but these proving too short, Cochrane ordered holes to be cut through the ship's sides, on a level with the berth-deck, and thus managed to keep the ship clear till the old pumps could be repaired. Nearly all the ammunition was spoiled, and in order to preserve the dry provisions, they were stowed in the hammock-nettings.

A party of men from the other ships having been transferred to the flag-ship to assist at the pumps, the squadron quitted Fonseca Bay on the 28th, and on the 6th of January, 1822, arrived at Tehuantepec.

On the 29th they anchored at Acapulco, at which place they found the *Araucano* and *Mercedes*, the latter having been sent on to gain intelligence of the Spanish frigates. The Governor treated Cochrane's squadron with civility, though not without fears that an attempt would be made to seize some Spanish merchantmen at anchor in the harbour. · The fort was consequently manned by a strong garrison, and other preparations made in case of hostile demonstration. The fear was groundless, but it owed its origin to false reports spread along the coast, to the effect that Lord Cochrane had taken illegal possession of the Chilian navy, and plundered vessels belonging to Peru, and that he was then on a piratical cruise, intending to ravage the coast of Mexico.

On the 2nd of February, a vessel arrived at Acapulco, and reported the Spanish frigates to the southward, whither, notwithstanding the unseaworthy state of the ships, Cochrane determined to proceed in search of them.

Despatching the *Independencia* and *Araucano* to California to purchase provisions, with instructions to follow the other ships to Guayaquil, the *O'Higgins* and consort **ran** down the coast, and when off Tehuantepec, encountered a gale which threatened their destruction. A sea struck the *Valdivia* and drove in the timbers on her port side, so that she was only saved from sinking by passing a sail over the damaged part.

On the 5th of March they anchored in the bay of Tacames, and learned that the Spanish frigates had some time before left for Guayaquil. On receipt of this intelligence they pursued their voyage, and on the 13th anchored off Guayaquil, where they found one of the objects of their search, the *Venganza*.

Their reception was not so cordial as on the previous occasion, two agents of San Martin having arrived there in the mean while, who, **by** promises, had gained over the government to the Protector's interests. Some attempts were made to annoy Lord Cochrane; but as, upon their manifestation, he laid the flag-ship alongside the *Venganza*, civility was enforced. The *Prueba* and *Venganza*, being short of provisions, had been compelled, by his close pursuit, to put into Guayaquil; but the *Prueba* had again left for Callao before Cochrane's arrival. Lord Cochrane then sent Captain Crosbie on board the *Venganza* to take possession of her, for Chili **and** Peru jointly.

His orders were to hoist the flag of Chili at the peak of the *Venganza*, conjointly with that of Peru.

This act gave great umbrage to the Guayaquil Government. Gunboats were manned, breastworks erected, and guns brought to the river-side; the Spanish sailors, who just before had sold their ship, from the dread of having to fight, being extremely active in these hostile demonstrations.

Upon this, the *Valdivia* was ordered to drop down with the flood tide in the direction of the gunboats which were filled with Spanish officers and seamen; upon which these heroes ran the boats ashore and scampered off, not stopping till they had gained the walls of the city.

The Junta, finding their warlike demonstration treated with contempt, remonstrated with Cochrane for taking possession of the *Venganza*, but without effect. He, however, proposed such terms as were most likely to be accepted and ratified by them. He proposed that the *Venganza* should remain, as belonging to the Government of Guayaquil, and hoist her flag, which should be duly saluted, upon condition that Guayaquil gave a bond to the Chilian squadron of 40,000 dollars that the *Venganza* should not be delivered to any government till those of Chili and Peru had decided on what they esteemed most just. The Government of Guayaquil was also bound to destroy the *Venganza* rather than consent to her serving any other state in the mean while.

This agreement having been signed, the Government of Guayaquil addressed a letter to Lord Cochrane, acknowledging the important services he had conferred on the States of South America, and assuring him that Guayaquil would always be the first to honour his name and the last **to** forget his unparalleled achievements. Alas **for** their honesty! no sooner had he sailed **from the** port, than the *Venganza* was given up to the agent of Peru, but the 40,000 dollars **were never paid.**

On the 27th March they left the Guayaquil river, and on the 29th fell in with Captain Simpson, of the *Araucano*, whose crew had mutinied and taken the ship from him. On the 12th of April they touched at Guambucho **for** the purpose of watering, when, to their surprise, the Alcalde produced a written order from San Martin, telling him that if any vessel of war **belonging** to Chili touched there, he was to deny assistance of every **kind;** but to this order no attention was paid.

The ships having taken **on** board whatever was required, and having repaired the *Valdivia*, sailed, on the 16th, for Callao. They reached their port on **the** 25th of April, when Cochrane found the other Spanish vessel, the *Prueba*, under Peruvian colours, **and** commanded by the senior Chilian captain, who had **abandoned his** squadron. The *Prueba* was immediately **hauled close** under the batteries, with guns housed, and ports closed, and so crammed with troops that three died in **one** night from suffocation. These steps had been taken to prevent her from sharing **the** fate of the *Esmeralda*. **To** calm their fears, **Cochrane** wrote to the **Government that** he had no intention of taking her, otherwise he would have done so at midday, in spite of all their precautions.

Lima was at this time in an extraordinary state, there being no less than five different Peruvian flags flying in the bay and on the batteries. The Protector had issued a decree ordering that all Spaniards who might quit the place should previously surrender half their property to the public treasury, or the whole should be confiscated, and the owners exiled. In the midst of this national degradation, the Protector had assumed the style of a Sovereign Prince, and had established an order of nobility, under the title of " The Institute of the Sun," the insignia being a golden sun suspended from a white ribbon, the Chilian officers who had abandoned the squadron coming in for a full share as the reward of their compliance.

Those who had condemned Lord Cochrane's conduct in taking possession of the money at Ancon, now admitted that he had adopted the only possible step to preserve the squadron of Chili. The officers of the liberating army told him deplorable stories of the state of affairs; and the regiment of Numantia, which had deserted from the Spaniards soon after the capture of the *Esmeralda*, sent an officer with a message, asking him to receive them on board, and convey them to Colombia, to which province they belonged.

Cochrane's appearance in the port of Callao caused serious, though, as far as he was concerned, unnecessary alarm to the Government. He, however, sent in a fresh demand on behalf of the squadron, and animadverted strongly on the events which had taken place at Guayaquil. Without replying to this by letter, Monteagudo came off to the *O'Higgins*, lamenting that the admiral should have resorted to such intemperate expressions, as the Protector, before its receipt, had written him a private letter begging **for** an interview; but that on the receipt of his note he became so indignant as to place his health in danger. Monteagudo further assured his lordship that in that letter he had made him the offer of a large estate, and the decoration of the "Sun" set in diamonds, if he would consent to command the united navies of Chili and Peru, in a contemplated expedition to capture the Philippine Islands, by which he would make an immense fortune. This disgraceful overture was treated with the contempt it merited.

Finding he could make no impression, and not liking the scowl on the countenances of those on board, the minister retired, accompanied by his military escort.

RETURN TO VALPARAISO.
[1822.]

In consequence of Lord Cochrane's refusal to comply with the wishes of the Protector, Colonel Paroissien and another were despatched to Chili with a long string **of the** most preposterous accusations, in which he was accused of committing every species of crime, from piracy **to** petty robbery, and calling on the Chilian Government to visit him with the severest punishment.

On the 8th of May, **the** schooner *Montezuma*, which had been lent **to** General **San** Martin by the Chilian Government, entered Callao under Peruvian colours. **This** insolence was too great for the admi-

ral's forbearance. He compelled her to anchor,
though not before firing upon her, then turned all
the officers ashore, and took possession of her. The
Protectoral authorities, by way of reprisal, detained a
boat belonging to the flag-ship, and imprisoned the
men. Rightly calculating, however, the consequences
of such a step, they soon set the crew at liberty, and
the boat was, on the same night, permitted to return
to the ship.

Heartily sick and tired of this contention, Lord
Cochrane took his final leave of Callao, and made
sail for Valparaiso, where he arrived the middle of
June, after an absence of a year and nine months,
during which the objects of the expedition had been
fully accomplished.

Lord Cochrane found on reaching Valparaiso, that
San Martin's agents had presented the Protector's
accusations against him to the Government at Santiago, though without effect, as Cochrane had taken care
to keep the authorities apprised of everything which
had transpired, and had exercised the most scrupulous
care in furnishing accounts of moneys and stores
taken from the Spaniards.

He announced his return, and briefly reported the
results of the expedition, enumerating his captures
and destruction, of which the following is a summary:—
Prueba, 50 guns ; *Esmeralda*, 44 ; *Venganza*, 44 ; *Resolution*, 34 ; *Sebastiana*, 34 ; *Pesuela*, 18 ; *Potrillo*, 16 ;
Prosperina, 14 ; *Araucana* ; seventeen gunboats ; the
armed ships *Aguila* and *Begonia* ; the block ships at
Callao ; and many merchantmen.

The inhabitants of Valparaiso greeted him with every manifestation of delight, nearly every house in the place being decorated with the patriot flag, whilst other demonstrations of national joy showed the importance **which the** Chilian people attached to the services which had been achieved, in spite of the obstacles they well knew had been opposed.

On the 4th of June, he received letters of thanks from the Minister of Marine, couched in the most gratifying terms; and in addition to this acknowledgment of the services of the squadron, a decree was issued commanding a medal to be struck in commemoration thereof.

San Martin, on the occupation of Lima, had, as before observed, caused a medal to be struck, claiming the success of the expedition for the army, which had done little or nothing towards it—leaving out **all** mention of the services **of** the squadron; the Chilian Government, on the other hand, gave the credit to the squadron—and omitted all mention of the army, which remained under the standard of the Protector.

The squadron had been almost self-supporting, for Lord **Cochrane** had raised a considerable revenue, for which he **had** scrupulously accounted, by granting licenses to the commanders and supercargoes of British vessels trading with Spanish ports. The duties thus collected were for the most part in contraband of war, while the compromise was received as a boon by the British merchants, and highly approved of by the British naval authorities.

San Martin, however, and others interested in a

line of policy which in its prosecution was inimical to
the true interests of Chili, afterwards charged these
proceedings against Cochrane as "acts of piracy."
But the Chilian Government was well satisfied with
all the steps he had taken for provisioning and maintaining the squadron, as well as with the seizure and
disposal of the public money at Ancon.

As he had not, however, received any official acknowledgment of the accounts of the squadron, beyond
the general expression of entire satisfaction on the
part of the Government, he applied to the Minister
of Marine for a more minute investigation into their
contents, as, from the charges made against him by
San Martin, he was desirous that the most rigid inquiry should be forthwith instituted. On the 14th of
June, the Minister replied,—

"The accounts of moneys applied by your excellency in the necessary requirements of the vessels of
war under your command, which you conveyed to me
in your two notes of the 25th of May last, have been
passed to the office of the Accountant-General, for
the purpose indicated by your excellency."

Aware of the dilatory habits of the departments of
state, he did not deem this satisfactory; and being
engaged in preparing a refutation of San Martin's charges, his lordship again urged on the
minister to investigate the accounts without further
delay, when, on the 19th of June, he acknowledged
the specific items; at the same time declaring his
high consideration for the manner in which he had
made the flag of Chili respected in the Pacific.

This was satisfactory so far; but, notwithstanding this full acquittal, the Government of Chili refrained from conferring either **upon himself or** the squadron the smallest pecuniary recompense, or returning the prize-money due to the officers and seamen, part of **which the** ministry had appropriated. On further pressing these claims year after year subsequent to his departure from Chili, Lord Cochrane was informed, sixteen years afterwards, that his accounts required explanation.

His refutation of San Martin's accusations **was** drawn up in the most minute manner, replying to every charge *seriatim*, and bringing to light a multitude of nefarious practices on the part of the Protector's Government which had been previously kept back.

The remaining **portions** of Lord Cochrane's services in Chili were of a political and desultory character. It was not surprising that in a country like Chili and Peru, then in a transition stage, and in which every ambitious man was seeking his own ends, careless who suffered, a stranger and foreigner should **have** been made the butt for the shafts of malice and detraction **by** one party, and worshipped as an idol by another. **Cochrane** boldly faced his enemies, and resisted falsehood **in** every shape. Had he chosen to play false by the **Chilian** Government, he might have enriched himself to **any** extent. General San Martin **wanted** only such an **ally in order** to convert Peru into a permanent empire, **and establish** himself as its king. He tempted and **tried** him in every possible way. But cajolery and menaces, open and covert opposition, failed alike to move him. Cochrane was true as steel. He had sworn to serve the republic of Chili, and he did so, fearlessly and honestly.

But who that has had any experience of infant states or republics, expects that virtue like Cochrane's was rewarded? In all such communities, San Martins and Zentenos are sure to abound; and although, in the long run, integrity may be duly appreciated, intrigue and deceit will pay best for the time.

There is no knowing to what lengths the persecuting spirit of Cochrane's enemies would have carried them, had not another struggling state solicited his assistance, and so removed him out of the way of their machinations. He listened to Brazilian overtures, and quitted the country after the most astonishing career of success that ever graced a modern warrior, a poor man—rudely and unjustly dispossessed of an estate conferred upon him as a reward for his services—his name a term of reproach among unprincipled foes, and robbed of the pecuniary compensation which had been sacredly promised. Had he been like those about him—avaricious and unscrupulous—this would not have been.

The storming of Valdivia, and cutting out of the *Esmeralda*, were feats of which Nelson would have been proud. The first is to be likened only to the capture of Banda by Sir Christopher Cole, the second to the recapture of the *Hermione* by Sir Edward Hamilton—actions which are admitted on all hands to be naval *chefs d'œuvre*.

Much was owing to **his** *prestige;* but more to his unsurpassed firmness **and** good judgment. With materials of a questionable **character, he** effected services which **have never** been outdone by disciplined troops **and ships'** companies.

His name, however, is now cherished in the country **which** he **was** so mainly instrumental in liberating from the galling Spanish yoke, as a household **word; and,** for many ages to come, will be venerated as a type of unflinching bravery and unexampled skill and integrity.

The seizure **of public money** at Ancon, one **of** the greatest offences alleged against him, was not only an authorized proceeding, but an imperative one; it was the only **means he** could command likely to preserve the squadron **under his** protection, from the rapacity and **villany of San** Martin. He passed through this phase of **his** adventurous life with honour; but we shall seek **in** vain for his reward.

SERVICES IN BRAZIL.
[1823.]

The **new struggle,** in which Lord Cochrane was called upon to **take a** prominent and, as it proved, vital part, was the attempt to free Brazil from Portuguese domination. **On** the expulsion of the royal family of Portugal by the **French army, in** 1808, Don John VI., it will be remembered, proceeded to Rio de Janeiro, and established there his seat of government; but in **1821** the king returned to Lisbon, leaving

his son and heir apparent, Don Pedro, as regent of
the Portuguese dominions in South America.

The example of Chili and Peru, probably, had
something to do with the events which took place at
Rio.   There was a Brazilian party desirous of throwing off the Portuguese yoke, as well as a royalist
party anxious for its continuance; and as Don Pedro
was suspected of siding with the Brazilian section,
the Cortes issued instructions to the municipal authorities to disregard the authority of the regent, and to
attend only to such directions as they should receive
direct from the Cortes. Don Pedro was thus virtually deposed; and an endeavour made to govern an
immense territory, some thousands of miles distant
from the parent country, without any regal representative.   The Cortes, sitting at Lisbon, supposed that
their edicts would be sufficient to reach and control
a tract of country stretching from the River Plate to
the Amazon. The consequence of this absurdity was
an open rupture. This was brought about by an
attempt on the part of the Cortes to annihilate the
nationality of the Brazilians altogether, by uniting
the native with the Portuguese army; and ended in
the declaration of their independence.

Don Pedro was at the same time declared Emperor;
but he refused to give his consent to the proceeding,
and made preparations for quitting the country. His
intention was, however, frustrated.   The popular
leaders held a meeting at midnight, and agreed to an
address intimating that his departure would be the
signal for throwing off all allegiance to Portugal, and

forming a republic; and Pedro was at length, induced to accept the title from the Brazilian representatives, of "Perpetual Protector and Defender of Brazil."

The Cortes endeavoured to crush this movement by main force. Troops and ships of war were despatched to compel obedience; and by resorting to these means cut off every hope of reconciliation. Don Pedro, naturally desirous to retain the country for the crown, to which he was heir apparent, instead of permitting it to fall to pieces as a republic, used every means in his power to reconcile the Cortes to the step he had felt compelled to take. But finding all his attempts vain, he suffered himself to be led a step further, and to accept the title of "Constitutional Emperor of Brazil."

It was now necessary to be prepared to resist force by force. Portugal was about to send ships and troops to overcome the so-called rebellion; and Pedro, in self-defence, collected the best squadron and troops he was able, and called Lord Cochrane to assist him by taking command of the former. Six months after the declaration of independence, Lord Cochrane, together with a number of valuable officers and seamen, several of the former holding commissions in the British navy, who had volunteered to accompany him, arrived at Rio de Janeiro.

The imperial invitation to join the Brazilian service, had been conveyed through the consul of Buenos Ayres, at the request of Bonifacia de Andrada, prime minister, and gave a distinct promise that Lord Cochrane should receive a full equivalent for the Chilian appointment which he then held.

On his arrival at Rio, however, on the 13th of March, attempts were made to put him off with an inferior rank and lower rate of pay, which he, of course, resisted.

The point was eventually settled in his favour, and Lord Cochrane became ,"First Admiral and Commander-in-chief of the Brazilian squadron," with a salary of 11,520 milreis per annum, at sea or on shore, and 5,720 milreis table-money, when embarked; and although attempts were subsequently made to render his position contingent upon the duration of hostilities, the original engagement was never really superseded.

The squadron of which he was appointed first admiral, consisted of the *Pedro Primeiro*, dignified as a 74-gun ship, but in fact a 64, on two decks,—a fine roomy ship, in reasonably good condition, victualled and stored for four months.

Another was the *Maria da Gloria*, of 32 guns, 24-pounder carronades and short 18-pounders, built in North America for the Chilian republic, who failing to pay the price demanded, the builders sold her to the Brazilians.

The *Piranga* was a fine frigate armed with long 24-pounders. Lord Cochrane hoisted his flag in the *Pedro Primeiro*, his old flag-captain Crosbie accompanying him. The *Piranga* was commanded by Captain Jowett, and the *Maria da Gloria* by a French officer, Captain Beaurepaire. Two or three other vessels were subsequently added.

With the above-mentioned three ships, Lord Cochrane sailed from Rio on the 4th April. It is hardly necessary to say that the crews of the men-of-war were of a very inferior description, composed of men of all **nations** and colours, for they were very badly **paid** when paid at all.

Cochrane had 130 black marines, just emancipated from slavery, on board his flagship, and 160 British and American seamen upon whom he could alone place any dependence.

The Portuguese squadron with which he had to contend comprised one line-of-battle-ship, five frigates, five corvettes, a brig, and schooner, and this force Cochrane discovered, on his arrival off the coast of Bahia, drawn up in line ready to receive him. The odds against him were **too great to** warrant his bringing on a regular action ; **but he** manœuvred so as to cut off the four rearmost ships, and would, no doubt, have captured some of them ; but after effecting the evolution of breaking the line, he found himself *alone !* The *Pedro* **had no** one to share her glory, or, what might have **been of** greater importance, render assistance. Signals **were** hoisted for them to come down, but the flags might as **well** have remained in the signal-lockers. The *Pedro* continued for a time blazing away with evident effect **at the** frigates separated from the main body, when suddenly **the** guns ceased firing. The cause of the cessation **was** quickly inquired into, when it was found that two Portuguese seamen, who had been stationed to hand **up** powder, had withheld the supply, and **made** prisoners of the powder-boys.

Thus alone and among traitors, Cochrane felt that he ought not to persist in following up the enemy, but rather to consult his own safety, and therefore hauled to the wind, and made sail to rejoin his recreant consorts. He had in fact put to sea with ships manned by men so disaffected that their commanders could not induce them to obey orders, and had some difficulty in preventing them from taking the ships into Bahia. The cartridges were so dangerous to use, owing to their casing, that the admiral was obliged to cut up old flags to render them serviceable, and the guns were without locks. The sails were rotten; every moderate breeze of wind caused heavy work for the sail-maker; in fact, no man ever had worse materials to work with. The discipline was upon a par with everything else. The marines knew nothing of the gun exercise, and very little of the use of small arms, yet had so lofty an opinion of their importance, that they considered it beneath their dignity to wash the decks.

Leaving the *Piranga* and another ship to blockade Bahia, Cochrane, taking with him the *Maria da Gloria* and the worst of the ships, proceeded to Moro San Paulo where he left the least efficient vessels to be converted into fire-ships, taking the best of the men into his own ship. He then resumed the blockade of Bahia, and succeeded in cutting off all their supplies.

On the 26th of May the Portuguese admiral again made his appearance, but although his force was so superior, evinced no desire to bring on an action.

Cochrane, knowing by experience the materials he had to work with, did not feel justified in taking the initiative, and after **some few** menaces **on** the part of the Portuguese admiral the squadron anchored in the harbour **of** Bahia on the 2nd of June. This was what **Cochrane** wanted. His fire-ships **and an** explosion-vessel had been prepared, and he hoped soon **to witness** a repetition of the Aix Roads affair. He was, however, rather startled at hearing that the fire-ships preparing at Moro San Paulo were about to be attacked by the Portuguese; but this design, if it was ever seriously intended, was soon abandoned. The next **report** was that the Portuguese would not wait to be burnt at Bahia, but that they would evacuate the port.

In the mean while, Cochrane determined to make a night reconnoissance **with** the flag-ship alone; and, accordingly, on the **12th** June, having previously taken the bearings **of the** high lands at the entrance to the river, he stood in shortly after dusk, and taking the top of the flood-tide, arrived within hail of the outermost ship. The wind failing, and the ebb-tide beginning to make, Cochrane was unable to do as much **as he** wished. He threaded the outermost ships, and **was** repeatedly hailed, but answering "an English vessel" **he** for the time lulled suspicion. Having observed enough to convince him that there would be no difficulty in destroying the Portuguese ships, huddled together **as they** were, he suffered the *Pedro* to drop down with the tide, checking her occasionally with a stream anchor out abaft, and recrossed **the** bar in safety.

Next day the fact of his visit became known in Bahia, and gave rise to a general panic. The admiral on the 29th, learnt that the consequent intention was to embark the troops on board the squadron, and proceed to Maranham, thereby abandoning the city to the Brazilians.

It is as well to state, in this place, that all the southern provinces had already declared for the emperor; but the northern districts, including Bahia, Maranham, and Parà, were still occupied by Portuguese troops. If, therefore, this step were taken, Maranham and Parà would alone remain in the direct interest of the Cortes.

This proceeding was actually taken. On the 2nd July the whole Portuguese force, naval and military, quitted the river and stood out to sea, accompanied by sixty or seventy armed transports and merchant ships, in which a great number of Portuguese families with their property had embarked. The ships of war numbered thirteen sail; and as Cochrane, at the time, had no other force beside his own ship and the *Maria da Gloria*, he was not in a position to make a regular attack; but resolved, nevertheless, to harass their rear. In order to prevent the merchant ships from leaving the coast of Brazil, Cochrane resorted to the plan of boarding them, and cutting away their main and mizen masts, so that they should only be able to sail before the wind.

On the 3rd, the admiral was joined by the *Carolina, Nitherohy,* and *Colonel Allen,* and leaving this reinforcement to deal with the merchant ships, Cochrane in the *Pedro* followed the war-ships. This temerity on his part greatly annoyed the Portuguese squadron; and, on the 4th, they angrily turned round upon their pursuer, and endeavoured to hem her in with the land. But Cochrane was too good a seaman, and his ship too well handled for his less accomplished foes. He succeeded in weathering the Portuguese admiral, and the latter, finding himself foiled, gave up the pursuit and resumed his course, after wasting several broadsides. The *Pedro Primeiro* did the same—that is, Cochrane resumed his chase of the thirteen **war** ships; and, moreover, the same night after dark, made a dash in among them, firing both broadsides. He then boarded some of the smaller ships, cut away their topmasts, disabled their rigging, threw their arms overboard, and compelled **the** officers to give their parole not to serve **against** Brazil until regularly exchanged.

On the night of the 5th the *Gran Para*, a Russian transport, was boarded and disabled in a similar manner. Shortly afterwards six large ships detached themselves from the convoy, and Cochrane being desirous **to** know the reason, made sail after them. Next morning he closed with the convoy, and singling out a large frigate-built ship filled with troops, opened fire upon her until she brought to.

The stranger was **a** large transport containing a detachment, a part **of** several thousand troops bound to Maranham. Lieutenant Grenfell, who boarded the transport, took possession of the private signals and instructions given by the Portuguese admiral, by

which Lord Cochrane learnt that the transports were
bound to Maranham; and, as it was important to prevent these troops from reaching their destination, he
ordered their main and mizen masts to be cut away,
arms and ammunition to be thrown overboard, took
possession of the regimental flags, and compelled the
officers to give their parole not to serve against
Brazil. The remaining five transports were treated
in the same way, for it would have been madness to
have attempted to make so many men prisoners.

The *Bahia*, Captain Haydon, shortly afterwards
hove in sight, upon which the admiral ordered four of
the troop-ships to be seized, and taken to Pernambuco.
The *Pedro* then resumed her chase of the Portuguese
squadron, and continued to follow them to 5 degrees
north latitude; when having split the mainsail in
tacking, Lord Cochrane considered it prudent to
look to his own safety. On the 16th at 3 A.M.,
however, he made one of his usual nocturnal visits,
and poured a parting broadside at half-musket shot
distance, into one of their frigates with evident effect.

Having thus chased the Portuguese squadron off
the coast, Lord Cochrane determined to proceed at
once to Maranham, where he arrived on the 26th.
The Portuguese admiral's instructions had made him
acquainted with the fact that reinforcements would be
expected at that port; and Cochrane therefore hoisted
Portuguese colours. The authorities, completely
thrown off their guard by this *ruse*, sent off the *Don
Miguel*, a brig of war, to the *Pedro Primeiro*, with
despatches and congratulations upon the safe arrival

of the presumed friend, and the deceit was not discovered until Captain Garcaõ, the Portuguese commander, stood on **the** deck of Lord Cochrane's flag-
ship, and had delivered his message and letters.
The latter put Lord Cochrane in possession of the
plans and intentions of the enemy, and acquainted
him with the fact that some reinforcements had
already arrived. Garcaõ's surprise and chagrin may
be coneeived at finding himself trapped, but Lord
Cochrane offered to release him upon condition that
he would be the bearer of a sealed despatch to the
governor and junta of the city. Before leaving, Lord
Cochrane duly impressed upon the mind of the
Portuguese commander, that the flag-ship was the
precursor of a large squadron; and **that** a fleet **of**
transports filled with troops which the flag-ship had
outsailed were **in the** offing, and would in a short
time land an army in **the** town. The Portuguese
captain was fully convinced of the truth of this well-
told and perfectly excusable fable; and was therefore
ready to confirm the statements similar to the above
which were embodied in Cochrane's sealed letter.

The effect was astounding. Already **news had**
reached of **the** evacuation of Bahia, and, considering
all lost, the Portuguese faction made conditional
proposals of capitulation. But as conditional proposals would not suffice, they were returned; and the
Pedro *Primeiro* entered the narrow river Maranhao,
which had never before been navigated by a line-of-
battle ship, and anchored off the fort.

The next **day,** 27th July, the junta, accompanied by

the bishop, arrived on board Lord Cochrane's ship, and gave in their unconditional adhesion to the Brazilian empire. The hesitation at first manifested was removed by a shot which Cochrane ordered to be fired over the town, after which all his demands were complied with, and the city, forts, and island, were all surrendered. Lieutenant Grenfell then landed, took possession of the fort, and substituted Brazilian for Portuguese colours. A party of marines also landed in the town for the preservation of order.

"Thus," wrote Lord Cochrane, "without military force or bloodshed, was a second great province secured to the empire, neither result being anticipated, nor even contemplated, in the orders communicated to me, which were to blockade the Portuguese in Bahia, and capture or destroy all ships met with ; anything beyond this not having entered the imagination of the government."

Cochrane immediately issued instructions to the civil authorities to make the necessary proclamations of independence, and published, as the First Admiral of Brazil, an address to the inhabitants of Maranham.

Liberty was with seeming liberality accorded to the Portuguese garrison to remain or leave as they pleased, with the honours of war, and the officers and men belonging to the vessels taken possession of were offered the option of entering the service of Pedro I., or of leaving with the garrison.

The declaration of independence was accordingly made on the 28th July, amidst the acclamations of the populace generally—those dissenting taking care to absent themselves from the ceremony. Naturally **so-**licitous to get the **Po**rtuguese troops away before the ruse was found out, Cochrane hastened their embarkation by providing **ships** for their reception. His instructions succeeded, **and** some of the troops embarked; **but the 1st** August having arrived, and none of the **pr**omised Braziliau transports of **troops,** the deception began to be suspected. Their unwillingness to depart was, however, quickened by the knowledge that the flag-ship's guns were pointed at the transports, which by this time were nearly full of troops, and by the assurance that unless the terms of the treaty were instantly fulfilled, they would be sunk. Captain Crosbie **at** the same time landed with a party of men and disarmed some troublesome militia. The transports eventually **put to sea** on the **20th.**

A large amount of government and public property was seized in conformity with the proclamation; and the brig-of-war *Don Miguel,* **a** schooner, and eight gun-boats were added to the Brazilian navy. The merchant vessels appropriated to the conveyance of the **garrison** to Lisbon were also **prizes,** but the captors were never paid for them.

Lord Cochrane then [reported the result of his almost incredible success to the Minister of Marine.

Parà was now the only province under the authority of Portugal, and before the *prestige* arising from his acquisition of Maranham faded away, he commissioned the *Don Miguel* under a new name of *Maranhao,* gave the command of her to Lieutenant Grenfell with the rank of captain, and despatched him to Parà with a summons to the junta and garrison to surrender. Grenfell was authorized to keep up the threat of the large reinforcements which were forthcoming, and was directed, if possible, to obtain possession of a new frigate just launched at that place intended for the service of Portugal.

In the mean time, the First Admiral had some difficulty to restrain the junta in order, which he had restored to power. They instituted a claim to the Portuguese property seized, demanding that it should be placed at their disposal. This demand was, however, resisted; but, as it was repeated, Cochrane ordered the property in dispute to be placed aboard two of the captured vessels, and taken to Rio for adjudication. But as this course would upon reconsideration have weakened his force, already too much reduced by manning the *Maranhao*, he directed the whole to be converted into money, and the amount remitted to the imperial government. The aggregate amount was several millions of dollars, all of which by a decree of the 11th December, 1822, promulgated for the express purpose of inducing foreign seamen to volunteer, as a matter of right belonged to the captors; but the stipulation, as the sequel shows, was ruthlessly disregarded.

Captain Grenfell's mission was eminently successful. The new frigate was in his possession, together with another vessel of war; and he also captured several merchant-vessels which he sent to Rio. He had carried out his instructions admirably. The phantom transports had been most effective; and

Parà also was added to the empire. The only blood drawn was from Grenfell himself, **who** was stabbed by a cowardly assassin **on** the discovery of the deceit which had been **practised**.

Lord **Cochrane now** thought it time to return to **Rio de Janeiro ;** but not wishing to allow the junta of **Maranham to** know his destination, he gave out that he should leave on the 9th September for Parà. **He** was, however, delayed by the misgovernment of the junta till the 20th, when he finally **left** the river.

HIS RETURN.
[1823 -5.]

The *Pedro Primeiro*, after her extraordinarily eventful cruise, **arrived at** Rio de Janeiro on the 9th November, after **an absence of six** months. **The** news of **Cochrane's wonderful** successes had preceded him, and honours **had been awarded** and complimentary addresses without end composed on the occasion. He was created Marquis **of** Maranham. On the arrival of the ship the emperor went on board to welcome **the** "First Admiral," **and his** every act received **imperial** approval. But a change **had** come over the government, and Lord Cochrane found himself under **the** direction of the party which, from the outset, had been most hostile to his appointment. Instead, therefore, **of** reaping **the rewards** and obtaining the prize-money **guaranteed** by royal proclamation, he found every opposition thrown in his path.

The proportion of the prize property captured at Maranham due to the flag-ship alone was £121,463 sterling, **exclusive** of the captures made by the squadron generally. The admiral requested that this might be paid. The emperor gave directions that his request should **be** complied with; but the **prize** tribunal appointed, consisting of thirteen Portuguese, delayed and resisted the appeal. Overtures were made to **Cochrane,** that if he would forego the claims of those under his command, his personal share would be paid. That they failed may be readily conceived. The squadron up to that time had received no pay, and the payment of three months' wages was offered to them. This was refused. And now his enemies attempted to subvert his authority, and trumped up every sort of false accusation their fertile imagination could conceive. The prize tribunal came to the determination to deprive the captors of their lawful due, by declaring the ships of war *droits* to the crown, thereby ignoring the proclamation of the 22nd December.

The Marquis of Maranham was made a privy councillor; but what availed that distinction, while his officers and men were penniless? Disgusted and disheartened by the faithless ingrates whom he had only too well served, he was at length driven, in March, 1824, to tender his resignation. His offer was met by explanations, promises, and evasions, but no money.

On the 24th May, Captain Grenfell arrived in the new frigate, which he had so cleverly captured at Parà, and had named the *Imperatrice.* In place of being thanked, **a** sum of 40,000 dollars, which he **had on** board, was forcibly taken out of the ship by the government during his absence, while reporting his arrival to Lord Cochrane. Grenfell was also ordered to be placed in **arrest,** and the First Admiral directed to do **the work** of a provost-marshal **by** executing **the warrant;** which he, of course, indignantly **refused** to undertake. The offence alleged against **this** meritorious officer, who subsequently became an admiral in the service,* arose out of his firmness in repressing some seditious proceedings on the part of the Portuguese faction at Parà. Grenfell, however, evaded his persecutors.

Pedro **was** powerless, though well disposed. He was a **mere tool** in the hands of the reigning faction; and his decrees were waste paper. Insult of every description was showered upon Cochrane, notwithstanding the **countenance** and support given him by the emperor. **An attempt** was even **made to search the flag-ship for certain treasure,** which Lord Cochrane was falsely reported to **have** concealed on board.

At length, the services of the squadron were again in request to quell disturbances which had broken out at Pernambuco. But the men could not be asked to lift **an anchor** while their arrears were unpaid. The emperor **at this** juncture offered 200,000 milreis in paper currency, which was about a tenth part of the prize-money **due. The** admiral finding he could get **no** more, consented **to** accept this instalment; and immediately issued **a** proclamation **to** the seamen, acquainting them with **the** emperor's concession.

---

* This gallant officer, now Admiral Grenfell, as the Brazilian minister, attended the funeral of the earl.

The consequence was, the return of all who had not quitted the country in despair. The money was duly distributed by the admiral and his officers; and, on the 2nd August, the imperial squadron sailed for Pernambuco, where they arrived on the 19th. Under the threat of a bombardment the revolt was suppressed and order restored, after which Cochrane left for Bahia, from whence he returned to Pernambuco. He had now become the pacificator. Every province was more or less disturbed; but the appearance of the squadron was the signal for quiet.

It is truly sickening to think that all this service was unrequited, or requited only by insult and opposition. Now and then reports that large expeditions were on their way from Portugal to reconquer the country, induced his persecutors and detractors to forego their annoyance; but no sooner did the danger vanish, than they were as bad as before. "Mercenary" and "robber" were common terms applied to him; although, had he been either, he would have had very little difficulty in filling his own coffers, and in providing for the wants of those under his command. His scrupulousness was his fault, in fact. The National Assembly awarded him thanks in abundance, and the emperor lost no opportunity of doing him honour; but he had enemies who were paramount, and bent on his destruction.

He now determined, a second time, to relinquish a position which was both onerous and unprofitable; and on the 1st January, 1825, placed his appointment at the disposal of the emperor; but the government could not afford to lose services so valuable in the still disturbed state of the **provinces**. He therefore again visited the various **parts** of the disturbed districts, until his health broke down under such continual work and **anxiety**, aggravated by **the** ingratitude of his **employers. After** disbursing a first instalment of prize-**money** among the crews of the different ships, he shifted his flag to the *Piranga*, despatched the *Pedro Primeiro* to Rio, and sailed for a northern latitude for the recovery of his strength. During his absence **from** England **a** foreign enlistment **bill** especially **aimed at Lord Cochrane** had been passed; but notwithstanding its threatenings, the defects of the *Piranga* and her want of provisions were such, that he considered it necessary to proceed to Portsmouth, and **he** accordingly anchored **at** Spithead on the 24th June, **in the hope of obtaining** supplies.

Shortly after his arrival at that anchorage, which he duly reported to the Brazilian envoy, he received a letter from that functionary stating that a report was **in** circulation that he, Lord Cochrane, had accepted **the command** of the Greek navy, and requesting to know **whether there** was any truth **in** the rumour.

Lord Cochrane, in reply, acquainted the envoy that that command had been offered him while in Brazil, **and** that subsequently to his arrival in England the **offer** had been renewed **by** the Greek Committee at Portsmouth, but that **it was** not his intention to **accept it** until his **relations with** Brazil were honorably concluded. This reply **was** no doubt intentionally misconstrued, **for** the envoy wrote again expressing "his regret" at the circumstance of his having quitted the service of his **august** sovereign. Lord Cochrane answered, stating that **his** previous letter had been misunderstood; when, acting **on** some correspondence he had received from Rio, the Chevalier Gameiro, the Brazilian envoy, gave him peremptory directions to return immediately to Rio, to give an account of some proceedings at Maranham. Previously to this, however, the Chevalier had written to the **first** lieutenant of the *Piranga*, Mr. Shepherd, informing him officially, that Lord Cochrane "had retired from the service."

Lord Cochrane replied to the order of the envoy to the effect that he would return to Rio as soon as the *Piranga* had been fully equipped. Upon this the envoy resorted to the extraordinary proceeding of stopping the men's wages and provisions, in consequence of which the men struck work. The fact at **the** bottom of all this trickery was the desire to get rid of Lord Cochrane, by summary dismissal, without satisfying his claims upon the government; for, as a peace was then negotiating, there was no further need of his services.

Peace was, in fact, concluded on the 3rd November, in which the independence of Brazil was conceded; and as, by some chicanery, Lord Cochrane's appointment had been limited to the continuance of the war, this opportunity was taken to break faith with him. A letter was, therefore, addressed to Lieutenant Shepherd, on **the** 7th November, 1825, acquainting him, under the **title** of "Captain, commanding the

Piranga," that he was **to place** himself under the orders of the legation, **and cast** off **all** subordination to the Marquis of Maranham.

Some months later Lord Cochrane received a letter from the Imperial Government, informing him that all **his pay** and other claims had been suspended till he should return to Rio de Janeiro, to justify himself and give **an** account of his commission. In the mean while, however, the *Piranga* had been taken from under his orders, and had sailed on her return to Brazil.

The result, therefore, of his service in Brazil was loss in everything **but** renown. **A** commission was subsequently appointed, and a report made in favour **of** Lord Cochrane's claims for a pension, and it was admitted that "he saved Brazil millions of dollars in military **and naval** expeditions," by his speedy **and** unexpected annexation **of** the Portuguese provinces; but he was excluded from sharing in the prize-money. His claims were never satisfied to the hour of his death; and the independence of Brazil, to the eternal **disgrace of all** who were in any way concerned in the Government, **or** who have since held the reins, was obtained **mainly at** the expense of the unrequited mental vigour **and i**nexhaustible resources of Lord Cochrane. The **title of** "Marquis of Maranham," **to** which were annex**ed** insult, fraud, treachery, and duplicity, almost beyond the **power** of conception, and the cross of the Imperial Brazilian order of El Cruzeiro subsequently conferred, can only be looked upon as a mock**ery** of his transcendent achievements.

SERVICES IN GREECE.
[1826–8.]

The overtures, which had been repeatedly made to
Lord Cochrane **to** form and command a navy to be
employed in the liberation of Greece, were now
seriously **entertained**. **If** mercenary motives had
ever held sway over this extraordinary man, such
could not have been the case on the present occasion.
The cause in which he was now called upon to lend
his aid was languishing for want of money, and all
who embarked in it must have done so with only
the most remote prospect of ever receiving remunera-
tion. There were here, at least, no mines of gold,
nor chests of silver, to quicken cupidity; and no inducement to embark in such a service save that of
pure fondness for adventure, and an abstract love of
freedom.

On the abrupt termination of Lord Cochrane's
connection with Brazil, the Greek Committee, in London, with the consent of the Greek deputies, Orlando
and Luriottis, entered into an engagement with him,
under which a fleet was to be created and placed
under his command. As the building of priames
and other vessels for war purposes had been strictly
prohibited by the Turkish Government in the Mediterranean, this fleet, which was to comprise steamboats and two large frigates, was ordered to be
built, the former in London, the latter in the
United States. Early in 1825 a loan of two mil-

lions sterling had been negotiated in London, of which one-tenth part had been remitted to Greece in specie, and all trace of it lost in its transit, or at least no accounts showing what became of it could be obtained. A further portion of £155,000 had been remitted to New York, to pay for the two frigates, each of which was to mount 60 guns; and the superintendence of the building was committed to General Lallemande. Only one of the frigates, the *Hellas*, was completed by the end of 1826, and then found to be not worth half the sum she was stipulated to cost. The building of the steamboats in London proceeded equally tardily and unsatisfactorily. The contract entered into specified that five vessels were to be ready, by the latest, in two and a half months from the 17th August, 1825, and were to have sailed in the month of November following. These ships were to cost another £155,000 of the loan.

The winter wore away, and May, 1826, had arrived ere the first of these steamboats was ready to leave the Thames. This vessel, named the *Perseverance*, sailed shortly afterwards under the command of Captain Hastings. Her machinery broke down almost as soon as she left the river, and when she reached Sardinia, which she did under canvas, her engines had to be taken to pieces and rebuilt before they were of the slightest use. She reached Napoli di Romania in November. Those which followed were not a bit better. The contractor for the engines had a son in the service of the Pasha of Egypt as an engineer, and it was conjectured that there was a deliberate intention **to** do the work in such a manner as to frustrate the **end in** view. The grossest frauds in connection with **the** loan and its expenditure were, in fact, practised, which **were** exposed shortly afterwards, to the inexpressible chagrin of the borrowers and lenders.

At length the admiral took his departure, and arrived at Poros in February, 1827, only to find the greatest disunion where unity was to be expected and necessary. His course was immediately taken. In a reply addressed to the deputation sent to him by the government to welcome him on his arrival, he said, **"I** was grieved from the first at seeing the bravest and most renowned military chiefs of Greece busying themselves about politics and the congress, and losing their time in disputing about the place of assembly, whilst the enemy is overrunning your country without the least opposition, while they hold three-fourths of the fortresses of **Greece,** and have surrounded its metropolis. **Athens** is in danger of falling into the hands **of the** enemies. The brave Fabvier, with a handful **of** heroes, full of enthusiasm for independence, has **advanced** to the assistance of its generous defenders, whilst the chiefs of Greece are disputing about politics."

Lord Cochrane advised them to **read,** " in full congress," the first Philippic of Demosthenes, which, with the change of names and dates, would apply closely to the suicidal course they were taking. His vigorous speech, added to a threat of immediate withdrawal, had the effect of bringing about a compromise between the disputants. Count Capo d'Istrias was appointed president of Greece for seven years, and Lord Cochrane was **named** commander-in-chief of the Greek fleet, in lieu of Miaulis, an arrangement in which **the latter** fully concurred. The aged Miaulis, moreover, used all his influence with the Hydriots to induce them to submit to the authority of the commander-in-chief. " I," said he, " as well as all the nation, have long founded my hopes on the arrival **of** the great man, whose preceding splendid deeds promise our country a happy issue out of the long and arduous struggle which it maintains. This man has arrived, and I congratulate the government and the whole nation upon it. The Greek marine may justly expect everything from such a leader ; and I am the first to declare myself ready again to combat, and with all my might, under **his** command."

It was now resolved to make a joint and determined effort for the relief of Athens, by a general attack upon the intrenchments of the besieging Turkish army. The fleet under Cochrane transported a large body of Hydriots and Spezziots, and by the end of April **the flower of** the Greek army was assembled under the walls **of** Athens, numbering about ten thousand men. Seraskier opposed the landing **of** **the** troops brought **in the** fleet, and some fighting was occasioned; but **the** Hydriots and Spezziots, having landed at different points, drove him from his positions, and the Greeks **in** the Piræus advancing from the other side to support their friends, the Turks withdrew within their intrenchments, and the

Greek leaders were left to form their own plans unmolested.

But Lord Cochrane's good genius of success seemed to have deserted him. He strove manfully, and devised schemes in the hope of aiding the cause he had espoused; but they resulted in ruin. The army landed at Cape Colias on the 6th of May, when the Greeks were defeated, dispersed, or cut to pieces. General Church, who, like Cochrane, had been endeavouring to aid the Greek cause, and with him had superintended the disembarkation, had to escape to the ships by jumping into the sea, and swimming for their lives.

Lord Cochrane repaired to the Greek islands to assemble his ships, but found his authority very limited indeed. The captains, who were, for the most part, owners of the ships, considered and calculated before obeying his orders, or took the initiative and got underway, as they thought proper. With his flag on board the *Hellas*, and accompanied by a few fire-ships, he sailed, however, and in the Gulf of Chiarenza fell in with two Turkish corvettes, which, after a short action, made their escape. On the 20th of May he captured a brig laden with powder and provisions, and then proceeded to Navarin to watch the Turkish fleet. The cause was *in extremis* when he took it up; and his connection with the Greek war of independence was made at too late a period.

He returned to England much disappointed, but conscious of having done his best; but not until the germ of independence had taken deep root.

FROM HIS RESTORATION TO THE SERVICE, TO HIS DEATH.
[1832-60.]

On the death of Archibald, earl **of** Dundonald, at Paris, in 1831, Lord Cochrane succeeded to the title—estates, unhappily, there were **none to** which to succeed. William IV., shortly after his accession **to** the throne, with a true sailor's feeling, considered that the halo of glory which the naval exploits of the earl had shed around the profession, apart from all **other** considerations, imperatively called for his re-storation to that service whose renown he had always so gallantly upheld. This was done in May, 1832, prior to which **a** free pardon under the great seal had been granted **him.** The **fire** of persecution had died out, and the **act of** placing the earl of Dun-donald's name upon the list of flag-officers was hailed with pleasure throughout the country.

Many held that it ought to have been accompanied by the grant of arrears of pay ; **but** as this concession would **have in**volved the necessity for similar payments in innumerable instances, the proposition was negatived.

In 1841 the **earl** was granted the good service pension of £300 **a** year, and in **1848** was appointed Commander-in-Chief **of the** North-American and West-Indian Stations, **upon which he** was employed **three** years. Subsequently, **in 1854,** he was made Rear-Admiral of England, with a further additional salary of **£342.** Every disposition was apparently shown to repair the injustice from which he had suffered. The Order of the Bath had been enlarged in 1815, and divided into three grades. The highest order, Grand Cross, was awarded to the earl in 1847, as an equivalent to the K. B. previously enjoyed by him; and shortly before his mortal remains were committed to their last resting-place in Westminster Abbey, the Queen caused the banner which had been torn down from its place in Henry VII.'s chapel by the king-at-arms, and the brass plate containing his lordship's arms, with the helmet, crest, mantling, and sword, which had been removed, to be replaced.

The earl married, in 1812, Miss Katherine Corbett Barnes, a lady of good family in the Midland Counties. The marriage displeased his uncle, the Hon. Basil Cochrane, from whom he had great expectations, and whose large fortune would have gone far towards recovering the Dundonald estates. But the marriage, like all his other engagements, was an affair of the heart; and, although tempted by offers of wealth, had he chosen to ally himself to the only daughter of an Admiralty official, he disdained all such overtures, and, happily for himself, consulted his affections. The amiable and heroic countess, who followed her husband's fortunes, and often shared his perils, died, leaving four sons, the eldest of whom succeeds to the title, and the two youngest are serving in the Royal Navy—one as a captain and **C.B.,** the other as a lieutenant.

The earl retained, very nearly to the last, his mental

and physical powers. **He was** in possession of several plans for the destruction of **enemies'** fleets, some of which were investigated **and favourably** reported in 1847 by **a select** committee, comprising Sir Thomas Hastings—**then principal** storekeeper **to** the **Ordnance**—Sir **John** Burgoyne, and Lieu**t.-Colonel** Colquhoun, **R.A.** He inherited his father's inventive genius **and his** misfortunes. His death took place in London **on** the 30th of October, '1860, he having previously undergone two operations for lithotomy; and he was **interred in** Westminster Abbey on Wednesday, **the 14th** of November, in the presence of a **large number** of naval and military officers of rank **and a large concourse** of sympathizing spectators.

A very distinguished naval officer of rank, who **recently served under the** flag of the late Admiral, **says** of him :—

"**I** find **it difficult to** express the very high estimation in which his lordship was regarded by all who had the honour of serving under his command. **Though** naturally reserved in his manner, his lordship **won the** affection of those around **him by** his truly **amiable** disposition and kind heart; whilst, at the **same time,** he commanded admiration and respect by the superiority **of his** mind, and the fame of his heroic deeds."

The pages of *Punch*, always abounding in pathos, **as** well as **wit,** never contained lines more worthy

of a poet's pen than the following tribute to our
hero's memory :—

Ashes to Ashes! **Lay the** hero down
  Within the gray old Abbey's glorious shade.
  In our Walhalla ne'er was worthier laid
Since martyr first won palm, **or** victor crown.

'Tis well the State he served no farthing pays
  To grace with pomp and honour all too late
  His grave, whom, living, Statesmen dogg'd with hate,
Denying justice, and withholding praise.

Let England hide her **face above his tomb,**
  As much for shame as sorrow. Let her think
  Upon the bitter cup he had to drink—
Heroic soul, branded with felon's doom.

A Sea-King, whose fit place had been by Blake,
  Or our own Nelson, had he been but free
  To follow glory's quest upon the sea,
Leading the conquer'd navies in his wake—

A Captain, whom it had been ours **to cheer**
  From conquest on to conquest, had our land
  But set its wisest, worthiest in command,
Not such as hated all the **good** revere.

We let them cage the **Lion** while the fire
  In his high heart burnt clear and unsubdued ;
  We let them stir that frank and forward **mood**
From greatness to the self-consuming ire,

The fret and chafe that wait on service scorn'd,
  Justice denied, and truth to silence **driven** ;
  From men we left him to appeal to Heaven,
'Gainst fraud set high, and evidence suborn'd ;

We left him, with bound arms, to mark the sword,
  Given to weak hands ; left him, with working brain,
  To see rogues traffic, and fools rashly reign,
Where Strength should have been guide, and Honour lord ;

Left him to cry aloud, without support,
  Against the creeping things that eat away
  Our wooden walls, and boast as they betray,
The base supporters of a baser court,

The crawling worms that in corruption breed,
  And on corruption batten, till at last
  Mistaken honour the proud victim cast
Out to their spite, to writhe, and pant, and bleed

Under their stings and slime ; and bleed he did
  For years, till hope into heart-sickness grew,
  And he sought other seas and service new,
And his bright sword in alien laurels hid.

Nor even so found gratitude, but came
  Back to his England, bankrupt, save of praise,
  To eat his heart, through weary wishful days,
And shape his strength to bearing of his shame.

Till, slow but sure, drew on a better time,
  And statesmen owned the check of public will ;
  And, at the last, light pierced the shadow chill
That foul'd his honour with the taint of crime.

And then they gave him back the knightly spurs
  Which he had never forfeited—the rank
  From which he ne'er by ill-deserving sank,
More than the lion sinks for yelp of curs.

Justice had linger'd on its road too long :
  The lion was grown old ; the time gone by,
  When for his aid we vainly raised a cry,
To save our flag from shame, our decks from wrong.

The infamy is *theirs*, whose evil deed
  Is past undoing ; yet not guiltless we,
  Who penniless that brave old man could see,
Restored to honour, but denied its meed.

A Belisarius, old and sad and poor,
  To *our* shame, not to *his*—so he lived on,
  Till man's allotted fourscore years were gone,
And scarcely then had leave to 'stablish sure

Proofs of *his* innocence, and of *their* shame,
  That had so wrong'd him ; and this done, came death,
  To seal the assurance of his dying breath,
And wipe the last faint tarnish from his name.

At last his fame stands fair, and full of years
  He seeks that judgment which his wrongers all
  Have sought before him—and above his pall
His flag, replaced at length, waves with his peers.

He did not live to see it, but he knew
  His country with one voice had set it high ;
  And knowing this he was content to die,
And leave to gracious Heaven what might ensue.

Ashes to ashes ! Lay the hero down,
  No nobler heart e'er knew the bitter lot
  To be misjudged, malign'd, accused, forgot :—
Twine martyr's palm among his victor's crown.

THE END.

COX AND WYMAN, PRINTERS, GREAT QUEEN STREET, LONDON.

" If the steamboat and the railway have abridged time and space, and made a large addition to the available length of human existence, why may not our intellectual journey be also accelerated, our knowledge more cheaply and quickly acquired, its records rendered more accessible and portable, its cultivators increased in number, and its blessings more cheaply and widely diffused."—QUARTERLY REVIEW.

LONDON : FARRINGDON STREET.

ROUTLEDGE, WARNE, & ROUTLEDGE'S
NEW AND CHEAP EDITIONS
OF
Standard and Popular Works
IN

NATURAL HISTORY & SCIENCE.	POETRY AND THE DRAMA.
BOTANY AND GARDENING.	DRAWING ROOM TABLE BOOKS.
AGRICULTURE AND FARMING.	PRESENT AND GIFT BOOKS.
SPORTING AT HOME OR ABROAD.	PASTIMES.
THE RIFLE.	HOUSEHOLD ECONOMY AND COOKERY.
HISTORY.	
BIOGRAPHY.	DICTIONARIES AND BOOKS OF REFERENCE.
FOREIGN COUNTRIES.	
GENERAL LITERATURE.	LAW.
RELIGIOUS AND HYMN BOOKS.	FICTION.
EDUCATION, LANGUAGES, &c.	

WITH A GENERAL INDEX.

TO BE OBTAINED BY ORDER OF ALL BOOKSELLERS, HOME OR COLONIAL.

In ordering, specially mention " ROUTLEDGE'S EDITIONS."

NATURAL HISTORY, SCIENCE, &c.

In post 8vo, price **6s.** cloth gilt, or **6s. 6d.** gilt edges.

A NATURAL HISTORY. **By** the Rev. J. G. WOOD. A New Edition, with many additions. Containing nearly 500 Illustrations, from original designs by WILLIAM **HARVEY,** engraved by the Brothers DALZIEL. Its principal features **are :—**

1st. Its Accuracy. 2nd. Its Systematic Arrangement. 3rd. Illustrations executed expressly for the Work. And 4th. New and Authentic Anecdotes.

" One of the best of Messrs. Routledge and Co.'s publications."—*Times.*

In royal 8vo, handsomely **bound in cloth**, price **18s.**

THE ILLUSTRATED NATURAL HISTORY.　First Volume—MAMMALIA. **By** the Rev. J. G. WOOD, M.A., F.L.S. With 480 Illustrations by WOLF, ZWECKER, HARRISON WEIR, HARVEY, COLEMAN, &c. ; engraved by the Brothers DALZIEL.

This superb Volume, containing **no less than 803 pages**, beautifully printed, and embellished with a profusion of admirable representations of animal life by the most eminent artists of the day, completes the important class of Mammalia. The Publishers refer with much satisfaction to the success of this great undertaking already achieved, and they trust that **the** execution of the work as far as it has now progressed, will be accepted by the subscribers as a sufficient guarantee for its adequate treatment until it be **completed**.

*** *The Illustrated Natural History—Birds—This Volume is now progressing in Monthly Parts, price One Shilling each. It will be completed in October*, 1861, *and will form a Volume, price 18s., uniform with that of Mammalia.*

In small post **8vo** (nearly ready),

NATURAL HISTORY NOTES. With Reflections on Reason and Instinct by the Rev. J. C. ATKINSON, Author of "Play Hours and Half Holidays." With 100 Illustrations by COLEMAN.

In cloth gilt, price **3s. 6d.**, or with gilt edges, **4s.,**

THE COMMON OBJECTS OF THE COUNTRY. By the Rev. J. G. WOOD. With Illustrations by COLEMAN, containing 150 of the "Objects," beautifully printed in Colours.

This book gives **short** and simple descriptions of the numerous objects **that are to be found in** our fields, woods, and waters.

Also, a Cheap Edition, price 1s., in **Fancy** Boards, with plain Plates.

In fcap. 8vo, price **3s. 6d.** cloth lettered,

THE COMMON OBJECTS OF THE SEA-SHORE. With Hints for the Aquarium. **By the** Rev. J. G. WOOD. The Fine Edition with the Illustrations by **G. B.** SOWERBY, beautifully printed **in** colours.

Also, price **1s., a Cheap Edition,** with the Plates plain.

"This **little work is of low price,** but of high value, **and is** just **the** book to be put into the hands of persons (and there are many **such**), whether young or old, **who** 'having eyes,' have hitherto 'seen not' **those** 'common objects' which bear within themselves whole cabinets of wonders.—*Globe.*

' Price **3s. 6d.** cloth gilt, or **4s.** gilt edges,

SKETCHES AND ANECDOTES OF ANIMAL LIFE. By the Rev. J. G. WOOD, M.A., F.L.S., &c. With Eight Illustrations by HARRISON WEIR.

"A fresh spirit pervades the **book,** as well in the narratives as the descriptive account of the nature and habits of the animals."—*Spectator.*

"Is replete with interest and information, and will be a valuable work to the rising generation."—*News of the World.*

Price 3s. 6d. cloth boards, or 4s. gilt edges,

ANIMAL TRAITS AND CHARACTERISTICS. Comprising Anecdotes of Animals **not** included in **the** "Sketches and Anecdotes." By the Rev. **J. G. Wood, M.A.,** F.L.S., **&c.** With Illustrations by HARRISON WEIR.

"Young people will spend their time pleasantly and **well** who should **be** found engaged over its pages, and those very wise people, their elders, if they took it **up, would** certainly be instructed."—*Examiner.*

Price 3s. 6d. each, cloth gilt, or 4s. gilt edges,

MY FEATHERED FRIENDS. Containing Anecdotes of Bird-life, **more** especially Eagles, Vultures, **Hawks,** Magpies, Rooks, Crows, **Ravens,** Parrots, Humming Birds, Ostriches, &c. &c. **By the** Rev. J. G. WOOD. With Illustrations **by HARRISON** WEIR.

"The author's endeavour has been to show *the life* and *the character* of **the** creatures described rather **than** their outward shape, the *strictly scientific* part of the subject having been treated of elsewhere. He has avoided the use of harsh scientific terms, and has, in every case where it has been practicable, exchanged Greek and Latin **words** for simple English. An attempt has also been made to show how the **nature** of the lower animals is raised and modified, their reason developed, **and their** instinct brought under subjection, when they **come** in familiar **contact with** man—the highest **of the** animal creation."

Fcap. 8vo, price 3s. 6d. cloth, or 4s. gilt edges,

WHITE'S NATURAL HISTORY OF SELBORNE. A New Edition. **Edited by the Rev. J. G.** WOOD, and illustrated with above 200 Illustrations **by W. HARVEY.** Finely printed.

"A very superior edition of this most popular work."—*Times.*
"Is a pleasant-looking volume, liberally illustrated with excellent pictures of nearly every animal or tree therein mentioned."—*Examiner.*

Foolscap, price 3s. 6d. cloth gilt, or 4s. gilt edges,

BRITISH BUTTERFLIES. Figures **and** Descriptions **of** every **native** species, with an Account of Butterfly Development, Structure, **Habits,** Localities, Mode of Capture, and Preservation, &c. With 71 **Coloured** Figures of Butterflies, all of exact life-size, and 67 Figures of Caterpillars, Chrysalides, Eggs, Scales, &c. By W. S. COLEMAN, Member of the Entomological Society of London.

*** A Cheap Edition, **with** plain plates, fancy boards, price 1*s.*

"**This** pretty and complete **little** manual of British Butterflies is another **valuable** contribution to **popular** scientific literature, and may be safely recommended to all who **have a** hobby for collecting that beautiful class of insects."—*Critic.*

Cloth limp, price 1s.

CAGE AND SINGING BIRDS: how to Catch, Keep, Breed, and Rear them; with Full Directions as to their Nature, Food, Diseases, &c. By H. G. ADAMS. With 22 Illustrations.

Fcap., **price 1s. 6d.** cloth limp.

THE RAT : its History and destructive character, with numerous Anecdotes, and Instructions for the EXTIRPATION of Rats from Houses and Farms. By JAMES RODWELL (Uncle James).

"This is one of the **most** interesting books upon a subject, **more or less** repulsive, we have ever **had** the good fortune to meet with. It is one of the most charming episodes in natural history possible to conceive. The author has a ' Vendetta ' against **the** Rat."—*Despatch.*

LOVELL REEVE'S POPULAR SERIES.

NATURAL **HISTORY** DIVISION.

Square, cloth gilt, price 7s. 6d. **each.**

BRITISH ORNITHOLOGY; containing a Familiar and Technical Description **of the** Birds of the British Isles. By P. **H.** GOSSE. With **19** Pages of Coloured Plates, embracing **100** subjects.

HISTORY OF BIRDS; comprising a Familiar Account of their Classification and Habits. By ADAM WHITE, F.L.S. With 20 Pages **of** Coloured Plates, embracing 110 subjects.

BRITISH BIRDS' EGGS. By RICHARD **LAISHLEY.** With 20 Pages of Coloured Plates, embracing 100 **subjects.**

BRITISH ENTOMOLOGY ; containing a Familiar and Technical Description of the INSECTS most common to the localities of the British Isles. By MARIA E. CATLOW. With 16 Pages of Coloured Plates.

BRITISH CONCHOLOGY. A Familiar History **of** the MOLLUSCS inhabiting **the** British Isles. By G. B. SOWERBY, F.L.S. With 20 Pages of Coloured Plates, embracing 150 subjects.

BRITISH CRUSTACEA ; comprising a Familiar Account of their Classification and Habits. By ADAM WHITE, F.L.S. With 20 Pages of Coloured Plates, embracing 120 subjects.

MOLLUSCA ; comprising **a** Familiar **Account** of their Classification, Instincts, and Habits, and of the Growth and distinguishing Characters of their Shells. By MARY ROBERTS. With 20 Pages of Coloured Plates, embracing 120 subjects.

[Continued.

LOVELL REEVE'S POPULAR SERIES—*continued.*

BRITISH ZOOPHYTES, or CORALLINES. By the Rev.
Dr. LANDSBOROUGH. With **20** Pages of Coloured Plates, embracing
120 subjects.

THE AQUARIUM, **of Marine** and Fresh Water Animals
and Plants. By G. B. SOWERBY, **F.**L.S. With 20 Pages of Coloured
Plates, embracing 120 **subjects.**

HISTORY OF MAMMALIA; comprising a Familiar Account of **their** Classification and Habits. By ADAM WHITE, F.L.S.
With **16** Pages of Coloured Plates, embracing 120 subjects.

SCRIPTURE ZOOLOGY; containing a Familiar History of
the Animals mentioned in the Bible. By MARIA E. CATLOW. With
16 Pages of Coloured Plates, embracing 120 subjects.

PHYSICAL GEOLOGY. **By J.** BATE JUKES, M.A., F.R.S.
With 20 Pages of Coloured Plates by Mr. **G. V.** DUNOYER.

MINERALOGY; comprising a Familiar Account of Minerals
and their Uses. By HENRY SOWERBY. **With** 20 Pages of Coloured
Plates, **embracing 120 su**bjects.

DR. BUCKLAND'S BRIDGEWATER TREATISE.

In **2 vols.** demy **8vo., price 24s.,** cloth extra,

GEOLOGY AND MINERALOGY, considered with reference
to Natural Theology. By the **late** Very Rev. WILLIAM BUCKLAND,
D.D., F.R.S. A New Edition, with additions by Professor Owen, F.R.S.,
Professor Phillips, M.A., M.D., Mr. Robert Brown, **F.R.S., &c.** Edited by
Francis **T.** Buckland, M.A. With a Memoir of **the Author, Steel** Portrait,
and 90 **Full-**Page Engravings.

"A work **as** much distinguished for the industry and research **which it**
indicates, **as for** its scientific principles and philosophical views. The extraordinary **and** inestimable facts which he has brought under the grasp of the
general reader, have **been** illustrated by numerous and splendid embellish-
ments; and, **while** his descriptions of them are clothed in simple and perspi-
cuous language, **the** general views to which they lead have been presented to
us in the highest tone **of a** lofty and impressive eloquence. We have our-
selves never perused a work more truly fascinating, or more deeply calculated
to leave abiding impressions **on** the heart; and if this shall be the general
opinion, we are sure that it will **be** the source of higher gratification to the
author than the more desired, though **on** his **part** equally deserved, meed of
literary **renown.**"—*Edinburgh Review.*

Fcap. cloth, boards, price **2s.**, or in cloth **gilt,** 2s. 6d.,

THE MARVELS OF SCIENCE, and **their** Testimony to
Holy Writ. A Popular System of the Sciences. By W. S. FULLOM.
Twelfth Edition, revised. 12 Illustrations.

In fcap. 8vo, cloth, price **2s. 6d.**,

GEOLOGICAL GOSSIP ; or, Stray **Chapters** on Earth and Ocean. By Professor ANSTED, **M.A., F.R.S.** With Illustrations.

CONTENTS.

Rivers and Water-Floods.	Origin of **Rocks** and Metamorphism.
The Surface of the Atlantic.	New Discoveries in **Iron** Ores.
The Great Deep and its **Inhabitants.**	Coal-Fields and **Coal Extraction.**
Statistics of Earthquakes.	Gold Deposits.
Origin of Volcanoes.	Water-Glass and Artificial Stone.
Antiquity of the Human **Race.**	Preservation **of Stones.**

&c. &c.

Post 8vo (in the press),

MINES, MINERALS, AND METALS. A Popular **Description** of them and their **Uses.** By J. H. PEPPER, late **Lecturer** at the Polytechnic Institution. With **300 Practical Illustrations.**

In square **royal**, price **5s.**, cloth extra,

BEACH RAMBLES, in Search of Sea-Side Pebbles and **Crystals**, with Observations on the Origin of the Diamond and other Precious Stones. By J. G. FRANCIS, B.A. With 14 Illustrations, designed by Coleman, and printed in **Colours by Evans.**

"What Mr. Gosse's books **are to** marine objects this volume is to the pebbles and crystals with which our shores are strewn. It is an indispensable companion **to** every sea-side stroller."—*Bell's Messenger.*

Price **2s. 6d.** cloth **gilt,** or **3s.** gilt edges.

THE ORBS OF HEAVEN ; or, The Planetary and Stellar Worlds. **A** Popular Exposition **of the great** Discoveries and Theories of **Modern Astronomy.** By O. M. **MITCHELL.** Eleventh Edition, with many Illustrations.

"This volume contains **a graphic and** popular exposition of the great **discoveries** of astronomical **science,** including those made by Lord Rosse (illustrated by several engravings), Leverrier, and Maedler. The Cincinnati Observatory owes **its** origin to the remarkable interest excited by the **delivery** of these Lectures **to a** succession **of** crowded audiences."

Fcap. 8vo, price **5s.,** cloth **gilt,** with Coloured Illustrations,

THE LAWS OF CONTRAST OF COLOUR, and their application to the Fine Arts of Painting, Decoration of Buildings, Mosaic Work, Tapestry and Carpet Weaving, Calico Printing, Dress, Paper Staining, Printing, Illumination, Landscape and Flower Gardening. By **M. E.** CHEVREUL, Director of the Dye Works of **the** Gobelins. Translated by JOHN SPANTON.

A Cheap Edition, without the Coloured Plates, price **2s.** cloth.

"Every one whose business has anything **to do** with the arrangement of colours should possess this book. Its value has been universally acknowledged, having been translated into various languages, although but recently into our own."

Crown 8vo, price **2s. 6d.** cloth, or **3s.** gilt edges,

POPULAR ASTRONOMY. A Concise Elementary Treatise on the Sun, Planets, Satellites, and Comets. With an Appendix, containing very complete Tables of the Elements of the Planets and Comets, and of the 33 Asteroids. By O. M. MITCHELL, LL.D., Author of "The Orbs of Heaven." 12 Illustrations. Revised and Edited by the Rev. L. Tomlinson, M.A.

Fcap. 8vo, price **2s.** cloth extra,

ARAGO'S POPULAR ASTRONOMY : Revised and Edited by the Rev. L. TOMLINSON. With numerous Illustrations and Diagrams. A valuable Chapter in this book is devoted exclusively to Comets, and was expressly compiled by Arago to dissipate the great apprehension of danger to the earth by the movement of these heavenly bodies.

Post 8vo, price **6s.** cloth gilt,

THE MICROSCOPE : its History, Construction, and Application. New Edition, with numerous Additions. By JABEZ HOGG, Author of "Elements of Natural Philosophy," &c., Assistant-Surgeon to the Royal Ophthalmic Hospital, Charing Cross.

"This book is intended for the uninitiated, to whom we cordially recommend it as a useful and trustworthy guide. It well deserves the popularity to which it has already attained."—*British and Foreign Medico-Chirurgical Review.*

Fcap. 8vo, price 6s. half bound,

A DICTIONARY OF TRADE PRODUCTS : Commercial, Manufacturing, and Technical Terms. With a definition of the Moneys, Weights, and Measures of all Countries, reduced to the British standard.

"Is a work of reference, such as is needed in every industrial establishment."—*The Times.*

Fcap. 8vo, price **1s. 6d.** boards, or cloth, **2s.**

NOVELTIES, INVENTIONS, AND CURIOSITIES IN ARTS AND MANUFACTURES. By GEORGE DODD, Author of "Curiosities of Industry," &c.

"Every novelty, invention, or curiosity that modern science has brought to light is here explained in an easy and natural style."

In post 8vo, cloth, price **6s.**,

THE BOY'S PLAYBOOK OF SCIENCE. By JOHN HENRY PEPPER, late Chemical Lecturer at the Royal Polytechnic Institution. With 300 Illustrations by HINE, includes the Manipulations and Arrangements of Apparatus required for the performance of experiments, illustrating the various branches of natural philosophy.

Fcap. 8vo, price 6d., limp cloth,

THE VILLAGE MUSEUM; or, How we gathered Profit with Pleasure. By the Rev. G. T. HOARE, of Taudridge, Surrey.

General Contents :—What is a Museum ?—A First Visit—The Shark—The Microscope—Antiquities—Works of Art—Hieroglyphics—China—Pictures—Models—Needlework—Zoological Gardens—The Use of Arms—Air Pump—Cotton and Manufactures—Precious Stones, &c. &c.

In 13 vols., demy 8vo, price 42s., cloth ; or in half-calf extra (13 vols. in 7), 63s. ; or the 13 vols. in 7, half russia, 70s.,

KNIGHT'S NATIONAL CYCLOPÆDIA OF USEFUL KNOWLEDGE; founded on the Penny Cyclopædia, but brought down to the present state of information.

Demy 8vo, cloth, price 5s.,

SUPPLEMENT TO THE NATIONAL CYCLOPÆDIA OF USEFUL KNOWLEDGE. By P. AUSTIN NUTTALL, LL.D.

This Volume (Vol. 13) comprises under a distinct alphabetical arrangement all the accumulated information of the last 12 years. Many articles, entirely new, have been written : and all the leading subjects of the twelve preceding volumes have been carefully written up to the present time ; it comprehends nearly 2700 articles replete with varied and useful information.

In 2 vols., royal 8vo, 1100 pages in each vol., price £2 2s., cloth lettered, or half-bound in russia or calf, £2 10s.

CRAIG'S DICTIONARY, founded on WEBSTER'S. Being an Etymological, Technological, and Pronouncing Dictionary of the English Language, including all terms used in Literature, Science, and Art.

To show the value of the Work, the General Contents are given :—

IN LAW — All the Terms and Phrases used and defined by the highest legal authorities.

IN MEDICAL SCIENCE — All the Terms used in Great Britain and other Countries in Europe.

IN BOTANY—All the Genera in Don's great work, and Loudon's Encyclopædia, and the Orders as given by Lindley in his Vegetable Kingdom.

IN ZOOLOGY — All the Classes, Orders, and Genera, as given by Cuvier, Swainson, Gray, Blainville, Lamarck, Agassiz, &c.

IN GEOLOGY, MINERALOGY, CONCHOLOGY, ICHTHYOLOGY, MAMMOLOGY—All the terms employed are carefully described.

IN MECHANICS AND COMMERCE—It contains a complete Encyclopædia of everything eminently useful to every class of society, and in general use.

IN QUOTATIONS—There are above 3000 Quotations from standard old authors, illustrating obsolete words.

IN DERIVATIONS AND PRONUNCIATION—All English known words are fully expressed.

Price 6d., sewed wrapper,

THE EARTH: Past, Present, and Future. A Lecture delivered by the Rev. GEORGE H. SUMNER, M.A., Rector of Old Alresford, Hants, and Chaplain to his Grace the Archbishop of Canterbury.

Post 8vo, price 9s., cloth extra,

SEAMANSHIP AND NAVAL DUTIES. By A. H. ALSTON, Lieut. Royal Navy. Comprising in detail the Fitting out of a Man-of-War; Her Management under all Circumstances at Sea; and the Employment of her Resources in all Cases of General Service. With a Treatise on NAUTICAL SURVEYING. With 200 Practical Illustrations.

BOTANY AND GARDENING.

REEVE'S
POPULAR NATURAL HISTORIES.
(BOTANICAL DIVISION).

Price 7s. 6d. each, cloth gilt, with Coloured Illustrations.

"A popular series of scientific treatises, which, from the simplicity of their style, and the artistic excellence and correctness of their numerous illustrations, has acquired a celebrity beyond that of any other series of modern cheap works."—*Standard.*

GARDEN BOTANY; containing a Familiar and Scientific Description of most of the Hardy and Half-hardy Plants introduced into the Flower Garden. By AGNES CATLOW. With 20 Pages of Coloured Illustrations, embracing 67 Plates.

GREENHOUSE BOTANY; containing a Familiar and Technical Description of the Exotic Plants introduced into the Greenhouse. By AGNES CATLOW. With 20 Pages of Coloured Illustrations.

FIELD BOTANY; containing a Description of the Plants common to the British Isles. By AGNES CATLOW. With 20 Pages of Coloured Illustrations, embracing 80 Plates.

ECONOMIC BOTANY; a Description of the Botanical and Commercial Characters of the principal articles of Vegetable origin, used for Food, Clothing, Tanning, Dyeing, Building, Medicine, Perfumery, &c. By THOMAS C. ARCHER, Collector for the Department of Applied Botany in the Crystal Palace, Sydenham. With 20 Pages of Coloured Illustrations, embracing 106 Plates.

[Continued.

REEVE'S POPULAR NATURAL HISTORIES—continued.

Price 7s. 6d. each, cloth gilt, with Coloured Illustrations.

THE WOODLANDS: a Description of Forest Trees, Ferns, Mosses, and Lichens. By MARY ROBERTS. With 20 Pages of Coloured Plates.

GEOGRAPHY OF PLANTS; or, a Botanical Excursion round the World. By E. M. C. Edited by CHARLES DAUBENY, M.D., F.R.S., &c. With 20 Pages of Coloured Plates of Scenery.

PALMS AND THEIR ALLIES; containing a Familiar Account of their Structure, Distribution, History, Properties, and Uses; and a complete List of all the Species introduced into our Gardens. By BERTHOLD SEEMANN, Ph.D., M.A., F.L.S. With 20 Pages of Coloured Illustrations, embracing many varieties.

BRITISH FERNS AND THE ALLIED PLANTS; comprising the Club-Mosses, Pepperworts, and Horsetails. By THOMAS MOORE, F.L.S. With 20 Pages of Coloured Illustrations, embracing 51 subjects.

BRITISH MOSSES; comprising a General Account of their Structure, Fructification, Arrangement, and Distribution. By ROBERT M. STARK, F.R.S.E. With 20 Pages of Coloured Illustrations, embracing 80 subjects.

BRITISH LICHENS; comprising an Account of their Structure, Reproduction, Uses, Distribution, and Classification. By W. LAUDER LINDSAY, M.D. With 22 Pages of Coloured Plates, embracing 400 subjects.

BRITISH SEAWEEDS; comprising their Structure, Fructification, Specific Characters, Arrangement, and General Distribution, with Notices of some of the Fresh-water ALGÆ. By the Rev. D. LANDSBOROUGH, A.L.S. With 20 Pages of Coloured Illustrations, embracing 80 subjects.

Cloth limp, price 1s.,

FAVOURITE FLOWERS: How to Grow them; being a Complete Treatise on the Cultivation of the Principal Flowers, with Descriptive Lists of all the best varieties in cultivation. By ALFRED GILLETT SUTTON, F.H.S., Editor of "The Midland Florist."

In small post 8vo, price 5s. cloth, or 5s. 6d. gilt edges; or in illuminated cover, bevelled boards, and gilt edges, 6s.,

A TOUR ROUND MY GARDEN. By ALPHONSE KARR. Revised and Edited by the Rev. J. G. WOOD. The Third Edition, finely printed. With upwards of 117 Illustrations by W. Harvey.